BLACK MASK

Matthew Moring
Editor

Keith Alan Deutsch
Editor Emeritus

Subrights & Permissions

For Reprints:
media@blackmaskmagazine.com

For Back Issues:
Please visit
www.blackmaskmagazine.com.

BLACK MASK (Vol. 37, No. 3), 2019. Published annually by Black Mask. Annual subscription $19.95 in the U.S.A. and possessions, $38.90 elsewhere payable in advance in U.S. funds. Subscription orders and correspondence regarding subscriptions should be sent to P.O. Box 835, Norwood MA 02062-0835. © 2019 by Steeger Properties, LLC, all rights reserved. Black Mask is a Registed Trademark of Steeger Properties, LLC. The stories in this magazine are all fictitious, and any resemblance between the characters in them and actual persons is completely coincidental. Reproduction or use, in any manner, of editorial or pictorial content without express written permission is prohibited. Submissions must be accompanied by a self-addressed stamp envelope. The publisher assumes no responsibility for unsolicited manuscripts or artwork. POSTMASTER: Send changes to *Black Mask*, P.O. Box 835, Norwood MA 02062-0835. Printed in the U.S.A.

Behind The Mask

IT'S TRUE—THIS issue is a bit delayed. But now that it's out and you see it's double-sized, with more stories than ever, we hope you'll find it well worth the wait.

This time around, we're including nine new stories in the *Black Mask* vein by Brian Townsley, Jane Jakeman, Brian Stanley, Hannah Honeybun, William Burton McCormick, Frank Megna, Jonathan Sheppard, Michael Bracken, Jim Doherty, as well as a new article on Raymond Chandler's *The Little Sister* by Katrina Younes.

We're appreciative of "Friend of *Black Mask*" Boris Dralyuk, who kindly supplied his translation of Isaac Babel's "Lyubka the Cossack" and arranged for its reprinting here. *Black Mask* readers are highly encouraged to pick up the recent Babel collection published by Pushkin Press, *Odessa Stories*.

And, as with previous issues, we've collected some of the best hardboiled detective fiction from the Popular Publications vaults, as written by some of the genre's best: Dashiell Hammett, D.L. Champion, Carroll John Daly, Frederick Nebel, T.T. Flynn, and Frederick C. Davis.

CONTENTS

THE GUILTY
Jonathan Sheppard

TWELVE GOOD MEN AND TRUE
Jim Doherty

PRIZE FIGHT

by Brian Townsley

ONNY TRIED desperately to focus on the passing landscape from the backseat of the cab in which he found himself. At least it was a cab, he reasoned. Of the three kinds of cars in which one suddenly finds himself in the backseat, the cab is clearly the best of the lot. There was no iron grate, no siren, and no goons on either side of him, so that was something.

He remembered sitting at the bar of the hotel where he was staying. He remembered the job going to shit. He remembered that it was 1951, already. He remembered his nine months of sobriety, before tonight. He remembered ordering rye with a beer back. More than once, he remembered that. There may have been more. Many more, even. Who knew? What he knew now, however, was that the Cathedral City nightlife was passing him quickly enough that he could hardly focus. He knocked on the window as a means of getting the driver's attention. He wanted out—*needed* out, in fact. He rapped his knuckles on the window and said what he was pretty sure was 'stop here.' The particulars were fuzzy, and his voice was difficult to discern, even to him, but he got his point across. The driver, a French gentleman who sang and hummed in his home language as he drove, stopped the vehicle and looked back at his sole customer, concern etched on the not inconsiderable features on his face. Sonny thought the concern ridiculous, of course, and asked 'how much' that sounded a bit more like 'dowmusssh' than he intended, but details were really not the point here. He tossed the bills at the man and exited the cab and found the level concrete a challenge.

Upon sitting on the curb, his reason for desiring fresh air was revealed as he projectile vomited heavily between his brogues in the gutter. It was mostly pink and thick and voluminous, filled with rye and chunks of bread and cheese snacks from the bar and it was hot and shot onto the concrete with verve. He heard women gasp behind him on the sidewalk and young men laugh out loud and without looking he knew other men were guarding the frail eyes of their dates as they passed. He laughed at this, which evolved into a cough and when he did this his head bobbed slightly as if a puppet, his pomaded hair nodding towards the pavement. He said something to them, these passing model civilians, but it was without handle and sounded a bit like a slurred blashphemy. But man, did he feel better. He reached into his pocket and removed his handkerchief and wiped clean his mouth and then the wing-

tips he had sullied with the contents of his stomach, which lay now steaming and given character on the pavement. He tossed the white cotton square into the gutter. No use in keeping *that,* he knew even without the gift of sobriety. His fumbled awkwardly at a pack of cigarettes until a single soldier was unearthed, at which point he stuck it in his mouth, unlit, and took in the evening.

He knew without looking at the signage that he was in the part of town in which he could not swing a dead cat without hitting a whorehouse or nightclub or saloon that did not have roots, or books, with the mob. The job may have fallen apart, but the night was still young. He spit once then, a thick gob that turned over upon itself and raised majestically above the street before catching the window of a passing car and was ferried away into the night. He stood, removed the fedora from his head and raked his slicked black hair with his fingers before rehatting, took note of his increased balance and the possibilities therein, and peered skyward at the bowl of stars presented. Then he lit his cigarette, inhaled deeply, and exhaled the remains into the desert night. A beginning, again.

CATHEDRAL CITY is so named because of the southern canyon which rims its borders and reminded travelers long before of a cathedral; the fact that the city was now well known for those actions one would not partake of in a cathedral was, of course, a paradox that the honorable founder Colonel Henry Washington could not have foreseen. For while the neighboring city of Palm Springs held the sobriquet of being the vacation home for the rich and beautiful on location from Hollywood, Cathedral City was surely the slutty younger sister, bereft of elegance, manners, and the money that often accompanies such things, but no less full of the lascivious desires therein. In short, Cat City was the place to go after dark. The mob had its hands in prostitution and nightclubs, after hours gambling and the habits that went with it.

Unlike the city which housed it, The Hotsy Totsy Club was appropriately titled. As Sonny took his bearings, the neon sign, which formed an X on the repeated O in the words, called to him like a lighthouse to the wayward stranger adrift. He checked for the brass knuckles in his jacket pocket and felt the weight of them before his hand had even found purchase. By the same measure, he knew without checking his shoulder holster that he had left the .45 in his room before he had gone down to the bar. Which had apparently led to too much rye, which had somehow led to him hailing a cab, which had led to his date with the curb, which led directly to the Hotsy Totsy. Quite the straight line, if you thought about it. So he was without his piece tonight. No better reason to avoid the need for one, he reasoned optimistically. Feeling an idiot nonetheless.

What he knew about the Hotsy Totsy was this: there was plenty to drink and eat, women of domestic repute if one was so obliged, card games on certain nights, numbers games most nights, and dog fights on a given night. Problem was, he couldn't quite remember what night it was at present, and reconciling that knowledge with the given night for said entertainment was downright hopeless.

The joint was set up thusly—it was a two-story establishment, the lower of which was mainly for drinking and the mentioned card game at the back on said given nights. He, however, did not have Katie with him and certainly would have to cheat at solitaire to pull anything nearing a victory from the 52 this fine evening. The upstairs was generally where guests frequented in couples. Even this thought briefly reminded Sonny of his deceased wife and with it brought no desire for cheap Cathedral City whores. Or even the moderately-priced ones. The back, which, truth be told, only the invited were able to frequent, featured other forms of entertainment. He sat at the bar with a crash and raised his finger while ashing his cigarette with his other hand. He had to really focus on this daring show of double-handed dexterity, and realized that was probably the extent of his coordination at present.

He looked around briefly, which he knew any good detective should do to 'take in the scene,' he had read Chandler and Hammett and Doyle and was aware of the fact that he should be able to discern slight mannerisms and throw barbs upon those who would engage him, but he found his vision blurry and even his thoughts still slightly slurred. There were, he noticed, many people here tonight. Most moving more quickly than he. So, no Sherlock tonight. More along the lines of a violent W. C. Fields, perhaps. He looked for the bathroom, primarily because of the rather morbid reality that he kept killing men in that particular room. The benefit was that there was indeed a sink to wash after said episodes, not that he had taken advantage of that particular,

but it would certainly be a benefit at some point. The negatives, well, there were really almost too many to count if he were to be honest. Regardless, he couldn't find the thing, so it followed that perhaps everyone in here was safe tonight.

The bartender appeared before him, placed both hands on the bar, and smiled the smile of a man not really smiling.

"I'll have a beer and a shot of rye," Sonny approximated.

The barman nodded, then flicked his forefinger at his own chin. As if to send a message. Sonny immediately believed that he was referring to one of his many tattoos, not that he had one on his chin, but the teardrop at the eye or perhaps the inkwork blasted about his hands as he smoked.

Sonny saw the gesture and stared back at the man.

The barman said, "You've got pieces of vomit on your chin, sir. This is a respectable establishment. Please…" and he trailed off, as if the words were in hiding.

"Fuck. Seriously? Hand me your fucking towel," Sonny said, and, when the man did not move, Sonny leaned forward and grabbed the towel on the barman's shoulder and brought it to his own mouth and chin and wiped vigorously. Sonny's eyes never left the other man's. When he had finished, he put the towel into the back pocket of his own trousers and said, "As for this being a respectable establishment, if it was, I wouldn't be here." He winked. It took some motor control, but he believed that he may have pulled it off. "Now, be a good little boy. Get me a beer and a shot."

The man turned reluctantly, as if thinking that perhaps he had a choice in the matter, and returned soonafter with the order. Sonny drank from the beer thirstily. He took the room in again. The lights were red and yellow and there were lots of them and most of the people seemed to be couples. He saw two obvious greaseballs, outside of the random spaghettihead out on a date, the first a short one at the end of the bar with his hands folded over his nuts, an old tough guy pose, probably the bar manager, and a much larger one standing near an emergency exit. Because those need guarding.

Sonny sipped his beer, then shot the chaser, and the night got longer.

THINGS HAD been going well earlier in the day. Sonny was still sober and following his mark around Palm Springs as if they were both on a date. Which, in retrospect, perhaps the mark may have enjoyed. The man was a young actor making his way about town, minding the Hollywood 90-mile rule and partying with the entertainment set at the pools and resorts. Sonny had been following him for two days for a director to whom the young man owed a not insignificant amount of money. Was Sonny proud of the work? He would have preferred multiple root canals without the aid of anesthesia. But the director was a friend he had helped out in the past, and this was cake work. This wasn't exactly dealing with goons or wiseguys or erasers. The guy was an actor, for chrissakes. Little girls are more dangerous. But then his mark had gotten into a tiff, no other word for it considering, with another actor at a pool party who just happened to be the squeeze for Rock Hudson, who, while not at all gay, was clearly concerned for his friend. Said friend had been pushed into the pool, no major crime there, but had hit his head on the concrete during the fall and cleared out the pool (of which a number of the Hollywood elite and near elite and not elite found themselves) as he bled. And bled more. He was going to be fine, to the happiness of Mr. Hudson, but the man Sonny was following, a young mister Charley Hutton, was currently in a Palm Springs cell, with nobody to bail him out and nobody waiting for him when he was to be arraigned for assault. Therefore, the job had gone to shit, and Sonny called Saul Bernstein to tell him the news. Then he checked up on Katie, seeing that she was fine. She was. She was playing a house game of poker. And having dinner with a young man Sonny needed to meet, and let the young man know that there were rules involved, here. He needed to do that. But, she was fine, as fine goes.

And then, for whatever reason, Sonny went down to the bar without his piece, and started drinking after nine months. Again. There was no analysis needed, of course—there were battles, and sometimes you lost. And here he was, at the Hotsy Totsy, with not enough middle fingers to raise at the world. There never are.

SONNY'S WAY of dealing with a closed door was generally to knock it over and with a closed window it was generally to break it, but instead he passed the large Italian man at the door a $50. Each party involved was as surprised as the next and so rather than requiring his brass knuckles, which sat at the ready, he slipped them from his fingers and found himself in the rear of the establishment, outdoors, near a manicured garden (a strange accessory, he realized even in his current state), and following a cement path. There were flowers and bushes of which he had no idea the name but it was clear someone had spent significant care on the area. There was, at one point, a man in a suit urinating on a large bush, but that did not seem irregular. The man even looked at Sonny and smirked, as if they shared a joke.

They walked further. It may have been the beer, or it may have been simply the distance, but the night had elongated with the walk. Then, without introduction, came a guttural hymn of the crowd, and a brief whine of the participants. Sonny, despite his state, recognized the evening for what it was. Dog Fight night. Now, he was not a fan of these events, but he had seen plenty of them in his time in Mexico, years before. They were mostly grisly and predictable affairs where men placed their dogs where they wished their dicks to be, and, paradoxically, generally the shorter, stouter dog came out on top. Many of these were pit bulls, or, as the Mexicans referred to them 'chamuco's,' who were bred for fighting their own. Unlike a terrier bred to hunt rats on ships or multiple breeds bred to herd sheep or cows or lions, these were dogs meant to fight other dogs. Which, in Sonny's condition, seemed both alien and, somehow, to make perfect sense.

The din became louder as he came upon the small amphitheater and two dogs were at work below. There were men of every race and color standing on the benches looking down upon the fenced pit, and the trainers of the dogs stood just outside. The descending standing levels allowed the fans access to the fights with clear viewpoints. Two bulls were in the ring at present, though it was clear to Sonny from the first view that the fight was done. He wished for an official, somebody to waive the fight off. The mostly white bull had the face and jaw of the brindle-colored bull firmly attached and the rear legs of the prey already on the floor. Two puddles of blood, nearly joining, lay beneath. It was a sad sight. Sonny didn't understand why the losing prizefighter of the dog match faced death while the human boxers went home to their wives and kids. It's all fighting. Live, or die.

As he was drunk and fixated on the bull fight in the ring, Sonny failed to see the two wop's until they lifted him by the armpits and carried him up the stairs of the amphitheater. It would be kind to say that there was something noble in it, but there really wasn't. They carried him as he impotently wacked his forearms about until they reached a plot of grass near the garden and dropped him. He got to his knees. Each of the meatballs stood next to him as he took it all in. He recognized the man in front of him then: Sally Campinella. He was still short, still ugly, Sonny noted. He was in a suit with a red flower at the top pocket. He couldn't remember what that was called. Sally said: "You can't just come down here, you motherfucker. What the fuck you think you're doing? Take in the sights? Some of the guys in LA still make you for the Big Vinnie hit!? And you're just gonna walk in here, like a swinging dick, and take in a dog fight?"

That was a lot of questions, right there, Sonny thought.

Campinella paused then, ran his thumb across his lips. Then he said, "If I had one iota, you tattooed freak: I'd plug your ass right here. Drunk, like you should be. I can smell you from here." He shrugged. "But I'm a nice guy. The old days is the old days." He smiled at Sonny, with teeth too large for his face. Then he hit him once, twice about the head, and Sonny felt his right ear bleed as the warmth of it ran down his neck. Then Sally turned, quickly, back towards the fights, and said, as he walked away: "do your shit." Now, Sonny had been drunk, as anybody near him would attest; and he had been distracted, as he had been carried off like a misfit child; but this newest insult, as if middle fingers had not been invented, woke him anew. One of the lugs stepped on his ankle and twisted his boot on it with his full weight. Sonny grunted and put his left hand out to the two lugs as if asking for time, just another second, while he reached for the brass knuckles in his coat pocket with his right hand and affixed them. He sprang upon the men then from his knees, breaking the tibia of the first man immediately (upon which he would never walk with a normal step again), and collapsing the face on the left side of the second as he sprung upward and towards him. It was a brutal three seconds. The first man, his leg bent slightly at an angle wholly unnatural, began sobbing quietly. The second man twitched slightly, face down. Sonny limped towards the small amphitheater again, feeling much less drunk, now. His ankle throbbed and he could already feel the swelling and his heartbeat down there.

There were two dogs beginning another dance anew: this time an undersized bull and a German shepherd, not a pup but barely into manhood. They barked, snapped, and growled at each other as they were held back. Sonny spotted Sally Campinella at about 0300. Sally was not looking at him, as the frenzy towards the alpha spectacle drew him as well. Sonny started walking that way upon the top row as the fight began. Both dogs were game, but it was clear within 30 seconds that the bull was taking the fight from the shepherd as he latched upon the neck and blood dripped, then ran onto the dirt below. The shepherd, however, was a savage as well. Despite realizing the game was up, he gripped the ear of the bull with his long snout, pulling blood, bossing the ring as he could. Sonny continoued around the uppermost row, then descended the benches gingerly with his gimpy ankle until he stood directly behind Sally C. Sally was enraptured with the fight, and he put his own hand up as if to protect him from the bull; Sonny grabbed his greasy, pomaded hair by the top of the head and pulled him backward and pummeled him once, twice in the face; he felt teeth and bone give; no words were needed.

He drew his hand back again and looked at the fractured visage below. Some partial person, now. The brass knuckles were slicked crimson and Sonny wiped those on the man's shirt collar. Then he stepped downward in the rows amid the crowd and climbed the fence into the ring. He kicked the bull with his right foot twice and when it did not give he punched it brutally in the ribs with his brass knuckles. The blow emitted an immediate howl and the bull released and retreated. The crowd had quieted, unsure of how to react. Sonny picked the bloodied shepherd up and put it over his two shoulders and walked through the fence from which both trainer and dog entered. Neither man approached him.

IT WAS a strange sight, this thick and bloodied man limping about the streets with a bloodier dog about his shoulders. The dog was licking the man's right ear and it made his fedora lean forward to the left, hanging about his head by gravity and angle alone. The man held his left hand out as if to hitch a ride, as if those about were so foolish as to take such a pair.

A cab did stop, however. It was the same French driver from before, Sonny realized, and of course it was. If he could handle Sonny nearly puking in his cab and now carried a dying dog on his shoulders it must indeed be a part of some larger mythic quest which, truth be told, may not have been the case. But fault the cabdriver none for the thought. Sonny leaned down into the backseat and (very awkwardly) placed the wounded dog on the red plastic bench seat and said 'animal hospital' in a much more sober manner than before and watched the night pass as the cab drove west.

SONNY HAD fallen asleep in a plastic chair in the lobby of the hospital as the medical personnel did what they could do for the wounded shepherd. He woke to a man in a lab coat standing above him. He had no idea the time. He grunted a sort of greeting and snorted and removed his hat. He cupped his eyes in his palms and raked his hands through his hair and looked back up again. The man in the lab coat was still there.

"Sir? Sorry to wake you… but I have news on the dog that you brought in," the man said.

"Yeah. Okay. Right, dog."

"The animal sustained a good deal of blood loss and some significant puncture wounds, but will otherwise be fine. You got him here in time." The man paused, and, seeing that Sonny was not responding, added: "He's shaved in some areas and bandaged in others, but… he'll be okay."

Sonny smiled at that. A grin nearing a grimace that made his face ache anew from the pounding he had taken earlier in the evening. He was sure, now that he thought of it, that he still had the caked blood on his face and neck. The man in the lab coat sat down in a plastic chair across from him and looked severe. Or whatever other expression passed for serious. He half-grinned, and began: "Sir, you look as if maybe you need some care as well. And…" he paused here, clearly searching for words he was uncomfortable finding, "well… about your dog. How *did* the animal get those type of wounds?" Sonny was tired and his head was aching and ringing and he felt as if he might come out on the right side of tonight regardless of the sobriety slip and it suddenly sprang to mind that honesty sometimes is the best policy. Sometimes.

He looked down at the fedora on the chair next to him and rubbed his stubbled cheek and flakes of dried blood fell to the floor. He nodded to the man, fumbled for a cigarette and lit it. Inhaled, exhaled towards the neon above. "Okay," he said.

"So here's the thing: I don't know this dog from Adam. He's a shepherd, I liked his spirit. He was going down, he knew it. But that fucker," he accentuated this by pointing with his cigarette towards where he imagined the dog to be, in the innards of the animal ER, "well, he just wouldn't give an inch. Here's the thing, doc. Are you a doc?"

The man nodded, once. He was young with curly hair and round spectacles and sat attendant. Sonny dragged the smoke, and continued: "I was at a dog fight tonight, and took a bit of a beating myself. Drunk myself into a stupor first. And this Dago goes by the name of Sally Campinella slaps me up a bit with his muscle and claims I had something to do with a murder of this shitbag Vinnie in LA, who was close with Mickey Cohen, and so he figures I deserve what I got coming. It's all shit. I kill people with some regularity these days, doc." He said this last bit with a clarity that surprised even him. As if he had confused the early morning lobby of an animal hospital for the confessional. "But dogs, now…" he continued, "dogs, well, they ain't got a choice. That's bullshit in my book." He dragged his smoke, exhaled. "And it's only my book we're talking here, right, compadre?" The doctor looked at Sonny as if there was a script for the scene and he had not been given it. He was surprised and embarrassed and interested all at once.

"I'm glad the dog is gonna make it. He'll come home with me. My daughter will like that." He smiled briefly at the thought. "As for me? Nothing that some iodine and an ankle brace won't cure." He looked the doc in the eyes then, and dragged his cigarette.

"Well," the doctor said, "I… uh, I'm glad that you brought the animal in when you did. The events that you describe make it difficult to quite understand… but, he couldn't have sustained that blood loss for much longer." He began to reach for Sonny's knee for sincerity, then thought better of it and rested it on his own, and continued: "This was a good thing you did. I… don't understand the rest of what you spoke of, but this was good."

Sonny smirked around the cigarette between his lips. "Yeah, maybe you should stick to animals, doc," he said, and stood, his ankle flaring immediately upon taking weight. He stretched his arms and shoulders, and looked down at the man still seated. "Hey, by the by, you wouldn't happen to have any leashes, would you?"

THE HOSPITAL ended up only being a few blocks from Sonny's hotel so he decided to walk the way home. What better way to get used to one another, he reasoned. He spoke to the dog the whole way home, telling the shepherd about his resolve in the ring and of Katie who would be another part of the new family and of his drinking slip which he hoped to keep between the two of them. Regret is best held for the loser, or the fallen, and thus each of them stumbled home in his way, leashed and limping, unable at times to tell one from another, but entirely together, a union at once primal and whole.

IN CUSTODY

by Jane Jakeman

OT ROOM for this one?"

"Get him away from my desk, Gregg! Christ, he's dripping everywhere! As if the rain's not enough—coming through the roof in this rotten old place."

"We'll be out of it in a week anyway. Due for demolition, minimum staffing, sell the site—story of local policing in our time, Sarge. Right you, get your nose off the sergeant's nice clean desk, you dirty young Mick."

DC Gregg pushed his prisoner away from the surface of the custody desk, smeared by snot and blood.

Rainwater continued to drip from the stained ceiling. The boy opened his eyes and struggled.

"God's sake, I can't breathe!" His voice was faint, squeaking like a hog-tied animal. His feathery red hair was darkened by liquids.

"He's going! Hold him up and get him out of my way!"

A fleshy hand grasped the collar of the boy's stained denim jacket.

"Don't worry about it lad, you're going to get special attention."

DC Gregg was strong enough to haul the boy upright with one arm. The collar of his grey-white nylon shirt had been torn open and a gold cross dangled from a thin chain. Gregg pulled at it and then let it swing back.

"Didn't I bloody know it! He's Holy Catholic Roller! Send for the chaplain! Want the last rites, do you, son?"

He turned towards the cells, pulling the boy around. "Which box you got reserved tonight, Sarge?"

Willis looked up at the bank of screens and muttered as if reluctantly, "The regular. Number five. But this is the last time, I told you before—I'll not risk it again. That spying bitch is in charge up at HQ—keep the bloody skirts out, I say. What did the kid do, anyway? What's the charge?"

Gregg dragged the boy towards the cells. "Christ, he's passed out. I've got a dead weight here. Sacks of potatoes, them sodding Irish. The charge? Resisting arrest, assaulting a police officer… you know the routine. Regular stuff. You bloody owe me, Willis."

Willis muttered under his breath. "That's paid off."

"What did you say? Leah still at Uni, isn't she? Could be locked up in a cell right now, that daughter of yours. Good job it was me got hold of her. And the white stuff. Give us a couple of ,imutes here, will you?"

He kicked open the door of cell five. Within, a low-watt yellow bulb illuminated a narrow metal bed, high walls, a tiny window-grating. Very little had been changed at this station since the nineteenth-century, except for the CCTV technology around the custody desk.

Willis was smarting at Gregg's words and his fist curled up in impotent rage, but he controlled himself as he called out, "This boy here. Name?"

Gregg fumbled with one hand in the boy's jacket pocket, produced a cheap plastic card holder and threw it towards the desk.

Willis picked it up and took out a credit card with a curly glittery logo on it. "Mr. Cashel Riley" said the name across the front.

"Have to enter you in the charge book, Mr. Cashel Riley," he said and looked at the bank of screens again as the cell door slammed shut.

One screen was blank.

THE CORONER droned on. "The forensic evidence showed that the deceased had suffered multiple injuries. If I may sum up your evidence, Dr. Alexander—"

He turned to the pathologist, who made a little bow of assent. "Of course, Mr. Compton."

"Good, now, Dr. Alexander has testified that there were two severe blows to the skull, one in the front to the face, one at the crown of the skull. The implement with which these were delivered cannot be determined, but that to the face could have been made by a blow from a fist. That blow would have caused difficulty in breathing, impacting on the nose and mouth. If the deceased had received attention, however, that and the impact to the head would not in themselves have been the cause of death. But there were also a number—Dr. Alexander says at least five—crushing impacts to the ribs, resulting in a fractured bone penetrating the right lung.

"How did the deceased come by these injuries? That we cannot answer with the slender evidence before us. Sergeant Willis has testified, and we have seen from the evidence of the CCTV record of the custody desk camera, that the deceased had what appeared to be a minor facial injuriy when he was brought to Hall Lane station at three-thirty a.m., according to the station records. DC Gregg, the arresting officer, assisted him into a cell. He was not thought sufficiently injured to warrant medical attention. However, at five a.m., he was discovered on the floor of the cell, having died of suffocation. Is that correct, Dr. Alexander?"

"Yes. He was found lying face-down in the cell and had suffocated in his own blood as a result of massive haemorrhaging from the pierced lung."

"And unfortunately there is no evidence of his final hours, as the camera placed to cover cell five was not operating, as DI Cumberland from the technical team has testified. Sergeant Willis has given evidence that a technological failure had occurred at Hall Lane. So we must assume that the deceased's injuries were far more serious than the two policemen concerned believed them to be, and that belief, sadly, meant they did not summon medical attention. I understand that Hall Lane police station is shortly to be closed as an economy measure and its equipment has not received the usual checks, so that failures in the electronic surveillance systems may have gone unnoticed."

GREGG WAS clearing out his desk at Hall Lane, carrier bags piling up next to the door. "Here, Willis, got another bin there? I've filled two up already. The junk, you wouldn't believe it, over the years." His voice echoed around the almost-empty station. "You going to lock up here for the last time, then?"

Behind the custody desk, Willis looked around at the peeling walls, the filthy cell-doors hanging open to reveal expanses of cracked white Victorian tiling within. The monitor screens of the CCTV cameras stared whitely out at the two policemen showing the unoccupied interiors.

"The 'tec blokes are coming tomorrow to take out the monitors," said Willis. "They'll be the last things to go. But for me, tonight's the end of it and I'll be bloody glad to see the back of this place. Mind you, we're fucking lucky not to be locked up ourselves. You went too bloody far that last time, but the coroner didn't even refer the case."

"Old Compton is a bit soft in the head, I reckon, but he's always on the side of us boys in blue, I'll say that for him. Hates the micks, too. All bloody bombers, he says."

He stopped and stared round. "Lighting seems to be flickering."

"Yeah, cables are dodgy. Sooner we go, the better. Gives me the creeps here, sometimes. They was hanging killers when this place was built."

"Don't be so bloody sensitive. They had it coming to them in those days, I 'spect."

Willis came round the desk and stood beside Gregg. "Yeah. Must be the draught making the lights swing."

Shadows continued to move around them, but suddenly a fuzzy white light began to flash in the bank of monitors.

"Jesus, gave me a start!" said Willis.

"Which one's that?"

Willis said slowly, "That's the monitor for cell five. I had it out when…."

The other screens were black, but one of them was now flickering and alive. Gregg raised his head to see the door of cell five swinging shut. There was silence for a minute. The two men stared at the expanse of scurfy metal.

A series of clicks came from the bank of monitors and lettering in red appeared on one. CELL FIVE HALL LANE 04/10/75 03.40 RECORDING

The image became steady, shapes forming in black,white and grey, and now there were recognisable bodies outlined in a soft silver. One of them was hauled through the door of the cell, the head turning briefly towards the camera, and then was twisted and flung towards the opposite wall. An arm appeared behind him and thrust out a hand outlined in muzzy platinum.

"Christ almighty, turn the damned thing off!"

Willis tore at leads around the bank of monitors, but the remorseless flickering on the screen continued. The first man, a thin youth, had slumped to the floor.

The second figure stepped forward, raised a boot and delivered a massive kick into the side of the prone boy. And again. Willis cried out involuntarily, "Stop, for God's sake, stop!"

But the kicking went on.

Finally, the second figure turned round. As he left the cell, the camera caught a full-face shot.

"Jesus, what's that camera doing? You must have had it running when I…."

"No way. There was no camera in cell five. You know that was our arrangement. I stuck to it."

"Then what…."

"I don't know. I don't bloody know what this is. But there's a date on the screen—the date you brought Cashel Riley in. And he's perfectly recognisable there."

"And so am I! This must be a recording—you'll have to destroy it."

Willis whispered, "But how the hell was it recording?"

Gregg looked past the monitor to the door of cell five, which was swinging open to reveal only a dirty tiled emptiness.

The screen had gone blank.

"All I could do was to tke the camera away and put it back after I—after I cleaned up," muttered Willis. "If it's a recording, I can't destroy it. I can't even play it back. There's no access from here, that's how they set it up." He thrust his face close to Gregg, as if trying to get something across to him.

"Everything goes straight online to Central. They run a tight unit down there. That's what the manual says, 'Facilities for playing back recorded images are housed in a separate area and operated only by trained staff.' I know the bloody stuff by heart!"

"For Christ's sake, can't you get them to do something?"

"No chance. They've got that new DI in charge of surveillance. She's a real ballcrusher." Willis turned back and waved an arm at the bank of monitors. "Looks like those damned things got more conscience than you, you twisted buggar."

Gregg had slumped down on his desk, turning as far away from the screen as he could, even though it was now blank. He said to Willis, almost spitting it out, "You've fucked me, then."

"No!" said Willis angrily. "No! Don't try to stick it on me. Why the hell did you do it?"

Gregg looked up and his heavy face weas distorted with anger as he said, "He was another of those Paddy shits. I can pick them out just walking down the street, even here in Gravesend. Just speak to them, like, hear the accent, get thinking of what happened—"

Willis yelled, "I don't want to hear that again! There's more to it than the story of your old grandad with his brains bashed out in Derry by the ruddy Black and Tans! I've heard it a hundred times. There's more to it than that, isn't there? You like doing it. You disgust me. I've had enough. I'll have to do the best I can for Leah, but I'm not scared of you any more."

He came closer to Gregg and leaned down, shouting at him. "It's something in you makes you do it. That's the truth, isn't it? I know it."

Gregg peered up at him and said very softly, "Know it? How the hell do you know it?"

There was a pause. Then Willis said, "I saw it just now You loved it. I bet you had a stiff on, didn't you?"

Gregg's hands were shaking on the desk. "You couldn't have seen a thing."

Willis whispered, "Oh, yes, you enjoyed it. You must have enjoyed it every time. I saw it all right. In your face. Your smiling face. On that screen, large as life."

Then the door started to open again and this time there was a phosphorescence illuminating the narrow space.

"Christ," screamed Gregg. "It can't be real! There's nothing in there!" He leapt up, shaking, and rushed into cell five.

Willis hurtled himself against the door, which slammed shut. Gregg yelled out, but as he banged against the steel sheeting he heard the scraping of the key turning in the lock.

Part of Willis' face, distorted by fear and anger, appeared through the hatch in the door. "You've been on my back all these years and this thing has got the evidence to send you down for a bloody long time—and I'm not going with you!"

The monitor for cell five came on again and showed Gregg helplessly banging his fists and then desperately butting his head against the unyielding door.

LAURA CUMBERLAND charged up the steps of Hall Lane, her blonde hair gleaming. "Now's our chance," she shouted at the team following her. "We'll have the place to ourselves. I've been waiting for this one. It's going to be difficult, we won't be able to keep it in the force eventually. But that's no reason to stop."

She reached the custody desk. "There's always been a question over this station. Too many arrests without follow-up or charge, too many camera failures."

She looked up and stopped short.

"God almighty, what's going on?" Her voice had fallen almost to a whisper.

One of the monitors over the desk was operating. It showed the interior of a cell with an upturned bed standing on end and a figure hanging from twisted cloth tied to the bars of the tiny window high up in the wall.

The screen continued faithfully recording. CELL FIVE HALL LANE 06/10/75 09.40.

Cumberland pushed open the door and looked around the cell, peering upwards for the small black eye.

There was no camera.

FIGHT MUSIC

by Brian Stanley

ONTY HAD started playing eights, that's eight-to-the-bar, when the fracas started. Alex was switching his brushes for his sticks, and didn't get to see what began the "incident." Kevin was… well, propped up on his stool with a back to lean on, and not doing much else. He held his bass against his shoulder with all the care of a corpse for his shoelaces being tied. Drunk? Stoned? Sick? All three? I really didn't know, but he was still able to play. Not as well as he can on nights when he's "on," but still as good or better than anyone else who plays here at The Spot when they're straight. That's why Monty started playing eights, just a basic pattern would be much easier for Kevin to follow, and the three of us wouldn't have to worry about him unless he collapsed.

I had just licked my lips and was about to start blowing "She Loves You," nothing fancy I admit, but it's the first tune I ever learned, and I've always kinda liked what I can do with it. The moment the reed touched my lips, the first shot rang out.

The guy in the white jacket with the dark hair looked like an absolute tough prick, but as cool as he might have thought he was in other situations, the sucker tripped on the last stair into the club and his gun went off, taking a chunk out of the ceiling. I wasn't looking at the entrance when the two men ran in, but from the corner of my eye I saw the blur of the running turn into a trip and then heard the incredibly loud bang, which focused my attention more on the tripping man than on everything else in the room. Things went in slow motion from there: Mr. White-jacket, dark-hair continuing his descent. His partner's jaw matching that descent—having his attention shift from the fat man at the table on the far side of the room to the thinner man falling next to him. The partner had a gun in his hand, too. He wore a lavender shirt, and sunglasses. Even though it was late and this place is so badly lit anyway, the guy wore sunglasses; well, then again, Kevin

had his sunglasses on the entire time, too. My hands lowered my horn as my eyes swept across the room from the doorway. Everyone in the room, the host at the stairway next to the two men; the young couple sitting at the table in the center of the room; Harry, the bartender; a cute, thin blonde sitting at the bar; the waitress and Billy the owner standing between the bar and the door to the kitchen; the young busboy standing on the other side of that door; the middle-aged couple sitting and the waitress at their table; the man sitting close to the stage by himself; and the fat man, the trashy-looking blonde, and the two guys in dark suits at the far table; all looked towards the origin of the loud sound and saw Mr. White-jacket kneeling on the floor, with a gun in

she got that fast?… Nah—way too tiny—that blonde) to the far end of the bar. Most impressive in a short black cocktail dress. Billy, pushed Sam the waitress against the wall, and then the brave, misguided soul, thinking this a robbery attempt, stepped forward to get the attention of the men at the stairs. The busboy pushed through the kitchen door, probably having been ready with this "la migra" maneuver since the day he started here. The middle-aged man jumped back in his chair, his arm sent Liz the waitress sprawling to the floor. His wife began to raise up her hands and open her mouth. I just stood watching the action in front of me. Alex stood up from behind his set to see the commotion better. The host just stood next to the two men motionless, a puddle beginning to form at his feet.

As Mr. White-jacket got to his feet, his head shaking off the impact of the fall, his partner, Mr. Lavender-shirt, sprang a step forward and fired a shot at the far table where the two guys in dark suits were reaching into their jackets. One was pushing the fat man down out of his chair, as he did this, and the other was placing his free hand securely on the edge of the table. The blonde put her hands on top of her head and sank to the floor, looking very jaded by what was happening. A bullet from Lavender's gun shattered her plate of pasta primavera on the table. Back on the bandstand, Monty hunched over his piano, feeling it could give him as much cover as anywhere he could duck to. Alex executed much the same manuever behind his drum kit. I began to fall down while trying to move backwards. Kevin just sat propped in his stool. I hit the ground with my right arm, and propelled myself back towards Kevin and Alex, while the dark-suited guy who was pushing the fat guy down got his gun clear of his holster and got a round off. Mr. White-jacket started firing again with his partner. The guy sitting by himself close to the stage right in front of me, pulled the shotgun out from under his trench coat.

I'm not sure if Billy realized that the two men who came in shooting weren't robbers, but his eyes grew large when they noticed him coming towards them, The fat man's table crashed as the the second bodyguard pushed it over. White-suit's eyes were big as he shot Billy twice in the face. Mr. Lavender shot him twice, too; but he had his sunglasses on. The first shot from the guy in the dark-jacket caught poor Billy in the back, but it didn't matter. He was already dead.

Meanwhile, the young guy had crawled under the table and pulled his girlfriend down by her legs as hard as he could. She

his hand. Things had seemed to move in slow motion as I said, and now for one instant, stopped altogether, then as if to make up for the lost time going so slowly, things began happening with an incredible, almost comic, quickness.

Monty's hands came down on the keyboard once, to punctuate the change in the room, now that everyone had taken a split-second to register the danger. The young girl at the center table just blinked unbelievingly as her date began arching down out of his chair. Harry dropped out of sight, just letting his knees sink straight down. The blonde at the bar impressed me, she must have been an amateur gymnast at least. She vaulted out of her stool, and immediately began crawling military-style (was that where yelped and stuck her arms in the air as her ass went to the floor. The middle-aged guy fell on top of Liz—his knee crushing her leg and his hand cupping her breast. Liz shrieked. His wife looked down to see that inappropriate sight for one second before the first shot from the second dark-jacket went through her neck and her head fell into the black forest cake on her plate.

The two men who had burst in now realized they had pretty much lost the element of surprise and were meeting a response to their attack. Mr. Lavender moved to the side of the bar, and Mr. White-jacket crouched and moved over behind the table that the couple was hiding below. The fat Italian had apparently recovered enough from the shock to speak. "Fucking cowboys!" he said, drawing a gold-plated automatic from his waist. The man alone dropped down behind his table with his back to the stage, his shotgun aimed towards the far table. He didn't have a clear shot from where he was, but was apparently content to stay there and wait. I looked behind me to see Kevin, still sitting tranquilly on his stool. "Kevin," I screamed, and he actually shifted a little to look at me as a shot ricocheted past the corner of the stage, "Get down. It's a FIGHT going on!" Kevin nodded, and I felt relieved that he'd heard me and be able to recover to be out of it another day, then he said, "Fight Song. Right." and began plucking the bass strings.

It was unbelievable. It was insane. It was surreal. It was the Haitian Fight Song by Charles Mingus. A very heavy bass and piano song and one of our better numbers. Two more shots (hitting a wall and a chair) accompanied Kevin on his first four riffs. Had he really thought I said "Fight Song"? I gaped at Kevin. I gaped at the chaos in front of me. I gaped at Monty and Alex, who were equally as disbelieving as I was. My heart stopped. My brain reeled. My hands brought my horn to my lips and I started blowing the chorus. He may not have noticed the gunshots or screamed, but Kevin heard me and stopped his solo to let me fall in. Monty's head popped up from behind his piano again. He looked like he was about to puke. Then he hunched his head back and began comping me. I wasn't as shocked when Alex joined in a few bars later.

Out in the club, the diners and employees were beginning to sense that (for now anyway) this fight was between the party of four and the two gentlemen who had burst in. Everyone was trying to make themselves as small and low as possible and hope it would end soon. Mr. White-jacket and Mr. Lavender had not said a word this entire time. The two bodyguards hadn't said anything either. The fat Italian would curse, or say something like "Caletti thinks he can rub me out! Ha!" and follow with a shot. Those shots were supposed to hit near the bar or the table, I would imagine, but all of them hit near the ceiling on the far wall. Every time he would shoot and shoot, the man with the shotgun would tense with energy. I blew a brief flurry of notes, and let Monty take a solo, noticing with the most relief I've ever felt that none of the participants in this gun battle had noticed our playing beside them. I felt sure I was right in playing along with Kevin, rather than trying to have stopped him. In as bad a situation as this was, I didn't want to make things worse by having him finally figure out what was going on. My mouth was dry, I swallowed, hoping to work enough moisture to join in on the next chorus. No sooner had I set my reed back to my lips than all hell broke loose… again.

"Punks," screamed the fat man as he emerged over the table,

"Lousy, disrespectful punks!" I realized he actually was offended as much by the cowboy tactics of the hit men as he was being their target. He fired three times at the bar and the third shot hit the paralyzed host in the chest. He'd been standing by the door this entire time, and now he collapsed; first to his knees, then onto his face. Mr. Trenchcoat, seeing his opportunity, rose up and pumped his shotgun. The bodyguard closest to him turned and started to bring up his gun and push down the fat man. The fat man and the other bodyguard gasped as the shotgun blast drowned us out completely, and turned the first bodyguard's chest bright crimson. Mr. Trenchcoat backed up towards the stage, cocking the shotgun again. Mr. Lavender was popping his head up to identify what had made that shotgun sound he had just been hearing, and the other bodyguard got off an instinct shot that broke the sunglasses right down the middle. Mr. Trenchcoat laughed, and I imagined him sneering as he aimed at the fat man. He backed up one more step for a better angle and stood right below me, in front of the stage.

I'm still not sure why I chose then to get involved. I guess it might've been to justify why we'd started playing in the first place when people were getting killed. It never occurred to me until later that if I hadn't done what I had, I would've been blown away by any stray shots or accurate ones that went through Mr. Trenchcoat. Alex, Monty and Kevin had been keeping time nicely, I don't know what they were expecting when I swung my sax up as high as I could, blowing a nice, high note… then smashing it as hard as I could into the back of Mr. Trenchcoat's skull. The thunk it made was louder than I was expecting, or maybe it wasn't because of all the other loud noises I'd been hearing. Pat, Sam, the old guy and the blonde all stared stunned. The fat man stared up at me, seeing the band on the stage for the first time. Mr. Trenchcoat fell to the floor in a heap. "Boss," said the second bodyguard as Mr. White-jacket came around the bar and shot him twice. The bodyguard fired a shot to answer him and the two of them hit the floor at the same moment. Monty and Alex had both stopped playing; Kevin still kept a rhythm on his bass. The fat man turned back to me from his fallen bodyguards and disbelieving date and our eyes met. I looked to my horn, a dent was in there from Mr. Trenchcoat's head, but it didn't look as bad as other horns I've seen. Pat and the old guy both got to their knees. Pat crawled towards Sam against the wall as the old guy looked at his wife's body still sitting in its chair. My eyes met those of the fat man again, as he nodded at me, then stepped forward, held the automatic over Mr. Trenchcoat, and shot him in the head. My saxophone dropped from my hands. Kevin stopped playing.

The cops seemed to be interrupting when they burst in a second later. The fat man tossed the gun to a table and just stared down at the body of Mr. Trenchcoat as the cops surrounded him. More and more of them came. Two of them tried to get the body of the middle-aged woman out of the arms of her husband. Another pulled the tablecloth over Mr. Lavender-shirt. I picked my horn up from the floor of the stage, relieved at not seeing any new damage from the punishment I had just inflicted on it. I blew a scale and was overjoyed to hear the notes sound alright. The policemen looked up at us, all annoyed. "Alright," said one, "Take five, guys." I looked to Monty, who looked to Alex. We all nodded in agreement that one absurdity deserves another. I looked at Kevin, who was just smiling in that altered state kind of way. Monty and Alex sat down. I counted off five beats.

The Dave Brubeck Quartet would've been proud.

INNOCENT MADE GUILTY

by Hannah Honeybun

EGAINING CONSCIOUSNESS, the throbbing from his cheek was mesmerizing; it was going to be swollen and black, not so easily hidden as the others. He couldn't tell how long he had been out for. The lights in the room were on, but a faint shimmering could be seen through the slits in the blinds at the far end of the room. He was lying on the dining room floor, blood caked to his forehead and the evening's meal splattered across the walls, like some new age art installation. The dizziness was overwhelming as he pulled himself up to sitting and then to standing, holding onto a nearby chair to stop himself from falling back down again, no doubt indication of another concussion. The house was silent, dead. His father must have already left for work. There was a dark red patch on the carpet where his blood had matted itself in with the fibres. That was going to leave a stain. The house was full of these blemishes, battle scars, much like his skin. A chipped skirting board, a dent in the kitchen island, a shattered door handle, the house was a storybook of violence. Using the furniture to keep himself upright he stumbled to the entrance of the dining room. The clock read 10:00AM in the hall. He was going to have another late mark at school. Still he couldn't just run there now, he would need a shower first, to clear the fuzziness from his brain, and reason out what had happened the night before, what had triggered him this time? At the foot of the stair he tripped, catching himself on his hands, he crawled up the remaining steps and into the bathroom.

If anyone noticed the bruises no one said anything. He wandered the halls of the school, alone, as was his tendency. He didn't like to talk to people, whenever anyone bothered him their speech was always some sort of synthetic sympathy. Joining a school mid-way through the final term would always have you set apart as an outcast, but when you were also the headmaster's son it made things even more complicated. It had never been his choice to return to St. Peters. He had been happy in Switzerland. There no one knew his family, and he was free to hide the horror that it was. Here there was no escaping it. When his mother had fallen into a coma there was no one left to protect him. His father had called him back faster than a bullet from a gun. So there he sat, in the back of a classroom, doodling in his notebook, silent and

terested in dating each other and who was making out with who on the latest episode of MIC than academia. His father had not bothered to find out where to place his son in St. Peters, he had ignored all his son's achievements, and instead had simply put him in with his age group. He was oblivious to the potential the Swiss had released in him. He had worked harder than any of his peers to become 'brilliant-minded' or that's what they had labelled him. The thought of getting himself a prestigious scholarship at university, and a good job following, drove him, single-mindedly to be the best he could be, simply to save her. If he could do all the former he could take them both far away, where his mother would never have to see his father again. He could finally be the protector. He had been enrolled into the advanced achievers course ready to start University next fall, three years earlier than most students, but it had all been for nothing. The reward for all that hard-work and effort had been revoked the moment he was called into the Principals office, and told he had to leave. His flight from Switzerland had been the next morning, and he was by his mother's bedside that night. It had all happened so fast he had scarcely drawn breath.

Outside the school buses were waiting. Ryan leapt onto one that was headed into town. He didn't want to return to the cottage, as usual he would put it off for as long as possible, and go to the hospital to see her first instead. His mother had fallen down the stairs, or that was the story that was being told. The blunt force trauma to her temple, caused by hitting the banister at a progressive speed. It fitted perfectly with the image his mother had always played, "Calamity Jane," appearing at school events bandaged and bruised like a vulnerable ripened peach, with the same worn down stories. She would laugh, and tug on his father's arm,

"I am simply a walking disaster!"

"I am thinking about padding the walls in the house!" he would chip in.

The parents and alumni would laugh along too. They were, after all such a beautiful couple. Him, tall and dark with a charmingly disarming smile. Her, slight and blonde with an impeccable taste in clothes, always lavishing a new hair style or a bright red lip. They were the perfect façade to their own dark story. Ryan however, had seen the end of the fire-poker. He had seen the piece of his mother's scalp still imbedded in the carved point. He had even seen the blood stain hidden underneath a new NEXT rug in their bedroom. He didn't doubt his father was capable of it. There had been moments before when he had thought he would kill her, but then she had sent him away. It was easy to forget how things were when you couldn't hear or see them anymore.

The nurses smiled their same pitiful smiles as he walked onto the ward. Her lifeless body still lay bleeping and breathing to the rhythm of machines. He wondered if he had been at home, if he had never left her would she be cooking him dinner right now back at the cottage, or would they both have ended up victims. It was impossible to tell, his father's temper was an unpredictable thing, there were many bruises and cracked bones he had obtained from stepping between her and his father's fists.

"Good Afternoon Ryan, good day at school?" A nurse stopped by the bed to check his mother's vitals.

"Fine," he said.

"That is quite a bruise, shall I take a look," she was examining his face curiously.

"No, it's ok," he replied.

estranged from everyone around him. The anonymous one with a dark secret no one cared to know.

"Don't forget to bring your essays on Greek mythology and religious practices," Mr. Michelson called out, as student scraped their chairs across the linoleum floor. The bell hadn't even rung, but the seconds were ticking down, and everyone was ready to leave for the day.

"Essay Mr. Dower," he said as Ryan walked passed him on his way out. "And next class, please try and pay attention."

"Yes, Sir," Ryan replied.

The teacher was right. He had missed the entire lecture, not that it mattered, he had covered the material a few years before in Switzerland. The Greeks and their religious actions had been a major breakthrough for him in his historical writing. The paper itself had been submitted for an international competition. His intellect was far beyond that of his classmates, they were more in-

"How did you get it?"

Ryan felt himself heating up. He wanted to tell someone, anyone. He wanted to scream, "It was him… he did this to me and to her," but who would ever believe him. Even if they did believe his accusation, on first examination of him they would find the scars like vines of ivy that wound their way up his arms, see the dark drawings in his notebooks, and read the encoded suicide notes on his computer. Even he knew he was unstable. Or it could always go the other way. A kindly Doctor would pull his father aside and tell him what had been said, and then Ryan would be the next one in a coma.

"Rugby," he said flatly.

"Of course!" the nurse went back to his mother's chart. "St. Peters has an excellent team don't they!"

He nodded.

Finally she left them alone, and Ryan unclenched. However much he wanted the secret out, he wanted it to remain a secret more. What would happened to him if it was all revealed? Where would he go? Things had to remain the same for him to finally get away. It would only take a few more years and he would be at university.

His visiting hour was almost up. He would need to leave now in order to get back to St. Peters before it got too dark. He leant towards her warm body, it always surprised him to discover she was still warm. He pressed his cracked lips to his mother's forehead planting a kiss. No words had been spoken or tears shed, yet he hoped that a solitary kiss would be felt and she would know he had been there with her.

Ryan removed his blazer. The sun was warm on his back, and he was starting to sweat through his white school shirt. He would have to get a bike soon so he could commute to and from the hospital without too much trouble. He wondered if there was one on site he could pilfer for himself. The walk was long, most of it took him along back country roads, and he was happy to have a bit of solitude before arriving home. He could prepare himself, although what for was always a mystery. He cut through the school hardcourts towards the School Master's cottage. The beat-up Toyota Yaris was parked in the driveway as it was most nights of the week. It belonged to Kimberley Bellingham, a sixth form student who, because of her excellent academic potential was receiving private tutoring from Dr. Dower. The fact that she was captain of the field hockey team, had legs for days and great tits had nothing to do with her privileged position. There was always a parade of them coming-and-going from the house. Beautiful young students, eager to please their Master. Ryan had gotten used to it, he may even say he was impressed by his father's ability to keep them all satisfied, and hidden from the prying eyes of his staff.

Ryan reached the house, the small cottage was built at the edge of the school grounds. Originally a Victorian estate the whole school had an air of arrogance to it, which suited his father down to the ground. The Master's cottage would have been the original gate keepers, and his father enjoyed the privacy the Masters house provided, many of the other teachers were living among the students in private suites. Ryan rattled his keys in the lock hoping Kimberley and his father would finish up what they were in the middle of before he opened the door. Inside the hallway was dark, the dining room door was closed, and the lounge curtains had been closed. He could hear the sounds of hushed talking coming from upstairs. The cottage, being the age it was did not have sub-

stantial soundproofing. Heading into the kitchen, Ryan tried to block out the scuffling coming from the bedroom upstairs as he poured himself a drink. Kimberley came down the stairs first, buttoning up her blouse as she went. She smiled at him with flushed red cheeks. His father lumbered down behind her, placing a hand on her buttocks he ushered her out the door.

"Bye Ryan! Good evening Doctor Dower" she said.

Ryan walked across the kitchen to the sink and placed the used glass in the washing up bowl. He wondered if his father had laid a hand on Kimberly yet, if she enjoyed his rough touch? It was of course inevitable, his father was a creature of habit.

The acrid stench of sweat seeped over to him. His father had come into the kitchen behind him. Ryan braced himself mentally; outwardly, he remained the small and defiant son he had always been. Whenever his father was close he seemed to shrink, concertina in on his own body. It didn't matter how small he could make himself his father's aim was always true, ribs, cheeks, balls, he never missed his target.

"How was mechanical mum?" His voice, dark and smooth made Ryan's hair stand on edge. His words were always coarse, always admonitory.

"The Doctor called today. They think we should switch her off".

"What?" Ryan spun around. "What do you mean switch her off?"

"Pull the plug, put her down…."

Bile rose up the back of his throat.

"You can't do that," he said, through gritted teeth.

"I can't?" his father questioned, stepping closer to his son.

Ryan felt the kitchen counter press in against his back, he was trapped.

"Please."

"You're begging me?"

"No"

"Beg me… go on…."

Ryan stared up into his father's eyes, they were a dark brown, so dark they could almost be black.

"Give her a little bit longer," he said.

"I can't hear you," his father loomed larger.

"Please. She'll pull through."

"What if I don't want her to pull through?"

That was it. He was going to be sick. Fear, concussion, or the simple smell of Kimberly on his father's skin. He turned and vomited into the sink.

"Disgusting!" his father repulsed away from him.

"Please, don't do it," Ryan begged once more, but it was a step too far. His father clamped a hand around the back of his neck and pushed his face into the warm liquid.

"I will do what I want, if I want to stop that bitch's bleeping, I will. Don't you dare ever question me again." He released him, but Ryan stayed where he was incase a sudden movement would cause his father to anger further.

"Clear that up, and the mess you left in the dining room," he said leaving the room.

Ryan stayed motionless until he heard the front door slam, upon which he fell to crouching in relief on the floor, holding his hands together trying to stop them shaking. A chilling sensation slowly consumed Ryan's body. He was being dropped from a great height. Gravity was pulling him down, everything was heavy and breathing became impossible. He was alone. His mother was finally going to be free, but what about him? Who was going to secretly ship him back to Switzerland? Stand in the way of his father's fist? He would not let himself cry, not in front of him, and definitely not because of him. Ryan pulled himself up and fixed on the tasks he had to do before his father returned. Eager to keep his mind occupied on anything other than his black future.

Once again Ryan felt as if reality was in fast-forward. The funeral came as a black wave. His father's crocodile tears careening down his face.

"It was the hardest decision I have ever had to make?" he repeated, everyone eating it up. Ryan mumbled his thanks to people who scurried past him, longing to be as far away from the reception as possible. The spectacle his father was making was impressive, he had to give him that, but then his thoughts went to his poor mother. The only woman in the world to be murdered twice by her husband, he couldn't even wait for her to die naturally. He had to have the final say. Standing by her bedside, watching everything shut down as machine-by-machine fell silent, Ryan was ashamed. He was ashamed he had not spoken up, but everything seemed too late. Like a pawn he had been moved into checkmate, and there were no further moves he could make to save them.

Kimberly's car was in the driveway when they pulled in.

"Doctor Dower, I am sorry for your loss," she said casting an eye around the vicinity. "Should I come for my tutorial at another date?"

"No, Kimberly, now is fine," his father replied, leading her into the house.

Inside, Kimberly made her way into the lounge, casually dropping her bags whilst his father hung back in the hall to speak to him.

"Better make yourself scarce," he whispered. "We are going to be doing some intense oral tutoring!"

Kimberly squealed as his father walked towards her, pulling off his tie and closing the door behind him. Ryan ran up the stairs, into his room, and flopped onto the bed, covering his head with a pillow. His father couldn't even pretend to be affected by his wife's death, she had been in the ground mere hours and he was back fucking a student in their front room. He was a psychopath, a cold-hearted killer, there was no other reasoning for it. A girly squeal escaped through the crevices of Ryan's pillow prism. What could he do to stop this? How would justice ever be served to his father? He was the only one left to bring it to him, the only one who knew what he truly was. He would have to take matters into his own hands, his mother's death had changed everything. He was not the same innocent boy who had returned from Switzerland, his father had killed him too.

It had been almost three months since Ryan had pulled himself off the dining room floor. He could hear them arguing through the wall. It had started with the small stuff. First of all he noticed his father lax up on his own beatings, choosing instead to ignore his son then engage him. Then he noticed her in school, favouring one arm over the other, a bruised wrist, and then a black eye. She was not coming over to the cottage as much, and when she did she always left in tears. Something hit against his wall, and Ryan hoped it was an objcet and not her skull.

"Don't come near me!" she shouted, her voice loud, they had moved into the hall.

Ryan heard her run down the stairs and the front door slam. He went to his window and looked out. She was sat in her car trying to compose herself. He could stay where he was, and watch her, or he could go down and do something; that was his choice. He had been waiting for this to happen, waiting for his father to step too far. His mother was dead and buried, but Kimberly was alive. She could still have a chance, if he did something.

Creeping past his father's bedroom door he scurried down the stairs, and out onto the driveway, careful to guide the door closed rather then let it slam. Ryan came to the passenger side door and tapped at the window. Kimberly jumped, but seeing it was him she released the lock. He climbed in.

"What?" she snapped.

"Drive. I need to talk with you, but not here."

Kimberly looked up at the house. Ryan followed her gaze, but there was nothing moving. They were not being watched.

"Quickly," Ryan said, and Kimberly started the car, driving them away from St. Peters.

Detective Mason Burrows stood below the large oak tree, the shadow of St. Peter's school and playing field loomed behind him. A crowd of students, and teachers were assembled around a makeshift police line. He could see phone-screens glinting in the morning sun, camera's poised eager to catch some gruesome detail to share with the world. He squinted up at the workers, swaying left and right to avoid being hit by the twigs and branches that were falling around him.

"Be sure not to hit the body," he called up.

It seemed a massacre ripping apart a tree in full bloom to unmask the scene of a crime, especially one so horrific. The body of a teenage girl was roped to a branch half way up the tree. She was fully clothed which was a relief, but the brutality of the murder was something else. He held up the evidence bag in his hand, inside were two pennies which had been placed on the victims eyes to hold down the lids. He wasn't sure what it meant, but it chilled him knowing that such detail had been taken over the murder of a child.

Evelyn Oxford, carefully sauntered over the debris in her heels, her tortoiseshell glasses already poised on the end of her nose for a clearer view of what was being uncovered. Burrows took a sip from his travel mug, wishing he had made his morning brew that much stronger. Oxford was a brilliant clinical psychologist, but her mumbo-jumbo made Burrows head spin at the best of times, and he was not a morning person.

"Teenage girl," he mumbled to her.

"I can see that Mason! Do we know anything else?"

"Not yet. We're waiting to get her down."

"All ready boss!" Someone in the tree called down.

"Go ahead," he called up. "And someone get those kids with cameras out of here!" he shouted in the direction of the uniformed officers with the crowd.

They carefully unwrapped the ropes from around the body and lowered her down to the ground. A makeshift tent was ready for the body, and Mason and Evelyn followed it in. The medical examiner pounced on the body as it was set down.

"Sixteen-eighteen year old female, strangled," he began. "Mutilated…."

"Pre or post mortem?" Mason interrupted.

"Most likely post. They are not deep cuts, just a multitude of them. Looks worse than it is."

"That's odd," Evelyn said, jotting something in her notebook. Mason rolled his eyes.

"What?" he asked, knowing he was falling into her trap.

"A remorseful killer?"

"There is no such thing," Mason snapped.

"I'll know more when I get her back to the lab," the medical examiner concluded.

Mason and Evelyn left him to prepare the body for transportation.

"Sir?" A uniformed officer approached them with an evidence bag in his hand.

"What is it?" he asked, taking the evidence from him.

"We found an abandoned car, a blue Toyota Yaris. The keys were in the ignition and those."

"Thank you," Mason said. "Looks like we have some ID. Kimberly Bellingham, seventeen years old, and there's a St. Peters school card. She's a student here."

"So what next?" Evelyn asked, handing him back the evidence bag.

"I think we need to talk to the head-teacher."

"I believe they call them Masters at institutions like this," she said.

"Whatever," Mason mumbled, marching off in the direction of the school.

Doctor Dower was pacing his office. Never before in the history of St. Peters had a body been found on the premises. The students were skipping classes to stand and gawp at the spectacle, most often joined by their own faculty member. A knock at the door distracted him, and he fumbled to get himself seated behind his desk.

"Yes?" he called out.

His secretary, Mrs. Bunson entered,

"It's the police," she said.

"Send them in."

Mason and Evelyn walked into the large office. A smartly dress, and remarkably handsome man was sat behind his mahogany desk. He rose from his leather chair and extended his arm. Evelyn sauntered past Mason and shook it, before seating herself. Mason followed suite.

"Doctor Dower," he began. "We have found a body on you back playing field."

"Yes, I am aware," he replied, curtly.

"We believe it to be the body of one of your students," he continued.

"A student!"

"Yes, a Miss Kimberly Bellingham," Evelyn said as Mason passed over the evidence bag with the school ID in it.

He felt his stomach fall. The body was Kimberly.

"Suicide?" he asked, staring at the ID, unwilling to look up in case he gave himself away.

"No, we believe it is a murder."

"MURDER!" Doctor Dower couldn't help himself now. He looked across at the two officers. "Are you sure?"

"We are," Mason said.

"Why would you mention suicide Doctor?" Evelyn began. She was like a serpent, when she had something, quick to strike, unwilling to let it go and unmatched in squeezing out the knowledge.

He knew he had spoken stupidly, why did he open his big mouth. The female officer was looking over her ridiculous glasses at him.

"You know, young girls," he shrugged.

"Perhaps you know this young girl particularly?" she said.

"What does that mean?" he spat, he needed to try and control his temper.

"Let's all calm down here," Mason said, eyeing the headmaster with suspicion. "We are simply wanting the students information so we can address her family."

Without replying, and still glaring at Evelyn, Doctor Dower pressed a button for his secretary. She knocked at the door before opening.

"Nia, please can you collect Kimberly Bellingham's file for the officers," he said.

The secretary nodded her head meekly at him and backed out of the room.

"Mrs. Bunson will help you with everything else, but if you please I have a school that needs to be counselled." He rose immediately, indicating that the conversation was over.

"Thank you for your time," Evelyn said, holding her hand out to him.

Dower looked at it before shaking indignantly, and the officers took their leave.

Outside the door Mason turned quickly to Evelyn, aware that the secretary was not in the vicinity.

"What was that about?" he whispered.

"Didn't you notice he immediately thought she had committed suicide?"

"Yes."

"So that would indicate that he may know a reason why she would have wanted to commit suicide!"

"You're grasping at straws," Mason said.

"Have I been wrong before?" she snapped back.

Mason eyed her wearily. She had a point. Evelyn had a bloodhound nose that could sniff out clues a mile away.

"No."

Mrs. Bunson scurried in with a file in her hands.

"Here you go officers," she said handing it across. "If there is anything else I can help you with?" she pushed her slim lined glasses up her nose, focussing on them.

"No, thank you," Mason replied. "That is all for now."

Opening the door for Evelyn, Mason followed her out of the office.

The medical examiner was waiting for them on their arrival back at the station. Evelyn was always highly fascinated by the morgue, Mason would prefer not to have to go down there at all, but make the examiners come up would be far more of a hassle apparently. He stood at the far side of the room, watching everything from afar.

"So I was correct at the crime scene, the wounds were all post mortem. See the killer wasn't violent, he was precise. The wounds are not deep or vicious they are barely skin-deep but they are ugly, grotesque looking in fact. There seems to be reason behind them. The marks over the breasts, the cuts on the neck, and the slashed face. There is no frenzy here, the killer took his time, and thought about what he was doing, and she is also missing some teeth."

Mason swore under his breath. Who could be disturbed enough to do this to a beautiful young girl, no more than a child.

"It is more of a ritualistic killing?" Evelyn asked.

"Perhaps, but there seems to be care made," he continued.

"Care!" Mason scoffed.

"Yes, look he has washed the wounds, and redressed her carefully."

"Was it something sexual?"

"I don't think so. There is evidence of sexual activity, but no signs of tearing or trauma."

"That is something," Mason said.

"Have you ever seen anything like this before?" Evelyn asked once more, scribbling in her notebook.

"Not in real life!"

"What does that mean?"

"Well the pennies on the eyes, and the careful damaging of the corpse, and of course the hiding of the body in the tree. These are all cultural references, some to the classics, and some to the native American."

"You mean the killer was well educated?" Evelyn commented.

"Exactly."

"A student perhaps?"

"Now finding a suspect is your job Detective!"

The medical examiner pushed the body back to the storage facilities. Mason knew that Evelyn was already forming some sort of profile in her mind, but he didn't have time to hear it. They needed to tell her parents, before someone else did.

This was always the worst part of the job, Mason thought as they approached the Bellingham's front door. It was in a quiet col-du-sac on a posh street out of town. The position of the house gave a beautiful view over the rolling hills of the countryside. In the distance a small tractor was working in a field. Mason took it in for a moment, wishing to put off the invasion of the Bellingham's peace a little longer. Evelyn however, was not in the waiting mood and she rang the doorbell. A strange tune reverberated around the house inside, Mason grimaced, he hated singing doorbells. A grey haired gentlemen, dressed in a formal suite and tie answered the door.

"Can I help you?" he said.

"Mr. Bellingham?" Mason asked.

"Yes," he replied, eyeing them a little cautiously.

"My name is Detective Mason Burrows and this is my partner Doctor Evelyn Oxford, may we come in?"

The man stepped aside,

"Of course," he said. "Maggie!" he shouted up the stairs.

Mr. Bellingham led them into the back kitchen. Breakfast bowls and cutlery were stacked beside the sink, and an aroma of coffee was coming from a french press on the side. They took their seats at a long pine table that dominated the kitchen space.

"What is this about?" he asked, perching himself against the kitchen counter.

"Perhaps we should wait for your wife," Evelyn said.

At that moment a tall, slender woman entered the kitchen. She was struggling to put on a pair of stilettos.

"Hi There!" she cooed, "I am running a little late for work. Is this urgent?"

"They are police officers," her husband replied.

"Oh! What's the matter?" her tone remained unchanged.

"You should probably sit down," Evelyn said, standing up herself and indicating the empty chairs.

"I would prefer if you would just tell us," Mrs. Bellingham replied moving to stand beside her husband.

"I am afraid that this morning we found a body on the grounds of St. Peters school," Mason began, and the air in the room stilled. "I am sorry to tell you that we believe the body to be that of your daughter Kimberly."

The parents stood stock still where they were, neither seeming to process the information. They had been struck dumb by it, like two shop mannequins.

"No, that's not possible," Mr. Bellingham said first.

"We found her car a sort distance from the scene," Mason continued.

"No, it's not possible!" his volume increased.

"We are so sorry for your loss," Evelyn said.

"Don't say that," Mrs. Bellingham snapped back at her.

"We will of course need someone to come down to the station to identify the body," Mason stood knowing that they needed to be moving on. The more time spent with the family, the less time spent investigating.

"The body… I… I…" Mrs. Bellingham whispered, her voice becoming thin.

The doorbell sung again, the sound even more jarring. Evelyn went to answer, and brought in the liaison officer.

"This cannot be happening?" Mr. Bellingham said, pulling his wife towards his chest. "I have a business meeting this afternoon…." his voice trailed off.

"PC Fysh here will help you with anything that needs to be done," Mason said, moving aside for the young officer to talk to the family.

Mason and Evelyn made their way out of the house, the sound of PC Fysh's voice steady, and slow. It was not until they made it to the car that they heard it, the sound they had been waiting for throughout the encounter, the scream of a mother realizing the loss of her only child. It was the most bloodcurdling sound, and one that Mason could never get used to.

Back at the station the events board was taking shape. Photographs of the crime scene were hung alongside photographs of evidence bags. Kimberley's school picture was positioned at the centre of it all. She was a beautiful child, Mason mused. The type of teenager, that as an adult male you would have to check yourself for double taking at. The mutilation of her face had disguised the beauty that had been there.

"How can we show that body to the parents?" Evelyn said, standing beside him, a fresh mug of coffee in her hands.

"I hadn't thought of that," Mason replied.

"Perhaps we can do dentals?"

"Some of her teeth have been removed."

"Shit!"

"Exactly."

The room behind was filling with the officers assigned to the case. They would need to get started soon. Mason had spent too long examining the board that he had neglected to refill his coffee. The beating in his head told him he was far too addicted to the black liquid, but it would have to wait.

"Good Morning everyone!" he said, calling the room to attention. "Thank you for all coming. Kimberly Bellingham, seventeen-year-old found this morning strangled and tied to a tree on her school grounds. The caretaker found the body, and time of death is around 8pm the night before."

"Raped?" Someone in the crowd called out.

"Not necessarily, but as you can see from the photographs the body was mutilated post-mortem. All the injuries are superficial and very specific as if the killer was making a point." Mason looked across the crowd of heads, all faces bent down over their notebooks scribbling away.

"We need to talk to everyone in her year group, find out who she hung around with, if there was a boyfriend, any disagreements. Jamie and Tiff I will leave that to you. I need someone to go over to the parents house and go through her room, we already have her cellphone but we will need her computer, Sooke and Haas that one is yours. Daniel, please can you get what you can off her phone. Finally O'Neil and Johnson go down to CSI and see what they pulled from the car. Evelyn?" Mason stepped aside.

"Yes, thanks. From what we can gauge the killer is meticulous, and possibly remorseful."

"Remorseful?" the same voice called out.

"The wounds were cleaned and the body dressed. Whatever the reason for the mutilation of the body, he feels it was important to do."

"He?"

"The body was hauled into a tree, I would think we are looking for a male. He is also knowledgable. The ritualistic style of the killing harks back to historical traditions. He is well read, educated, so make sure you are talking to the teachers, find out what the kids are studying. This is a targeted killing, of that I am sure. Any questions?" she scanned the room. The only response was ceaseless scribbling in notebooks.

"OK! You know what to do."

The room erupted in action as each team member took to their given task.

"And us?" Evelyn turned to Mason.

"I think we need to speak to the Master again."

"Already?"

Mason indicated for Evelyn to follow him into his office, an evidence bag was laid on the table. Inside was a student agenda.

"Every week the same thing, tutorials with Doctor Dower, and look," he passed the book to Evelyn. Everywhere the name was mentioned Kimberly had decorated the surrounding area with love hearts.

"A student crush?"

"Perhaps, but you yourself said you didn't trust him."

"I did, but sleeping with a student?"

"It's happened before, older man falling for his younger student."

"Hmmm," Evelyn concluded.

"Not convinced?" Mason asked.

"Why would he kill her and dump the body on his own school grounds?"

"Why did he think she had committed suicide?"

"Touché, using my own suspicion against me! Still I think we need to air on the side of caution and talk to the faculty first."

"Fine, let's start at the bottom and work our way up," Mason walked to the door of the office, holding it open for Evelyn. Talking to every member of staff in an institution such as St. Peters would be time-consuming, but perhaps Evelyn was right. Flying into the Master's office with swords drawn was probably not the best idea. Love hearts did not mean he was crooked. Evidence was needed, and staff gossip was always a good source for that.

Ryan could hear his father pacing in the room beside him. He was muttering unintelligibly to himself. Ryan had barricade his door with a chair. His father had returned from his office earlier than usual and had gone straight into the kitchen, poured himself a whiskey, but before he had drunk even half the glass he had thrown it across the room. Then he had thrown the decanter, eventually swiping everything off the kitchen counter, including his mother's teapot. Ryan had watched from the stairs.

"What are you looking at?" his father had snarled, making a run at him. Ryan had made it safely into his room before his father, who had remained outside it banging for several minutes. When he had been unable to get inside he had gone into his room where Ryan heard him now.

Ryan had wanted to know what was going on. Everyone was talking about it, but no one seemed to have any real informa-tion. The police had emptied the contents of Kimberly's locker, and were questioning her classmates. The playing field remained cordoned off and guarded by uniformed police. He had gone to his father's office at lunch to see if he could find out anything, but there were two people inside, questioning him. The secretary had told him they were detectives. Ryan did not want to be caught snooping so had left quickly, but had seen the two detectives later in the afternoon inside the staffroom. It would only be a matter of time before they connected his father with Kimberly, or at least he hoped they would. She had not been the most discrete character, and he was confident in her ability to have left an evidence trail of the affair.

The pacing next-door had stopped, and Ryan wondered if it was safe to leave his room. It was dark outside, although the sky was bright behind the school. The darkness illuminated by the police lights that remain on the crime scene. So what next? Would they come and arrest his father? Would they charge him with murder and rape? He hadn't really thought what would happen to him when his father was taken. He was after all, still a minor. He didn't really know if there were any relatives who could take him in, no one had ever been to the house before. Then again, his mother had kept everyone at an arms length for fear of her marriage being discovered for what it really was. Would he go into care? Even that sounded a better situation from the one he was currently in.

Ryan's stomach rumbled, he would need to go down to the kitchen soon to eat. He pressed his ear flat against the wall that separated his fathers room from his own. There was no sound. Ryan carefully removed the chair and checked the hallway. It was empty, had his father left without Ryan noticing? Ryan was at the top of the stairs when he heard his father's door click. His hands immediately around his neck.

"What did you do?" he shouted. "What the fuck did you do?"

Ryan couldn't breath. The stairs in front of him went in and out of focus.

"I don't know what you mean," he choked out.

"Kimberly…" he said. "You got in her car!"

His father had watched them that night.

Ryan tried to make a reply but his air was gone, and he lost consciousness.

It was not the first time his father had choked him. He woke up at the top of the stairs. His father's figured loomed beside him. How was he supposed to get away this time?

"Why did you do that?" his father asked.

Ryan did not know how he had known he was conscious again, but once more his father turned on him.

"Why did you do that to her?" he said again.

When Ryan didn't reply a second time his father launched himself. Grabbing Ryan by the arm he pulled him up, Ryan felt the bone snap out its socket. Noticing the limp arm in his grip, Ryan's father let it go. Lifting the same hand he slapped him across the face, hard. Ryan fell. His father used his legs then, kicking out at his son. Ryan felt his ribs snap, one, two, three, four.

"Please," he whispered trying to curl up in a ball.

"Murderer," his father shouted, kicking again and again.

"Like father, like son," Ryan hissed back.

The foot caught him in the temple, his neck snapping back from the force, and everything went black.

"What have we got?" Mason stood in front of his wearied officers.

The case was twenty-four hours old, and none of them had

had more then a few hours off. There were too many people to interview. Too many people involved in the school, too much information to be compiled.

"The Master was sleeping with her," a uniform called out. "We have evidence on her phone, email, and in her diary."

"Great, but did he kill her?" Evelyn said.

"We spoke to some nurses at the hospital his wife was at. They had their suspicions she had been abused. That and her medical records…" another officer said.

"So?" Mason questioned, this was all good but not enough to arrest the man for murder.

"Well some people think he killed her, and set it up as an accident," the officer concluded.

"Do we have a file on this?"

"We do."

"I want to see it," Mason was passed a handful of paper which he added to his ever growing pile.

"The Year Elevens are studying Greek History," someone offered up.

"Really?" Evelyn perked up.

Mason's eyes rolled, they were set for the Master, but she was once again leading them on a goose-chase. She was never happy with where the evidence led. Mason wondered if perhaps she had joined the force simply to enact a TV crime show where the obvious answer was always incorrect.

"Is that everything?" Mason looked out. There was no reply.

"Keep digging at the wife angle, and try and find the car on some sort of CCTV!" he said, indicating for Evelyn to follow him.

With the door of the office safely closed he turned to her.

"What is with you?" he said.

"I want to lock up that Dower as much as you do, but why would he damage the body like that?"

"I don't know. Some sort of fantasy?"

"No, the evidence doesn't point to sadism, but something else entirely…" she wavered off.

"Fine, you want to speak to a class of year elevens?" he said, half hoping she would say no, but instead she was at the door, keys for the car in hand.

"Yup," she smiled.

Mason grabbed his coat off the back of his door, the paper work would have to wait.

Doctor Dower looked in the small glass window that was set into the history room door. Mr. Michelson was writing on the board, oblivious to his presence.

The class however, had noticed and there was a whispering taking over their silent study.

"QUIET!" Michelson said, turning from the board.

Dower knocked, and opened the door allowing the Detective and his colleague in.

"Doctor Dower," Michelson said, putting down the chalk.

The students stood up from their desks and viewed them all curiously.

"You may be seated," Dower said. "These Detectives would like a few words with the students," he said, looking at Michelson.

"Of course. What about?"

"History," Evelyn said stepping forward. "Good Morning Everyone!"

The teenagers mumbled at her.

"Is everyone present today?" Dower asked.

"Everyone, but Ryan…" Michelson replied.

"Who is Ryan?" Mason enquired.

"My son," Dower disclosed, but the tone of his reply was not missed by Evelyn who shot a look over at Mason.

"He's sick today," Dower continued. Mason nodded.

"If it's information on the Greeks, Ryan is your man," Michelson continued.

"Really?" Evelyn turned to the teacher.

Michelson rummaged through some papers on his desk. After a quick scan he found what he was looking for, and passed it to Evelyn. It was Ryan's essay. Evelyn skimmed it quickly and passed it off to Mason.

"We will need to speak to your son," Mason said to Dower, not looking up from the paper in his hands.

"Perhaps tomorrow…" he said.

"No now!" Mason said, leaving the classroom of prying eyes.

Ryan heard voices, but he could not will his eyes to open.

"Call the paramedics," Evelyn said. "Ryan? Ryan can you hear me?"

Ryan could feel someones hands on him.

"Dislocated collarbone, broken jaw…" Evelyn listed the visible injuries to Mason, who explained the situation to the emergency responder on his phone.

Ryan tried to move, the sensation made him feel sick.

"Don't move. It is going to be alright!"

"He's fine," his father's voice spoke.

"Be quiet Doctor Dower, and stay over there," Mason's voice was calm, but the look exchanged between the two men kept Doctor Dower from answering back.

"Is this how you treated your wife?" Evelyn asked.

Dower did not reply. He would not rise to their bait.

"And to Kimberly?"

"I did not kill Kimberly," he spat. "He did! I saw him get in her car!"

The information was lost as paramedics barrelled up the stairs, Evelyn stepped away letting them work. Mason did not waste anytime, but approached Dower, cuffing him and reading his rights.

They waited for Ryan to be loaded into the ambulance before they turned for the station. The case had seemed so cut and dry, but now Mason was doubting his suspect. The abuse of wife, and child was certain, perhaps Dower even abused Kimberly, but murder? The man didn't seem capable. He liked to exhibit his power on weaker suspects, killing them would defeat his purpose. There would be no control if the person were dead.

Evelyn was tapping a pencil on her teeth beside him, her notebook open. She had a theory. Once they had dropped off Dower at the cells he was sure she would eat his ear off with her hypothesis. For now the car was silent. Each passenger consumed with their own thoughts.

"Go on then," Mason said, walking back to the car.

"What?" Evelyn replied.

"Don't be ridiculous! I know you have an idea!" Mason opened the door for her.

"I thought you never liked my ideas!"

Mason slammed it shut. He reminded himself to breath as he walked to the drivers side. If he didn't let Evelyn play for a few moments, then she might never tell him her theory. He knew that all too well from previous experiences.

"Do you really want to know?" she said, as Mason turned the keys in the ignition.

"Of course I do!" he replied.

"I think Doctor Dower killed his wife, and beat Kimberly…."

Mason went to speak, but Evelyn held up her finger with it's perfectly painted, red nail.

"But, I don't think he killed her," she dropped her hand.

"That's it?" Mason said, keeping his eyes on the road.

"I have another idea, but I want to speak to Ryan first," she replied.

"I guess I will have to wait for you to share that then?"

"Exactly."

Mason switched on the radio, an unfamiliar song filled the car with sound. That would keep them occupied until they reached the hospital, he thought. He would need distracting, or he might lean over and strangle the information out of Evelyn. Their partnership was an odd one, he respected her brilliance, but then there were times when she would just drive him to the edge of his reason.

Ryan could see the detectives at the door. They were talking in hushed tones with his Doctor. A drip was hooked into his left arm filling his blood stream with steady medication. The pain he had been in when regaining consciousness was now just a distance throb. They had arrested his father, he had heard that much, but now they were here for him. He thought about the things he could say, and the things he should. All that remained was for him to choose which quorum to share. The door swung open and the detectives came in.

"Hello Ryan, it's good to see you again. I'm Evelyn Oxford and this is Detective Mason Burrows."

Her heels clicked across the floor, Ryan counted the steps it took her to reach his bed.

"Thank you," Ryan said.

"For what?" Mason asked, taking the seat closest to him.

"For finding me," his words were slurred and the motion of talking painful with his jaw wired shut, even with the heavy meds.

"You're safe now Ryan," Mason said. "Your father will never be able to hurt you like that again."

Ryan put his head back on the pillow. The room was spinning once again, waves of nausea flowed over him, and he breathed deeply. The detectives waited for him to open his eyes again. Ryan almost wished they would disappear, give him freedom for a bit longer, but as his eyes opened there they were still, watching.

"Why did your father do that to you Ryan?" Evelyn asked.

Ryan considered the answer. He could confess out right, or he could make them dig.

"Why not?" he said, "We've been my father's punching bags for a long time."

Evelyn glanced across at Mason.

"And your mother?" he asked.

"Yes, and my mother," Ryan replied, he closed his eyes once more, he didn't want them to see his emotions, which were still too raw.

"Did he kill your mother?" Evelyn asked.
"Yes," he said.

A weight lifted off his chest.

"But he didn't kill Kimberly did he?" she continued.

The weight returned, would it feel that good to confess everything, he thought.

"Why did you kill Kimberly, Ryan?" Mason asked.

Ryan didn't move.

"I don't know what caused this to happen, but I know it was a tragedy. This young girl has been robbed of her future. She will never be able to become a Doctor, a teacher, a politician, a wife or a mother…" Evelyn took over now, probing further.

His eyes flickered.

"Why did you do it?" Mason asked again.

"I had to!" Ryan said, so quietly Mason leant forward to make sure he didn't miss anything.

"Help us understand," Evelyn said, placing her hand on his.

"She wouldn't listen… I tried to tell her about what he would do. I had to save her from him."

The room was spinning fast now. The colour had faded from his cheeks, and he felt he was going to throw up, but he had to finish what he had started.

"Steady Ryan."

"He would have done to her what he did to my mum!"

"Calm down, Ryan!" Mason could see the boys condition turning, he was still to weak to be pushed. A machine began bleeping frantically at them.

A nurse entered the room.

"You need to leave now," she said, checking Ryan's drip.

"Please wait!" Ryan grasped at Evelyn's arm.

"I need to say this, or I might not have the nerve again."

"You need to rest," the nurse answered him.

"We can talk again tomorrow," Evelyn said, patting his hand.

"No, I need to say it now!"

"What do you need to say?" Mason said.

"I didn't mean to kill her. I only wanted to save her."

"We understand, but you are too fragile. Rest and we can talk again."

"But you don't understand do you!" Ryan gasped trying to stay conscious as everything him around him became liquid.

Mason and Evelyn began walking towards the door, watched fervently by the nurse. Mason paused.

"Not now Detective," the nurse approached him.

Ryan was struggling against his machines. The nurse pressed a button by his bed calling for assistance.

"I had to protect her from him. Always."

Another nurse rushed into the room, knocking against Evelyn who quickly stepped out the room. Mason watching the boy a few moments more as he fought against the nurses trying to hold him down. Everything about him was desperate. He was not what Mason would ever consider a killer.

For a moment they stood there in silence, unsure what to say next. In truth the tragedy of this crime was not that one life had been extinguished, but two. For her part, Evelyn wanted to lay the blame fully at Doctor Dower's door, but she knew that was impossible. He would go down GBH, but not for murder.

"Is that what you thought?" Mason interrupted her thoughts.

"It is what I feared, yes."

"He will be charged," Mason said.

"I know," she replied.

"There was one thing I don't understand, what did he mean by always," he mused.

"It's a Greek belief that when you die, the manner of your corpse will be the same in the afterlife. Ryan maimed her so Dower would not touch her on the other side and she would be safe. It was an act of protection."

"Poor kid," Mason muttered.

"What life was he ever destined to have with that man as his father," Evelyn concluded.

A uniformed officer approached them from the end of the corridor, nodding at the detectives he took his post up at Ryan's door. The boy would not leave the hospital with his freedom.

Ryan lay his head back on the pillow, allowing the morphine to distract his thoughts. He was guilty, he knew that, but as the words had fallen from his mouth, so had his fifteen-year burden. His father had finally been revealed for what he was, and they were freed from him, all three of them. ◖◗

The Evolution of the Femme Fatale in Raymond Chandler's *The Little Sister* BY KATRINA YOUNES

AT FIRST, she is the sweet kitten. But then she rages at you, and turns on you. The femme fatale, according to Janey Place, is "the dark lady, the spider woman, the evil seductress who tempts man and brings about his destruction" (Place 47). She is a typical client in a hardboiled detective story. Normally, we view the femme fatale as sexy, walking into a PI's office wearing all black, holding a cigarette and speaking seductively, lips smeared with a delicate red lipstick that probably costs more than what the PI would charge her for a job. But, there are other ways she can appear in a PI's life. A femme fatale may take many different forms, according to what a situation may require of her. Rather than simply fixating on her physical appearance to identify her,

one should also look to her qualities and characteristics, especially as they are brought out whilst the PI is with her. The perfect example of an unobvious femme fatale is Orfamay Quest from Raymond Chandler's novel *The Little Sister* (1949).

The novel follows PI Philip Marlowe as he depends, yet again, on his keen powers of observation and intimate knowledge of The City of Angels. The action begins with Orfamay Quest, "a small, neat, rather prissy looking girl, with primly smooth brown hair and rimless glasses" (6) from Manhattan,

Kansas, seeking Marlowe's services. She asks him to search for her brother, Orrin, who travelled from Kansas to Bay City for work. Soon after he takes on the job, Marlowe stumbles upon a drunken superintendent, with an ice pick in his neck and a "retired optometrist," also with an ice pick in his neck. Most importantly, Marlowe also encounters Los Angeles starlets Mavis Weld and Dolores Gonzales, who, although do not have ice picks in their necks, are ice-cold femme fatales. Reading these three women of *The Little Sister* more closely shows Chandler turning the sexually attractive yet dangerous and deceiving figure of the femme fatale inside out.

PART I: ON THE FEMME FATALE'S ATTRACTIVENESS

Gonzales versus Orfamay

ONE OF the most prominent characteristics of a femme fatale is her coded physical appearance. Her sexual appeal is a ruling convention in noir. She attracts the male protagonist, as a black widow would the male of her species, to mate with him and kill him or have him killed. Of the three women in *The Little Sister* that charm Marlowe, Orfamay, Gonzales and Weld, it is really only Gonzales who is described as being a sexy, typical-looking femme fatale. Even then, *sexy* is a very weak word to describe her: "The bell chimed and a tall dark girl in jodhpurs opened the door. Sexy was a very faint praise for her. The jodhpurs, like her hair, were coal black. She wore a white silk shirt with a scarlet scarf loose around her throat…. She held a long brown cigarette in a pair of tiny gold tweezers" (69). If Marlowe's words fail him, the affective pull of her physical appearance does not.

In stark contrast, Marlowe's characterization of Orfamay seems almost totally desexualized. When they first meet, he describes her as a "small, neat, rather prissy-looking girl with primly smooth brown hair and rimless glasses" (6). Interestingly, in a comment through which the novel seems

to reflect on the conventions of its own genre, not to mention the direction that the action will take, Marlowe adds that "nobody ever looked less like Lady Macbeth" (ibid). The wife of the eponymous tragic hero of William Shakespeare's famous play, Lady Macbeth is of course a powerful and fatal character. She advances her own ambition by controlling and manipulating the kindness of her husband, whose manhood she constantly belittles. She is thus the famous ancestor of the femme fatale. But in Marlowe's first impression of her, Orfamay matches nothing of this description.

Chandler develops the contrast between Orfamay and Gonzales through his respective descriptions of their mouths. When Marlowe first interacts with Orfamay, she calls him and speaks to him in a "small, rather hurried, little-girlish voice" (4). Although her voice sharpens a bit during the phone call, she still uses her manners in saying things such as "I beg your pardon?" and "Goodness" (4-5). Orfamay's mouth is 'clean' so to speak, insofar as the words coming out of it are polite, although at times harsh: "Her mouth was small, firm and tight" (37). She is a reserved woman, and she makes that clear. Even when she and Marlowe kiss a few times, it is more of a delicate kiss, not followed by her stealing his wallet: "She reached a quick arm around my neck and started to pull. So I kissed her. It was either that or slug her… she let out a long easy sigh" (40).

Gonzales' lips, to the contrary, are not only painted red, but she even tried to bite Marlowe's tongue: "Her mouth was as hot as ever a mouth was. Her lips burned like dry ice" (72). She then goes on to take his wallet, forcing him to chase her wildly around the room. Even then, Gonzales' kiss was better than the one he shared with Orfamay, as he frankly tells Orfamay (91). If we turn back to Marlowe's characterization of Gonzales, especially compared to the characterization of Orfamay, it appears that Gonzales is the most dangerous femme fatale of the two. But what about Weld? How does she fit in?

Weld versus Gonzales

WELD IS the third of the three women

that Marlowe meets: "Her hair was fluffed out carelessly and she hadn't bothered with make-up. Shew wore a hostess gown and very little else. Her legs ended in a little green and silver slippers. Her eyes were empty, her lips contemptuous" (72). Much like Orfamay's, the description of Weld's mouth is not sexualized; and it does not interact with Marlowe's mouth in the same way as Gonzales' does. Weld's mouth, for example, twists in a "wry disgust" (75). Furthermore, Weld does not kiss Marlowe when she first meets him. She slaps him. Actually, she slaps him twice. The first time is so hard that it sounded like Gonzales slamming the door (74). Upon first meeting, Marlow thus associates Weld with Gonzales. While she does not look like Gonzales, i.e., the description of her physical appearance is not sexualized in the same way, her *act* of slapping makes Marlowe associate the two. This comparison can mean that Weld possess the same strength as Gonzales, but in her confidence and behaviour rather than in the way she dresses or puts on makeup. Somehow the physical appearance of Gonzales, in contrast to Orfamay and Weld, posits her as the most dangerous woman of the three. But, appearances can be deceiving, especially when genre convention leads us to believe that we know what a femme fatale is supposed to look like.

PART II: ON THE FEMME FATALE'S DECEPTIVENESS

Deceptive Body Language

CHANDLER'S NOVEL ultimately shows that a femme fatale is not always going to dress for her target's convenience. She is not always going to look like Gonzales, for whom *sexy* is too faint praise. She aims to become difficult to read. She may very well look like the complete opposite of Lady Macbeth. This breaking of convention suggests that immediate sex appeal is a less important characteristic of the femme fatale than her dangerous ability to deceive, to wear a mask, to mime her own opposite and thus to elude control. Luce Irigaray, in *The Sex Which is Not One* (1985), notes how it is useless "to trap women in the exact definition of what they mean, to make them repeat (themselves) so that it will be clear; they are already elsewhere in that discursive

machinery where you expect to surprise them… woman always remains several, but she is kept from dispersion" (29-31). Irigaray's argument is a perfect fit with my own. In attempting to distinguish who the femme fatale of *The Little Sister* is, it would be a mistake to simply look at the physical characteristics of the available candidates. Rather, the narrative suggests that we focus on her actions to identify her.

One prominent and intriguing action is the use of body language. A femme fatale generally likes to wrap men around her finger. In *The Little Sister,* one of the most interesting body part in the novel *is* the finger. Orfamay, Gonzales and Weld use their artful digits in different yet similarly seductive ways to lead and mislead both Marlowe and the reader.

Almost every interaction between Marlowe and Orfamay is a roller-coaster ride. In one such scene, she acts sweet, like a kitten, then gets angry at him for his drinking, smoking and crude wit. After a few exchanges that would be frowned upon in Kansas, Orfamay apologizes and puts on her charm. She "timidly" asks " 'Are you mad at me?' " ands makes "a little circle on the desk with the point of a finger" (94). Marlowe doesn't fall for her performance, or at least not all of it. He tells her to "quit acting innocent" and to "get the hell out" (94). The incident eventually ends with her saying "I hate you!" and leaving (96). Interestingly, Orfamay does the exact same thing with her finger during the last interaction with Marlowe, when, finally caught, she apologizes for her deception. As Marlowe observes: "she… drew a line along the desk with her fingertip. That was just like the first time too" (229). The femme fatale is deceptive to the very end, already "elsewhere in that discursive machinery where you expect to surprise them" (Irigaray 31).

Weld and Gonzales also deploy their fingers for seductive purposes, in immediately sexier ways. In one incident, Marlowe visits Weld whilst she is on set. She invites him into her dressing room and after exchanging some hellos, "[s]he reached up and pulled a finger down the side of my cheek. It burned like a hot iron" (132). After asking Marlowe how much he makes, "[s] he did that with her finger again and I just didn't grab hold of her" (132). Her actions evince both her sexual desire and her desire for dominance, and Marlowe's inability to stop her suggests his momentary acquiescence to both of her desires. About 30

pages later, Marlowe is talking with Gonzales in his office when, as "[s]he got rid of the brown cigarette stub in [Marlowe's] ash tray" she touched his hand "lightly with a gauntlet finger" (161). A subtler gesture than Weld's, though no less affecting and fatally attractive.

The main difference between the three women is that Orfamay does not touch Marlowe. Rather, she touches his desk. Does this aid in her feigning deception? Both Weld and Gonzales make bodily contact (cheek and hand). With Orfamay, she was apologizing for having lied to Marlowe about murder having taken place. She said that she only said so to scare him (94). Unlike in the previous scenes where she and Marlowe make up in a way, she left angry and annoyed, perhaps indicating that Marlowe is no longer putting up with her "bubblingly" laughter and cute movements with her finger (94). He has always known what kind of a person she is, but now, it seems he begins to see the deception in her coyness. With Weld and Gonzales, Marlowe does not react so negatively at their cute and seductive finger movements. The attraction prevails. The scenes go on longer than that with Orfamay and there is even some sort of a reflection on Marlowe's part on having seen and felt their fingers on him. For example, Weld's finger "burned like a hot iron" but, when she did it again, he "didn't grab hold of her" (132). With Gonzales, the touching using the finger is described as "light" and as she sat back, "[t]he little lights began to dance in her eyes" (162). And yet if the attraction, and the temptations, are greater in the last two cases, Marlowe still resists. In all three instances, Marlowe never touches them back. His self-restraint protects him from their more or less deceiving physical and personal charms.

Marlowe's Illiteracy

AT THE end of the novel, we discover that the two women most imbedded in the criminal action are Orfamay and Gonzales. As John Athanasourelis explains in his study *Raymond Chandler's Philip Marlowe* (2012): "although Weld, like Linda Conquest, consorts with gangsters, there's no evidence of any wrongdoing on her part. Far from it; she has tried to help the murderous Orrin and she's willing to take responsibility for Steelgrave's murder in order to protect Orfamay. It is hardly accidental that Orfamay turns out to be one of the novel's true criminals" (119). Chandler thus does an excellent job of deceiving the reader into judging Orfamay a mere nuisance, whose lies are probably inconsequential. Of all the Marlowe adventures, *The Litte Sister* seems the most innovative in its deployment of the trope of the femme fatale.

Yet, the detective, in the end, prevails: a convention that is not broken. Even though Orfamay acts so "ordinary," Marlowe intuits a deception in her performance in acknowledging her to be most one of "the most unusual girls" he has ever met (230). Moreover, when Marlowe confronts her about all the secrets she tried to hide (wanting money from Weld, informing Steelgrave where Orrin is, etc.), she boldly asserts, her femme fatale will to power intact: "I could tell the police… they'd believe me" (236). Why would they believe her? Because she can play the sweet kitten so convincingly. Her performance of the feminine is the complete opposite of Gonzales (the typical looking femme fatale) and Weld (a Hollywood starlet)—although perhaps no less clichéd. But glimpsing something of the actor behind the performance Marlowe scornfully observes that she and Orrin "belong to that class of people that can convince themselves that everything they do is right" (233). Marlowe appears to end up despising Orfamay even more than Gonzales, who also proves to be a criminal, indeed the engineer of the crimes and Steelgrave's murderess. Is this because Orfamay's deception was so difficult to apprehend, because until the end she was always elsewhere than the place he sought to surprise her?

CONCLUSION

IT IS conventional in noir that the femme fatale vying for the hero's romantic attentions will likely have a sweeter and purer rival. *The Little Sister* misleads its readers, as it does Marlowe himself, into thinking Orfamay might ultimately be that rival. But the actual characterizations of Orfamay, Gonzales and Weld underscore Chandler's acknowledgement (and aid in establishment) of "the fact that old-fashioned reliance on stereotypes established by detective writers is impossible" (Athanasourelis 120-121). In this novel, Chandler turns the dangerous and deceiving femme fatale inside out, as if "convinced that a new, more flexible stance that is critical of received standards was needed to realize the social potential of the [hardboiled] genre" (ibid). Granted, she is still brought under control at the end by her male antagonist. But in her increasing multiplicity, she is becoming more troublesome and difficult to read than ever. ◖●◗

Works Cited:
Athanasourelis, Paul John. *Raymond Chandler's Philip Marlowe.* McFarland & Company, Inc., Publishers, 2012.
Chandler, Raymond. *The Little Sister* [1949]. Vintage Books, 1988.
Irigaray, Luce. *The Sex Which Is Not One.* Cornell University Press, 1985.
Janey Place. "Women in Film Noir." *Women in Film Noir.* ed. by Elizabeth Ann Kaplan. British Film Institute, 1998.

LADY DEATH

by William Burton McCormick

Rīga, Latvia

Latvian journalist Santa Ezeriņa pushed five thousand counterfeit Euros over the sticky nightclub table into the trembling hands of a mobster and prayed he fell for the deception. Under low light, with heroin and alcohol in his veins, it was a good bet this Lithuanian drug dealer she knew only as "Jonas" would miss the money's falseness. A bet her editor was all-too-eager to risk Santa's life over. A bet she needed to win to survive the night.

Jonas thumbed through the bills, biting his lower lip as he counted, his long yellow incisors giving him a primitive, animalistic expression. The psychedelic lights of the dancefloor behind Santa turned in their direction, adding a touch of the surreal to Jonas's form, the thug transformed into a third-rate imitation of a Picasso figure. A *Guernica* character without the Spanish master's genius.

Jonas smiled and pocketed the money. As his coat opened, a stray beam gleamed off the revolver hanging at his ribs.

Santa forced down her fears, focused on business.

"It's your turn," she said flatly.

Jonas waited for the revolving lights to pass, then opened the weathered manila folder at his elbow. Inside, folded in rows of three, lay sixty paper cocktail napkins, thin and cheap like those found in down-market cafés along nearby *Čaka iela*. Pen scribblings in a blocky handwriting decorated the napkins, each scrawled with dates, times, and—most valuable to a journalist like Santa—clear and evident names.

Santa took a sip of her rum before examining further. Collectively, these napkins recorded the comings and goings at the Kaunas mob headquarters, a virtual criminal timesheet of the Lithuanian underworld since early winter. This she anticipated when she bought it with her newspaper's "money."

But as Santa sifted through the little note-napkins before her, she recognized more than well-known criminal names. Businessmen, judicial leaders, priests, celebrities from Hollywood to Bollywood attended the mob bosses of Kaunas, Lithuania. One napkin noted a three-hour stay by a Vilnius judge in March, another revealed a meeting with two Polish politicians in April. Several members of the Latvian *Saeima* had visited in May, the writing alleging these members of Santa's own parliament left with "donations" of two hundred thousand U.S. dollars each.

If published, these would shake up far more than the Kaunas mob.

"Tell me again, where you got these, Jonas?" she asked.

"Vikas Andriulis, the son of Kaunas kingpin Tomas Andriulis, had some beef with his pop. I don't know who Vikas was negotiating with—Interpol, the Lithuanian cops, maybe the Latvian cops, since we run so much H up into Rīga—but Vikas started writing down the names of everyone who saw his old man. Vikas plopped his fat ass in the restaurant that fronts the Kaunas mob headquarters, jotting everything on napkins, and shoving them in his pockets when anyone looked. I caught him doing it and stole the whole collection before he could give those notes over to the 'good guys.' Figured if his pop was getting pinched, why couldn't I profit by it instead of Vikas?"

Vikas Andriulis was found with his head crushed in a machine press three weeks ago in Warsaw. The police in Poland and the three Baltic Republics blamed rival gangs. The newspapers worldwide blamed Vikas's father Tomas.

Santa's instincts blamed the man sitting across from her.

"I could've gotten more money, you know?" Jonas fidgeted in his chair, sweating, growing agitated. Santa wondered if whatever he was hopped-up on was kicking-in or maybe wearing-off. "Hell, you think I planned to risk my neck for a crappy five thousand? I gave you a steep discount, lady."

"Yes. We paid practically nothing."

"You oughtta be more grateful. I'm handing you the scoop of the year for your 'practically nothin'." Under the table, Santa felt the toe of his shoe slide up her shin in a clumsy attempt at a caress. She moved her leg away.

Pimpis!

A haggard-eyed waitress appeared, her baby-bump belly spilling up over the tight black spandex pants the employees were forced to wear at *Klub Hot Brasilia*. She deposited a tubular stein of beer, fifty centimeters high and brimming over with foam, onto the table. Jonas reached into his coat, pulled out a fistful of the fake Euros Santa had given him.

She didn't want those bills examined by anyone sober. Not while she was present.

"Let me get this," Santa said handing the woman her last genuine Euro bill. "To show that gratitude."

Jonas leered at Santa, puckering his mouth over those yellow teeth. "How about a kiss of gratitude, instead, sweet lips?"

"Not on your—"

The beer stein exploded. A bullet, fired from a gun somewhere behind Santa, passed through its glass to lodge a slug in Jonas's chest. He lurched to the side, pupils dead as doll's eyes. Three more shots desolated his shuddering body, turned a man into bloody meat as he collapsed to the floor.

Screams erupted. Tables overturned. Clubgoers slipped and fell, shoving their fellows aside in blind panic, the crowd scattering throughout the basement bar in desperate search for safety.

And in the center of chaos, all Santa Ezeriņa could think was:

Not again....

"DID YOU see the gunman, Miss Ezeriņa?" asked Senior-Inspector Roberts Kalvans, a diminutive fortyish police investigator Santa knew too well. This was the fourth time she'd crossed paths with him this year alone, their meetings too frequent for their mutual liking. Yet, here they were once more.

The basement discothèque cleared of customers, if not quite gun smoke, Santa remained in the same chair as the moment of the murder, a well-needed drink in her hand. At her feet, Kalvans's men examined Jonas's body. They were not happy.

Neither was she.

"No," she said, finally answering the Senior-Inspector's question. "All I saw was the victim twist when the bullets struck him. He fell back in his chair, kicked the table, spilling our drinks and collapsed on the tiles. I never glimpsed the killer."

Kalvans shoved his hands into his pockets, leaned hard against the wall. "Spilled your drinks? You've a full glass in your hand, now."

Santa smiled despite her mood. The same old dances with Kalvans, the eternal jousting. "Maximo rum is rarer than gunfire in a criminal dive like this one, Inspector. In a crisis, you hang onto what's important."

"Understood," he said softly.

She wondered if he did.

Kalvans glanced down at the body as his men fished the revolver, brass knuckles, a syringe kit and a bag of powder—heroin?—out of Jonas's pockets. No money, real or counterfeit to be seen. Thankfully.

"Any idea who the deceased is?" asked Kalvans.

"No clue," she lied. "A chance meeting in a bar. You know how it is these days."

"I've been married twenty years tomorrow, Miss Ezeriņa. I don't really know 'how it is these days' in singles bars. What did he say to you?"

"He remarked I had kissable lips. I believe those were his last words."

"Knowing your reputation, probably, the last words of a few other Lotharios too, eh?" He smirked. "And in the killing's aftermath you stayed in your chair? While panic broke out around you?"

"Where's safer than remaining with the body? It's the one place the assassin won't be found.'

"He could've shot you next."

"If I were a target, crouching beneath the table wouldn't save me, Inspector. There's only one way out of this basement bar—the front steps. And the killer must use them for his own exit. Fleeing in the same path as an assassin only extends my danger. Unwise."

"You think well under duress."

"Only one in four can. I'm the one."

"Yes. You just might be...."

She didn't like how he said that.

Another policeman approached Kalvans, a familiarity in his manner that implied a long working relationship. In a throaty voice the officer said: "The coat check boy has a description of the shooting suspect, Senior-Inspector. Big guy, older, white, in a black suit with yellow or orange pinstripes. Memorable because he refused to check his suit jacket. On a hot night like tonight, with the air conditioning broken, everyone else did.... The boy thought this unusual."

Santa found this worrying. Not the description of the killer, that was helpful. But that the coat check boy was talking at all. She'd bribed him to keep quiet, to omit

certain key events. Like how she'd been alone with body for three or four minutes when the customers and staff fled the club, or that she retrieved her money from the victim and slipped that napkin-filled folder into her purse.

No, she didn't like him squawking to the police. She should've used a real hundred Euro bill to bribe the boy rather than a fake. But Santa was flat broke, without options....

Such was life at the *Baltic Beacon* newspaper. High danger, low salary.

Kalvans nodded at the officer's report, returned his attention to Santa. Something whimsical came across his face, an expression she instantly disliked.

"You probably know, Miss Ezeriņa, our men call you *'Nāve.'* "

" 'The Death Spirit?' You really know how to sweet talk a girl." She feigned surprise. This was nothing new. *Nāve,* when used as a proper noun, was the personification of death in Latvian folklore. A female spirit wrapped in white burial linens, usually carrying a sickle. Her culture's version of the Grim Reaper. A lady Death.

It was not a compliment.

"Wherever you go someone perishes, Miss Ezeriņa. You're worse than Angela Lansbury."

"You've been watching American reruns again, Inspector."

"There is nothing on now that Latvia is out of Eurovision. And my wife wants to learn English." He shrugged. "You'll never shed the *Nāve* moniker, if you keep materializing next to corpses, Miss Ezeriņa. I promise you that."

She stared at him, felt the weight of his words. The truth behind the jest.

"It's a habit I'm trying to break, Inspector."

FORTY MINUTES of police questioning later, Santa walked alone along *Čaka iela* towards the home of her newspaper's publisher and editor, Daks Sīkstums. It was nearly four a.m. and while the summer sun was beginning to brighten the horizon, shadows still pooled deep and purplish in the alleyways off the great stone buildings lining either side of the avenue. An unpleasant walk, a sweltering Saturday night with the mosquitos biting and drunks shouting suggestive calls as she passed. But she and Daks had to get this story written, out to the *Baltic Beacon* presses and ready for the Sunday edition in six hours.

Their lives, frankly, depended upon it.

Santa had lied to the police. Nothing

personal against Kalvans but she didn't want that folder, the basis of her story, sequestered as evidence. When those names were published the politicians and crooked cops on the mob's payroll were ruined, the Lithuanian underbosses and likely the big boss himself, Tomas Andriulis, were all compromised and soon be dead. The bad guys punished one way or another. The ensuing mob war to fill the vacuum might choke off a fraction of the heroin on these streets and reduce the trafficking of Ukrainian and Belorussian girls through the Kaunas-Rīga pipeline that lead to forced prostitution in the brothels of Stockholm, Oslo, Helsinki and beyond.

And hopefully all the mobsters would be too busy killing each other to put a price on her or Daks.

Fifty-fifty chance. At best.

She turned from wide *Čaka* to a smaller avenue, then off the street entirely into one of those open and grassy lots that occasionally separate the contiguous blocks of the city center. Daks's home was a little wooden house hidden within the shadows here, squeezed in by the higher buildings behind and on either side of the isolated land. A single-story relic of the nineteenth century before the great building boom of the early 1900s transformed Rīga into an architectural wonder. The weeds high, the yellow and green paint peeling from a weather-worn exterior, the house looked its age, even older. Only telephone lines and the glow of electric lights from the windows hinted that Santa remained in the modern age.

Santa slid the emergency key Daks had given her long ago into the lock, turned it and entered the sparse interior.

"Daks!? You here?" she shouted. "Daks?"

No reply.

The bedroom and kitchen were empty. He was out.

Santa sighed. Daks had a habit of gettin' his wires crossed, it was one of the many reasons the *Baltic Beacon* barely survived under his tutelage. Daks was probably at the *Beacon* offices waiting for her.

She called the *Beacon*. No one picked up.

Her instincts rebelled at this, but she pushed away her fears for now. She'd give him fifteen minutes to appear, then head to the offices and start working on the story without him….

Santa pulled the wad of counterfeit Euros from her purse, set them on a little table in Daks's central room. The sooner she rid

herself of these, the better. It was all Daks's 'money,' anyway, scamming Jonas his idea. She wondered where Daks got these fakes originally and how often he used them….

She'd check the bills in her pay pouch carefully next Friday.

A breeze ruffled the money on the table. Daks had left one of the windows open near the entrance to the kitchen.

He knows better than that, she thought. In this part of Rīga, at this hour, no ground floor window should ever be open even on a sweltering night. It's not safe.

"Men…" she said with disgust. She removed one of the rubber bands that held back her hair, collected and bound the bills into a money-roll. Then Santa walked over to close the windowpane. She passed Daks's darkened water closet, the door ajar. The hall's light reflected off the surface of a puddle inside.

Strange. Had a pipe broken? Santa opened the door fully. Crimson liquid flowed out over her shoes.

"Oh God…."

"ANOTHER MEETING, another murder, Miss Ezeriņa," said Senior-Inspector Kalvans, his back to Santa, stirring sugar into his coffee in Daks's kitchen. "And only five blocks from the last one too. You're quite the prowler tonight, *Nāve.*" He turned to her, sipped his drink. "Need I stick a guard on you?"

"I don't need protection," she said tersely, head-in-hands at the kitchen table.

"You misunderstand. To protect the populace *from* you, Miss Ezeriņa. There are two million more Latvians out there for you to endanger."

"Not funny."

"It wasn't meant to be."

"I don't appreciate your implications, Inspector. I did the proper thing. Called the police when I found Daks dead. Cooperated all night. With both killings. I'm practically a saint."

"Many terrible things happen under the light of your halo, Saint Santa…."

Another officer came into the kitchen. She remembered him as the one who'd spoken with the coat boy at the discothèque, the same relaxed manner, the same husky voice. His informality bothered Santa with her friend, boss and mentor dead in that toilet room. So, casual about murder, the police….

And they called her "Death."

"Two gunshots fired at close range, Senior-Inspector," said the officer. "By the angle

of the entry wounds, it's a fair bet Daks Sīkstums was on his knees begging for his life when killed." He glanced at Santa, then back to Kalvans. "Sad way to go, even for a sleezy tabloid chief like him."

"Sleezy…" she muttered.

Kalvans waved the man away. Took a seat at the table near her. His voice turned softer:

"Miss Ezeriņa… Santa…. If you are straight with me, I'll be straight with you. The unidentified man killed in the discothèque…were you interviewing him for a story? There are no cameras in that filthy disco, but several witnesses saw you talking to the victim for as long as twenty minutes before the shooting. Tell me truthfully, were you obtaining information for the *Baltic Beacon?*"

"No."

He did not believe her. Nor should he.

"Let's say I'm right and it was for the *Beacon.* Now the editor of that same newspaper is dead. Connect the dots for me, please."

"Daks made a lot of enemies with *Beacon* exposés. The murders could be a coincidence…."

"When our Ballistics department tells me the same gun killed both men, Miss Ezeriņa, will you still maintain it was a coincidence?"

She sighed. Felt impossibly old for a woman not yet thirty.

"We'll burn that bridge when we get there, Inspector."

YET ANOTHER hour passed before Santa was free of the police. The sun was high above the horizon now, but overcast skies left the streets too dark for her ease. A busy Saturday night had passed into a lazy Sunday morning with no one about, yet each person she did encounter was assumed by her raw nerves to be a mob assassin. Santa's head swam with exhaustion and perpetual alarm as she tried to drive out thoughts of poor Daks laying in a pool of blood in that water closet and think logically about what she must do.

She'd go to *Beacon* offices. Write up the article, include every crooked name, have it finished by noon. Then do an obituary for Daks. A coda for his life in black and white, an appreciation of a relentless and daring, if flawed man. When the print edition was on the trucks and going out to all of Latvia, when no censor honest or criminal could keep the truth hidden, she'd claim to any who asked that the napkin notes were passed to her by an anonymous source, hours after the killings. Kalvans might suspect, but he couldn't prove otherwise. Which was fine with her.

Daks would approve.

Santa passed a group of drunks camped on the sidewalk waiting for the 'OK' brand liquor store to open. One called to Santa as she passed, asked for a handout, begged her to wait. He spoke a bit too clearly for her liking. Too sober-sounding. When he rose to follow her, she changed sides of the street.

So, did he.

This persistence disturbed Santa. As did his closing pace. Fortunately, she'd reached her destination, the long granite building that contained the *Baltic Beacon* offices. Santa pressed in the stubborn pins of the entrance combo-lock, slipped into a blackened hallway, pulled the door closed, then ascended a mammoth spiral staircase to the top floor. She heard that vagrant pounding on the street entrance below as she unlocked the door to the newspaper's offices three stories above him, passed inside, and relocked it. Set the bolt tightly.

A wide, deep room of old desks and shoulder-high partitions stretched out before her. Here and there a lighted desk lamp defied the blackness, left on by carelessness or, preplanned protest to the long hours for *Beacon* staffers. With the Sunday edition only hours away, it was possible someone else might be in.

"Alberts? Līva?" she shouted. No answer.

Unsurprising. Who's the girl that risks her life all night while others sleep? The one who gets labeled "*Nāve.*"

She flipped the main light switch and made her way to her own desk as the ceiling lamps slowly came to life. The office was sweltering despite countless opened windows. Santa switched on the powerful fan beside her chair, felt the breeze cool her body, blow away some of the troubles of the past night. She removed the last rubber band, unpinning her hair, felt the tension in her mind and muscles melting away.

Until something caught her eye. A sputtering celling-light, slower to activate than the others, revealed a thick-shouldered man sitting in a chair by the nearest partition.

For an instant, she believed it was some new colleague working odd hours. The *Beacon's* frequent turnover meant there were always unfamiliar faces in the office. But

then the man raised a silencer-fitted revolver and said in Lithuanian-accented Russian:

"Hand over Vikas Andriulis's folder, Santa."

Face-to-face with Daks's murderer, no doubt. "What makes you think I have anything from Vikas Andriulis?"

"Our mutual friend 'Jonas' gave it to you. When you pass counterfeit bills to coat boys, they change loyalties. Make calls. Tell truths." He fidgeted a little in his seat, the chair's wheels squeaking as he did. The motion carried him out behind the partition, closer to the light. A thick, square man in black suit with yellow pinstripes, a matching yellow tie hanging down over a hefty stomach to drape across a muscular thigh. He looked every bit the mob goon he must be.

"Speaking of those fake bills. Hand 'em over too."

Santa reached into her purse, found the money-roll of counterfeit Euros, tossed it to the goon. She made her aim slightly off, prayed his gun might waver as he reached out to catch the money, give her an opening....

It was not her day. He caught the money-roll in one hand with little effort, the gun ever steady and aimed right at her torso. The goon grinned and slid the Euros into his jacket's pocket.

"Now the folder, Santa."

"And if I don't give it to you?" she asked through parched lips.

"You get shot. Die slowly."

"And, say, I cooperate?"

"You die faster."

"Well, that's unsporting of you."

"Sport's got nothing to do with it. This is all business." He cocked the pistol. "I'll count to three... One... two...."

"Okay, okay. Here it comes." Santa lifted the folder from her purse. She held it out to him, the slightest tremble in her hand. Santa's tremor increased as her thumb flipped open the cover in front of the fan face, the napkin notes flowing out like a swarm of sixty white butterflies over the man.

In the blizzard of swirling napkins, she heard his bullet strike the fan blades with a horrible metallic crunch, as Santa threw herself down and towards him, shoulders striking against his lower abdomen, legs churning across the floor, driving him and the chair backwards.

They hit the wall hard, his chair's backrest reclining violently out through the opened

window. Santa grabbed the assassin's legs, flipped him backwards, heels up, dumped the goon out through the window.

He nearly fell. A thick hand on the windowsill was all that saved him from a three-story fall. She heard his gun hit the pavement far below.

Santa grabbed his tie with one hand, slammed down the windowpane with the other. It dislodged his grip. The assassin hung in space, his tie pinned under the closed pane, its end held by Santa on her side of the glass, straining with all her strength to maintain her grip.

"Who sent you?" she shouted, trying to hold his weight, twisting the tie around her fist.

He dangled helplessly, face turning purple.

"Who?" she repeated. "Tomas Andriulis, the Kaunas boss?"

"Yeah," he grunted.

"Tell Tomas, I'll never be silenced! Daks Sīkstums won't be silenced even in death! Tell—"

He reached around to a pocket, pulled a knife, smashed the glass....

She let go of the tie. It slipped beneath the windowpane.

He plummeted. Landed gruesomely in the back courtyard. Did not move.

Okay... You... you'll be silenced then....

Out of a tunnel from the main street, that vagrant stumbled quickly to the body. Searched his things, withdrew the thick money-roll Santa had given the killer, a look of triumph on his whiskery face.

"Those bills are fake!" shouted Santa through the broken pane. "Counterfeit!"

Without a glance at her, he shambled away again into the tunnel.

Well, she hoped he got a drink or two before they busted him.

She sighed. *Journalism doesn't pay enough for this....*

Santa turned off the electric fan, collected all sixty napkins from the floor, locked them in her desk drawer. Then she picked up the telephone receiver and made a reluctant call. Two rings and he answered. Even at this hour.

"Inspector Kalvans? Santa Ezeriņa... yes... happy anniversary, by the way... no, self-defense this time... no... that's a bit rude, stop calling me that word.... It's 'Santa,' Inspector... 'S-A-N-T-A!'" ◣

SUCKER PUNCH

By Frank Megna

OHNNY DiMARCO couldn't believe his ears. He held the phone in front of his face as if it were a strange animal before saying, "Are you serious? You want me to fight in Miami next Friday?"

The promoter at the other end of the line, Wild Bill Brennan, assured Johnny he wasn't kidding. "Whatya want from me? The bum we booked dropped out at the last minute. Claims he broke his hand. All I know is, I need a replacement or I'm up Shit's Creek. I hear you're in shape. You ain't retired again are ya?'

"Not Officially." It was the literal sense of that statement that was the problem. Even though it was common knowledge that Johnny DiMarco was a partner in Kranski & Associates, a PI Agency, there was good reason for Brennan to think he could still match him in a semi-main event.

The Brooklyn Bomber, a moniker Johnny never liked, had fought only twice in the last 5 years (since his "first" *unofficial* retirement). However, both fights had taken place in the previous eleven months: One was a knockout win over a promising young prospect; the other a hard fought draw with Bobby Czyz—another over-the-hill New York legend. Brennan figured Johnny was still trying to prove something and was a good bet to take the bait.

"So who you lookin to bolster?" Johnny asked sarcastically.

"Since when are you a setup? If I'm not mistaken you're still ranked somewhere around 18th according to the WBC."

"16th," Johnny corrected him. The fact that he wasn't ranked in the top 50 by any of the other ratings organizations didn't enter into the discussion. "So who's your boy?"

"Mo Rodriquez," Brennan answered softly.

Johnny exploded, *"The Cuban Heartthrob!* He's got something like 20 straight knockouts, ranked in the top ten by everybody and his uncle. What am I fodder?"

Moises Rodriquez was not just a rising young star in the Cruiserweight division, he *hurt* people. Brennan knew exactly what he was doing trying to match him against Johnny on short notice. Even if he got lucky, and there was little doubt Johnny DiMarco could still fight, The Cuban Heartthrob had guaranteed big paydays ahead. When he beat DiMarco, the publicity alone could get Rodriquez a title shot.

It was also true he had not yet fought anyone of Johnny Di-Marco's stature—or more accurately, *former* stature.

Coyly Brennan said, "I ain't heard you say no. Think it over. I hear you're up to your ass in snow up there. Might be a nice little vacation."

Brennan was right about the snow. A week in the Miami sun might be a nice vacation—if it didn't include getting your brains scrambled.

"Give me a day or two, Bill. I gotta talk it over with Willie." He already knew what his manager/trainer Willie Gaspin would say. Brennan agreed saying he couldn't wait much longer.

Johnny hung up and impulsively swung himself around and around in his swivel chair. He wished his tiny office had a window; he had an urge to stand in front of it and gaze at the view of Downtown Brooklyn. Tony's office had the view from the 17th floor of the Crestline Building overlooking Court Street.

Just then, Gloria Frankel, Kranski & Associates' receptionist-secretary-researcher and junior partner, walked in. Gloria was short with dark curly hair and a nice figure. She never knocked. Johnny thought of her like a kid sister. "You'll make yourself dizzy," she said catching him mid-spin.

"My equilibrium's shot anyways," he joked.

She lowered her voice, "There's a funny little man here to see you. He says he's a friend."

"Oh yeah? Funny lookin is ok, long as I don't owe him money. What's his name?"

"Kenneth Felk." Johnny's face said he had no clue who that was. She tried to elucidate, "Brown hair, about fifty. He said he owns a steakhouse on the East Side. Smiley's?"

A light bulb popped on. "For Christsakes—Kenny from Smiley's. Sure. I know the guy for seven, eight years. I forgot his last name. Probably wants to say hello."

Johnny had a feeling Kenny wasn't just there for a friendly chat. That wasn't the type of relationship they had. He was maybe a once-a-month customer and Kenny an attentive restaurant owner who liked to sit down for an after-dinner aperitif. Kenny wasn't even a boxing fan and usually made small talk about current events or the weather. It was never more personal than that.

As soon as Gloria led Felk in, Johnny could tell there was a problem. He was an expert at reading body language. Twenty plus years in the fight game had trained his perceptions into an *emotion seismograph*. He could read an opponent's insides, his

confidence level as soon as they met in the center of the ring for the ref's instructions. What he picked-up now in Kenny's suppressed movements was abject fear.

"Relax, take off your coat," Johnny said while nodding to Gloria to close the door behind her. "This snow's been crazy, huh?" Kenny Felk tried to smile as he sat down. The smile made his teeth press down on his lower lip. He reluctantly unbuttoned his overcoat to reveal a cream-colored Valentino suit. It was an odd choice, Johnny thought, embarrassed for the guy's fashion sense.

Felk started with his usual chitchat about the Yankees.

Johnny cut to the chase: "Kenny, what's on your mind?"

"I've got a problem and I feel you're the person to help."

"Tell me about it." He was trying not to listen and not think about Wild Bill's offer.

Felk fidgeted in his chair a couple of seconds, and then said, "It's Gina."

Johnny dropped his chin reflexively. He knew Gina was Kenny's wife and that their marriage was a few years old. He and Mary had been invited to the wedding but couldn't go for some reason.

When Johnny first met Gina, he was surprised by how young she was. There was a twenty five-year age difference. She was long-legged, blue-eyed and framed with shoulder-length hair the color of wheat. A knockout

Johnny had heard about how they met: She was a former Rockette with a torn Achilles looking for work as a hostess—until she could dance again. Kenny hired her on the spot.

At the time Kenny Felk, pulling fifty, still lived with his mother in the family brownstone in Yorktown. The old lady took an instant dislike to the former Rockette but that didn't stop Kenny from falling head over heels. Four months later, wedding bells rang. Gina took over the brownstone, bought all new furniture and hired a new hostess to meet and greet at Smiley's. A few months later, Felk's mother died from heart failure.

"Gina just left. Disappeared. No warning, nothing," Kenny stammered on the verge of tears. "Maybe she's in some kind of trouble?"

"How long has it been?"

"Four months."

"Why'd ya wait so long, Kenny? Did you go to the police?" Johnny knew the police wouldn't care.

Felk winced. "No police. I can't deal with strangers. I waited hoping she would just come home one day."

Johnny tried to be professional: "What about her clothes, jewelry?"

"Gone."

"Sounds kinda permanent. What about her family, her friends?" Johnny inquired further.

Felk assured him he had asked everyone he could think of but admitted he didn't know much about Gina's family background.

Johnny had some awareness of the symptoms lawyers referred to as *alienation of affections*. Most of the work he did at Kranski's entailed process serving to warring spouses. Occasionally, he even tailed a wayward husband to prove there was some hanky-panky at the root of the *alienation*. There almost always was. "Was she acting any different towards the end?"

"She was a little more… quiet," Kenny said as if he understood for the first time what that meant.

"Look Kenny, let's do a little background check on Gina. We'll give it to one of the computer guys Tony has on the payroll and we'll see what we come up with. How's that?" Johnny smiled to convey assurance. "I'll ask Tony to handle this; after all, he's a real Private Investigator."

Felk looked at the floor. "I'd rather you handle it personally."

Johnny tried to explain he might have a fight coming up and, besides, he wasn't good at investigating anything, "Me, I couldn't find my own ass with both hands. Believe me."

Felk started to cry. "I thought of all people I could have turned to, you'd be the one to understand how it feels to lose a wife."

Backed into a corner, a jolt of pain worked its way through his insides. Johnny did know what it was like to lose a wife. And it was sudden. Mary died in his arms from an aortic aneurism. It happened two years earlier. Kenny Felk was among the hundreds who attended the memorial service. As he remembered it, the newly married Gina Felk was with him.

"Alright, Kenny, I'll do what I can." He told Felk to sit with Gloria and give her as much information as he could, including cell phone numbers, credit card and bank statements.

"I brought most of it with me," Felk said patting his breast pocket. He went on to explain he had an idea of what to expect After all, he watched those cop shows about tracking missing persons.

"You got a recent picture, by any chance?"

Felk nodded and reached into his pocket coming out with a 4X6 snapshot. "It was taken on her last birthday."

Johnny looked at the photo of a semi-smiling Gina. He read discontent in those bright blue eyes—but pretended he didn't. "Good. Most of this computer tracing stuff escapes me but I know what to do with any leads that turn up. I'll get back to you in a couple of days. Who knows, she might even come home by then."

Felk thanked him and left to see Gloria.

Johnny started spinning in his seat again. Now he had two separate energy streams propelling him in circles.

IT WAS around 8pm when he walked into the *4 Corners*. It wasn't the sweet smell of success that assaulted the nostrils; it was the body odor of struggle and dreams. Rarely, were they the same thing. A legendary institution for half a century, it was the entire second floor of a pre World War I warehouse on Rivington Street on the lower East Side. Johnny had been a regular since he was a scrawny fourteen-year old. The gym was only half-filled with fighters and trainers practicing their nightly rituals. Ropes were skipping, bags pounded, shadows boxed….

Johnny spotted the old man tutoring a pair of amateur welterweights in one of the training rings. It must have been after a sparring session. Both kids, dripping sweat, were gloveless and sans headgear. He loved watching Willie Gaspin handle young fighters: it was listening to a symphony while watching a sculptor chisel marble. Willie was seventy-five years old and at five foot ten, two hundred pounds, no ballerina; he moved with the grace of a tomcat as he demonstrated proper boxing technique: adjusting stances and hand positions.

After catching sight of Johnny, he dismissed his charges with: "Tomorrow, right after school. No excuses. Now go do your homework." The boys almost genuflect and head for the showers chirping like sparrows.

Back in Willie's tiny rear office, the two men sized each other up.

"You got that worried look," Willie started, "what's cooking?"

"I missed your sweet face," Johnny smirked.

"Don't *hock mir a chinik*. Spit it out."

"What kinda shape you figure I'm in?" Johnny's tone was serious.

"Fair. Don't tell me—"

"Brennan called."

"*Oye, gevald!* I heard he needed a short-notice *shmuck* for his prospect. Are you nuts?" Willie threw his hands up and asked: "Is he nuts?"

"I'm contemplatin his offer."

"A man offers you a ditch and you're so ready to jump?" Willie shouted, "You're no where near Main Event condition! You will never see Main Event condition again in this lifetime. Stay retired, *meshugener!*"

It was the same speech the last time he came out of retirement to fight Bobby Czyz in Vegas. Willie was right then too. There was no reason to jeopardize a career that listed 34 victories, 7 losses and 4 draws. He had no future in the sport.

"So you don't think I gotta chance against this kid?" Johnny tried to sound insulted.

"If I'm not senile, your birthday was last May. Is forty younger than thirty-nine? Disregard the advantages this Rodriquez has in reflexes, in reach, in brute strength—"

"But not in smarts, not in knowledge. Am I right? These kids got no discipline to learn the craft," Johnny tried to convince himself

Willie begrudgingly conceded, "He's raw, unskilled. Not in your class. But that's besides the point, you are *retired*. You promised. I owe it to Mary—"

Johnny reacted with a flash of anger: "Don't start preachin!" He hated feeling as if he were betraying a sacred trust. On the other hand, Willie felt it was his duty to protect him. Too many ex-pugs wandered around in a fog of regret and brain damage.

Willie sighed. "Like always, I'm there if you give me no choice. That's thirteen days from today; we don't have a minute to waste. Strip down and workout."

"Tomorrow night." Johnny patted the old man's shoulder, "I know it ain't easy, Will. I ain't even made up my mind yet. Besides, I took a case that might throw a monkey wrench into the whole thing."

"Then there's hope. I had my way, I'd call Brennan and tell him to shit in his hat and punch it!"

Johnny was half-hoping the Gina Felk thing would be the perfect distraction. One where he could walk away from Rodriquez without any lumps and still keep his pride. He went home to Bensonhurst to sleep on it.

Tony Kranski's office looked like it belonged to somebody important. It was spacious with an impressive desk dominating a pair of crisp leather armchairs, an Italian coffee table, couch and rolling-cart bar. The walls were covered with boxing memorabilia—most of it from DiMarco's career.

Tony Kranski had a habit of rubbing his bald spot while chewing over the details of an investigation. Johnny watched his partner go through his nervous hand gyrations as Tony thumbed through a report with his free hand. "It was a planned exodus this Gina went on," he muttered. "She changed her forwarding address on various accounts and bills way ahead. It wasn't difficult to get her new address. Like she didn't give a shit. But, it could be just a mail drop."

"I'll check it out right away," Johnny said and shifted gears "Look, Tone, I might need to get out of town for a little while"

"I heard." Tony didn't try to mask his disgust, "You ain't playing with a full deck you fight that kid."

"Jokers wild!" Johnny wiseassed. "Comeon, Tone, I'm just toying with the idea."

"Hey, you're a big boy. But you're also my business partner. You owe me to not take any crazy risks." Tony went back to head rubbing: "One funny thing on her recent credit card history," he used a pencil to circle something: "She's been frequenting this one particular gas station in Astoria—near her new address." He handed the paperwork to Johnny.

"What's so funny about that?"

"She doesn't have a driver's license. Another thing," Tony said with a pronounced head-rub, "the address is a 'care of Kurtz'. No first name."

It took inside 40 minutes to get to Astoria. Rush hour would be worse. He figured it paid to get an early start. He had plans to get to the 4 Corners before it got crowded, before five pm. A little over a week and a half to get into fighting shape. A pipe dream.

Gina's new home was a neat five-story brick apartment house, on 29th Avenue. Inside the vestibule, Johnny scanned the buzzers and found one with the name "Kurtz" next to it: Apartment 3C. There was an intercom, the kind with a handset and keypad. He decided to see if anyone was home. The wall speaker sang out the buzzes. After six, it went dead.

Johnny stepped outside, it was sunny and warm for mid-February. The snow was melting. Who needs Miami anyway? He considered his options. He decided to go to the gas station a couple of blocks away and flash Gina's picture, see if he could get a reaction.

A middle-aged woman wearing a scarf over her face came out of the building. She was carrying one of those heavy-duty shopping bags, obviously on her way to the grocery store. She stared at Johnny suspiciously. He surmised she was the attentive type. "Scuse me, you live in this building?"

Her eyes darted up and down his length before her muffled voice said, "And who are you?"

"Name's DiMarco." He held up a picture ID. "I'm a private investigator. Don't wanna bother you but mind if I show you a picture?"

"I'm sorry, I'm busy," she defensively took a backwards step.

"It'll only take a sec. Promise, I don't bite." He tagged-on an irresistible smile radiating legitimacy. It was Johnny DiMarco's secret weapon. Most women reacted with sympathy.

The allure of a nice man with such a beat-up face was hard to resist. "I don't like getting involved," she said waveringly.

"No involvement necessary. Just tell me if she lives in the building." He flashed Gina's picture.

Her eyes answered first. The woman pulled the scarf down, "She lives here. Third floor, apartment C." Her voice had an edge to it.

"She lives with somebody right?" Johnny probed

"Yes, moved into Mr. Kurtz's apartment. A couple of months ago I think."

"And you know this guy Kurtz?'

"Not really. He's lived here about a year."

Johnny winked playfully: "Kinda young, good lookin type I'll bet, huh?"

"Some would say so. He works just down the street at the Arco station. He keeps to himself."

"You been a big help, miss. I think I'll take a walk over and say hello to Mr. Kurtz." Johnny took a step away when the woman added:

"There's another man living in 3C. And sometimes a woman too."

"Another man? And a woman?" Johnny asked turning back to her. She had more on her mind.

"The woman comes and goes. Sort of the plain Jane type. He's a short, stocky man with slicked-back, greasy hair. He's seems very unpleasant. Snapped at me one time. I live on the same floor, thought I was being nosy. Staring too hard I guess. I'm pretty sure he lives there. I'll bet whatever you're investigating, he's responsible."

Johnny wondered if she was right. "The nasty type, huh? And he moved in at the same time as the girl?"

"No, about a few weeks later. I hope you don't think I'm a busybody. I just notice things."

"No way. In this day and age, you'd better keep your eyes open. Am I right?" He leaned in conspiratorially: "You wouldn't have a name on the second guy by any chance?"

She shook her head and re-wrapped the scarf around her mouth. "They're just strange. I've lived here twenty years and most of the tenants have been friendly. Nice, like you." Her eyes narrowed: "Should I be worried?"

"Nothin' like that. Enjoy the rest of your day," he reassured.

At the Arco station, Johnny walked into the cashier's office. There was a tall skinny guy wearing a blue uniform jacket behind the counter, a cigarette dangling from his lip. Soon as he saw Johnny he asked, "What pump, Chief?"

"I'm on foot. Listen, does a Mr. Kurtz work here? Johnny asked without a hint of menace.

"You his parole officer?"

"Naw, I'm a friend of a friend of his."

The cashier winked. "He's in the garage, working on a Taurus."

"Thanks," Johnny said thinking he knew what the wink meant. He was dealing with an ex-con. Why is it women run off with creeps?

There were a couple of mechanics in the six-car garage. He spotted Kurtz with his head under the hood of the Taurus, leaning onto the engine. He walked close enough to touch his back before saying, "I hear you do good work."

Kurtz turned over and raised-up to eyeball Johnny. He had on coveralls with a name-patch that read: *Lon*. He was bigger than Johnny, well built, maybe two-forty, and the type who lifted heavy weights: prison-muscled. He was about thirty and handsome. In his hand, he held a ratchet wrench more like a weapon than a tool. "Yeah. I do good work. Who sent you?"

"Howya doin Lon?" Kurtz must be the guy Gina was shacking-up with but who was the other man and how did he fit into this twisted fairytale. "Gina Felk's husband sent me."

Kurtz's shoulder twitched with the impulse to swing his wrench. Johnny saw it and took a step back. He also saw that Kurtz had self-control. He didn't want to go back to prison.

Kurtz snarled: "Figured somebody would show up. The husband's got enough bucks to hire a punk like you. Tell him she don't want him anymore."

"Listen, Romeo, I could care less how you see things." Johnny tried to reason: "It's my job to find Gina and talk to her. She owes her husband that much. Put yourself in his shoes."

"Fuck him! Rich cocksucker. He don't deserve her."

Johnny fought the urge to deck Kurtz. He had learned long ago that you can't educate jerks with three-punch combinations. Even if it felt good. "Where is she?"

Kurtz ignored him by turning back into the engine.

Johnny shifted his stance and quickly scanned his surroundings, just in case. "So you wanna tell me you love her at least—or is it her credit cards and jewelry that give you a hardon?"

"What!?" Kurtz snapped like a switchblade.

"You heard me."

"There's nothing between Gina and me. I'm just giving her a place to stay."

Johnny tilted his head to show consternation. "You telling me you ain't shacking up?"

"She's my sister Jo's friend. They're both staying with me." Kurtz puffed-up his chest like he was thinking about getting tough.

"Funny, that's not what I heard."

The rising vocal level of their conversation had attracted notice from the other mechanics.

"I don't give a rat's ass what you heard," Kurtz bellowed.

"Is the other guy the boyfriend? Is that what you're telling me?"

"Back off before I crack your head open like a cantaloupe," Kurtz warned tensing up.

Johnny had a strategy: full-court press. He took a step into the ex-con and calmly announced: "Get used to this *faccia*. You're gonna be seeing it in your dreams."

Kurtz goes off like an alarm clock. He cocks his arm back and swings the wrench at Johnny's head. DiMarco reacts by stepping inside to the right while simultaneously throwing a left hook to the solar plexus—it took years to perfect that blow. The punch lands first and Kurtz sank to his knees struggling to breathe. Johnny crouched down and patted the paralyzed Kurtz gently. "I hate like hell to have to get physical. And you oughta know better being on parole. You listening Lon?"

Kurtz, clutching his gut, made a gurgling noise that Johnny interpreted as listening.

"Believe it or not, I'm kinda a respected citizen in this city. I even got some fans among New York's *Finest*. Now, I don't like makin' idle threats, but I could file a complaint and put your sad coolie back in a dark, cold prison cell. *Capice?* Parole violation. So now, where is Gina Felk?"

Kurtz had regained enough oxygen in his lungs to wheeze, "I don't know. Swear. With my sister…."

Johnny took out one of his business cards and placed it between Kurtz's clenched fingers. "Be sure she either calls me or her husband. Okay?"

"Yeah." Kurtz grunted and glanced at the card. "DiMarco? The fighter. Thought you looked familiar."

"Thanks. You want a hand up?"

Kurtz shook his head and Johnny left.

All the talk about Kurtz's sister had Johnny wondering what the deal was. Could it be Gina Felk was just unhappy in her marriage, that there was no love interest alienating her affectations? Not that either possibility would be a comfort to Kenny Felk.

Johnny called Tony Kranski and asked for a background check on Lon Kurtz—just to cover himself. "Also anything on a sister," he added. Tony promised a rundown first thing in the morning. With that, Johnny decided to head to the 4 Corners for his workout

He went through his paces at the gym: warm-ups followed by three rounds of rope skipping, then, two rounds on the heavy bag. There was nobody to spar with so he went directly to the speed bag for a couple of rounds. His lack of timing showed. There was no music, no grace in the rapping sounds.

Willie watched him every step of the way saying little but radiating sourness. "You're sadly mistaken, you think you're in shape enough to fight," he summarized.

"Thanks for the vote of confidence," Johnny said as he headed to the showers. The old man was right. The match with Rodriquez was suicide.

Bright and early the next morning Johnny rolled out of bed for roadwork. The stiffness (from the previous night's light exercise) permeated every joint. Another bad sign. Still, he forced himself to jog/half-walk three miles along Shore Parkway under the Verrazano Bridge. It was murder every step of the way.

He made it to Kranski's around 10am hobbling like the forty-year old man he was. Tony was waiting with the Lon Kurtz report in hand. It had to wait.

Sitting in Johnny's office was Gina Felk.

He sized up Mrs. Felk as she sat down in front of his desk. She was decked out in a tailored spring suit. It was maybe a little too colorful and premature considering winter hadn't ended yet. She was much prettier than he remembered: her hair brighter, eyes greener, lashes longer. Her lips were lush. It would be easy to listen to her.

"Kinda surprised to see you here, Mrs. Felk," he muttered with only a hint of sarcasm.

"I thought it was best. I'm glad you found me," she said surprisingly.

"Is that right?"

"I certainly can understand your disbelief Mr. DiMarco. You're Kenneth's friend. But I assure you it's true. I've been terrified."

For the first time he heard the lilt of her slight Southern accent. "Kenny ain't exactly the type to beat an unfaithful wife."

She dropped her head and slowly fluttered those long lashes:

"I've made a terrible mistake. I didn't trust what I had. The goodness of it."

"Where'd you meet this guy Kurtz?" Johnny asked as if he could steer the conversation. "Were you prison pen pals?"

A tiny ironic smile emerged. "No. I met Lon through his sister, Jo. We knew each other from Fayetteville—that's in North Carolina, where I'm from…" She drifted off into private thoughts for a few seconds and came back with, "I became infatuated with Lon. He can be quite charming." She went on to explain she quickly realized that Lon Kurtz was a violent, cruel man. He hit her and promised he would kill her and her husband if she tried to leave. She didn't know where to turn.

"The police?"

"He is my closest friend's brother and I didn't want to put him back in prison."

"So what's different now?"

"You. I didn't think Lon was afraid of anyone. He's afraid of you." She leaned forward, "Tell me the truth Mr. DiMarco, do you think Kenneth will still want me when he hears where I've been?"

"Can't say." Johnny felt himself being drawn into the *vortex* of her wounded beauty.

Gina read men like well-lit road signs: "Would you? If you were in Kenneth's place, want me back?" It was of a purr than a question.

"Tough to figure feelings like that." He caught himself mid-fall. Women were not part of his life. There was still too much grief. "Who else lives with you and Kurtz?"

"Why… no one. Jo visits all the time. Even she wants me to get away from Lon. I can't face this alone. Will you help me?"

"What I can do is talk to your husband. We'll go from there. You ready to return home?"

"On a moment's notice."

He told her he would see Kenny that morning at the restaurant and that Kurtz would back off if that were what she really wanted. "I won't have to beat his brains in neither. He'll get the message. He's a survivor."

"So am I," she assured him. "I understand now why Kenneth talked the way he did about you. As if you were a fist full of nails and an ice cream cone rolled into one." She laughed at the image.

His skin was too leathery to blush. But he did anyway.

She gave him her private cell phone number. "Lon doesn't have it. Neither does my husband. I'm not going back to Astoria—ever! Please, you be the one to call me. I don't know how I would react hearing Kenneth's voice right now." She stood up to leave. *"Tuscaloosa's Calling Me But I'm Not Going,"* she joked.

Johnny had no knowledge of Seventies musicals. He cautiously came out from behind his desk and reflexively reached-out to shake her hand: "Where you gonna be?"

"Take in a movie or a trip to a museum, I guess. Or maybe a long walk in Central Park." She took hold of his large hand as if it were wounded prey and said, "I'll just wait to hear from you."

Before she let go, he concluded Kenny would have no choice but to take her back. She was irresistible.

Gina darted-in and kissed his cheek, "Thanks Johnny," she murmured.

Alone, he was still bobbing in the ripples left in her wake.

Tony walked in and, thankfully, broke the spell: "Wouldn't mind hanging my hat on her bedpost," he quipped. In his hand was the paperwork on Kurtz.

Johnny sat on the edge of his desk still half-musing about Gina Felk. He tried to shake it off by asking, "What'd he do time for? Raping a nun?"

"The last go around for armed robbery. Got him six upstate: Attica. Enjoys damaging people," Tony said and handed Johnny the two page report. "What you call a *conflicted personality.*"

Johnny flipped through the pages picking up information. "He's a tough monkey. Likes to use a baseball bat, huh… three different times. What's this?"

Tony nodded knowing what Johnny had keyed in on.

Johnny was following his own train of thought: " 'Male Prostitution'. Is that with…? He found the answer to his own question: "Arrested with males?"

"Maybe he's a switch hitter? Get it? Baseball? Batter? I spoke to a friend of mine who works as a psychiatric consultant for the New York prison system. Pulled our boy's file."

"Yeah? Don't give me that psychological bullshit," Johnny wisecracked.

"Let's put it this way, Kurtz had a good time in Attica. Had a harem of punks who called him 'Da-Da'." Tony shook his head sadly, "What the hell does a classy babe like Gina Felk see in a chicken hawk?"

Johnny sighed airing his utter confusion. *Marone.* Who knows?"

"He's only been out of the joint eleven momths. Thirty-two years old and lived in homo-paradise a total of nine years of his life. He's a fruit. Go gigure."

"I don't judge. Live and let live I say."

"Yeah, that's one of the things wrong with you. Too liberal in your permissive attitudes."

"Besides, it ain't about sexual orientation, it's about power," Johnny said. When Tony looked at him sideways he added: "I musta read it somewheres."

The intercom buzzed and Gloria's voice followed: "A Mr. Brennan on line three for you Johnny."

"Okay," he said to the intercom. "Do me a favor Tone, get one of your pals in the Department to straighten out this Kurtz."

"No problem. Parole officer too. Kurtz won't bother her anymore. Guarantee," Tony said absolutely.

Johnny took Brennan's call.

HE WALKED into Smiley's Steak House on East 79th Street as lunchtime was starting. The host, a Donald Trump wannabe wearing a gray pinstripe suit, greeted Johnny and asked, "How many are we today, sir?"

Guess Kenny's learned his lesson with lame dancers, Johnny thought as the host waited for an answer. "I'm here to see Kenny—Mr. Felk. Just tell him it's Johnny DiMarco."

The host wasted no time dialing-up his boss. A minute later, a leggy waitress wearing some kind of lavender miniskirt appeared and led Johnny to a table at the rear of the restaurant.

"What would you like Johnny," Felk said trying not to seem nervous. "Marsha, bring Mr. DiMarco a menu."

"Naw, I'm good. I can only stay a couple a minutes. I gotta an appointment with a cranky old man." Johnny noticed Marsha's eyes bug misinterpreting his words. "My trainer. I gotta go to the gym."

Marsha smiled her relief. Felk head-tilted. The waitress took the hint and left.

"I found her, Kenny. It wasn't too hard."

"But she doesn't want me. Why should she? She's young, has her life in front of her—"

"Hold your horses there, my friend. She wants to come back. She… still loves you. She told me so herself," Johnny embroidered. "You want her back, right?"

Kenny Felk's face did a back flip. He didn't want to know any details about who Gina had been with or why. Nothing. He started to cry. Tears of joy. "You're a great friend Johnny. Thanks."

Johnny squirmed but felt good about helping his friend.

"I'll cook for her. Myself, the whole nine yards. Tell her to be home by dinnertime. I just want her back in my life."

Johnny simply said the "other party" would no longer be in the picture: "It's been taken care of." He went on to explain he had to get to the gym, that he would have to decide by the next morning whether to take the Rodriguez fight

The last thing Kenny said was, "I'm throwing your victory party!"

"Yeah? But only if I beat Rodriguez!"

JOHNNY GOT to the 4 Corners by 2 pm. Before stripping down, he called Gina Felk. He got her voice mail. He figured she was at the movies and had turned off her cell. He gave her the good news that Kenny was busy preparing a *welcome home dinner.* Just the two of them. He wished her luck and said he'd call later just to be sure she got the message.

Willie grimaced hard throughout Johnny's workout. Particularly during the 2 round sparing session he had arranged with a nineteen-year old amateur heavyweight. The kid had won the New York City Golden Gloves tournament the year before and was preparing to turn pro. He made Johnny work. Not that he was able to dominate—far from it. DiMarco used every trick in the book, frustrated the kid, made him miss, sidestepped, spun him and easily kept his young sparring partner off-balance. When he wanted, Johnny hit the kid with light counter-combinations. Nothing damaging, just enough to demonstrate who was boss. The kid wasn't in the same league. It was also clear, Johnny DiMarco's days were numbered.

When the sparring ended Willie laconically said, "You still figure you got a prayer?"

Johnny knew in the ring prayers alone never get answered.

After showering, he sat in front of his ancient locker. As he solemnly dressed his aching body, he listened to the banter of the young men surrounding him. Most were still teenagers. They all had a jovial freeness Johnny DiMarco could no longer remember. Turning forty will do that to you. Pathetic.

He decided to call Gina again just to be sure she had gotten his message. He heard the same voice mail response. Funny. He called Kenny at home and heard another automated voice say that no actual person was available. Strange. "Maybe they went out to eat," he said to himself. But it didn't feel right. He decided to take a cab up to Yorktown for a look-see.

Half an hour later, he was standing on East 74th Street in front of the Felk brownstone. It was three stories high and as far as Johnny knew, only Kenny and Gina Felk lived there. He could see light coming from the ground floor bay windows. Maybe they just decided to have a quiet, romantic evening and turned off the phones. No reason to bud in, he figured. Besides, he was dead tired and depressed as hell. The Brooklyn Bomber realized he would have to turn down Brennan's offer and that he would never fight again.

His thoughts turned to finding the nearest bar, when out of the corner of his eye Johnny noticed the brownstone's front door opening. A short man wearing a dark brown leather coat stepped out and quickly closed the door behind him.

"Scuse me buddy, anybody home?" Johnny asked moving towards the man.

"No. There's no one inside," the man answered tersely and turned to leave.

Johnny stopped him with: "What're you doin in there, pal?"

"The plumber," the short man spit out without looking back.

Johnny didn't like that answer and quickly grabbed him by the collar spinning the guy around. Now that he was facing him, Johnny noticed the slicked-back hair. "Where's your tools?"

"Inside. I'm coming back. The toilet's backed up so the customer and his wife went out until it's fixed--"

"Is that right? So where you goin?" Johnny yanked him closer with the question.

The short guy spun his wheels and said, "The hardware store—"

"Bullshit!" Johnny shoved him towards the brownstone's front door. "Let's go—inside! You can show me the problem."

"Take it easy," the guy grumbled and reached for the door handle. The door was unlocked. Not a good sign.

They went inside. Johnny kept his grip on the guy's collar and steered him down the entrance corridor toward the lighted parlor. When they turned into the room, Johnny saw a pile of clothes lumped-up in a corner. Upon closer inspection, he realized it was Kenny Felk lying in a bloody heap. "What the fuck! You did this?"

The short guy said nothing. Johnny spotted the murder weapon, a Louisville Slugger, near Kenny's feet. "Where's Gina?" he asked through clenched teeth.

"Fuck you, DiMarco!"

Johnny's temper was about to express itself as a short left hook. Instead, his fist opened mid-flight and he ripped at the creep's coat tearing it open: "I said where's Gina!"

"Waiting!" the terrified little man said and squirmed. That's when Johnny saw a woman's breast pop out and it didn't belong to Janet Jackson. The terrified little man was a woman.

JOHNNY DIDN'T get home until after midnight. The homicide detectives went over every detail of his involvement in the case. Because Jo Kurtz was in custody, although she wasn't talking much, they had pieced together a murder theory: First, Gina Felk was involved in a lesbian relationship. They had met while Jo Kurtz, a corporal in the Army at the time, was stationed at Fort Bragg in Fayetteville. Second, Jo Kurtz and Gina conspired to get rid of Kenny Felk. Third, they had worked it out so that Lon Kurtz, whose fingerprints were the only clear ones on the murder weapon, would be the obvious fall guy. (Jo had never liked her brother.) And, four, Gina and Jo would live happily ever after on Kenny's estate— worth around 12 million.

All they had to do was wait for a snoop like Johnny DiMarco to show up to put the plan into gear.

The following morning, after checking with the lead detective in the Felk murder case, Johnny called Brennan.

"I want the fight," he told the promoter.

"Beautiful," Brennan said ecstatically. "I knew you would."

THE GUILTY

by Jonathan Sheppard

1. The Girl and the Detective

MANDY WAS bored.

She sat in the little steel box next to the gas pumps at her Dad's filling station, her chair tilted back, one foot up on the counter in the little cashier's cage. It wasn't actually a cage, but it felt like a cage. Who was she kidding, the filling station, the whole goddamn town felt like a cage to her. Mandy was sixteen, and single, and living in a small town, dying to break free. She wanted to meet a good-looking boy with a tattoo and she wanted him to drive her away in his old beat-up muscle car. Or she wanted to get a scholarship to Harvard (fat fucking chance!) and escape that way. It didn't much matter how she got out of Drought Creek. She just needed out.

At the edge of the big wide tarmac, near the two phone booths (one of which still worked), the Greyhound bus pulled in for it's five-minute stop. Mandy leaned on her chair and chewed her gum and looked at the bus. Thought about grabbing the cash from the till and running out there to the bus and getting on and never coming back. Instead, she spit out her bubble gum and fed herself another stick and cursed under her breath.

And then something unusual happened.

A man got off the bus.

She'd seen the bus driver get off a few times to take a leak, or buy a can of soda, or something like that. But no, this guy was getting off getting off. He had a small duffel bag over one shoulder, and what looked like a map in his other hand. She watched him take a few steps away from the bus, and adjust the fedora on his head. He was definitely dressed city-like, black suit and raincoat and a snazzy-looking grey fedora. He was tall, thin, maybe in his late 30s or early 40s. He looked good to Mandy, but, then again, most men did.

Mandy chewed her gum, and waited for something to happen.

The bus door closed, and she heard the bus's engine kick over, and

a few seconds later the bus was rolling out of town. She watched the tall man in the hat walk over to the two pay-phones. He tried the nearer one first, saw that it wasn't working, and then moved over to the other one. She watched him feed a few coins into the phone, and dial a number. He said a few words into the phone, and then listened as someone answered. And then he hung up. The whole conversation took maybe 15 seconds.

The tall man laid the phone carefully back in the cradle and picked up his duffel bag and turned, walking straight towards her now. He looked right at her, with eyes that were cold and clear and seemed to see right through her. He walked across the tarmac, around the pump, and up to the window.

"Afternoon," he said.

She hesitated.

"Uh—hi." She cleared her throat nervously. "Something I can do for you?"

The tall man held up the paper map in his right hand. "Is this

"I don't know of anything, here in town. Sorry to say. Maybe you'll find something."

"Sure hope so," he replied, lifting his hat a little and re-settling it on his head.

He glanced down at the map, then up at the road.

"Town's this way?" He pointed with the map hand.

She nodded. "Not far. Five, ten minute walk."

He tipped his hat to her.

"Thank you, Miss."

She watched him lift his duffel bag and sling it over his shoulder, and start walking. Little clouds of dust jumped where his boots touched the ground. The wind caught his coat, and it flapped in the wind, and for a brief moment, Mandy saw the man's pistol. Not like the one the Sheriff carried. It was a shiny silver revolver, like the one the Sheriff carried, but shorter. The one the Sheriff carried was as long as her forearm, maybe.

The tall man rearranged his coat, and tugged his hat down on his head and kept walking towards town.

Mandy thought, she should mention this to her parents.

2. The Innkeeper and the Detective

THE HOTEL Grande Americaine was a big old monstrosity of dark wood and brass, built in a time when there was a lot more money to go around. Jerome owned the hotel, not because he'd saved up his money and bought it, but because his parents had, and then they'd been polite enough to die. In any other city, Jerome could have sold the Hotel Grande Americaine and made himself a lot of money. But not here in Drought Creek. Here, the best he could hope for was that a few folks would drift through town looking for work, that the local men would keep the whores busy Friday and Saturday nights, that the roof wouldn't leak when it rained. Not for the first time, Jerome looked to the heavens and thanked his parents for leaving him this mess.

He lifted the hotel ledger and opened it, and the saucy magazine tucked inside it. It fell open to the page he'd been looking at earlier. A dark-haired woman wearing a bathing suit leaned on a wall next to a pool of blue water. She wasn't doing a very good job of wearing the bathing suit. Most of it seemed to be slung around her waist loosely, like the gunfighters in movies wore their gunbelts. Her name was Marie Something-or-other, and her smile was white and her nipples were a dark shade of pink and Jerome was far more interested in her than in the Hotel Grande Americaine.

Drought Creek?"

"Unfortunately."

He half-smiled at that.

"What brings you here?" she asked, forgetting herself. "Sorry, uh. I just don't understand why somebody would come to this town on purpose."

He watched her with those eyes for a second.

"Looking for work," he said. "Haven't had much luck with that lately."

"What kind of work you do?"

"Why?" he asked. "Are you hiring, young lady?"

She laughed.

"Sorry. I'm being nosy. This place is boring."

He nodded.

"This and that. I was a truck driver for a while. Worked in a factory. Farmhand, once or twice. Whatever way I could put food in my belly and a roof over my head."

Jerome sat on the stool behind the reception desk, imagining Marie Something-or-other walking through the door and asking him to show her his best room, something else happened.

Jerome almost got his wish.

Almost.

Taking off his hat and shaking the water droplets from it, a man stood in the doorway and glanced back out into the street. It wasn't raining, exactly. More like drizzle. A few scattered drops here and there.

Jerome couldn't remember the last time he'd seen a good rain.

Jerome couldn't remember the last time he'd seen a good anything.

Until now.

The man walked over to the reception desk, hat in one hand, travelling bag in the other. Jerome studied him, and he studied Jerome. They spent a few fractions of a second sizing each other up. Then Jerome suddenly remembered he was a hotelier, and straightened up and put on his best smile.

"Welcome, sir, to the Hotel Grande Americaine."

The tall man's hand moved first toward his hip, and then stopped. He then reached for his shirt pocket, and took some money out of there. He peeled off a few bills and laid them on the leather blotter on the counter.

"I'd like a room, please," he said.

Jerome nodded.

"Any preference, sir? Ground floor? Or up high someplace? One bed? Two? Will anyone be joining you?"

The tall man seemed to think about it for a moment.

"Up a floor or two. Looking out over town. I think that'll do nicely. And, no, I'm not expecting anyone to join me."

"Would you like someone to join you? I'm sure it could be arranged…."

As soon as he'd said it, he felt that it was a mistake. He wasn't sure exactly why, but it felt like he'd screwed up.

"No, thanks," he said. "Just the room."

He counted the money the stranger had put down.

"How many nights might you be staying, sir?"

The tall man shrugged.

"A week, maybe."

Jerome put a key on the blotter in front of the newcomer.

"Room 309. Front and centre, sir, just up there." He pointed in the general direction of the room, back toward the front of the building. He gestured frantically at the porter.

"I can carry my own bag," the tall man said. "Thanks anyhow."

He waited until the tall man had gone up the stairs to re-count the bills in his hand. A couple of minutes of re-counting, and shuffling from foot to foot, and re-counting the money later, he put the money in the lockbox and picked up the phone to call his brother.

3. The Whore and the Deputy

IT WAS a Thursday afternoon, and Deputy Jack Ford, one third of the Drought Creek Sheriff's Department, loved Thursday afternoons. They were the best part of the week for him. He was on bag-man duty. He spent Thursday afternoons driving around to the various businesses that paid for his (and the Sheriff's) protection, or for him to look the other way, and picking up his take.

He walked up the front step and knocked on the door of an old house on Tudor Street, not far from downtown. The woman who opened the door a minute later, was well dressed in a dark blue skirt and jacket, her dark hair piled up on top of her head. Cassidy was well into her forties, but she was still a good-looking woman. She smiled and opened the door.

"Deputy Jack. Won't you come in?"

"Think I might," he replied, spitting out the toothpick he'd been chewing on and following her inside.

They walked through a long, narrow sort of lobby, and into her office at the back of the house. Another girl sat on the sofa in there, in her underwear, reading a fashion magazine. She was young. Not an ugly thing by any means. But the Deputy liked Cassidy better. He watched her move around behind her desk and open a drawer, take out an envelope with his name written on it in red ink. She came back round the desk to hand it to him. It was thicker than the last two envelopes he'd picked up. He thumbed through the cash inside quickly, saw nothing out of the ordinary.

"There you are," Cassidy said with stage-courtesy. She was acting. But then, women in her line of work were almost always putting on one kind of performance or another.

He sat down on the day-bed there beside the window, and sighed a little, tried to relax. He unbuckled his gunbelt, and set it aside within easy reach.

It was quiet in the room for a minute.

"Carol?"

The girl perked up, looking at her employer.

"Miss Cassidy?"

"I've given the Deputy our weekly contribution. And yet, you'll notice, he's still sitting here." As she said this, she walked over closer to where Jack and young, virginal Carol sat. "Do you know why he's still here?"

Cassidy sank to one knee beside Carol, her other foot still planted on the floor. She watched the wheels turn in young Carol's head. She raised a hand and hid her mouth, and stage-whispered:

"He's waiting for you to fuck him, Carol."

"Oh," Carol said.

"No," the Deputy said, putting a hand on Miss Cassidy's shoulder. "You."

She gently swept his hand off her shoulder.

"She needs the practice."

He put his hand on her hair.

"You don't need the practice. You've forgotten more than she'll ever learn."

Cassidy and the Deputy stared into each other's eyes. She was a strong-willed woman. But she was also in business. She fake-smiled, and climbed on the Deputy's lap.

A couple of minutes later, the phone on her desk started ringing. Carol, who was watching her work, eventually decided after the second or third ring that perhaps she should answer the phone.

She got up and grabbed the phone from it's cradle.

"Miss Cassidy Teller's office," she said brightly.

"Is Deputy Ford there?"

She glanced over at the Deputy, who was fooling with Cassidy's hair.

"He is."

"Put him on the phone right now. It's his brother."

She lowered the phone from her ear.

"Deputy?" she asked. "Deputy, the Sheriff's on the phone. He says it's important."

"Goddamn it."

He got up and grabbed the phone from Carol's hand. Cassidy wiped her mouth carefully.

"Sir?" he said, composing himself.

The Sheriff told him about something he'd just heard. That there was a new fella walked into town this morning from the bus stop. Girl there said he was strapped. Six-gun on his hip. The Sheriff was right, it was a little concerning. The Sheriff told him the man had been seen at the Gas N' Go, walking towards town, an hour earlier.

"I'll find him, sir. I'll see what's up."

He put the phone back in the cradle, and turned back to Cassidy, intent on getting her to finish what she'd started.

The phone rang again.

It was his brother, this time.

Goddamn it.

4. The Deputy and the Detective

A NEW man in town with a gun on his hip. Deputy Jack Ford didn't like that at all. He and the Sheriff were supposed to be the only two tough guys in town. The cocks of this particular walk. At least in theory. Not always in practice. Mr. Crowe employed some unsavoury types sometimes. But these were desperate times, and good help was hard to find out here. Then a thought occurred to him. Maybe this guy was a new gunhand Mr. Crowe had hired.

His brother, Jerome, was sitting behind the counter, with a cup of coffee and that ledger of his, which Jack would have bet a day's pay had some kind of girlie or pulp magazine hidden inside. He walked straight to the desk, where his brother handed him the master key.

"Three-oh-nine," he said.

The Deputy pocketed the key and headed for the stairs.

"Good afternoon to you too," Jerome said to his back as he walked away.

Up the stairs two at a time, to the landing, pause, take a breath, up the next flight. He walked down the corridor until he got to 309. He almost inserted the key in the lock, before thinking that maybe he should observe at least a little of the protocol. So he knocked instead. Leaned into it and knocked hard, as only a cop can knock hard.

After a brief pause, he heard a voice from inside.

"Hello?"

"Drought Creek Sheriff's Department. Open up, please."

Another brief pause.

"Coming."

And then the door opened.

The Deputy walked into the room without waiting for an invitation. The guy's hat and necktie hung on the back of a chair, and his coat hung on the hanger next to the front door. His bag was open on the bed. And, the Deputy noted, his shiny revolver lay on the bed next to the duffel bag.

"Afternoon, sir. Could I see some identification, please?"

He rattled that all off quick.

The city slicker put a hand in his shirt pocket, and took out a business card. He passed it to Ford between two fingers.

"What am I supposed to have done?" he asked calmly.

"Walked into town with a gun on your hip. You scared that girl out at the filling station."

"I've got a permit for the pistol. It's in my wallet."

The Deputy looked at the business card he'd been handed. "This says you're an insurance man. You're not no insurance man."

"Why not?"

"Because you're not built like any insurance man I ever saw. Because of the gun, and because I can see that tattoo through your shirt sleeve in this light. Marine?"

"Navy, actually"

"Well, either way, you're not any insurance man."

He dropped the business card on the floor, and grabbed a fistful of the man's shirt.

Deputy Jack Ford's day had already taken one left turn. Just then it took another one.

This reedy-looking guy bent his knees and dropped a little lower than his full height, and he knocked the Deputy's grip loose with a forearm that he swung hard. Then he shoved, hard, and Ford stumbled back a step. Two. He realized he was in a fight, then. It had been a long time since anyone had fought him. Usually they were terrified of him. He got his guard up, but he was slow doing it. The same arm that had knocked his loose, came in straight and hard and fast, and the fist at the end of it exploded into his lips, cutting them on his teeth and sending him back hard against the wall. He grunted and pushed off from the wall, swinging a wild haymaker that the tall man ducked under, and answered with a rabbit punch to his ribs. Jack lost his breath, stumbled. He tried again, and got an elbow across the jaw for his trouble.

Jack had had enough. He reached for the .44 that hung on his right hip.

The stranger got to his revolver first. And he swung it, hard, clipping Jack above the ear. Everything went silver-white for a second, and then Jack was sitting on the floor looking up into the barrel of the tall man's gun.

"Shit," Jack said. "You don't fight like an insurance man, neither. Just who the fuck are you?"

"I'm the Fuller Brush Man," the newcomer said.

5. The Sheriff and the Detective

HANK WHITFIELD, Jr. had been the Sheriff of Drought Creek since Noah got into the boat-building business. Or so most people in town believed. It wasn't far from the truth, though. Two world wars had happened during his time in office. He'd buried a son, three deputies and his wife. At his age, he didn't care about much besides keeping the town safe, making some money, eating good steaks and drinking good bourbon. Drought Creek was a quiet town, most of the time, and he was generally left to his own devices. It was only these past few weeks that things had gotten at all stressful for him.

And now this.

He got up from behind his desk and buckled on his .45, took his hat from where it lay on top of the filing cabinet, and walked out. When his secretary raised her eyebrows, he told her he was going to take a walk over to the Hotel and see what was keeping his Deputy.

When he got outside, he found it was raining. Since he didn't care to get wet, he walked around the side of the building and got into one of the two marked cars there. He fired it up and drove the four hundred yards to the Hotel Grande Americaine.

He pushed through the bat-wing doors into the lobby.

Jerome, the nerdy little man behind the desk, his Deputy's

kid brother, was used to this by now. He pointed upwards and told the Sheriff the room number.

The Sheriff looked around in vain for an elevator he knew wasn't there, then sighed and headed for the stairs.

About ten thousand steps later, it seemed, he was on the third floor. He walked to 309, where he saw the door was standing open. Settling his left hand on the .45's grips, he stepped through the door.

Jack was sitting on the edge of the bed, looking sort of deflated. It wasn't a look the Sheriff liked on him. He seemed to be alone. All the little hairs on the Sheriff's neck stood on end. He started to turn, pulling the .45 from the ornately tooled leather holster on his hip.

Not fast enough.

None of it fast enough.

The man who stepped out from the corner of the room, behind the door, pointed a Colt .38 at him with one hand. In his other hand, he held what the Sheriff recognized as the Smith & Wesson .44 his Deputy usually carried.

"Afternoon, Sheriff."

He let his 1911 settle back into his holster. He wasn't quick enough on the draw. Not now. Probably not even fifteen years ago, when he'd been in his prime. This fella had him, dead to rights.

"Yeah, let's leave that right where it is. There's been enough gunplay already. And besides…." He held up the .38 and the .44. "… I'm fresh out of hands."

The Sheriff took a deep breath, and asked:

"Who the hell are you?"

"My wallet's on the side table there. I didn't get a chance to reach for it before your man tried putting his hands on me."

The Sheriff walked over to the side table and picked up the wallet lying there, opened it. There was a badge in there, a police detective's badge, numbered 139. And a PI's licence. The man over there in the corner, pointing two guns at him and his Deputy, had been a lawman himself until recently. And now he was a private op, by the looks of things.

Fuck.

This wasn't good.

"What are you doing in my town, Mister…" He studied the PI licence. "Mister Keel?"

"Oh, come on," the PI said, laughing a little. "You know why I'm here. You both know why I'm here."

Sheriff Whitfield and Deputy Ford looked at each other.

"The reporter?" the PI said. "Oakes. Rebecca Oakes. She came out here on a story? And then disappeared off the face of the earth? Poof. She's gone."

"Not ringing any bells for me. Never met the lady. Assuming I believe you, stranger, what's your interest?"

"Miss Oakes writes, mostly, for the Picayune. Which is owned by a corporation called Warrick Holdings. Warrick paid me very well to come out here and be interested." The detective paused for a breath. "Your department is pretty well known, Sheriff, for bells not ringing, murderers going free, envelopes of cash passing from hand to hand. Warrick, to be blunt about it, doesn't trust you to conduct a thorough and professional investigation."

The Sheriff didn't like that.

"So here comes you," he said.

"So here comes me," the PI repeated.

"You don't have any authority to operate in my county," the Sheriff said.

"Try and stop me."

With a thumb, the PI broke open the Deputy's .44, and spilled the bullets on the carpet at his feet. He snapped the gun closed with a flick of his wrist, did a quick road agent's spin and handed the empty roscoe back to it's owner. With his other hand, he holstered his own revolver behind his hip.

That was when the Sheriff went for his 1911.

"Maybe I stop you right now." He thumbed back the hammer on his .45. "This is my town, sonny boy."

The PI didn't reach for his revolver. He took a step forward, bent his head a little, and pushed the bridge of his nose into the ugly snout of the chrome .45.

"Enough talk, Sheriff. If you're gonna kill me, do it. Do it right now."

Seconds ticked by. There wasn't any air in the room anymore.

The PI stood up to his full height. Straightened his tie.

"Tomorrow morning, first thing, I start looking for whoever killed Miss Oakes. Stay out of my way."

6. The Sheriff and the Deputy

IN THE parking lot behind the Sheriff's Department, Sheriff Whitfield leaned on the trunk of his cruiser. Jack Ford stood not far away, fidgeting. Not exactly pacing, but you could see he wanted to pace.

"Fuck. Fuck."

"Calm down," the Sheriff said in his calm,

gravelly voice. "We are the law in this town. Me. And you. We wear the stars, we carry the guns. We decide how shit goes down."

"Yeah. We've got this whole fucked-up little town locked down. Always have. But we don't have him locked down. How the hell did he get here? Who dropped the dime?"

Ford was hysterical, almost, it seemed.

The Sheriff was disappointed. They didn't make 'em like they used to.

"Nobody dropped the dime," the Sheriff said. "It's just the newspaper, protecting their interests. If you disappeared out on patrol one night, I'd round up some boys and find you, one way or another. He's just doing the same thing."

Ford fished out his steel-and-leather hip flask with a shaking hand. Unscrewed the top. Drank some of the cheap bourbon inside.

Not this again, damn it.

"I killed her, boss."

"I know you did. I gave you the order. You're a good soldier. Always were."

Ford drank more of his Four Roses.

"What if… what if he…."

"There's no what if. You hear me, Jackie Boy? There is no what if. If this city slicker detective finds anything we don't want him finding, we just give Mr. Crowe a call. He'll handle it. He's got people for occasions such as this."

Ford had seen the kind of heavies that hung around with Mr. Crowe. They gave him the willies. Gave him the willies, even with a star on his chest and a .44 hanging from his hip.

"Finish your drink. Go see one of Miss Cassidy's girls. Or go on home and get some sleep. I don't much care. Get yourself right. We're gonna have a full day tomorrow, Jackie Boy."

The Sheriff packed his pipe, and leaned there against the cruiser and had a smoke. Ford went inside and changed back into his civvies. Came out a few short minutes later and drove away. The Sheriff smoked his pipe, and watched the sky fade from purple to black.

Ford had been his Deputy for seven years now. He liked the kid. Hoped he wasn't going to become a problem.

Exhaling a long line of smoke, the Sheriff tapped the ashes out of his pipe and went inside to place a call to Mr. Crowe.

7. The Old Lady and the Detective

MADELAINE KINGSHOTT saw the

clouds gathering in the northern sky, but wasn't daunted by them. Storms blew through with frequency, and they rarely stayed long. At least, not this early in the year. She wasn't going to let it stop her taking Sky for her walkies, No Sirree. Sky was her dog, an old, thin Husky she'd adopted from a dog-pound a couple of towns over. After her husband passed, she'd found that she needed some kind of company. The house was too quiet and too empty otherwise.

She leashed Sky, and put on her jacket, and they set out from her house walking down the hill towards downtown. She lived on a quiet side street not far from the centre of Drought Creek, two blocks from the Public Library where she'd worked for 27 years. She still worked there, technically, but only a few hours a week. Her young assistant, David, had taken over as the Librarian when she'd drawn her pension.

Madelaine enjoyed her daily walks with her dog, even if it did mean stooping now and then to clean up one of Sky's little messes. That was alright. It was part-and-parcel of owning a dog.

They'd take their walk, and she'd stop at Mel's for a morning cup of tea, like usual. Maybe she'd have one of those sausage biscuits Mel made. They were delicious.

Sky barked at something or other, pausing for a moment, and then carried on. Probably a squirrel or something.

Thunder rumbled, far off in the sky.

When she got down the street to Mel's, she looped Sky's leash over the closest fire hydrant. Sky sat down, tongue lolling, watching the street. Sky was a calm dog, who took things as they came. It was one of the reasons they got along so well. She went inside to get breakfast, and a bowl of water for the dog.

She was sitting at one of the tables outside, waiting for her tea to steep, when she saw the man come walking over from the hotel. He wore a good suit and a purple tie, a little loose in his collar. He tipped his hat to her as he walked by, scratched Sky's ear. He went inside and ordered a coffee. A minute later he returned, and sat at one of the other tables. He bent over the coffee and breathed it in, and it seemed to give him back some of the life he'd misplaced. He lifted the cup and drank.

"Morning," she said, pleasantly.

He looked at her over the rim of his mug.

"Good morning," he said after a brief pause. "Don't think I've seen you here before. You new in town?"

"You might say that. Just in town for a few days on a job."

"Ah." She sipped her tea. "Well, you've come to the right place. Mel's has the best breakfast in town."

He gestured with his mug towards the man behind the counter.

"He bribing you with free tea and scones to say that?"

They both laughed a little.

"You working for Mr. Crowe?" she asked.

"Who's Mr. Crowe?"

"Well, he's the man who runs this town."

"Good to know. No, I'm not working for any guy named Crowe. I work for a newspaper company, actually. Warrick."

"Warrick Holdings. Yeah. They own half the newspapers in the state."

He looked at her, raised an eyebrow.

"I was the town librarian for many, many moons," she explained.

The stranger smiled a little.

"My first job, in high school, was helping out at the Library where I grew up."

"Well, I'm sorry to say they're not hiring. I'm amazed there's still enough money to keep the place open."

"I'm not in that line of work anymore," he said.

Now it was her turn to raise an eyebrow and wait.

He paused for a moment, and seemed to make a choice.

"I'm a detective," he said. "My name is Keel. Do you mind if I ask you a question?"

A detective? She was amazed. Pleased, even, a little. She was fair certain she'd never spoken to an actual detective before.

"Fire away," she said.

He reached under his jacket and took out an envelope, showed her a picture. It was a picture of a young woman, thirty or so, with a lot of curly brown hair. Kind of ordinary-looking, but certainly not homely.

"Have you seen this woman? Her name is Rebecca Oakes. She's a newspaper reporter. Works for the Picayune, upstate."

She recognized the woman right away. Her hair was a little different, but it was her.

"Yes. Yes, she came into the library when I was there talking with David. David's my, er, successor."

"Would you remember when this was?" She thought about it.

"Not this past Saturday, the one before that." She counted on her fingers. "Ten days ago."

"You spoke to her?"

"Just to say hello. David spoke to her.

She was doing some kind of research, or so I gathered. Looking into something in the town's history. Looking at newspapers, I know that much. Had a stack of them on her work table."

The detective had pulled out a little notebook from another of his pockets, and was writing notes in it with a short chunk of carpenter's pencil. When he was finished, he set the notebook and pencil down and took another sip of his coffee.

"Is that helpful?" she asked.

"It's very helpful," he said. "Thank you, Miss Librarian."

She raised her teacup.

"Happy to help, Mr. Detective."

"Do you remember anything else about her? Anything at all? Sometimes little details can be a big help."

She thought about it.

"Nothing that sticks out in my memory. I'm sorry."

He took her hand, kissed the back of it like a proper gentleman. Placed a card on the table next to her mug.

"I'm Keel," he said. "I'm staying at the Hotel Grande Americaine. Room 309. If you think of anything else, anything at all, please call or drop by."

She tucked the business card in her jacket pocket.

"And I'm Madelaine Kingshott," she said. "Pleased to meet you, Mr. Keel."

He picked up his cup of coffee and drained it.

"I should be on my way. Things to do."

"You should get Mel to fix you one of his bacon and egg sandwiches before you go. They're delicious."

"I just might."

8. The Sheriff, the Deputy and the Kingpin

IN THE morning, Jack Ford was drinking coffee and eating Aspirin, sitting slumped at his desk, trying to get himself going. There was paperwork to do. Reports to type up. And there was a damn detective in town, about to ruin everything. He wished he could've poured a little whiskey in his coffee. It might have helped with the headache. But now wasn't the time. At the Drought Creek Sheriff's Department, they were expecting company.

The Sheriff was in his office, wearing one of his white uniform shirts. His Stetson sat crown-down on top of a filing cabinet next to his desk. Irene, the secretary who kept the place running, was nibbling on a Danish and correcting one of his reports with a red pencil. It annoyed him, at first, when she did that. But he knew it was for the best. His reports might end up in the hands of a judge or the State Police. He didn't want to be looking like a fool.

At a little after nine, someone opened the door from the parking-lot side. A big, bearded man in a suit. He held the door in one hand, an umbrella in the other. The man who walked into the building was huge, both in height and in weight. Jack was six-foot-one, and Mr. Crowe towered over him. He also weighed probably twice what Jack weighed. His hair was slicked back and he had a thick, brush moustache. He was wearing a suit that probably cost more than Jack's car, and took off his hat as he walked in out of the rain.

Mr. Crowe said not a word to him, and walked past him, straight into the Sheriff's office without knocking. He seated himself without waiting for an invitation.

"Coffee," he said to Irene.

Deputy Ford looked back at the two men standing around the doorway, the two big bearded men in their expensive suits. He could see the shapes of guns under those jackets. Mr. Crowe referred to these men as his "assistants." Anybody with a set of eyes could see what they were. They were his hired killers. Ford had been a cop long enough to know the type.

Mr. Crowe and the Sheriff talked a few minutes. Neither of them seemed particularly happy.

Then the Sheriff looked up, and waved Ford in.

Taking a deep breath, Ford picked up his coffee and carried it with him into the Sheriff's office.

Mr. Crowe eyed him in that way he had, equal parts distaste and disinterest.

"There was a job needed doing. I could have had Phil out there do it for me. Would have been no skin off his nose. But no. You wanted to do it yourself. Wanted to impress me, I suppose? Looking to move up in the world. Is that right, Deputy?"

Ford looked at his shoes.

"Pretty much," he said.

"Pretty much," Mr. Crowe repeated. "Look at me, Ford."

He raised his eyes and met Mr. Crowe's.

"Did you kill that girl?"

"Of course I did! Sir. I did as I was told."

Mr. Crowe arched an eyebrow.

"Are you certain?"

The deputy bit back words that he knew would have gotten him killed, probably immediately, by Phil over there.

"I'm certain, Mr. Crowe. I shot her myself, kicked her off the bluff into the river below. I watched her go. She's gone."

"Shot her how many times?"

"Just once." He stammered. "I—I only need one. I shoot straight."

"Did you confirm the kill?"

He nodded.

"I don't believe you, boy. Did you climb down the bluff and see the body in the river? Did. You. Confirm. The. Kill."

Ford looked at his shoes again.

"No."

In a flash, far faster than he'd thought the fat man could move, Crowe had snatched the Sheriff's .45 off the desk, and was pressing the barrel to his temple. Ford pissed himself a little. Felt his eyes getting wet at the corners.

"Don't you fucking lie to me, boy."

"I… I didn't because I didn't need to. There was no need. The fall or the bullets would've killed her."

"Bullets?" Mr. Crowe snapped. "You said you shot her once."

"I did," Ford stammered. "I think I did."

"You think. You think?"

Ford said nothing.

"You have a few drinks before you drove her up there? A little liquid courage? I know you're a boy who needs liquid courage. Can't seem to manufacture any of your own."

Mr. Crowe picked up the decanter behind the Sheriff's desk, splashed some expensive bourbon into a jelly glass. Slammed it down on the table in front of Ford.

"Drink some of that, and give me a straight answer, now, boy."

With a shaking hand, he picked up the glass. Sipped some of it. The bourbon burned down his throat. It burned good.

"I had a couple of drinks. I needed to. I'm not… I never killed no woman before."

"You're not what?"

Without moving his head, he turned his eyes to look over at the huge man who pointed the .45 down at his temple.

"Please don't kill me, Mr. Crowe."

Mr. Crowe let the hammer down on the .45.

"I don't think I will," he said.

He picked up the leather holster and slid the .45 back into it, returned it to where it'd been near the Sheriff's elbow. The Sheriff, who hadn't done a goddamned thing to help him.

"Perhaps I'll let this fellow Keel do it for me," Mr. Crowe said.

9. The Librarians, The Detective and the Killers

JUST AFTER lunch, Madelaine Kingshott waited in front of the library on a bench, reading a favourite old paperback. After a few minutes, she looked up to see the fellow she'd met that morning, Mr. Keel, walking across the park toward her. He had his jacket off and folded over his arm, his tie loosened in the collar. As he approached, he took off his Wayfarers and tucked them in one of his pockets.

"Good book?" he asked.

"One of my favourites," she said, letting him see the cover.

"Huh," he said. "I read that, back in high school."

They went into the library, up the short flight of steps and around the corner to where the main desk was.

She introduced Keel to David Thomson, the young fellow who'd replaced her. David wore a striped tie with a pale blue short-sleeved shirt. His glasses were horn-rimmed.

"How can I be of help, sir?" David asked, adjusting his glasses on the bridge of his nose.

The detective took a picture from his shirt pocket and showed it to the librarian.

"Do you recognize this woman?"

David took the picture and looked at it for a second.

"Yes," he said. "She was in a few weeks back. From out of town. Had a lot of questions. Was doing research for a book or a magazine, something like that."

"How good is your memory of that day? Do you remember what she was looking for?"

"My memory is still fairly sharp," he said. "We don't get a lot of out-of-town visitors here. And… she was pretty."

Keel looked at the picture a moment before tucking it away.

"She's certainly not ugly."

He took a small notebook from one of his hip pockets, flipped it open.

"So, what was she looking at here?"

"Newspaper archives. Maps. Business stuff. She was interested in the town's history, particularly the mining and smelting operation just north of town. That's owned by a Mr. Crowe."

Keel wrote down the name.

"Mr. Crowe is… well, I can't say for sure, but the rumour is…."

"Even rumours can be helpful sometimes. Let's hear it."

"Rumour is he's sort of the man behind the curtain around here. The Sheriff and the Mayor run Drought Creek, but he really runs it."

"Gotcha."

Keel scrawled some more notes in his little book.

The bell over the door jingled behind them. Keel glanced back over his shoulder, saw a guy in a black suit and a Marine Corps haircut walk into the building and beeline to the magazine rack. He picked up the latest issue of National Geographic.

Keel went back to his line of questioning with the librarians, old and new.

"Is there anything else I can do?" David asked.

Keel thought about it.

"Is there? Do you remember anything else?"

David thought about it.

"I'm not sure… let me have a few minutes."

Keel took a seat at one of the worktables nearby and went over his notes, patiently letting David have his minutes. While he was doing that, a second man came into the library. He was essentially a copy of the first one. Same high-and-tight haircut, same beard, same build. The two of them walked across the library, directly toward where David and Madeleine, the two librarians, were leaning on the counter talking quietly.

Keel took cover behind a bookshelf for a moment. He took a breath. He drew his .38, and cocked it.

One of the two goons took a Luger out and lay it on the counter. His hand covered it, and it was pointed straight at David.

Keel stepped out from behind the shelf, then, aiming his revolver at them.

"Now, let's be reasonable, gents. You're here for me. Leave them out of it."

The one with the Luger shifted it on the counter so it was pointed at Madeleine, then back at her younger counterpart. He smirked a little. He was playing a game, and enjoying it.

"I don't get paid to be reasonable," he said.

Keel shot him, then. In the neck. His head snapped sideways and he fell against David's desk, the Luger skittering to the floor. As he fell, his partner, over a few feet the other side of the retired librarian, went for his gun. He never cleared leather. Keel shot him twice in the chest. He fell on his ass, cracking his head against the counter. The Colt in his hand fell in his lap, dead fingers still gripping.

It was the loudest five seconds in the long history of the Drought Creek Public Library.

When the door opened and the detective stepped out of the library, the Sheriff was ready. He pressed his back against the side of the building, and sidestepped closer to the doorway. He shoved the barrels of his big old scattergun against the detective's ear. The detective stopped where he was. His revolver was broke open in his hands, he'd been reloading it as he walked.

"Take one more step and, by God I'll blow your guts all over that tree there," he growled.

Keel stayed where he was. He was still. The gun in his hand was still. He barely seemed to breathe or blink.

"You're under arrest," the Sheriff said. "Drop that roscoe. Hands on your head."

Keel dropped the revolver at his feet. Put his hands on top of his head.

"You mind me asking what I'm under arrest for?"

"The two men lying dead in there."

"They came here to kill me. Didn't seem overly concerned with the safety of the two locals in there, either. But you knew that, I think."

The muscles in the Sheriff's jaw bunched up and worked.

"How do you figure that?"

"Just based on how quickly you showed up. Or were already hanging around. Almost as thought you set this up."

The Sheriff swung the shotgun hard, burying the stock in Keel's side. Keel fell to one knee. The Sheriff held out a hand to him. It wasn't to help him up. It held a pair of handcuffs.

10. The Drunk and the Detective

GARY WANTED a drink very badly, but he also never wanted to smell another drop of alcohol as long as he lived. Gary was coming up on the third day of his hangover, despite the plentiful water and aspirin provided by the Sheriff's Department. The food wasn't the best, but it was food. And anyway good food would probably have been wasted on Gary's stomach, which was not unlike an ocean in a storm.

Gary lifted his head off the pillow on the cot in the holding cell, squinting his eyes against the light that flooded in from the other room as they opened the door. The asshole Deputy and the only-slightly-less-asshole Sheriff came in, steering a clean-cut looking guy in a good suit towards the other cell. They stopped, put him against the wall. The Sheriff stood back a bit, .45 in his hand, while the Deputy started frisking the clean-cut guy. He started with the ankles and worked his way up, slowly.

"We going to find anything else on you?" the Sheriff asked.

Mr. Gentleman's Quarterly didn't answer him.

The Deputy worked his way up, unclipping the holster from Mr. Gentleman's Quarterly's belt, and the little leather pouch that contained twelve extra bullets for his revolver. He also liberated a wallet, a notebook and two pens, a folding knife, and a pair of Wayfarer sunglasses. All of that went into a paper bag, and the Deputy took it away somewhere.

Then the Sheriff gestured toward the holding cell with his .45.

"In you get," he said.

Mr. Gentleman's Quarterly stepped into the holding cell and pulled the door closed behind him. He moved around the little cell, examining the cot, the toilet/sink, and looking out the little window at the street behind the Sheriff's Station. Then he sat down on the bunk. His eyes moved around the place, taking in details. They took in Gary, in the next cell. He didn't say anything.

After a couple of minutes, the Sheriff and the Deputy went into the other room, where their desks were. Gary waited another minute or two after that, before introducing himself to the fellow in the next cell, with a bow and a wave of his hand.

"Good evening," he said. "Gary Hill. Town drunk. At your service."

Mr. Gentleman's Quarterly looked at him, stone-faced, for a moment, and then he started laughing.

"Hi, Gary," he said when he'd calmed down. "I'm Keel."

"Keel… that a first name? Last name? What are you in for anyway?"

"It's a last name. I didn't tell you my first. Don't take that personal, I don't tell it to most people. And I'm in here because a couple of men tried to kill me, an hour ago, over by the library."

"You're in here because a couple of men tried to kill you?"

Mr. Gentleman's Quarterly lowered his voice a little, giving it a slightly conspiratorial tone.

"I killed them first."

"Really?"

"Really." He raised his voice, just a little. "They weren't very good. I've mixed it up with guys who'd have eaten them for breakfast."

"Huh," Gary said. He was amazed. He didn't meet a lot of genuine tough guys. Plenty who talked the talk, but not one who walked the walk. This guy seemed like he might. "So, what's the plan?"

"What's your plan?"

"Oh, me? I don't have a plan. I just want to get some orange juice, or maybe a bit of the old hair o' the dog. You wouldn't happen to have…."

Mr. Gentleman's Quarterly shook his head.

"Not when I'm working." He scratched his jaw. "I'm not sure what the plan is. For now, I wait to talk to my lawyer. If I get to make a phone call, I call my boss and let him know what's what."

Gary nodded.

"We gonna escape?" he asked.

Mr. Gentleman's Quarterly smiled a little in the dark.

"I'll have to get back to you on that one, Gary."

Gary lay back on his bunk, thinking about a bottle of good bourbon. And then about a bottle of cheap bourbon. And then a bottle of fortified wine, which he might actually be able to afford. Gary the Town Drunk was a realist.

His new friend Mr. Keel sat on his cot, back against the brick wall, waiting. Watching.

Some time later, Deputy Ford came back into the room.

He tossed a set of handcuffs at Keel's feet.

"Put those on. We're goin' on a trip."

Keel picked up the cuffs, snapped one onto one of his wrists.

"Where we off to?" he asked.

Ford held up the picture he'd taken from the detective's shirt pocket earlier.

"Rebecca Oakes. I'm going to show you where she was last seen."

The detective, Keel, took a deep breath.

The Deputy opened the cell, gestured for Keel to come out with his .44.

Keel walked out of the cell slowly, and looked over at the Deputy, who was planning to murder him.

"Lead on, Macduff."

11. The Sheriff, the Deputy and the Detective

DEPUTY FORD turned on the radio in the car, turned the dial to some local music station. Turned it off again a moment later.

Turned the windshield wipers to a faster speed. The detective sat beside him, hands cuffed in his lap. His suit looked a little rumpled from spending most of the day in a holding cell, but otherwise he still looked a lot calmer and more focused than Ford felt.

"You kill her? Or did the Sheriff?" the detective asked conversationally.

The Deputy looked like he was going to say something, for a moment, but then stopped himself.

They drove on in the silence.

"As far as I know," the detective said, "you haven't done anything yet. Not too late to turn this around."

"Shut up," Ford growled.

They drove out of town, up a long winding road into the forest. The road curved around a lake, tall waterfall at one end. It was kind of picturesque. Keel might have liked to come there with a canoe and fish for an afternoon, under other circumstances. They wound their way up the ridge, through the tall pine trees. Passed a wide dirt road with a gate across it and signs. Some sort of factory. Keel could see the buildings back in the woods a bit.

Eventually they came to a turnout. Ford put the car in park, got out. Came around and opened Keel's door.

"We walk from here," he said.

Keel gestured with his cuffed hands.

"Lead the way."

"No," the Deputy said. "You go on ahead. I'll be right behind you." His hand settled on the grips of his .44.

Keel started walking up the path worn into the hillside. Pine needles scratched at his ankles, his wrists.

"Where we going, Deputy?"

"The Bluff," the Deputy answered. "'Bout a five minute walk up this way. Best view in the county, looking out over the lake and the falls. Pretty secluded up here. The odd high school couple drives up here to make out, but that's it. Otherwise, it's quiet."

"Great place to get rid of a body," Keel said.

"Oh, don't you worry about that," the Deputy said. "Soon enough, all your troubles are over, Mr. Keel."

"Not until I find Miss Oakes, they're not."

"Like I said, I'm gonna take you to her."

They continued up the hill. Keel thought about his situation. His revolver and his pocket-knife were gone. He was miles from town. He could make a break for it, but, over unfamiliar terrain, in his loafers… Ford would probably just shoot him in the back and leave him to bleed out in the forest.

"So," Keel said. "We get up there, you're gonna kill me and dump the body off the Bluff, right? That's the plan? Probably get busted up pretty good on the rocks down below. Look like an accident or something. City-slicker detective didn't know what he was doing, took a tumble…."

The Deputy looked at him.

"Come on, Deputy. Neither of us is stupid. I know what's cookin'."

With the barrel of his .44, Ford nudged him in the back.

"Walk," he said.

"Fine, I'll walk. You talk."

Ford said something under his breath.

"Fuck it," he said, a little louder. "You just gotta know, don't you? Well, I guess, you only got a few minutes left. I might as well put your mind to ease."

Keel turned, feet shifting on the loose dirt under him.

"Please do."

Ford nudged him in the belly with the .44. "Walk, I said."

Keel started walking again.

"Yeah. I killed the reporter. Brought her out here, like you said. Figured this'd be as good a place as any."

"What'd you kill her for?"

"Not my idea. Sheriff's orders."

"Somebody gives you an order to kill a woman, you follow it? That's the kind of man you are?"

Again, the .44 nudged him in the back.

"I'm whatever kind of man I need to be, to survive and make some money. You don't know what it's like, law officering in a town like this. Crowe runs the whole goddamn shooting match. Calls all the shots."

"Crowe? Who the hell is Crowe?"

"Oh, come on. You don't know? Alistair Crowe, the Titan of Industry? Owns all the steel mills and factories in this part of the state? Has more money than God?"

"I'm not from around here."

They climbed.

Keel stumbled a little, grabbed a tree to stay upright. They were getting close to the summit.

"Oakes came to town chasing some kind of story," Keel said. "Found something you didn't want getting out."

"Not my idea. Not my secret. Crowe's."

"Oh, give me a break. You're all fucking in on it together. What was it?"

"What wasn't it? Crowe bringing in illegals as labourers. Safety concerns. Sanitation problems. Chemical leaks into the surrounding lakes and wildlife. The man's rich for a reason. He cuts any corner he can to make a buck."

"Sounds like a charming guy."

"Brother, you have no idea."

"Remember what's on the agenda when we get up the hill? I'm not your fucking brother, Deputy."

The Deputy took a step forward, his .44 in his hand swinging as though he planned to throw it like a baseball. He swung at Keel hard, like that.

One of his feet went out from under him on the loose dirt and gravel, and he stumbled.

The opportunity had come, and Keel was ready for it. He grabbed a fistful of the Deputy's hair, and drove his knee up into Ford's face as hard as he could. Broke his nose, flattened it out to one side. Blood spurted from Ford's nose and mouth. He fell over on his side, trying to raise the .44 and point it at Keel. Keel took it away from him.

"Change of plans," Keel said grimly. "On your feet."

Deputy Ford spat out blood, slumped against the tree he'd hit when he went down.

Keel was fresh out of patience.

He cocked the .44, aimed it down at Ford.

"Up," he barked. "Move. Or I'll leave you here, you sonovabitch."

They continued up to the top of the Bluff.

It was a beautiful spot, Keel had to admit. The cliff was a sheer drop to the narrow end of the lake, far below. The waterfall was barely visible at the other end, off in the distance.

"So, this is the spot, huh?"

"This is the spot," Ford replied.

"How many people you kill up here for Crowe and the Sheriff?"

Ford shrugged.

"A few."

"Sheriff ever come along? He the sort that does his own dirty work?"

Keel noticed, too late, the shape of the big man moving through the trees off to his left. Big man with a shiny chrome .45 in one hand, and Keel's own snub-nosed .38 Special in the other.

"Sometimes," the Sheriff said, "When I have to."

And then he emptied Keel's .38 into Deputy Ford.

Keel took three quick steps to his right, getting some cover against a big elm tree. Aiming the long-barrelled .44 at the Sheriff.

The Sheriff tossed Keel's empty .38 on the ground, near his dead deputy. Pointed his other gun, the big chrome .45, at Keel.

"So what's the story going to be? Your Deputy and I killed each other?"

The Sheriff shrugged.

"Something like that."

"Only one problem with that story," Keel said. "I've got your boy's .44 here. You shoot me with that .45, the story falls apart a bit."

Keel sidestepped to another tree, looking for better cover, keeping the revolver pointed at the Sheriff with every step. The Sheriff was a little closer now. Perhaps twenty-five or thirty feet away.

"It does present a bit of a problem," the Sheriff said. "But I've been running this town twenty-six years, Mister Detective. I'll figure something out."

"Running it for Mr. Crowe."

The Sheriff laughed. "That's supposed to stick in my craw? Get me angry? Get me to make a mistake? Hell yes I run the town for Crowe. Everybody works for somebody. Besides, he keeps me in whiskey and cigars and women."

The woods were quiet for a moment.

"Enough talk," the Sheriff said, and aimed at Keel, and started shooting.

Keel snapped off his first shot at the Sheriff and broke left, moving fast, ducking for cover. He swung around another tree and fired back over his shoulder as he ran. One of the Sheriff's bullets tore through a tree next to his head, showering him with splinters of oak. They hit his face, his eye. They hurt. But he didn't stop. Keel tripped over a stump, fell, shoved himself to his feet again. He fired again, on the run. The Sheriff squeezed off rounds fast. Keel heard the Sheriff's .45 click empty. Heard him reloading. Keel braced against a rock, fired another two shots back at the Sheriff. One went wide. One, he was pretty sure, clipped the Sheriff's calf.

And then the Sheriff was shooting at him again.

Keel ran, firing another shot, but one of the Sheriff's bullets battered through the darkness and drew a line of hot red pain across the side of his head. Keel hissed with pain, and stumbled, and fell off the Bluff into the darkness.

12. The Detective and the Cabin

KEEL DIDN'T seem to be dead.

He wasn't entirely sure how or why he wasn't. After the bullet clipped his ear and the ground went out from under his feet and the darkness swallowed him, he'd been

pretty sure that was it. And then the water. The cold, mountain lake. He'd almost drowned. But he'd dragged himself up on the rocks, coughing and shaking. He broke open the Smith & Wesson .44, and found that he had two rounds left. The .38 was lost, now. And his spare gun was in his suitcase, back at the hotel twenty miles away. It might as well have been on the moon, for all the good it did him.

His jacket was stained with blood and torn. He discarded it. His tie wasn't in very good shape either. He tore it up into a few pieces and pressed one of them to his ear. It bled profusely. The bullet had clipped the top of his ear off. It hurt, but he'd had worse. As long as he got it stitched up, it'd be fine.

He made his way along the shore, glancing up occasionally at the bluff. He didn't see or hear anything up there. He wasn't sure exactly how long a fall it'd been, but it had to be 150 feet at least.

Then, as he was stumbling along the shore of the lake, he noticed something.

Far along the curve of the lake, he could see a little cottage. And, he thought, the shape of someone standing there on the shore, watching. As soon as he looked that way, the shape disappeared back into the little cabin there.

Lacking a better idea, Keel headed that way.

13. The Detective and the Reporter

KEEL MADE his approach to the cabin slowly, and carefully. Both because he didn't want to spook the person hiding inside, and because he was tired and sore and bleeding. He briefly considered marching in there with his gun drawn, but then changed his plans. He tucked the .44 in his belt, and tried to look as non-threatening as he could. Hah. That was a laugh. Wet, bloodstained, with a big roscoe tucked in your belt.

There was definitely someone in the cabin, but the lights were off. No smoke came from the tin chimney at the side. There were no other signs of life around: no car, no campfire, no picnic table. The moon shone down through the trees, lighting the way. Keel moved up quietly, and raised his fist to knock on the door.

He never got the chance.

Wild-haired and wilder-eyed, a woman looked at him over the barrels of an old Iver Johnson shotgun. Her clothes were dirty, her hands shaky. She wore a tattered white blouse and green slacks torn at the knee, and had a blanket thrown over her shoulders.

"Don't come any closer," she said. "I'll kill you."

Keel smiled then, he couldn't help it.

She misinterpreted his smile, his laugh, as a threat. Prodded at him with the old shotgun.

"Who are you?" she asked. "That bastard Sheriff send you?"

"No," Keel said. "Well, in a manner of speaking. He sent me off the Bluffs."

"It's what he does with anyone who causes problems for him."

"But you survived the fall."

"So did you."

"Broke my leg. But otherwise, came through it OK."

She moved the blanket-coat so he could see her leg, all splinted up. She'd done a good job of it. Better than he'd have done, if it was his leg. That made sense, though. He'd read her file. Rebecca Oakes had been a nurse during the War. She knew how to survive, how to take care of herself.

Keel extended his hand in the dark.

"Miss Oakes, ace reporter for the Picayune, I presume."

She wasn't ready to let go of the shotgun just yet, but she did lower it so it wasn't aiming at his face.

"You seem to have me at a disadvantage, sir."

Keel still held his hand out to her.

"Sorry," he said. "Keel. Private eye. I was sent out here to investigate your disappearance."

"You have a first name, Keel?"

"It doesn't get much use, in my line of work. But, yes. It's Liam."

"Well, come inside, Liam Keel, private eye. And shut the door behind you."

A handful of little candles burned inside. The cabin looked like it'd been abandoned for a while. There wasn't much there. A table, two wooden chairs, a few books, a fishing rod in the corner. He saw the spot on the wall where the shotgun had been hanging, over the door.

On the table sat a box of bird-shot she'd found for the shotgun, and a sheaf of paper covered in notes and scribblings. The story she'd been working on. The one that had gotten her killed. Gotten them both killed. She gathered up the papers, squared their edges.

"There's no food to speak of," she said. "Some stale old crackers. A few cans I don't trust. Got rust on 'em. I caught a couple of fish, but I ate 'em."

"That's alright," Keel said. "I'll be OK. Who's cabin is this?"

"I got no idea," she said.

"So… what are you still doing here?"

"Lying low," she said. "Staying alive. If you haven't noticed, Mr. Keel, the local cops aren't the friendliest."

"I do get that feeling," he said.

She noticed his ear, then.

"Hold on a second," she said. She took a green metal box off the wall. A first aid kit. Had a quick look at what was inside it. It was old, but fairly well stocked.

"Let me tend to that ear for you," she said. "Can't have you bleeding all over."

While she worked on his ear, he tried to relax a little. He was cold. He wished they could've lit a fire.

"In the morning we can head out," he said. "Back to town."

"Back to town? Are you insane? We head for the city. For the Picayune, and the Police too. The real Police, who don't try to shoot you and dump you off cliffs."

"My suitcase is at the hotel. And my extra gun."

"Don't need a suitcase if you're dead."

He waited for her to continue.

"You know going back means a fight, don't you?."

"I do."

"You want it, don't you. You want that Sheriff dead."

"After what he did? You're damn right I do."

She thought about it for a moment.

"A corrupt Sheriff, his deputy, a titan of industry, and who knows who else. Maybe the whole fucked-up little town."

"Be a hell of a story," he said.

"Front page," she answered. "Above the fold."

She sighed.

"What the hell."

She handed the old shotgun across to him.

He broke it open, looked at the twin shells inside. Then he snapped the gun back together, and found a spot to sit in the windowsill, and fell asleep. She watched him for a moment, and then laid down herself.

14. The Girl and the Innkeeper

MANDY WAS annoyed.

The sun wasn't even up, and she was out cleaning the windows of the little metal box. The box was her cage, her cell. She wanted to run away to the city. She definitely wanted to go back to bed. As she was lifting her rag

from the water bucket, she saw a pickup truck stop a little way down the road, and two people climb out of the back. They were walking her way. She dropped the rag into the bucket and straightened up, cracking her back.

She recognized the stranger who'd come to town a couple of days earlier, the handsome guy in the suit with the gun on his hip. He didn't seem to have the gun anymore, and his suit was the worse for wear. A woman walked along with him. She looked rough, too.

The stranger walked up, and smiled at her.

"Morning, young lady."

She looked at him, taking his measure.

"You remember me?," he asked.

"I do," she said. "You look like ten miles of bad road. What happened to you?"

"All manner of unpleasant things," he said.

She bent to pick up the rag.

He took out his wallet.

"How would you like to make some fast money?"

She narrowed her eyes.

"Daddy pays me to clean…."

He held up a $20 bill.

She dropped the rag in the dirt.

He handed her the $20, and told her what he wanted her to do.

JEROME WAS sitting behind the counter at the Grande Americian, his ledger open in front of him and a fresh magazine open inside of it, wishing he was anywhere in the world other than Drought Creek, when a young woman came walking in the front door. He'd seen her around town once or twice. Her name was Mandy or Amanda or something like that. Her parents owned the gas station. Jerome gassed his car there regularly, but he never paid them much mind.

The girl walked up to the front desk

She stood there for a moment, chewing her lip, looking uncertain, and then she stepped forward and slapped both fists down on the counter, not very hard. Her eyes glistened wet.

"Which room is Richie in?" she asked.

Jerome put his ledger down, inadvertently displaying the centrefold of the magazine inside. But the girl didn't seem to pay it any mind.

"Where's Richie. Tell me which room he's in. Tell me."

"I'm sorry, young lady…."

"Don't you be sorry, you just tell me what I wanna know. Richie told me he was checked in here. You tell me what room.

Richie and I are in love. He says he's going to marry me, and take me away from this terrible little town—"

She went on, crying and stomping her feet and slamming her little fists down on the table. Jerome tried his best to calm her down. When Keel slipped in the back way and hot-footed it up the stairs, Jerome never noticed. An African elephant could have stomped through the lobby and he'd not have noticed.

15. The Showdown

IN THE tiled bathroom of the gas station, Keel washed his hands and face and got into some clean clothes. He lifted out the cardboard false bottom from his suitcase and retrieved the Mauser and the two spare stripper-clips. Then, feeling a lot better, he went back out of the washroom. Mandy and the reporter, Rebecca Oakes, were waiting there, talking to each other about something. Women's business. None of his.

Then he walked to the payphone, the one he remembered was working. He fed in a few quarters Mandy had taken from the cash register and given to him. He called a friend in the State Troopers, stationed in a town forty miles north.

"O'Grady?" he said. "It's Keel. Morning."

"Keel. It's seven-thirty in the morning. What do you want?"

"You remember that favour I did for you last year? I need to call it in. I need to call it in right now."

The sleep and the grumpiness went out of O'Grady's voice.

"What do you need?"

"I'm in a town called Drought Creek. I need you to get five or ten men you trust, and get down here. Right now."

"Okay."

"Okay?"

"Okay. I'm on the way. I'll be there as quick as I can."

"How long?"

"An hour, maybe."

"Get here," he said, and hung up the phone.

He deftly lined up the stripper clip and thumbed the bullets down into the gun, thumbed back the hammer. It was more gun than he was used to carrying, but, then, he was in more trouble than he was used to being in.

Speaking of trouble, he could see a couple of cars approaching, coming out from Drought Creek.

Rebecca held the shotgun out to him.

"No," he said. "You hold onto that. You two get out of sight, now."

She looked like she wanted to say something, but he interrupted her.

"You want that story to get out," he said. "It doesn't get out if we're all dead."

"What are you going to do?"

"Talk to them, I guess."

"And if that doesn't work?"

"Then I'll kill as many of them as I can. Stay out of sight. Anyone comes through that door and isn't me, you shoot 'em."

She nodded.

"Go on, now."

She headed back around the corner of the building. He walked out to meet the two approaching cars.

They stopped a little short of the gas station. The rear doors of one car opened, and two big men in grey suits climbed out. One had a moustache, the other was growing a beard. They were almost copies of the two he'd killed at the library. A fat man in an expensive suit sat behind the wheel of that car. Crowe, he suspected.

Out of the other car climbed Sheriff Whitfield.

"Keel!" the Sheriff shouted. "You're supposed to be dead!"

"Sorry to inconvenience you," he called back.

Just then, Mandy's father, the man who owned the gas station, came striding out.

"What's this all…."

He stopped very suddenly, and looked down at the star of red spreading across his belly. One of the grey-suited killers had snapped around and shot him instinctively. He slumped to the ground next to one of the pumps.

Keel pointed the Mauser at that grey-clad killer, and shot him in the head, twice, as fast as he could pull the trigger.

And then the fight was on.

The Sheriff and the other killer started firing at Keel. He turned his body side-faced to them, making himself a harder target, and he walked slowly toward them, answering their hail of shots with his own. A bullet zipped by his left eye so close he felt it pass. But he kept moving. The killer's revolver clicked empty, and Keel shot him three times while he tried to reload. He sat down in the dirt, and didn't do much after that.

The Sheriff, meanwhile, was ejecting an empty magazine from his .45 and feeding in a fresh one. Keel still had a few shots left in the Mauser's box magazine. He

squeezed them off, one by one, driving the Sheriff back to take cover next to his car. The Sheriff put his arm up over the hood, and fired blind.

Keel retrieved the extra stripper-clip from his hip pocket and clacked it down into place, and shoved down hard with his thumb. He was pulling back the bolt when the Sheriff fired a blind shot around the side of the car and hit him somewhere in the leg. Keel felt the impact, and felt the leg go out from under him, but not much more than that. The pain would come later. The fall probably saved his life—bullets zipped through the air over his head.

He rolled onto his side, not thinking about his leg, and tried again to pull back the bolt on the Mauser. This time, it worked.

When the Sheriff poked his head around the side of the car, Keel blew most of it off.

The dust settled. Keel got his good leg under him, and hobbled over and leaned on the Sheriff's car. Miss Oakes came out from the side of the building, still holding the shotgun, and Mandy trailed along with her.

"Are you alright?" the reporter asked the detective.

"Well, I'm sorry to say we won't be going out dancing tonight."

Mandy ran to her father, who was bleeding badly, but hadn't cashed in his chips just yet.

Keel shifted the Mauser to his other, less bloody, hand.

The driver's door of the other car opened, and the fat man in the expensive suit got out. He held a Colt .25 automatic in one fat hand. It looked tiny. He raised it, tiny or not, and squeezed off a shot at Keel. The shot buried itself in the dirt near Keel's feet. Keel winced and raised the Mauser again, aiming for the centre of Crowe's chest.

And then Rebecca Oakes, the investigative reporter from the Picayune, stepped around the side of the building, and fired both barrels into Crowe.

And then there was nothing left to do but wait.

In the distance, they could hear sirens.

16. Epilogue

MUCH LATER, Keel hopped on one foot over to the window and opened it a little to let some fresh air in. It had been raining, and the air smelled sweet. He got back on his bed before the nurse came around and yelled at him again. O'Grady came in then, bringing coffee and a sandwich from the hospital cafeteria. They'd already talked, Keel had given him most of the details of the last few days.

O'Grady took the Drought Creek Sheriff's tin star out of his pocket, and looked down at it on his palm.

He showed it to Keel.

"You know, I hear Drought Creek is looking for a new Sheriff."

Keel laughed.

"I'm sure one will turn up, 'fore long."

"You headed back to the city?"

"Soon as the leg heals up a bit. I don't do so well out here in the sticks."

O'Grady's curiosity got the better of him.

"What was that lady reporter in talking to you about earlier?"

"Job offer," Keel said, taking a bite of his sandwich.

"A job offer?"

"She's always running off to one place or another, trying to get some kind of scoop. Apparently that's what they call it. You know, the big story. The headline."

"Yeah, she has a tendency to get herself into trouble that way."

"Well, apparently she wants to go get herself into trouble down near the border. Mexicali, I think she said. Something about union busters and Federales."

"You gonna take it?" O'Grady asked.

Keel shrugged.

"We'll see how the leg is in a few days. I'm thinkin' about it. Been a while since I've had a good churro."

THE MALTESE TERRIER

by Michael Bracken

ALLY JENSON arrived at work Thursday morning to find the office door unlocked, the lights on, and her boss shot dead behind his desk. She had been employed by Diamond Investigations—a one-man operation run by Dick Diamond—ever since graduating from secretarial school three years earlier. She still didn't know if she had been hired for her figure or for her way with figures because she couldn't type worth a damn. And, with her boss facedown on the green blotter amidst a Rorschach test of his own blood, she never would.

The shapely blonde knew better than to touch anything, but that didn't stop Sally from grabbing the steno pad from her desk and making notes about what she saw: Diamond's overcoat askew on the coat rack. His fedora upended on the filing cabinet. An open bottle of cheap whiskey on the desk. Two empty shot glasses, one with a red lipstick imprint near the rim. Half a dozen cigarette butts mashed in the amber ashtray and a single butt with matching red lipstick caught in one of the notches. Several strands of long white hair caught under the left front leg of the guest chair. A handwritten notation in Diamond's open appointment book read *bread, eggs,* and, in a different colored ink, *milk.*

When Sally returned to her own desk, she noticed the stationery drawer—the place where she kept the firm's envelopes and letterhead—had not been completely closed by the last person who opened it, and she knew that wasn't her. She pulled it open, rifled through the contents. When she saw nothing out of place, she took the spare .38 and the manila envelope filled with the firm's emergency cash from the false bottom of the drawer. She walked them down the hall to the insurance agent's office, where Maria Delgatto, graduate of the same secretarial school as Sally, tucked them into her desk drawer and let Sally use the phone to call the local precinct house. When she finished, Maria phoned Tony Scarpinato, the freelance shutterbug she'd been seeing.

Two bored homicide detectives arrived in due time, took one look at Diamond's body, and confirmed what Sally already suspected: She was unemployed.

"Looks like Dickie boy died of lead poisoning," Lieutenant Wilber Garrison said.

Sergeant Donald "Dolphin" Williams laughed, and it was obvious how he'd obtained his moniker. When he finished, he asked, "This how you found him?"

"I haven't touched a thing."

"You know who he met with last night?"

"Death," the lieutenant said.

Williams laughed again.

Sally shook her head. "I thought he was done for the day."

"And you? Where did you go?"

"Home."

"Where's that?"

While the lieutenant nosed around Diamond's office, stepping on the white hair, flipping pages in Diamond's appointment book, and squinting at the lipstick on the shot glass, Williams took down Sally's home address and the number of the pay phone in the hall outside her efficiency apartment.

"Blow, sister," Williams told her when he finished. "We can take it from here."

Sally collected her purse and headed toward the elevator. She took one last look at the office as the elevator door closed, saw Scarpinato snapping pics, and wondered if she would ever again see the gilt lettering on the half pane of glass topping the office door:

Diamond Investigations

Dick Diamond, Private Investigator

SALLY SPENT her morning in her former employer's one-bedroom apartment, letting herself in with the spare key he'd entrusted to her several months earlier, and she went through his things before the police thought to. Nothing in Diamond's apartment seemed out of place, but she knew he paid the super's teenaged daughter to clean the place once a week. On the coffee table, the previous morning's newspaper was folded open to a story with accompanying grip-and-grin photo of local businessman Heinrich "Henry" Milch receiving an award from the Police Benevolent Association.

Diamond's spare suit hung in the closet along with two pressed white dress shirts and a pair of chinos. His dresser drawers contained a dozen yellowing white A-shirts and a similar number of white boxer shorts, black dress socks, and spare pair of garters to hold them up. His jewelry box contained a stickpin, some tie clips, a pair of cuff links, and half a dozen prophylactics.

She found nothing of interest in the nightstand and nothing stuck between the mattresses. In the small bathroom, she found only his shaving kit, shower supplies, and a packet of headache powder, so she moved on to the kitchen.

Two bread heels occupied the breadbox. In the icebox, one egg, two bottles of beer, and a quart of milk kept company with an uncooked steak. She found two bottles of expensive whiskey in the cupboard, and she took the unopened one with her when she left. She also took the steak.

On the way to lunch, Sally stopped at her apartment long enough to put the steak in her icebox, and she met Maria at the Automat to collect the .38 and the envelope of cash taken from the false bottom of her desk drawer.

Maria was built like a fireplug. The red dress she wore only accentuated the resemblance and drew attention to her as she made her way to the table where Sally waited with a half-eaten ham-and-cheese on rye, a tuna on white, and two milks. The shorter woman had carried Sally's things out of the Bancroft Building inside a box that once held No. 10 envelopes, and she placed the box on the table between them. "Tony cancelled lunch so he could get his pics developed for newspaper's evening edition."

"You can't stand in the way of the news," Sally said. She felt the weight of the box's contents as she pulled it across the table.

Maria looked around before leaning forward and whispering, "What are you going to do with a gun?"

"I don't know yet," Sally told her, "but I certainly wasn't going to leave anything for the coppers to filch."

"If I can do anything—" Maria offered.

"I need you to keep an eye on the office," Sally told her friend. "If you see anyone nosing around, let me know."

"I can do that," Maria said, "but do you really think the killer will come back?"

"I don't know what to think," Sally said. "Dick did all the investigating. All I did was answer the phone and keep the books."

"So, what're you going to do about finding work?"

The office rent was paid through the end of the month, as was her apartment rent. Sally didn't need to find a new position immediately—if managed carefully, the firm's off-the-books emergency fund would provide for her short-term well-being. "I'll be okay," she said as she tapped the box. "I have a few dollars stashed away."

As they ate, Maria told Sally about all the police in and out of the Diamond Investigations office that morning. "They removed several boxes of stuff after the coroner took away the body, but mostly they talked to people in the building, asking did we see anything or anybody unusual yesterday."

"What did you tell them?"

"I told the lieutenant that I see strangers going in and out of your office all the time. What makes one any more unusual than another?"

AFTER LUNCH, Sally carried the envelope box to her apartment before opening it. She checked the revolver to ensure it was loaded before hiding it in her breadbox. She added fifty dollars from the emergency fund to the paltry three dollars in her wallet and put the rest of the money in a coffee tin on one of the upper kitchen shelves.

She cracked open the bottle of whiskey taken from Diamond's apartment and poured a shot. As she nursed it, she considered her options. She always figured Diamond would get himself killed. He was known for cutting corners, most of his clients were shady characters, and the string of dames who visited his bed couldn't be counted without an adding machine. Sally knew she could mope around and feel sorry for herself, or she could find out who terminated her employment.

After finishing the shot, Sally grabbed her purse and headed toward the Bancroft Building. The regular Joes had all gone home by the time she arrived, and the neighborhood had turned dark and quiet, except for the neon light advertising O'Malley's, the watering hole at the far end of the block.

She pushed her way in, caught the attention of most of the men there, and made her way to the bar as they parted to let her pass. She motioned for the bartender.

He said, "What'll you have, sister?"

"Dick Diamond was found dead morning."

"I heard," the bartender said. "He left an open tab."

"Did you see him at all last night?"

"He came in around seven," the bartender said, "and left with a bottle of the cheap stuff."

"Why didn't he go to the liquor store? It's only a few blocks away."

"He said he didn't have time."

"He say anything else?"

The bartender narrowed his eyes. "Who are you?" he asked. "I've seen you around, but we ain't never been introduced."

"Sally Jenson," she said. "I worked for Dick."

The bartender laughed. "That's funny," he said. "I wish I had me a gal who worked for dick."

Sally glared at him until he grew uncomfortable.

He turned and raised his voice. "Any of you guys see Dick Diamond after he left here last night?"

A chorus of negative responses deflated Sally's optimism, and she turned to leave.

"Hold on," the bartender said as he reached over the top of the bar to catch her elbow. When she turned back, he said, "There's a rummy sleeps in the alley next to the Bancroft Building. You need to give him something to loosen his tongue."

Sally bought a bottle of cheap whiskey that matched the bottle on Diamond's desk, thanked the bartender, and made her way down the street to the alley. She hurried past it during the day, but at night she had even less desire to approach it. She stood at the end of the alley and looked into the darkness.

A ragged voice called to her. "You need something, dollface?"

"I brought you this." She offered the whiskey bottle to the darkness.

"What's the catch?"

"I need to ask you a few questions about last night."

"Then bring me that bottle and ask your questions."

"I—I can't see you."

"It's probably better that way, dollface. Just follow the smell. I ain't bathed in a month."

Sally stepped carefully into the alley and a moment later felt someone take the bottle from her hand. She asked the rummy if he knew Dick Diamond and, when she learned that he did, asked if he'd seen her boss the previous evening.

"I seen Diamond come out of O'Malley's, must have been a quarter past seven. He shoves something in the mailbox and double-times it back here and into the building. A few minutes later, a Packard pulls up and some dame gets out and heads inside."

"Recognize the dame?"

"Never seen her before. Never seen the dog before, either."

"Dog?"

"She carried some kind of terrier tucked under her arm."

"Did you see her leave?"

"I had just cracked open a bottle of rotgut and from then on I wasn't paying attention to nothing else but my new best friend."

"Can you tell me anything about the woman?"

"I've seen lady wrestlers with better figures."

"Meaning?"

"Stout. Like a whiskey barrel, and her pins were nothing to write home about neither, not like yours."

"Thank you," Sally said. "Was she a blonde, brunette, or redhead?"

"Didn't see her hair. She wore a hat, one of those fancy things with a wide brim, and the collar of her overcoat was turned up."

"Anything else you can tell me?"

"You want the bottle back so's you can get your deposit?"

"No," Sally said as she began edging toward the light at the end of the alley. "You keep it."

"You want me to keep a look out for this dame?"

"You see her again, you let me know." Sally gave him the number for the pay phone outside her apartment, unsure if he would remember the number without her writing it down.

With no idea where to go next, she went home. She pan-fried Diamond's steak and later put herself to sleep by downing several shots of Diamond's whiskey.

SALLY WISHED she had the packet of headache powder from Diamond's medicine cabinet because her head throbbed when she awoke the next morning. She showered, dressed, and made her way to the diner on the corner intent on having two eggs over-easy, toast, and copious amounts of black coffee.

"Shame about your boss," the waitress said when she brought the eggs and toast.

Sally looked up at Gretta. "What do you know about it?"

"Only what's in the paper." Greta walked away and returned with that morning's edition. The front-page headline, bannered over one of Tony Scarpinato's photos, read *Shamus Shot, Police Perplexed.*

As Stella sopped up her egg yolks with her toast and downed a second cup of black coffee, she read the brief news report. She didn't learn anything about Diamond she didn't already know—he served in the European theatre during World War II, opened Diamond Investigations upon his return to the states, never married and had no children—but she was perplexed that police claimed to have no clue who killed Diamond or why. What she saw in Diamond's office and what she learned from the rummy who lived in the alley next to the Bancroft Building, convinced Sally that a stocky, white-haired woman who favored red lipstick, filtered cigarettes, and cheap whiskey killed Diamond. Like the police, though, she did not know why her employer had been killed.

She decided to share her information with the cops and find out what information they failed to share with the newshound who inked the article about Diamond's death. She made her way to the precinct house, but before she could talk to Lieutenant Garrison, Sergeant Williams pulled her aside, into a small room often used to coerce confessions from the guilty and the innocent alike.

Sally asked why the newspaper article claimed the police had no leads. "You saw the lipstick on the shot glass and the cigarette filter, didn't you?"

"It don't mean nothing," Williams said. "Could've been yours, sweetheart. Could've been anybody's."

"You talked to everybody, didn't you?"

"Nobody saw nothing."

"But there's a witness," Sally insisted. "He saw a woman enter the Bancroft Building between seven-fifteen and seven-thirty."

"Who?" Williams demanded. "Who's the witness?"

She told him about the rummy who lived in the alley next to the building.

"A drunk? Who'd believe a drunk?"

"I—"

"Go on home and tend to your knitting, sister," Williams growled. "We'll take care of this case."

"It sounds like you don't intend to do a thing."

Williams grabbed Sally's arm and pulled her to her feet. He pressed his keg-like belly against hers, pushing her back against the wall. His breath stank of coffee and nicotine when he growled, "You go home now and forget this conversation, or you'll live to regret it."

He stared deep into Sally's eye. She stared back, and he blinked first.

The sergeant stepped back, opened the interrogation room door, and hustled Sally through the precinct house to the exit. As he pushed her outside, onto the front steps, one of the other officers made a joke about dizzy dames and Williams laughed.

The sergeant's dolphin laugh was the last thing Sally heard before the door closed behind her.

SHE SPENT the rest of the day asking questions of her dead boss's clients and trying to shake the feeling she overlooked something. When she returned home that evening she was no closer to having answers to any of her questions. No one knew anything and few of them cared.

Sally poured herself a shot of Diamond's expensive whiskey and was sitting at her kitchen table nursing it when the pay phone outside her apartment rang several times. One of her neighbors answered it and a moment later banged on her apartment door. "It's for you!"

She stepped into the hall and pressed the receiver to her ear.

"Sally? It's Maria. I tried calling earlier, but you weren't home."

Sally listened while Maria told her about a man seen hanging around the second floor of the Bancroft Building that afternoon. "He seemed awfully interested in your office."

"Who was he?"

"I don't know," Maria said. "I've never seen him before."

"What about women? You see any women hanging around?"

"Nobody I didn't already know."

Sally wondered if the rummy in the alley had seen anyone, so she grabbed her purse and returned to the Bancroft Building. The alley was just as dark as the night before, and she entered gingerly. She didn't know the man's name, so she called, "Are you there?"

She heard rustling but no response. Then she stumbled over a body, skinned her palms, and tore a gash in her stockings. She remained on her knees and felt around in the darkness for breathing, for a pulse, for any sign of life. She found none. She righted herself, intending to seek help. Before she took her first step toward the mouth of the alley, someone behind her pulled a foul-smelling gunnysack over her head and wrapped thick arms around her, pinning her arms to her sides. She struggled, but it did no good. The man trapping her arms was too strong, and her kicks at his shins were ineffectual.

He carried her to a waiting car and threw her in the back seat. She tried to pull off the gunnysack and received a slap against the back of her head hard enough to make her eyes water.

"You should have let well enough alone."

Sally recognized the voice, but she wasn't certain from where, and neither the man sitting next to her nor the driver spoke again until they reached their destination.

Dragged from the car, she could tell from the echo of their footsteps and the smell of grease and gasoline that they were inside some kind of garage.

She was pushed into a kitchen chair and her arms tied behind the back of the chair.

A new voice said, "You're Dick Diamond's Gal Friday."

Sally knew of no reason to deny the man's statement. Though she could not see who was speaking, she turned toward the sound of the voice. "I was Mr. Diamond's secretary."

"But no longer."

"That's correct, sir, I'm not. Mr. Diamond was killed, and I—"

A smack to the back of Sally's head silenced her. She heard a small dog yap. She couldn't tell how close it might be.

"I talk," said the voice. "You listen."

"I—" She stopped herself.

"Mr. Diamond possessed something I wanted. I asked for it politely, but he refused to give it to me. He said he no longer had it. I'm thinking maybe he gave it to you." The voice moved and Sally turned her head to follow it. "Did Mr. Diamond ask you to hold something for him?"

Sally said nothing and received a smack on the back of the head. The familiar voice said, "That was a question. Answer it."

"Mr. Diamond never gave me anything but long hours and low pay."

The man behind her laughed and she took another smack in the back of the head. She'd heard the laugh before, in the Diamond Investigations office and again at the precinct house.

The unfamiliar voice continued. "You best be telling the truth. If you're not, the next time we talk will be the last."

"You're going to kill me, too?"

"I don't know what Mr. Diamond saw in a mouthy broad like you," the voice continued, "but maybe we can change your attitude."

"You going to hit me again?"

"I wouldn't ever hit a woman," said the voice, "but my associates have no such compunction."

Sally prepared for another smack in the back of the head and wasn't at all prepared for the fist buried in her stomach. A small dog yapped while repeated blows from a pair of saps rained down on her until she lost consciousness and the only thing keeping her upright was the rope binding her hands to the back of the chair.

SALLY CAME to on a deserted street, laying facedown in the gutter, bleeding from the corner of her mouth, her entire body numb from the beating she'd taken. Her hands were free, so she pulled off the foul-smelling gunnysack and looked around. She found her purse two feet away, but the streetlights were broken or burned out and she didn't at first recognize her surroundings.

She grabbed her purse, struggled to her feet, and stumbled toward the nearest cross street. When she reached it, she recognized where she was and knew she was much closer to Maria's apartment than her own. By leaning against storefronts and parked cars and lampposts, she stumbled her way there and leaned into the intercom buzzer.

Maria answered. "Tony? You forget something?"

"This isn't Tony," Sally said. "I need to come up. You alone?"

"What are you doing out at this time of night?"

"Buzz me in and come help me up the stairs."

As soon as the buzzer sounded, Sally pushed her way into the apartment building's foyer.

Maria, wearing a pink bathrobe and fuzzy pink slippers, hurried down from her third-floor walk-up and helped Sally climb the stairs and into her apartment. Sally stumbled, almost knocking from the wall one of the framed black-and-white photographs taken by Maria's boyfriend.

After she closed the door behind them, Maria asked, "What happened?"

Sally told her.

Sally didn't realize how badly the two goons beat her until she stripped off her clothes and saw bruises covering much of her torso. They had been careful to avoid bruising any part of her visible were she wearing modest clothing, and she was only bleeding from her mouth because she hit her face on the curb when they pushed her out of their sedan.

Maria used a wet washcloth to dab the blood from the corner of Sally's mouth. A moment later, she drew a warm bath and helped ease Sally into the tub. While Sally soaked, Maria sat on the toilet lid.

"Why are you doing this?" she asked. "You didn't even like Mr. Diamond."

"When a woman's boss gets killed, she's supposed to do something about it. It doesn't matter what she thought of him. He was her boss and she's supposed to do something about it."

Maria shook her head but held her friend's hand until morning.

SALLY TOOK a cab to her apartment building mid-morning Saturday, paying the driver with some of Diamond Investigations' emergency cash. As she walked past the row of mailboxes in the lobby, she realized there was something in hers. She took out a wad of envelopes, carried them upstairs to her efficiency apartment, and dumped them on her kitchen table. Most of the envelopes contained bills and junk mail, but one was a Diamond Investigations envelope addressed to her in Dick Diamond's sloppy handwriting. She opened it and withdrew a key with the number 17 etched into it.

She stored her suitcase in a bus station locker when she first arrived in the city from Quarryville, so she recognized what the key opened. She changed clothes, poured and drank a shot of Diamond's whiskey, and put the .38 from the breadbox into her purse.

Not knowing if she was being watched, Sally wasn't planning to take any chances. She called a cab, met it in front of her apartment building, and instructed the driver take her to the bus station. She sat in the waiting area and watched all the people entering and leaving until she convinced herself no one had followed her. She opened locker 17 and removed a white No. 10 envelope. She hurried into the ladies room, pushed into a stall, and opened the envelope to find a strip of 35mm negatives.

She held them up to the light but couldn't figure out what she was seeing. She stuffed the negatives back in the envelope, put the envelope into her purse, and made her way to the bank of pay phones, where she dialed Maria's number.

Her friend answered on the third ring.

"I need Tony's help."

"With what?"

Sally told Maria about the strip of negatives. "I need him to make prints."

"I'll let him know you're on your way and I'll meet you there." Maria gave Sally her boyfriend's address, and fifteen minutes later the three of them were in Tony's apartment looking at the filmstrip.

Tony took the negatives into his bathroom, long ago converted into a darkroom. Sally tried to follow him, but he pushed her back. "It's barely big enough for me in there. Just wait a few minutes and I'll bring out the prints."

Sally paced Tony's living room until he returned with several 8" x 10" photo prints. They were still damp, and he placed them one at a time on his kitchen table. The three of them bent over each print and stared at it. The photographs were taken through a bedroom window and showed a stocky, dark-haired woman undressing. Some of the photos caught a reflection in the bedroom mirror of a man sitting on the bed watching the woman. His face was indistinguishable in the first few photos.

Maria glanced at Sally. "Your boss was a peeping Tom."

Tony smirked. "Just wait."

He placed the last print on the table. In the photo, the woman had pulled off the last of her unmentionables, revealing external plumbing.

The two women straightened up in surprise. Then Sally sorted through the prints until she found one where the woman's face was quite clear.

Sally turned to Maria's boyfriend. "Do you still have Thursday morning's newspaper?"

"Under the sink."

Sally dug through the stack of newspapers, found Thursday's, and thumbed through it looking for the article about Heinrich Milch receiving an award from the Police Benevolent Association. When she found it, she jabbed her finger at the newspaper photo as she showed it to the other two. "This is the same man, isn't it?"

They agreed it was.

Maria looked at her. "You think Mr. Diamond was blackmailing Heinrich Milch?"

"I don't know," Sally said. "I don't know if I'm strong enough for this if he was."

"A woman can do anything a man can do, Sally," Scarpinato said, surprising her. "It doesn't take a dick to get things done."

"You're right," she said.

As they examined all the photos a second time, Sally slowly realized why Diamond had added milk to his shopping list even though he had an unopened quart in his icebox.

AFTER SALLY took the Diamond Investigations emergency money from her purse and divided it amongst them, they took separate cabs from Tony's apartment.

Her cab dropped Sally off in front of an impressive brownstone. She carried her purse and a manila envelope containing the prints Tony made earlier that day. The negatives were safely tucked away.

She climbed the steps and rang the bell. A moment later a man the size of a Clydesdale opened the door and stared down at her. He said nothing but his eyes narrowed as if he recognized her.

A longhaired white Maltese terrier yapped its way into the foyer, and she recognized the hair trapped under the chair leg in Diamond's office.

"I've come to see Mr. Milch."

"He isn't—"

"Who is it, Gunter?" A man built like a whiskey barrel joined them in the foyer, scooped up the Maltese terrier, and took a long look at Sally before he said, "I'll see the lady in my study."

The man blocking the doorway led her through the house to the study, where Heinrich Milch sat behind a desk nearly as large as Sally's efficiency apartment. He held the terrier in one arm and a tumbler three-fingers-full of whiskey in his other hand. He raised the glass a few inches and said, "May I offer you something to drink?"

Before Sally could respond, Milch called, "Dolphin."

Sergeant Donald Williams joined them in the study. "I told you she'd be trouble."

"Fix the lady a drink."

As Williams turned to the bar and began pouring whiskey into a tumbler, Sally tossed the manila envelope on Milch's desk. He put down his tumbler, upended the envelope, and let the photo prints spill across his desk. "Ah," he said. "You found the pictures. These could prove quite embarrassing if they were made public." He looked inside the envelope. "And the negatives?"

Sally reached into her purse, as if in response to his question, and his eyes widened. Instead of negatives, she pulled out Diamond Investigation's spare .38, spun around, and leveled it at Williams. The sergeant had halved the distance between them while her attention was on Milch, and he wasn't bringing her the tumbler of whisky he'd poured. He held a sap in his hand, one she felt multiple times the night before.

Williams nodded toward the revolver. "What do you think you're going to do with that?"

"Well, I'm not going to use it to pick my teeth."

He laughed his dolphin laugh. "You ain't got the balls to pull the trigger."

"I don't need balls." She had the last laugh when she put a slug through Dolphin's blowhole. The sergeant dropped to the floor.

The doorman burst into the room and stopped the moment he saw the .38 in Sally's hand.

"I believe the young lady has us as a disadvantage, Gunter," Milch said.

Gunter held his arms out to his sides, ensuring that Sally realized his hands were empty. She motioned with the barrel of the .38, so he moved past Williams's body to stand next to Milch's desk.

"You were Diamond's last appointment the night he was killed," Sally explained. "He wrote it down as *milk,* but that's what *Milch* means in German, isn't it?"

The stocky man holding the Maltese terrier said nothing.

"And it isn't what you're wearing in these photographs that would prove embarrassing," Sally continued, "it's the person in the room with you."

"And that would be?"

"Look closely, Mr. Milch. His reflection is caught in the mirror."

Milch handed the terrier to Gunter and pushed the prints around the top of his desk as he examined them.

Sally, Maria, and Tony had spent all afternoon tracking down the name of the man whose image was reflected in the mirror. "You don't just have the police under your thumb, Mr. Milch, you have a United States Senator in your back pocket."

Gunter threw the dog at Sally, and it hit her square in the chest as she swung the .38 up and to the left just before squeezing the trigger.

The big man dropped.

The Maltese terrier yelped as it hit the floor. Then it attacked her ankles.

She kicked at the dog. When she returned her attention to Mr. Milch, he held a semi-automatic pistol taken from his desk drawer.

"I ought to shoot you," Sally said, "you and your little dog, too."

The two stared hard at one another, weapons at the ready.

Sally heard a sound behind her, but didn't dare look over her shoulder.

Milch tossed the pistol aside and called to the terrier. "Adolph!"

The dog quit harassing Sally's ankles, ran to the man behind the desk, and jumped into his lap.

A hand reached over Sally's shoulder and took the .38 from her hand. She turned to find herself facing Lieutenant Wilber Garrison.

"Your friend Maria told me what you were up to," he said. "We'll take it from here."

Garrison did, and Sally collapsed into an overstuffed chair as the room flooded with police, thankful that Maria caught the ear of an honest flatfoot after they separated earlier that evening.

Scarpinato was standing outside the brownstone taking photographs when the police escorted Heinrich "Henry" Milch away in handcuffs, when the bodies of Dolphin and Gunter were carried out, and when Lieutenant Garrison escorted Sally Jenson to a waiting patrol car. Several of his photographs appeared in the next day's morning edition under the headline *Shamus Secretary Solves Shooting, Police Purge Proceeds.* The accompanying article described how Sally solved the murder of her boss and how solving the murder led to uncovering massive police corruption. The article hinted that the corruption might even reach into the upper reaches of statewide politics.

MONDAY MORNING, Sally stood at the Diamond Investigations office door and watched the gold gilt drying after a sign painter replaced Diamond's name with hers.

Diamond Investigations

Sally Jenson, Private Investigator

An unfamiliar man stopped, removed his hat, and said, "I was here Friday, but you were closed."

Sally stepped aside and let her first client into the reception area where Maria Delgatto, her new secretary, sat behind her old desk.

Being a dick, Sally decided, wasn't all that difficult.

TWELVE GOOD MEN AND TRUE

By Jim Doherty

**OR THE** record," said Alameda County Superior Court Judge Tom Couper, "please state your full name, age, marital status, whether or not you have any children, and your occupation."

"Daniel M. Sullivan, Jr." I replied. "I'm 23, single, no children. I'm an undergrad at UC Berkeley, majoring in Legal Studies, and I support myself at a several part-time jobs."

"What are your part-time jobs?"

"I'm a reserve officer with the Berkeley Police. Prior to that I was a part-time civilian student employee with the UC Police. I'm also a member of the Board of Directors at the Berkeley Student Cooperative. I'm also licensed as a real estate salesman under my father, who's a broker in San Francisco, but I don't work at it very often. I've also done a little free-lance fiction writing. Sold a few short stories, but they haven't paid nearly enough for me to make a living at it."

"And you go to classes, too?" said the judge, eliciting a few chuckles from the courtroom.

"Well, I have to admit my GPA isn't as high as it could be," I replied, eliciting a few more chuckles.

"Besides what you've already mentioned, do you have any relatives or close friends in law enforcement or the legal profession?"

"Yessir. My dad, Dan Sullivan, used to be a San Francisco police officer. He had to retire very early in his career on disability, which is why he went into the family real estate business. My grandfather on my mom's side, Frank Lowney, was a detective in the Southern Pacific Railroad Police. His son, my uncle, Frank Lowney, Jr., is a trial attorney here in Oakland. Specializes in medical malpractice."

The judge asked, "Is that Francis Xavier Thomas More Lowney?"

"Yes, it is, Your Honor. Apparently you know him even better'n me. I had no idea Thomas More was his confirmation saint."

"Patron saint of lawyers," Judge Couper explained. "Sorry to interrupt. Please continue."

"Yessir. My uncle by marriage, Johnny Evans, retired from the Navy as a Senior Chief Master-at-Arms, kind of a nautical military police topkick. My cousin, Rob Lowney, is a deputy district attorney in San Diego County. Another cousin, Finn Lowney, is a correctional officer over at San Quentin. And I have two cousins by marriage, Vince Williams and Clem Michaels, who're both reserve police officers. Vince is with the Concord PD and Clem's with the Marin County Sheriff's Office. Vince is also an attorney in Lafayette, specializing in civil litigation and real estate law. Clem's wife, Barbara, my cousin, is in law school, but she's not a lawyer, yet."

I paused for a moment, then added, "Your Honor, if I have to list all my friends in law enforcement we'll probably all be here a long time."

That generated more chuckles.

IT WAS late Thursday afternoon. I'd been on jury duty almost two weeks. Since juries aren't typically assembled on Fridays, this would likely be my last day of service.

During my term of duty, I'd been on panels from which juries were being chosen six times, and had been called up to the jury box for the *voir dire* process three times, four including this session in Judge Couper's courtroom, but had yet to actually be selected to serve on a jury.

I wasn't really surprised. This was the second time I'd been on jury duty since registering to vote at the age of 18. The first time was last year, at Federal District Court over in San Francisco. There I'd been *voir dired* three times during my term of service, but had never been chosen then, either. This time it was California Superior Court at the René Davidson Courthouse in Oakland.

In either court, whether the case was civil or criminal, it made no difference. Once the defense lawyers found out I was a cop, from a family of cops and lawyers, they always exercised their right to an unexplained peremptory challenge on me.

Almost always, anyway. There was that time last week when the defense counsel smiled broadly, looked me right in the eye and, in response to the judge's question about any further challenges, replied, "Your Honor, this jury is satisfactory to me as constituted."

The Deputy DA's jaw dropped, and he looked at his adversary in surprise, then looked at me, then down at his notes. Then he took a second look at the defense attorney, a second at me, and a second at his notes. Then he repeated the process yet a third time.

The upshot was that the prosecutor wound up using one of *his*

challenges to bounce me off the jury. The defense lawyer'd totally gamed him into voluntarily burning off one of his own limited store of peremptories on a candidate who most would've regarded as a clearly pro-prosecution juror, simultaneously allowing the defendant's representative to preserve one of his.

Ah, the drama of courtroom strategy.

Anyway, the salient point was that, however he'd managed it, he'd gotten me off the jury.

And I was dead sure I was going to be bounced off of this case, too. On this case, I wouldn't merely be undesirable to a defense lawyer.

I'd be sheer poison.

HAVING GOTTEN my personal details down on the record, the judge went on to ask the money questions. Had I ever served on a jury before (I hadn't, though I'd been on jury duty before). Could I judge the case impartially and according to his instructions (I could). Was I personally acquainted with either prosecution or defense counsel (I wasn't). Did I know any of the listed witnesses (I didn't).

"Mr. Sullivan, inasmuch as this is a drug case, can you tell us if you've ever worked in narcotics enforcement?"

"Not as a regular assignment. I've occasionally worked with the Special Investigations Bureau, BPD's vice/narcotics detail, on drug sweeps, and a few times I've gone along with them to provide a uniformed presence when they were serving a search warrant. I've also made undercover drug buys in the South Campus area, specifically in and around People's Park, but that was working under the Telegraph Avenue Foot Patrol, not SIB."

That was one of the items that would make me poisonous. It wouldn't get me challenged for cause, because the defense couldn't really claim that just being involved in drug enforcement biased me in this specific case. But it was sure to get me peremptoried.

"Do you know any of the jurors who've already been seated?"

"No, sir."

"Is there anything else you think we should be aware of?"

"Yessir. I recently lost a loved one to drug use. He overdosed on some tainted heroin."

My cousin, Chuck Evans, the son of my mom's sister, Marie, and my Uncle Johnny.

"I'm very sorry for your loss. You don't need to go into details, but do you think that loss would render you unable to judge this case impartially?"

"No, sir, I don't. But I thought I should mention it in the interests of full disclosure."

"Thank you. Do you have any scheduling conflicts that would keep you from being able to serve on this jury?"

"Well, Your Honor, I do have mid-terms coming up next week. But, if I'm chosen, I don't think I'd have any trouble getting 'em postponed. To tell the truth, I could use the excuse."

More titters from the audience.

I WAS then turned over to the attorneys. The Deputy DA, Colin Kent, asked a few perfunctory questions, establishing that there was no reason to challenge me for cause, which would force counsel for the defense, Stewart Goldblum, to expend one of his shrinking number of peremptories.

Goldblum came out swinging.

"Mr. Sullivan," he said, "steeped as you've been in law enforcement, practically from the cradle, do you really think you can render an impartial verdict in this case?"

"Yessir, I do."

"Don't you think your background, both professional and familial, disposes you to… makes you feel as if you have a duty to favor the prosecution?"

"Quite the contrary. I think my background, both professional and familial, has instilled in me a deep sense of duty, as you say. But, as a juror, my duty would be to examine the evidence in this case impartially, and render a verdict of guilty only if the prosecutor has met his requirement to prove his case beyond a reasonable doubt."

"What would you do if you were pretty sure the defendant, Mr. Jason, was guilty, but you did not believe the prosecution had quite met its burden of proving the case 'beyond a reasonable doubt?' "

"I'd vote to acquit."

"What would you do if it was a very close call?"

"I'm not sure what you mean by a very close call. But let's say 'reasonable doubt's' a line on the road, several miles out, and at the starting point, the DA fills his tank with evidence, the fuel that propels his car. If the car has enough gas to get him past that line, I vote to convict. If he runs out of gas short of making it, I vote to acquit. If he just barely makes it over, so that nothing but the front point of his bumper is past the line, I vote to convict. If he's a micro-millimeter short of the line, or even right on the line, but not beyond, I vote to acquit. So, assuming this is going to be a close case, I guess the question is, how sure are you of my ability to tell where that line in the road is, and to tell where, in relation to that line, that car is when the Mr. Kent runs out of gas. But I would do my best to make those judgments impartially."

GOLDBLUM WAS a flamboyant looking guy. In his 50s, he was still boyishly handsome, and acted like he knew it. His ties were carefully knotted, his three-piece suits carefully tailored. He'd worn a dark gray glen plaid yesterday and had carried a leather attaché case with the same pattern. Today's suit was navy, with white pinstripes so prominent they almost stood out like neon against the ultra-dark blue. His leather attaché case was also navy, and also decorated with pinstripes.

The guy actually had briefcases to match his suits!

His longish, wavy gray hair was styled, deliberately styled I later found out, in a manner resembling actor Michael Douglas's signature coiffure. I learned afterwards that over in San Francisco, where he had his offices, he was known as "the lawyer with the Michael Douglas haircut."

When I'd gotten back to my room the night before, I'd been tempted to Google him, but scrupulously decided to wait until I was actually finished with jury duty. Later on, though, I found out that he was something of a celebrity over in The City, a larger-than-life criminal law specialist in the tradition of such bygone Bay Area legal legends as Jake Ehrlich, Mel Belli, and Nate Cohn. Like me, he also dabbled in fiction writing, and had recently had a novel, a romantic thriller called *The Only One of Its Kind,* released to a certain amount of fanfare some months prior to this trial.

Me? I'd managed to sell some short fiction to websites nobody but other hopeful writers looked at, and counted myself lucky if I got paid five or ten bucks per story.

I was surprised, and almost embarrassed, that I'd never heard of him before.

I'd seen him driving down Oak Street earlier that morning. I'd been walking down the same street to the courthouse at Oak and 13th from Broadway, where the AC Transit 51 bus had let me off. He'd been driving a Lamborghini. A Gallardo. It occurred to me that an Egoista might've been more appropriate, but, of course, the Egoista was a concept car, never actually put into production. The Gallardo was blazing red with gold wheels inside the tires.

Apparently his extravagance didn't extend to having different colored cars to match his suits.

He was obviously annoyed that I wasn't giving him any ammo that he could use to challenge me for cause. Unless he could disqualify me, he'd have to use one of his peremptories. And I was guessing he didn't have that many left.

THE JURY examination had begun yesterday afternoon. The pool was unusually large. Out of the first twelve called up for examination, Kent had successfully challenged one for cause, and made two peremptories. Goldblum made no challenges for cause, but made seven peremptories, all of them white people.

Goldblum's client, Dallas Jason, was a light-skinned African-American, probably in his mid-20's, just a few years older than me. He was wearing a conservative business suit, his hair was cut short, and he was freshly shaved, but the clean-cut look he was trying to convey was undercut by the gang tats visible on his face, including a teardrop under his left eye. In gang parlance, that could mean he'd killed someone in the past. Over time, though, other meanings had attached to the symbol, the mourning of a friend who'd been killed, for example, or the wearer's having been the victim of sexual abuse in prison. And, since a few rock stars had adopted the look, the more sinister implications had been diluted. Still, I was rather surprised that Goldblum hadn't had Jason put on some make-up to hide the tats.

Two potential jurors had survived the first round. Ten more were called up. Kent peremptoried three, Goldblum four, along with getting Judge Couper to approve one challenge for cause. Three of Goldblum's peremptories were white, the fourth was an Asian woman whose brother was on SFPD's Chinatown Squad (or Asian Gang Task Force, to give it the official, and more politically correct, title). A black woman whose son had died of a drug overdose, and who admitted that it would be difficult to be impartial in a drug case, was excused for cause at her own request.

In California, the lawyers on both sides of a criminal trial are entitled to ten peremptory challenges each, for a total of twenty, unless the potential penalty is death or life imprisonment. Then each side gets twenty, for a total of forty.

Goldblum had already peremptoried eleven, and that surprised me. The charge against Jason, possession of cocaine for sale, a violation of Section 11351 of the California Health and Safety Code, only carried a maximum penalty of four years.

Unless, perhaps, this was his third strike. Jason must've racked up a couple of felony convictions. I wasn't supposed to know that. But you can't unknow things you already know. I knew what being allowed more than ten peremptories meant. And I knew the possible meaning of the teardrop tattooed under Jason's eye.

But I also knew that neither of those things meant he was guilty in this case. That would have to be proved beyond a reasonable doubt.

Not that I was ever going to get the chance to make that judgment.

THE REST of the day and most of the next went like that, with Goldblum doing his best to keep whites off the jury, and Kent spending his peremptories more thriftily than his opponent. I'd stopped counting after the second round.

By three o'clock the next day, eleven jurors had been seated. Now they only needed one more juror, and two alternates. Judge Couper sent the eleven who'd already been picked home for the day, telling them to be in court Monday at nine AM for opening statements.

Then he had the court reporter pick six names out of the bin. There was time for one more round before the close of business.

I was the first one whose name was pulled, five more joined me.

GOLDBLUM LOOKED down at his notes, than up at me again.

"You mentioned a loved one who'd died in a drug-related incident."

"Yessir."

"Could you tell us all more about that?"

"My cousin. Chuck Evans. Charles Evans, that is. He was a fireman back east. He was injured on the job, and had trouble controlling the pain afterwards. When the prescription for his medication ran out, he found heroin easier to acquire than illicit pain pills. His life went into a tailspin as he struggled with the addiction. One night he got hold of some tainted heroin, went to bed after shooting up, and never woke up."

That was going to be biggest issue. Being white made me undesirable. Being a cop, from a family of cops, made me unacceptable. Having done some work in drug enforcement, however peripherally, made me positively toxic. But having a loved one who'd OD'd?

That made me by God radioactive!

"Do you think you'd be inclined to find my client guilty so you could exact some measure of vengeance for the death of your cousin?"

"I'll find your client guilty if the DA proves his case. If he fails to meet the burden of proof, I'll vote to acquit. Chuck doesn't come into it."

"Do you intend to make law enforcement your career after you graduate?"

"Yes, I do."

"And, despite choosing a profession that amounts to putting people in jail, you'd really vote to acquit, if the prosecutor doesn't meet his burden? You really believe that everyone deserves to be presumed innocent until proven guilty?"

"Let's say that I think innocent people deserve to be presumed innocent and that, as a practical matter, the only way to make sure an innocent person gets that presumption is to extend it to everyone who's accused of a crime."

"So you're saying you don't think guilty people deserve that presumption?"

"I'm saying that I think the system can't work unless that presumption goes for everyone. It's based on society's recognizing that the system is designed by humans, and therefore flawed. So, as a society, we've made the value judgment that, if errors are going to be made, it's better to err on the side of mercy. Better for guilty people to be acquitted, than for innocent people to be convicted. That's why we presume everyone's innocent. That's why the burden of proof's on the prosecutor. And that's why the prosecutor's bar is raised so high. I agree with that value judgment."

Sorry, sport, you're just going to have to burn off a peremptory.

He sat down, obviously disgruntled.

Kent, on the other hand, looked as wonderfully gruntled as it was possible to look.

IT TOOK about and hour and a half to examine the other five potential jurors. Two were thirty-ish mothers, one black and one Hispanic. A third was a teacher at an inner city high school in Oakland, black male. Four and five, an engineer and a bank teller, were white males.

After they'd all answered the questions put to them by the judge and both attorneys, the judge called the lawyers up for a sidebar. During the ensuing private conference at the bench, Goldblum gesticulated emphatically and insistently, and the judge calmly shook his head negatively. Kent said little. Finally the judge turned to Kent and said something to him. Kent responded, and the judge nodded.

The two lawyers went back to their respective tables, and the judge turned to the jury box.

"Mr. Sullivan, Mrs. Grayson, and Mrs. Vega, would you all please stand."

We all did as the judge directed.

"Mr. Sullivan," he said, "you are our twelfth juror. Mrs. Grayson, you are our first alternate. Mrs. Vega, you are our second alternate."

I could feel my mouth dropping open and my eyes opening wide in surprise.

How the hell had that happened?

WHEN I came through the security checkpoint at the main entrance to the courthouse on Monday morning, I saw that one of the deputy sheriffs working the metal detector was the same one who'd been serving as one of the bailiffs in Judge Couper's courtroom the week before, I greeted him, and asked him why the change in assignment.

"Sometimes they like to move us around, get us used to different duties," he said. "But I'll probably be up in Judge Couper's court later today. He requested extra deputies."

"I was really surprised I made the final cut," I said.

"There's a story behind that," he replied. "The judge'll probably tell you about it after the case is over."

He paused for a moment as he helped another party enter, then said, "I found one of your stories on the 'Net last night."

"Which one?"

"The one about the treasury agent whose counterfeiting case turns out to be related to a sex murder."

"Oh, yeah. I was kind of proud of that one. You know that actually happened. The real-life cop was named Carmine Motto. I just changed the names and smoothed out the edges to make it a readable piece of fiction. Where'd you find it? That website's not up anymore."

"It was on one of those 'Net archive sites. 'Time Machine' I think it was called. I really liked it. Do you have any others out?"

"Yeah, but they're mostly written under a pseudonym."

Turned out he was interested in writing, too, and had completed some short pieces, but, like all writers of short stories, was having a hard time getting them sold. We chatted a few more minutes. I suggested a few websites, and he wrote 'em down.

"Since you're assigned here," I said, "you must be finished with jail duty."

"Thank God," he said. "Hated Santa Rita, and Dyer was even worse."

Santa Rita was the main county jail way out in Dublin, nearly thirty miles southeast. Dyer was the North County Jail over on 6th Street, here in Oakland.

"How much longer before you're on patrol?"

In some counties, sheriff's departments make a distinction between patrol deputies, who do police work in the unincorporated areas of a county, and correctional or court deputies. But deputy sheriffs in Alameda County are all-purpose, and since jail duty is a lot less popular than patrol or investigation, and court duty only slightly less unpopular than jail duty, a deputy can spend years working as a turnkey or a bailiff before ever getting a beat. And, if he or she ever gets promoted to sergeant, the cycle starts all over again.

"Maybe next year," he said, grimacing.

"I know what you mean about hating correctional work. I went through the academy at Santa Rita a little less than a year ago. Left me with a firm conviction that I never wanted to work there."

"Your department send you?"

"They sponsored me, but I paid the freight myself. Being a graduate of a full-time basic academy automatically made me a Level One reservist. I also thought having a full basic school under my belt would make me a more attractive candidate once I start looking for jobs as a regular after college."

"Good idea," he said.

The crowd at the checkpoint was starting to get heavier, so I left the deputy to his duties, told him I'd see him later, and went up to the courtroom.

THERE'S AN old saying among lawyers, often attributed to poet Carl Sandburg.

When the law's against you, pound on the facts. When the facts're against you, pound on the law. When the law and the facts're both against you, pound on the table.

Well, right from the moment he began his opening statement, I figured Goldblum must've thought the facts and the law were both against him, 'cause he came out in full table-pounding mode.

First thing he did was take a copy of the information form binding his client over for trial after the preliminary hearing, and tear it in half.

"This means absolutely nothing," he said, tossing the two halves onto the podium contemptuously. He went on to assure us, at some length, that there was no case to answer against his client and that, once both sides rested, we'd have no choice but to find his client innocent.

Now, of course, simply having an information filed doesn't make a man guilty, but it's not quite true that it means absolutely nothing. It means at least that the prosecution has proved that a crime has been committed and that there's enough probable cause to bind the defendant over for trial.

Kent's opening statement was, by contrast, not nearly as dramatic, but was a brief cogent description of what facts he intended to prove. And was confident that he would prove. He finished with an explanation of why his proving these facts, and proving them beyond a reasonable doubt, should lead us to a verdict of guilty.

The low-key approach of Kent would provide a sharp contrast with the comparatively histrionic approach of Goldblum throughout the course of the trial.

MOST OF the prosecution witnesses were agents of the Alameda

County Narcotics Task Force, which, as its name implies, operates throughout the county, and is staffed by officers from many of the local agencies within the county, but primarily by members of the Sheriff's Office and the Oakland Police Department. Berkeley PD, which, as I'd mentioned to the judge, has its own, very active drug and vice unit, the SIB, works with them occasionally, but, as far as I know, doesn't contribute personnel. Which was good, from my perspective, since it meant I didn't personally know any of the cops involved in the case.

Dallas Jason had come under their radar by accident. The main target in the investigation this particular team from the Task Force was conducting was someone else entirely. A major trafficker against whom that they'd been trying to build a case for months. They'd been surveilling said major trafficker, and had followed him into the parking lot of a Lucky supermarket on 18th Street in Oakland, when they observed a car, driven by a guy they'd never seen before (who would turn out to be Jason) pull up alongside him, driver-side to driver-side. Jason passed what appeared to be a large amount of cash to the major dealer, who, in turn, passed back a large package in a plastic shopping bag, wrapped up in duct tape.

The team leader, deciding that they needed to identify this new player in the game, instructed one of the surveillance cars to follow the unknown party.

When they were about a mile away from the supermarket, the unit following Jason called for cover from uniformed patrol, and pulled him over. When the patrol unit arrived, the two Task Force agents removed Jason from the car and began searching it. One of them found the package, which turned out to be packed white powder, weighing a bit more than two pounds, hidden in a secret compartment in the passenger side door.

Jason and the suspicious package were then transported to one of the Task Force's offices, where one of the two officers made a preliminary test on the powder, while the other questioned Jason.

The powder turned out to be cocaine, though the strength level would be determined by a more comprehensive test conducted at the crime lab.

Jason, for his part, after being properly Mirandized, admitted that he'd been buying coke from the major leaguer for some months. Up to today, he'd been buying half-kilos. This was the first time he'd bought an entire kilo, but his profits from the half-kilos had been substantial enough that he felt he could expand his business.

That pretty much was the prosecution's case right there. Jason had been seen buying something from a major dealer. The package he'd bought had turned out to be coke. And he'd admitted that he'd bought it wholesale in order to resell it retail. All the elements needed to prove possession for sale.

But there were complicating elements. Jason was, relatively speaking, small fry, not the big fish the Task Force was hoping to hook, and if they charged him, it would be clear to said big fish that law enforcement was on to him, because arraignments, and prelims, etc., are all public.

So, to keep things on the down-low, the two narcs thanked Jason for being so cooperative, and told him he was free to go "for the time being." If, later on, the DA decided to press charges they might have to pick him up again, but, just for now, they weren't going to book him. They were, of course, going to hold onto the coke, which would be booked into evidence. He was also told that it probably would be a very bad idea to mention this encounter with the forces of law and order to his associate, since he wouldn't want to be blamed for making said forces aware of the wholesale drug business said associate was operating.

So, for several months after this, Jason got to breathe free air, while the case against the major trafficker was built little by little. When the Task Force finally had enough to bust the major trafficker, the DA decided that Jason could now be charged without jeopardizing the case against the main villain in the story.

That was as far as the prosecution got that first day. The team leader testified about Jason's having been observed exchanging money for a package at the Lucky parking lot. One of the two cops who followed Jason testified about finding the kilo in the hidden compartment and later testing it. The other cop testified about Jason's admission that he'd been dealing retail for some time. A technician from OPD's Criminalistics Division testified that the coke was about eighty per cent pure, which would mean it would stand up to being "stepped on," or cut, to a degree that the would make the two-odd pounds much heavier, and much more profitable at the retail level.

The courtroom was filled with gangbanger types, apparently associates of Jason who were there to lend moral (a rather ironic term to use in this context) support. Accordingly, after court was recessed for the day, all of us jurors were walked out of the courtroom by deputies in order to keep the 'bangers from trying to intimidate us.

THE DEPUTY who'd been working the metal detector that morning walked me down to the ground floor, along with a few other jurors.

"Your car at the Alcopark?" he asked. The Alcopark is a large parking garage on 12th Street, a short walk from the courthouse.

"Took the bus," I said. "But I should be able to get to up to Broadway safely."

"Walk with us as far as the garage, anyway," he said.

It occurred to me I didn't know his name, yet. So I asked.

"Jack Loughlin," he said.

"Ah. Another Irish cop!"

"From a family of cops, just like you."

"If you're really this concerned for our safety," I said, "maybe I should come armed."

"Wouldn't be a bad idea," he replied.

THE NEXT morning I got up a little earlier, slung on a shoulder holster, slid my

nine-mil into it, and then walked down to the Public Safety Building on Martin Luther King Boulevard. I signed in on the Duty Roster in the Reserve Office, putting "Court (René Davidson)" in the "Activity" section. Reserve cops aren't authorized to carry off-duty like the regulars are, so, in order for me to be able to legally pack my weapon to and from the Court House, I'd have to be signed in.

I walked from the PSB over to University Ave, and caught a 51 bus. About a half-hour later I entered the Court House, went to the holding cells, stowed my pistol in a gun locker provided for cops, then went up to my assigned courtroom.

KENT RECALLED the lab tech from the OPD Criminalistics Division, who'd already testified as to the strength of the cocaine found in Jason's car. This time he questioned the tech about the shopping bag in which the coke had been wrapped.

It had apparently come up missing when the evidence was signed out, and no one knew what happened to it. It wasn't really that big a deal, but it was the kind of tiny little spark that Goldblum could fan into a bonfire if Kent didn't put it out first. The tech sheepishly admitted that, after unwrapping the package, he'd put the shopping bag aside, while he conducted his tests. He admitted that he'd forgotten about it after those tests were completed, and speculated that someone probably saw the bag left unattended, assumed it was just trash, and threw it away.

Since the shopping bag was, technically, part of the evidence, its coming up missing was a careless error. And that could suggest carelessness with more important parts of the evidence. By dealing forthrightly with it during the direct examination, Kent was making it more difficult for Goldblum to turn it into a major issue.

Turning it into a major issue was exactly what Goldblum tried to do on cross, but, since Kent had already dealt with the issue, all Goldblum could manage was to get the lab tech to admit what he'd already admitted during direct examination, which didn't really have a lot of impact the second time around.

When Goldblum finished his cross-examination, Kent rested.

GOLDBLUM'S ONLY witness was the narc who'd interviewed Jason. Jason had admitted that he'd bought the coke to resell

it, and this admission was absolutely crucial to the prosecution's case. Unlike many other states, in California possession for sale is not presumed just by the large amount of the drug possessed. That's a good piece of supporting evidence, but it's not absolutely conclusive. Jason's statement that he'd been in the retail coke business for some time was what made the case solid.

If Goldblum could torpedo the narc's testimony, the prosecution's case would probably go toes up, and Jason would go free, since simple possession was not a lesser included offense listed on the information.

Goldblum started in by asking why Jason had been interviewed by only one officer.

"Everybody else was busy with other tasks. There were only a few of us, and each one had a particular job to do. Testing the dope. Listing and booking the evidence. It was just the way the labor got divided."

"Isn't it customary for interrogations to be conducted by more than one officer? To at least have another officer present?"

"It's common. I wouldn't say 'customary.' It depend on the assets a given agency, or a detail of a given agency, has available."

"Well, Officer, I've heard of very few cases in which there weren't at least two officers present to witness an interrogation," said Goldblum.

"Objection," said Kent. "Mr. Goldblum is making an argument, not asking a question."

"Sustained," said Judge Couper. "Save your arguments for summation, Counselor. When you're addressing the witness, make sure you're asking questions, not making comments."

Goldblum apologized, then requested that, inasmuch as the witness had originally been testifying for the prosecution, the defense be allowed to treat him as "hostile," which meant he could ask leading questions that the witness would only be allowed to answer with a simple "yes" or "no." The judge gave Goldblum permission to do so.

Goldblum proceeded to ask a series of "Is it not true that…" types of questions that gave the witness very little wiggle room in framing his answers. Despite this, he was unable to shake his testimony.

Finally Goldblum asked, "Is it not customary for interrogations to be recorded?"

"Yes it is."

"But there was no recording equipment available at this location."

"The department had not provided any."

"I didn't ask why there was no such equipment available. Only whether or not it was available. Now, since, as you say, the department had not provided any such equipment, this interview was not recorded, is that correct?"

"No, it's not correct."

"Didn't you just tell us that no recording equipment was available?"

"No, I didn't. I said the Department hadn't provided any. I used my own device to record the interview."

"What… your…" Goldblum sputtered for a few moments. Then, collecting himself, managed to ask, "What kind of device did you use?"

"My cell phone."

"Did you book your cell phone into evidence.?"

"No, I didn't."

"Did you at least save this recorded conversation on your cell phone?"

"No, I didn't."

"Well, then, your having recorded it is hardly relevant, is it?" he said with a sneer. "No further questions."

Kent's first question on cross was, "Did you make a permanent recording of the conversation?"

"I did."

"How did you do this?"

"I downloaded the recording from the phone to a laptop, and then from the laptop onto a CD-R. I booked the CD-R into evidence."

"Is this the CD-R you downloaded the recording onto?" he asked handing it the witness.

"Yes, it is."

"Your Honor," said Kent, "I move that this CD-R be marked for identification as Peoples' Exhibit 5, and entered into evidence."

"Your Honor, I object!" said Goldblum. "This item was not revealed to me during discovery."

"That's not true, Your Honor," said Kent.

The jury was excused from the courtroom while this point was argued.

WE SPENT about fifteen minutes in the jury room, then were recalled to the court. The upshot of the argument we were not allowed to witness was that the disk was admitted into evidence, and we were allowed to hear it.

Jason clearly admitted buying the coke wholesale to peddle it retail, an admission that, not only was he knowingly in possession of the stuff, but that it was his intention to sell it.

Kent ended his cross-examination, and turned the witness back to Goldblum, who declined the opportunity to do any redirect.

The attorneys then gave their closing arguments.

Kent, as was customary, went first. His summation was brief, and to the point. The defendant was observed by several witnesses buying something that was later found to be more than two pounds of cocaine. That cocaine was found hidden in a secret compartment of the defendant's car. The defendant admitted that he'd bought it, and that he intended to resell it. All the elements of the crime of possession of cocaine for sale had been proven beyond any reasonable doubt. In consideration of this, we, the jury, had an obligation to find the defendant guilty.

Goldblum went next. He had very little to work with at this point, but he did his best. His summation went on longer than Kent's, and was more emotional. There was, he insisted, every reason to discount the testimony of the cops. While failing to give specific reasons for discounting that testimony, he returned, over and over, to the point that the cops had let the defendant go after supposedly finding him in possession of a large amount of an illegal drug, and then eliciting a confession. That simply didn't make sense. Narcotics officers didn't let dealers free. It simply was not credible. Moreover, the way the physical evidence, the actual kilo of coke, was tainted by the missing shopping bag made all of it suspect, and, on that basis, should be disregarded completely. The fact that the defendant was released after giving a statement suggested that the he was told he would be freed in exchange for his confession, so the confession should be disregarded. Since it was a case of *quid pro quo,* it couldn't be regarded as truly voluntary. He went on in this vein for ten minutes, and concluded by insisting that simple justice demanded we find his client innocent!

Kent's rebuttal was remarkable in its brevity.

"Once again, Mr. Jason was seen buying the cocaine. He was found in possession of the cocaine. His car even had a special secret compartment for *hiding* the cocaine. And he admitted that he bought the cocaine in order to resell it at a profit. Those are the elements of the crime. Knowingly being in possession and having intent to sell. That's all there is to it. The reason he was not immediately charged has been explained over and over. He wasn't the focus of the investigation. Had he been charged immediately, it would have jeopardized the case they were trying to make against the wholesaler. Quite frankly, Mr. Jason just wasn't that important. You may disagree with the investigative strategy of the officers, but that doesn't change the evidence. You may criticize the carelessness with which the shopping bag was misplaced, but to dismiss the cocaine on that basis is ludicrous. It's like throwing away a birthday present because you can't find the wrapping paper. The lost shopping bag doesn't alter the main points. He was in possession. He intended to sell. That's been proven. All the defense can offer is smoke and mirrors. And smoke and mirrors, ladies and gentleman, does not add up to reasonable doubt."

With that, the case was turned over to us for deliberation.

AS SOON as we entered the jury room, I went to the washroom to take a leak. I returned to find that, in my short absence, I'd been elected the jury foreman.

"You sure?" I asked. "There's no one else interested?"

No one volunteered, so I shrugged my shoulders and took my seat.

"Okay, then let's get started. First of all, I want to remind you all that we've got a big responsibility here. The decision we make will have a profound impact on the defendant. If we find him guilty, he'll be going to prison for a long time. So we have to be very clear that if anyone here votes 'guilty,' it's got to be because he or she is convinced, beyond any reasonable doubt, that he really *is* guilty. If we have a reasonable doubt, we have to find him innocent. And if it turns out we made a mistake, it's better to that we mistakenly let a guilty man go free than an innocent man be punished. Are we all agreed on that?"

A series of nods, "yeahs," "sures," and one "damn right."

"Second, we decide the facts, and nothing else. The judge decides the law. We make our decision based on the evidence we've seen and heard. We don't judge whether or not that evidence should be allowed in. Are we all agreed on that?"

"How about that search of the car?" asked one. "They didn't even have no warrant!"

"That's exactly what I'm talking about. Whether or not that search was legal isn't our call. It's the judge's. And he let it in, so we have to go along with that decision. If the judge was wrong, it's up to Jason's lawyer to appeal his decision. But it's not an issue we're supposed to deal with here. If we saw the evidence in court, we can assume, in fact we should assume, that it was legally obtained. Any evidence that wasn't legal should've been suppressed before it got to trial. Any evidence that wasn't excluded we can, and should, use to make our decision. Agreed?"

More nods and verbal affirmations.

"Last thing. The only fact we're trying to decide is whether or not Mr. Jason did what he was accused of. Just as we don't decide whether or not the evidence is legal, we don't decide whether the law he's accused of breaking is right. I've heard people say that liquor store owners and bartenders do as much harm to society as any drug pusher. Some of you may agree with that. And you may be absolutely right. Laws aren't automatically wise or correct simply 'cause they're laws. But that's not the issue we're facing here. Whether we like it or not, owning a liquor store or a bar is a legal business. The people who do that have licenses. They pay taxes. They own or rent the property they use to conduct their business. And whether we agree with the law or not, selling cocaine, or possessing it with the intent to sell, is *not* a legal business. The only job we have here is to decide whether or not Mr. Jason's guilty of breaking a law that's on the books. Not whether it should be on the books. Can we all agree on that?"

Another round of concurrence.

"Okay. Just so we know where we all stand, I suggest we start by taking a preliminary vote."

Blank sheets of paper were passed around, written on, and collected. The tally, without any discussion, was nine "guilty" votes to three "not guilties."

Just about at that point lunch arrived.

AFTER WE'D eaten, I called the jury to order again, and said, "Right now we stand at nine to three in favor of conviction. I'd like to hear from the three who voted for acquittal, and find out their reasons."

I looked at the faces of the other people seated around the table. Of the "twelve good men and true" assembled, fully seven were actually women, three black, two white, one Latina, one Asian. Two housewives, an elementary school teacher, a nurse, a CPA, a veterinarian, and the owner of an employment agency. The remaining five, three black, two white, included a bus driver, a Realtor, a janitor, a construction worker, and me. If Goldberg hadn't been

quite successful in assembling a jury with a black majority, he'd at least managed a non-white majority. But I didn't think that, in the end, the case was going to hinge on race.

Nevertheless, as it happened, the three "not guilty" votes were all black. Two said they weren't comfortable voting "guilty" until after there'd been some discussion and argument about the case.

The third said she just didn't believe the police witnesses, and she personally knew of cases where innocent young men had been framed by the police, and she didn't want to be part of that.

Well, I guess every jury has at least one of those.

MS. "I-DON'T-TRUST-THE-COPS" notwithstanding, the next hour or so went very well. Everyone had their say. Everyone gave their analysis of the evidence. Everyone was, not merely civil, but unfailingly courteous. Everyone seemed determined to fulfill their responsibilities faithfully and carefully.

I'd always believed in the jury system as a concept, but seeing it in action, with real human beings doing their best to ferret out the truth, and come to a just and correct verdict, I found myself in a sort of awe at how well it all worked.

Two and a half hours later, we stood at eleven to one. Mrs. Edwards, the lady who didn't trust the police witnesses, was the sole hold-out.

"Why should I trust that they're telling the truth!" she said. "I just don't believe them."

I'd been mostly silent to this point, picking speakers, stopping interruptions, and generally guiding things, but, at this point, I felt compelled to make an argument.

"Mrs. Edwards," I said, "I'm certainly not going to sit here and tell you that, never in the history of law enforcement, has a cop ever framed a suspect. But let me ask you this. What do they get out of it in this case?"

"What do you mean, 'What do they get out of it?' They get themselves a conviction."

"Sure. But of who? It's not like this guy's Al Capone, or John Gotti, or Pablo Escobar. He's just a two-bit street dealer." I paused and then corrected myself. "An *accused* two-bit street dealer. He wasn't even the focus of the investigation. And, if you're right, it means that every single one of these cops is conspiring to frame him. Every single one's deliberately perjuring themselves. If they're caught lying on the stand, they lose their jobs, their pensions, and, most likely, go to

jail. Why would they risk that for someone as unimportant as Jason? They didn't even bother booking him when they first hooked him up. He wasn't even important enough to take the chance that his arrest would foul up the bigger investigation. What do they gain that makes it worth the risk?"

She thought about that for few moments, and said, "Well, you might have a point there, at that."

"One more thing to think about. And, in a way, it's even more important. Even if he's guilty, what do they lose, really, if he gets off? They'll get him next time. If he's guilty, and we let him off, there's always a next time. Even if they never get him, they'll get some other two-bit dealer. God knows, there's no shortage of them."

She was weakening. I don't think she really believed he was innocent at all. She just had this notion that she *should* believe he was innocent. Maybe she saw herself as the Henry Fonda character from *Twelve Angry Men,* making a lone stand for truth and justice, and slowly persuading the other eleven of the righteousness of her position.

But in this case, truth and justice were on the side of the prosecution. And, slowly but surely, everyone in the room was coming to that conclusion.

After three hours, we had a unanimous verdict.

WE FILED into the courtroom, and took our seats in the jury box. When everyone was seated, I handed our verdict to Jack Loughlin, who was one of the bailiffs. In the jury room, I'd filled in Jason's name on the form, circled "guilty," and signed it as the foreman, then passed it around so everyone else could sign it.

Jack handed the verdict to the clerk, who made a note, and then handed it to the judge.

Judge Couper read the verdict, turned to us, and asked, "Mr. Foreman, have you reached a verdict?"

I stood up and answered, "Yes, Your Honor, we have."

"On the sole charge of possession of cocaine with intent to sell, a violation of Section 11351 of the California Health and Safety Code, how do you find?"

"We find the defendant guilty."

There was a loud rumbling of discontent from the gangbanger-filled gallery, and one female voice screamed, "Oh, no!" but the judge gaveled them all down.

Goldblum asked that we each be polled,

so the judge called my name, and asked me to stand up again.

"Mr. Sullivan, what was your verdict in the jury room?"

"Guilty, Your Honor."

"Is that your verdict now?"

"Yes, it is."

He repeated the process with the other eleven. When everyone stated that his or her individual verdict was guilty, and still was, he pronounced the verdict as valid, and had it entered. Then he told Jack to take us back to the jury room.

"Aren't we done?" I asked.

"Yeah, but the judge likes to come back and thank the juries for their work. Plus we need to get you all your checks."

"Okay."

"Listen," he said to the whole jury, "you all did a great job, guys! Really excellent work. Thank you."

"Wonder what that was about?" said the real estate agent, when Jack left. "I mean he's a cop, so it figures he prefers 'guilty' verdicts. But that seemed particularly enthusiastic."

"Hard to say," I replied. "Maybe there's more to the case than we realized."

A few minutes later, Judge Couper entered, thanked us all, and made a point of shaking hands with each individual juror.

"Deputy Loughlin seemed particularly pleased by the verdict," I said. "Is there something else going on here?"

"Jason's been charged with murdering another inmate while he was awaiting trial for this case," said the judge. "This is Jason's third strike, which means he could get twenty-five to life. It puts the DA's Office in a much stronger negotiating position regarding the murder."

So I was right about the strikes. Which reminded me of another question.

"Judge, how the hell did I get on this jury, anyway? I was sure Mr. Goldblum was going to bump me."

"He'd used up all his peremptory challenges seating the first eleven. You didn't give him any reason to challenge for cause, though he certainly tried. Since you were the first of the six candidates for that twelfth position, you were going to be the juror, and the next two chosen would be the alternates. Mr. Kent wanted you on this jury. He still had three peremptories left, so he used them to keep the cop on the jury, and the two mothers of small children in reserve."

I chuckled at the irony, and said, "I'll be damned."

AFTER WE were all released, and had shaken hands and wished each other well, I went down to the holding cells, retrieved my weapon, holstered it, and went to the lobby. Jack Loughlin was about to walk a group of us over to the parking garage.

"You coming?" he asked.

"Need to talk to you about something," I replied. "I'll wait 'til you get back."

He shrugged and said, "Okay."

When he came back some minutes later, he asked, "What's up?"

"Has Goldblum left yet?"

"He was still talking to his client when I left. He's supposed to take the 187 case, too. But Jason's thinking of firing him and getting someone else after Goldblum screwed up so bad on the recording of the confession."

"How'd that slip by him, anyway?"

"Kent sandbagged him. A disk with the recording was included in the discovery material Kent sent over, and marked correctly. But it wasn't highlighted. He sent so much material that Goldblum just overlooked it. Goldblum also tried to get the coke suppressed at the evidentiary hearing, claiming the search of the car was illegal. That didn't fly either. The cops'd seen the transaction. They pulled him over on a public road. And the premises searched was a moveable conveyance, so they didn't need a warrant. Kent was able to give chapter and verse on all the precedents that supported him. Between the coke and the confession, Goldblum was sunk right from the jump."

"Which brings me to my point. Who do you think Jason and his posse really blame for the 'guilty' verdict? Us or Goldblum? I don't know that much about him, but judging from that car he drives, he must be one of the most expensive criminal defense lawyers in the Bay Area."

"He is," said Jack.

"And I imagine he gets paid whether or not the trial ends in an acquittal. Think about it. None of us jurors knew Jason. We had nothing against him personally. We were just judging from the evidence. From their perspective, who was it that let the evidence in? The guy they were paying all that green to keep it out, that's who. You've been looking out for us, but, was I you, I'd also follow Goldblum out of here when he leaves."

"You might have something, at that," said Jack speculatively. "You pick up your iron?"

"Yeah," I said, patting my jacket to indicate where it was holstered.

"Mind sticking around for ten or fifteen minutes?"

"Not at all."

SHORTLY AFTERWARDS we saw Goldblum emerge from an elevator and leave the building. We followed him at some distance as he walked west on 12th Street to the Alcopark garage. Still keeping our distance, we entered the garage behind him.

He was parked on the first level, and had apparently made special arrangements with management. His Lambo was straddling two separate parking spaces so no one would park too close to him.

"That's far enough, lawyer," came an angry voice. "Keep away from that fancy car o' yours. Don't wanna mess it up by gettin' blood all over it."

It was a feminine voice, the voice that had screamed "Oh, no!" in the courtroom when the verdict was read. As we moved closer, we could see her, holding a Glock, "gangsta" style, with the barrel tilted to her left, parallel to the floor.

"You messed up! Told us you could get him off. 'Stead he got his third strike and he still facin' a murder rap!"

"I said I could get him off if I could get the evidence suppressed. I tried. I still might have a chance on appeal. If I can get an appeals court to declare the search of the car illegal, then the conviction will be overturned. We still have options."

There was, not unsurprisingly, a note of desperation in his voice as he tried to reason with the woman.

"You ain't gettin' no other chance. I'm dismissin' you with extreme prej-oo-diss. We gettin' us a lawyer know what he's doin' once I take care o' you."

As she spoke, Jack and I drew our weapons and approached her from behind. When we were within ten feet of her, Jack said, "Police. Put the gun down now."

"Puttin' nothin' down 'til I put this lyin' sack o' shit down."

"That'll just get you dead and won't help your man. Put that gun down before you make things worse. Now!"

"Can't make it no worse. Dallas got three strikes on him now. He goin' way forever even if he skates on that killin'."

Jack seemed flummoxed, and it suddenly occurred to me that, even though he was a full-time cop, and I was only a reserve, I had more experience in situations like this than he did. I'd been working the street. He'd been in jails and courtrooms.

I spoke up, "Lady, there's two of us, and only one of you, and you're facing the wrong way."

"Still kill *him.*"

"How's that supposed to help Jason? He'll still need a lawyer. You think anyone else'll take his case if he knows that bringing home the wrong verdict earns him a bullet?"

"He *promised* he get him off."

"I promised to try," said Goldblum.

"Be quiet, Mr. Goldblum."

He nodded.

"Okay, lady," I said. "You listen close, 'cause I'm through talking after this. If you don't put that piece down by the time I count to ten, you're going to be breathing out of the back of your neck. Make up your mind fast, 'cause I'm counting by fives."

I paused for a brief moment to give her time to consider, then said "Five! *Ten!*"

"Don't shoot! Don't shoot!" she screamed, dropping the pistol. I winced a little as she did that. There's very little chance that a well-maintained weapon, manufactured by a reputable company, will accidentally discharge when they're just dropped instead of carefully placed. Nevertheless, the recommended command is always, "Put the gun down," rather than "Drop it."

Jack holstered his pistol, stepped forward, cuffed the woman, then called for back-up on his radio, specifying that a female deputy would be advisable.

When the prisoner was safely secured, and her weapon under control, he turned to me and said, " 'You'll be breathing out of the back of your neck. Make up your mind fast 'cause I'm counting by fives.' Man, that was great! You use that line in one of your stories?"

"Heard it on some old TV show. Might've been *Police Story* or *SWAT.*"

"Hope using it doesn't get you in trouble for plagiarism."

"Fair use," I said. "You agree with that, Mr. Goldblum?"

"Excuse me," he said. He was leaning against his Lambo, breathing hard, still pretty shaken up.

"Can I get in trouble for using a line from an old TV show? Or is that fair use?"

"I'm not a copyright lawyer," he said.

"Never mind," I said. "It wasn't really a serious question."

He looked up, noticing me for the first time, and said, "You're Sullivan. The jury foreman."

"Yeah."

"What are you doing here?"

"Helping to save your life. You're very welcome, by the way. And the memory of your gracious expression of appreciation will keep me warm on cold nights."

"No, no, I'm sorry. I just meant, why you? He's a deputy, but you were here on jury duty."

Jack said, "He's the one who had the idea you were more likely to be under threat than any of the jurors. I asked him to back me while we followed you out of the building." He paused, looked speculatively at Goldblum, and said, "Let me ask you something. You religious? Keep kosher, fast on Yom Kippur, like that?"

"I... sometimes go to Temple on Sabbath," he said.

"Well, tomorrow, I'd see if you can find a minyan to join up with for Morning Prayers. And, if you do, offer up a special prayer of thanks."

"For you guys saving my life," he said, nodding.

"Nope," said Jack. "If Dan hadn't've been on the jury, it never would've occurred to me to make sure you got to your car safe. We were totally focused on protecting the jurors. You should thank God you ran out of peremptories before Dan got called up to the box."

LYUBKA THE COSSACK

by Isaac Babel (English translation by Boris Dralyuk)

I N MOLDA-VANKA, on the corner of Dalnitskaya and Balkovskaya Streets, stands the house of Lyubka Shneyveys. In this house you'll find a wine cellar, an inn, a feed store and a dovecote for a hundred pair of Kryukov and Nikolayev doves. All these things, along with plot forty-six at the Odessa quarries, are owned by Lyubka Shneyveys, nicknamed Lyubka the Cossack—all, that is, except for the dovecote, which belongs to Yevzel the watch-man, a retired soldier with a medal. On Sundays Yevzel heads out to Okhotnitsky Square and sells his doves to city clerks and kids from the neighbourhood. Besides Yevzel, Lyubka's courtyard is also home to Pesya Mindl, the cook and procuress, and to Tsudechkis, the manager, a Jew about as puny and with the same little beard as Ben Zkharya, our Moldavanka rabbi. I've got a lot of stories about Tsudechkis. And the first of these stories is how he came to manage the inn for Lyubka, nicknamed the Cossack.

About ten years ago Tsudechkis brokered a deal for one of the local landowners, helping him buy a horse-drawn thresher, and in the evening he took this landowner to Lyubka's place, so they could celebrate in style. This buyer had whiskers reaching all the way down to his chin, and his boots were patent leather. Pesya Mindl served him gefilte fish for dinner, and after dinner a fine young lady by the name of Nastya. The landlord spent the night, and the next morning Yevzel woke Tsudechkis, who had curled up on the doorstep of Lyubka's room.

"Listen here," said Yevzel, "last night you were talking big, saying how you helped that landowner buy a thresher—well, let me tell you, he spent the night, then ran off at dawn like the scum that he is. Now, hand over two roubles for the meal and four for the young lady. You're a slick one,

old man. Plain to see. You know the score."

But Tsudechkis wouldn't hand over the money. So Yevzel shoved him into Lyubka's room and locked the door behind him.

"Listen here," said the watchman, "you just sit tight, and when Lyubka comes back from the quarry, she'll wring your neck, God help her. Amen."

"You convict!" Tsudechkis said to the soldier, glancing around the room. "You know nothing but your doves, convict, but I've still got faith in God, and he'll lead me out of here, same as he led all the Jews out of Egypt, and then led them out of the desert…."

The puny broker had a lot more to say to Yevzel, but the soldier pocketed the key and stomped off in his big boots. Then Tsudechkis turned and saw the procuress Pesya Mindl sitting by the window, reading *The Miracles and the Heart of the Baal Shem.* She was reading the gilt-edged Hasidic book and rocking an oak cradle with her foot. Lyubka's son, Davidka, lay in the cradle, crying.

"So that's how things work in this penal colony," Tsudechkis said to Pesya Mindl. "You've got a child lying there, crying its heart out, a pity to watch him, and you, a fat woman, sit there like a stone in the forest, won't even give him a bottle…."

"Give it to him yourself," said Pesya Mindl without looking up from her book. "If he should take it from you, you old trickster. He's as big as a Russkie and all he wants is his mama's milk, but his mama, she's bounding around the quarries, drinking tea with the Jews at The Bear, buying up contraband at the harbour. Believe you me, she gives as much thought to her son as to last year's snow…."

"Yes," the puny broker said to himself, "you're in the pharaoh's hands, Tsudechkis." He walked over to the eastern wall, muttered the whole Morning Prayer, adding a coda or two, and then took the crying infant in his arms. Davidka looked up puzzled and waved his little crimson legs, which

were bathed in infantile sweat, while the old man began walking up and down the room, swaying like a *tsaddik* in prayer and singing a song without end.

"A-a-a," he sang, "other children get big holes, but Davidochka gets rolls, so he sleeps both day and night… A-a-a, other children get tight fists…."

Tsudechkis showed Lyubka's son a little fist with grey hairs and kept going on about the holes and the rolls until the boy fell asleep and the sun reached the middle of the gleaming sky. It reached the middle and began to tremble like a fly sapped of its strength by the heat. The wild peasants from Nerubaysk and Tatarka staying at Lyubka's inn clambered under their carts and fell deep into a wild, babbling sleep. A drunken workman trudged into the gateway, dropped his plane and his saw, and collapsed to the ground—collapsed and began to snore for the world to hear, enveloped by July's golden flies and its azure flashes of lightning. Nearby, in the shade, sat the wrinkled German settlers who'd brought Lyubka wine from the Bessarabian border. They lit their pipes, and the smoke from these sinuous chibouks mingled with the silvery stubble on their unshaven elderly cheeks. The sun hung from the sky like a thirsty dog's rosy tongue, off in the distance the colossal sea rolled onto Peresyp, and the masts of faraway ships rocked gently on the emerald waters of the Odessa Bay. The day sat in a glorious barque, gliding towards evening, and it was only when evening loomed, at five o'clock, that Lyubka returned from town. She arrived on a little roan nag with a big belly and a shaggy mane. A thick-legged fellow in a cotton shirt opened the gate, Yevzel gripped her nag's bridle, and then Tsudechkis shouted to Lyubka from the place of his confinement:

"My respects, Madame Shneyveys, and a good afternoon. I see you decided to go off on business for three years and dump a hungry child in my lap…."

"Shut it, mug," Lyubka shot back at the

old man and climbed down from the saddle. "Who's that yapping in my window?"

"Tsudechkis, that slick old man," the soldier with the medal informed the mistress, and then launched into the whole story with the landowner, but he didn't get to the end, because the broker interrupted him, screeching at the top of his lungs.

"A shame, I tell you, a *shanda!*" he screeched and threw down his skullcap. "Dumping your child in someone's lap and disappearing for three years… You get over here right this minute and give him your teat…."

"Don't you worry, I'm coming, you swindler," Lyubka muttered and headed for the stairs. She burst into the room and popped a breast out of her dusty shirt.

The boy reached out to her, gnawed at her monstrous nipple, but got no milk. A vein swelled on the mother's forehead, and Tsudechkis told her, shaking his skullcap, "You want to snap everything up, greedy Lyubka; you drag the whole world towards you, like children drag a tablecloth to get at breadcrumbs; you want the finest wheat, the finest grapes; you want to bake white bread in the heat of the sun, while your bundle of joy, your little *bubbeleh,* wastes away without milk…."

"You want I should give milk?" the woman hollered and squeezed her breast. "The *Plutarch* pulled into the harbour today and I covered fifteen versts in the heat. While you, you old Jew, give me the old song and dance. Go ahead and pay up the six roubles…."

But Tsudechkis still wouldn't hand over the money. He undid his sleeve, bared his arm and shoved his bony, grimy elbow in Lyubka's mouth.

"Choke on it, felon," he said and spat into a corner.

Lyubka stood there with someone else's elbow in her mouth, then took it out, left the room, locked the door behind her and went out into the yard. Mr. Trottyburn, a veritable pillar of red meat, had been waiting. Mr. Trottyburn was the chief engineer on the *Plutarch.* He had brought two sailors with him. One of the sailors was an Englishman, the other a Malay. All three of them had dragged the contraband from Port Said into the yard. Their crate was heavy. It slipped from their hands, hit the ground and out rolled cigars tangled up in Japanese silk. A gaggle of women flocked to the crate, and two wandering gypsies, wobbling and rattling, came sidling up.

"Shove off, crones!" Lyubka hollered

and led the sailors off into the shade of an acacia tree. They sat down at a table, Yevzel poured them wine, and Mr. Trottyburn unwrapped his wares. He drew out cigars and delicate silks, cocaine and metal files, loose-leaf tobacco from the state of Virginia and black wine purchased on the isle of Chios. Every object had its price; they washed down each figure with Bessarabian wine, which smelt of sunshine and bedbugs. Dusk rolled across the yard, dusk rolled like an evening wave across a wide river, and the drunken Malay, completely bewildered, touched Lyubka's chest with a finger. First he touched it with one finger, then with each of his fingers in turn.

His tender yellow eyes hung over the table like paper lanterns over a street in China; he sang something very quietly, then Lyubka pushed him with her fist and he fell to the ground.

"Knows what he wants, the little guy," Lyubka told Mr. Trottyburn. "Gonna lose the last of my milk to this Malay, when that Jew up there, he's eating me alive for it…."

And she pointed up at Tsudechkis, who was standing by the window and washing his socks. A small lamp was sending up smoke in the room, the tub foamed and hissed, and Tsudechkis, sensing that the people below were talking about him, leant out the window and cried out in despair.

"Help me, people!" he cried, waving his arms.

"Shut it, mug!" Lyubka laughed. "Just shut it."

She threw a rock at the old man, but missed her first shot. So then the woman grabbed an empty bottle of wine. But Mr. Trottyburn, the chief engineer, took the bottle from her hands, aimed and lobbed it squarely through the open window.

"Miss Lyubka," the chief engineer said, rising from the table and aligning his drunken legs. "Many respectable people come to me for goods, Miss Lyubka, but I don't give my goods to any of them—not to Mr. Kuninson, not to Mr. Batya, not to Mr. Kupchik. I only do business with you, Miss Lyubka, because I find your conversation most delightful…."

Having firmed up his tottering legs, he grabbed his two sailors—one English, the other Malay—by the shoulders and led them in a dance around the cooling courtyard. The people from the *Plutarch*—they danced in meditative silence. An orange star had rolled down to the very edge of the horizon and stared at them, wide-eyed. Then they got

their money, grabbed one another by the hand, and went out into the street, swaying like a hanging lantern on a ship. From the street they could make out the sea, the black water of the Odessa Bay, the toy-like flags atop the submerged masts and the piercing lights burning in spacious interiors. Lyubka accompanied her dancing guests to the crossing; she stood alone in the empty street for a while, laughed to herself, and turned back for home. The sleepy fellow in the cotton shirt locked the gate behind the mistress, Yevzel brought her the day's receipts, and she headed upstairs to bed. There she found the procuress Pesya Mindl already asleep, and Tsudechkis rocking the oak cradle with his bare puny feet.

"You've tormented us, shameless Lyubka," he said, and took the child from the cradle. "Lousy mother—here, watch and learn…."

He placed a small comb on Lyubka's breast and laid her son in the bed next to her. The child reached for his mother, pricked itself on the comb, and began to cry. Then the old man offered Davidka the bottle, but he turned away.

"What's this witchery, you old cheat?" Lyubka muttered, dozing off.

"Quiet, you lousy mother you!" Tsudechkis answered. "Watch and learn, damn you…."

The child pricked itself on the comb once more, then hesitantly took hold of the bottle and began to suck.

"There," said Tsudechkis and laughed. "I weaned your child. You could learn a few things from me, damn you…" Davidka lay in his cradle, sucking his bottle and drooling in bliss. Lyubka woke up, opened her eyes, then closed them again. She glimpsed her son and the moon breaking in through her window. The moon went leaping through black clouds, like a stray calf.

"All right," Lyubka said. "Pesya Mindl, you open the door for Tsudechkis. And let him come get a pound of American tobacco tomorrow…."

And the next day Tsudechkis showed up for his pound of loose-leaf tobacco from the state of Virginia. He got a quarter-pound of tea in the bargain. A week later, when I came to buy doves from Yevzel, I saw that Lyubka's inn had a new manager. He was as tiny as Ben Zkharya, our rabbi. Tsudechkis was the new manager.

He stayed at this post for fifteen years, and during that time I heard a lot of stories about him. And if I can, I'll tell them in order, because these stories, they're very interesting.   ◗●◖

LOCK THE DEATH HOUSE DOOR!

by D.L. Champion

1. Battersly Takes Steps

LOOKED OUT the dirty window at the warm June sunlight. It swept like a golden stream, through the perennial depression of Centre Street. It touched the grim solidity of the Tombs, softening the severity of those ancient bricks. It fell upon the roof of Police Headquarters opposite, deftly fashioning a tawny noose about the black dome. Then, emboldened, the rays swept across the windowsill, penetrating the ugly gloom of the tenement flat where I sat with Allhoff.

"Allhoff," I remarked, "it's one hell of a fine day."

Allhoff sat on the other side of the room, his little body huddled close up against the desk. At his right a stained and battered coffee pot gurgled on its electric base. Before him were a sheaf of departmental papers and a chipped cup.

As I spoke he half turned in his chair and his bitter eyes surveyed the unswept room. It was furnished with half a dozen rickety chairs and three desks. Off to the left a door stood open, revealing an unmade bed. A pile of soiled linen lay on the floor. Allhoff turned back to his desk. He picked up the cup and sipped coffee audibly before he answered.

"I hadn't noticed," he said dryly. "I don't suppose Morris Manning has, either."

I glared at him. He possessed an uncanny faculty for puncturing high spirits. Unerringly he had said the one thing that could have depressed me this morning. Morris Manning was in the death house. I had aided Allhoff in putting him there. Justice, I believed, would be served by his execution. Yet it was not pleasant to contemplate. In twenty odd years on the force, I had sent a dozen men to their deaths. But I had never ceased feeling squeamish about it.

"Damn you," I said. "Did you have to say that?"

He smiled unpleasantly and with vast satisfaction. He reached for the coffee pot and refilled his cup. Then with an air of phoney ingenuousness, he said: "Where's young Battersly?"

I eyed him suspiciously. "He's at lunch," I told him. "He had an early date for lunch. He told you that before he left."

"So he did," said Allhoff with a beaming benignity that aroused my worst fears. "And I wonder who he's lunching with?"

"You know damn well who he's lunching with," I said. "Now what sliminess have you got up your sleeve?"

ALLHOFF CHUCKLED horribly and drank his coffee. As he replaced the cup on the unwashed saucer, young Battersly came in. He wore, it seemed to me, an air of apprehension, paradoxically mingled with an expression of triumph. He wore, also, a smear of rouge on the collar of his uniform.

It was Allhoff who noted the last item. He pushed the cup and saucer away from him, stared at Battersly and made a clucking sound with his tongue.

"Well, well," he said, "so you're going to marry an orphan."

That crack was hitting so far below the belt that even I felt the blow. I threw an angry glance at Allhoff, then looked over at

Battersly. To my surprise he did not wince. He met Allhoff's eye squarely and his voice was steady as he spoke.

"She's not an orphan, Inspector," he said quietly.

Allhoff lifted his cup in both hands, like a chalice. "She will be," he said. "She will be in less than twelve hours. Her father's fast in the death cell. And this time the locksmiths are laughing like hell at love."

He turned his head swiftly like a cat and stared at Battersly. The kid's face was white and I saw his Adam's apple move. But he did not lower his gaze. His head remained erect. For the first time, he had not wilted under the lash of Allhoff's tongue.

Allhoff noticed this, too. And it annoyed him. He spoke again in a savage high-pitched tone.

"When you wipe away her tears tonight, remember, her old man'll be sitting in a chair with a million volts shooting through his body. Remember, too, that I put him there. When you kiss her, remember you're kissing the daughter of a killer, a low cold-blooded killer." He broke off and peered into Battersly's face. He smiled as if what he saw there pleased his twisted soul. Then he said in a softer, unctuous tone: "But, of course, you still believe Manning's innocent, don't you?"

Battersly nodded his head. His fists were tightly clenched at his sides as he held himself in check. His voice was strained but expressionless as he spoke.

"I believe Mr. Manning's innocent, Inspector," he said. With a touch of defiance, he added: "And I'm not the only one."

"No?" sneered Allhoff. "Who else? Ruth Manning?"

"Not only Miss Manning," said Battersly. He paused for a moment, then burst out impulsively. "There are others, Inspector. Lots of others."

"Who? The Seven Dwarfs?"

Battersly's knuckles were white. For the first time he showed a little of the anger within him.

"All right," he snapped, "if you must know. There's the commissioner for one. The district attorney for another. The governor, the attorney general. The—"

Allhoff blinked his agate eyes. "Do you mind telling me," he asked with ornate politeness, "what in the name of God you're talking about?"

Battersly cleared his throat nervously. Before he could answer, the telephone jangled. I picked it up and said "hello." The voice at the other end announced that the D.A.'s office was on the wire. It uttered a half dozen sentences that didn't make sense to me and concluded by inquiring whether or not the inspector desired to do anything about the Manning pardon.

The last crack left me almost speechless. Finally, I said, "Hold the wire," and turned to Allhoff. "It's the D.A.'s office," I told him. "They want to know if you care to do anything about the Manning pardon."

For the first time in my life I saw Allhoff utterly and completely amazed. His little eyes grew wide as if belladonna had been poured into them. His jaw sagged, revealing snagged yellow teeth. His face was that of a surprised mummy.

"The *what?*" he gasped. "The what pardon?"

I was as bewildered as he, but I leaped at the opportunity to needle him. "Manning," I said. "Morris Manning. Remember? The guy who didn't notice what a fine morning it was."

He was too dazed to swear at me. "For the love of God," he said, "have they gone crazy over there?"

"It's possible," I told him. "But that doesn't seem to be the point. The crux of the matter is that they're digging out a pardon for Manning."

ALLHOFF DIDN'T answer for a long moment—just looked at me. Then he looked at Battersly. I followed his gaze. Battersly stood by the window with folded arms. There was a faint triumphant smile on his lips—and a light of bitter victory in his eyes. Allhoff saw these things and his quick brain gave him the answer.

"All right," he said to me. "Tell that C.C.N.Y. lawyer to come over here with the details. I'd like to know what the hell it's all about."

I transmitted the message and hung up. Allhoff had turned half around in his chair. His narrowed eyes were fastened upon Battersly. There was a maniacal glint in his gaze. I knew what was coming within the next ten minutes or so and I was aware of a familiar sickening emptiness at the pit of my stomach.

"So," said Allhoff. "I send 'em up the River and you bring 'em back. I strap 'em in the chair and you cut 'em loose. Now what the hell is it all about?"

"I knew he was innocent," said Battersly. "You only sent him up on circumstantial evidence. When Miss Manning asked me to help clear her father, I went along with her."

"Well, well," said Allhoff, "and what a great golden heart you have!"

Battersly bit his under lip. "Well, anyway," he said, "we did what we started out to do."

"We?" snapped Allhoff. "Who?"

"Miss Manning, Mr. Scranton and myself."

"Scranton?" said Allhoff. "You mean Manning's shyster mouthpiece?"

Battersly nodded. "We've proved Mr. Manning is innocent," he went on. "We got a confession in the bargain. We've broken the case."

Allhoff picked up the coffee pot. It rattled against the rim of his cup for a moment. Then he turned around again.

"So," he said again, "you've broken the case. And would the supersleuth explain to a blundering flatfoot precisely how you did it?"

Battersly flushed and shuffled his feet uneasily. "Well," he began, avoiding Allhoff's unblinking eyes, "when Miss Manning first came to me, I decided to take steps to—"

He broke off, horrified at his inadvertent phrase. This was exactly the opening Allhoff had been sparring for. I mentally cursed Battersly for his stupidity. The emptiness in my stomach became a vast unwholesome vacuum.

"*You—took—steps,*" said Allhoff, and his tongue rolled purringly over the words. "*You—took—steps.*" His voice slid up into a crescendo lilt and there was stark insanity in his eyes as wild words tore from his rasping vocal cords. "God damn you! You took steps! You dare say that to me? You dirty yellow dog! You stole my legs. Now you try to steal my brain. I put a killer in the chair. You take him out. You lousy—"

Frenzied epithet jerked apoplectically from his contorted lips. His eyes were two black pits of madness. Battersly stood pale and silent at the window. Allhoff's words fell like slimy missiles on our ears. Then, suddenly, I knew I could stand it no longer.

I stood up. "Allhoff!" I cried. "Allhoff, for God's sake, man, shut up! For the love of heaven, shut up!"

He broke off for a moment and glared at me. Then he pushed

his chair away from the desk, looked down, regarding the two leather stumps attached to his body where his thighs should have begun. He wriggled them grotesquely.

"He took steps," he muttered. *He* took steps! I took steps myself once. Once before—"

He raised his eyes and looked at Battersly again. His lips tightened and he inhaled deeply, preparing for a fresh outburst.

I plucked Battersly's sleeve. "Get out," I said. "Quickly. No matter what he says. I'll take the responsibility."

Battersly nodded. He strode, white-lipped, toward the door.

"And where are you going?" roared Allhoff. "Back to the jailbird's daughter? Back to your bride? Well, carry her across the threshold on my legs. My legs!"

He broke off and roared with hysterical laughter as the door closed behind the younger man. Then he bent over and patted the leather pads of his stumps with dreadful affection.

"My legs," he muttered to himself. "My legs. Good strong legs. Damn him!"

HE SWUNG around abruptly and returned to the papers on his desk. I sighed and took a bottle from the desk drawer. I drank a good four ounces of whiskey without bothering with a glass.

The alcohol didn't do much good. For three years now, I'd sat at my desk in this dreary tenement flat watching Allhoff grow madder and madder. There was no longer any doubt in my mind that he belonged in an asylum. His brilliant mind teetered back and forth across the borderline of insanity.

When he had lost those legs of his he had lost something vastly more important along with them. Part of his reason had gone, too. His sole aim in life now was to torture young Battersly. Allhoff had fulfilled it well. The kid had already paid for those legs tenfold.

It had happened some years ago when Battersly was a raw recruit. During a raid, led by Allhoff, Battersly's nerve had failed him at the last moment. Failure to carry out his assignment, had resulted in a score of machine-gun bullets burying themselves in Allhoff's legs.

Gangrene had followed—and then amputation.

Technically, Allhoff was no longer a member of the police department. Half a man could not be carried as an inspector on the rolls. However, Allhoff still possessed his diabolically keen mind. The commissioner, no genius himself, couldn't afford to let that go.

Circuitous bookkeeping in the departmental accounts saw to it that Allhoff drew an inspector's pay twice each month. Since he didn't move around much he had leased this disreputable tenement opposite headquarters for reasons of convenience. And through all these years he had remained the commissioner's right-hand man. Heaven help the blundering rookie who made the error of thinking otherwise.

With sadistic cunning he had insisted that Battersly be assigned as his assistant. He had won that point and had devoted himself, thereafter, to torturing the youth. He had exacted a terrible psychological revenge. I was the unwilling witness to Battersly's ordeal.

There was no out for me. Another year and a half and I could retire on pension. Until then I was forced to sit here, performing paper work for Allhoff. The commissioner ignored all my transfer requests. I damned well knew why.

I had come up with Allhoff some twenty years ago. I didn't know him any too well—no man did—but I was better acquainted with him than any one else on the force. I was here to act as buffer between him and Battersly. I was here to temporize when the going got too tough. I was the oil on the troubled waters, the peacemaker. In short, I had the damnedest sucker job in the entire department, and I was heartily sick of it.

2. *The Man Who Wanted to Burn*

IT WAS late afternoon. An hour before, Allhoff had heard the story the assistant D.A. had related about the contemplated Manning pardon. He had listened with cold restrained fury. Then he had snatched up a telephone and gone to work, with the result that now the tiny disorderly room was crowded.

Young Battersly stood by the window. His arm rested about the shoulders of a well-dressed girl. Ruth Manning was pretty enough in a hard, worldly sort of way. She wore no rouge, and her face was powdered to death's-head white. Her eyes were black and somber. It seemed to me that there was an anxious shadow in them as she stared fixedly at Allhoff.

Seated directly before Allhoff's desk was Morton, a plainclothesman I knew slightly. Morton wore a handcuff about his left wrist. The length of the chain away a gaunt thin man of some fifty odd years moved uneasily on a straight-backed chair. At Allhoff's side stood Scranton.

Scranton's legal reputation was terrific and he knew it. He was short, bald and cocky. His suit was somewhat on the loud side and his tie stood out like a neon sign. There was a confident grin on his face. His assured strutting manner reminded me of Hermann Goering.

We all remained silent waiting for Allhoff to speak. His yellow face was set and hard, his little eyes expressionless as he reached across the desk and picked up the bubbling coffee pot. His hand trembled as he filled his cup. I, alone, knew what terrible beating fury welled up within him.

He lifted the cup, drained it, replaced it on the saucer. He looked around the room with bitter gaze and his eyes finally focused on the handcuffed man. He picked up a pencil, poised it above a scratch pad.

"Name?" he snapped. "What's your name?"

"Searle, sir," said the gaunt man. "Robert Searle."

Allhoff scribbled a notation and grunted.

"Now," he said. "You made the statement to the district attorney that on May eighteenth this year, you shot and killed Arthur Richardson?"

Searle nodded his head slowly. "That's right, Inspector," he said. "I killed Richardson."

Allhoff scribbled something on his pad. A tiny click sounded in the room as the pencil point broke. Allhoff threw the pencil irritably on the desk. He lifted his head and stared squarely at Robert Searle.

"You make this confession of your own free will? Under no duress, under no threat, without inducement?"

Searle's head moved slowly up and down. His lips moved and he spoke so softly that I could scarcely hear the words.

"Yes," he said. "Of my own free will, I confess to killing Richardson."

"In that event," said Allhoff blandly, "you're a damned liar."

Searle looked startled. His faded blue eyes opened wide and he sat up in his chair.

"But, Inspector," he began, "I—"

Allhoff bounced up and down in his chair. His fist hammered on the desk.

"Shut up!" he shouted. "You lie, I say. Manning killed Richardson. I proved it and a jury agreed with me. Manning killed him and he'll burn for it. God, I—"

Scranton moved closer to the desk and spoke with a soothing bedside manner. "Now, wait a minute, Inspector. Just wait until you hear our evidence. Manning's conviction was just one of those things. An honest mistake. There's no hard feeling on his part, I assure you. All of us make mistakes occasionally."

Allhoff swung around and glared at him. "I don't," he snapped. "I've never been wrong in my life."

It was useless to argue that point with him. He actually believed it. Scranton regarded him quizzically. Allhoff leaned back in his chair and looked around the room.

"Now listen," he said. "When I send a guy up, he stays up. When I break a case, it stays broken. I cleaned up this Richardson killing once before. Since there seems to be some doubt about it, I'll do it again for you."

HE TOOK a notebook from his desk and opened it. Then he resumed.

"Manning had ten million dollars and a steel mill. He also had a factory superintendent named Richardson and very little respect for Federal law. He was shipping steel and running guns to half a dozen countries in violation of a Presidential embargo. Richardson discovered this. He promptly blackmailed Manning. Manning paid until Richardson's demands became exorbitant. Then he killed him."

Allhoff stopped for a moment and drank coffee.

"The records found in Richardson's possession proved the motive. The bullet in Richardson's skull was fired from a revolver recovered from a sewer a hundred yards from the scene of the crime. The serial number on the gun checked the gun as belonging to Manning. What the hell more do you want? Manning belongs where I've got him—in the death house. And if you spring him, Scranton, I'll put him back there. Pardon or no pardon, Manning's going to burn."

"Now wait a minute," said Scranton. "There's more to it than that."

"Right," said Allhoff. "There's the fact that a love-lorn copper from my own office fell for Manning's daughter. Hence, he decided Manning was clean and I was a damned fool. There's the fact that Manning has all the money in the world to spend to get out of stir. There's the fact, Scranton, that you're an unscrupulous little shyster whose ethics go down as the fee goes up."

Scranton bridled at that. "Listen, copper," he said. "You're not bullying a wet-eared rookie. You're talking to a member of the bar. I didn't come here to be insulted."

Allhoff looked up quickly. "I'm glad you mentioned that," he said. "Just what the hell are you doing here? I'm supposed to be questioning Searle. Where do you fit in?"

"I represent Searle," said Scranton acidly. "I'm his lawyer."

Allhoff's little eyes narrowed. There was an odd expression on his face as he said: "Searle's lawyer? I thought you were Manning's lawyer."

"Well," said Scranton, "Manning's a square-shooter. He appreciated the fact of Searle's confessing. Searle has no money. Manning wanted him to have good legal advice. He asked me to take the case."

ALLHOFF DREW a deep breath, picked up the coffee pot. "So," he said slowly. "You represent the guy you're trying to get out of the death house. You also represent the guy you're trying to put in, in his place. Scranton, the smell of fish is overpowering."

"Damn it," said Scranton, "do you want to hear the evidence or don't you?"

"All right," said Allhoff wearily. "I suppose I've got to listen to it in order to break it down again. Go on."

"To begin at the beginning," said Scranton. "Miss Manning, here, certain of her father's innocence, enlisted the aid of Patrolman Battersly."

"Old golden-heart," murmured Allhoff. "The Galahad flatfoot."

"The three of us worked together on the case," went on Scranton. "We searched first for a possible suspect. We discovered that for some months prior to his death, Richardson had been carrying on an affair with Searle's wife. They were in love. We discovered other evidence which clinched it. We confronted Searle with our proof. He confessed."

Allhoff looked up sharply. "Why?" he snapped. He transferred his gaze to Searle. "Why?" he said again. "Why did you confess?"

Searle blinked his washed-out eyes. The muscles of his gray-yellow face moved convulsively.

"Well," he said, "they had me dead to rights. Besides, I didn't like to see an innocent man suffer for my crime."

"My God," said Allhoff. "The place is lousy with golden hearts. Can't you do better than that?"

Searle's face seemed to become more jaundiced than ever. He looked nervously at Scranton.

He said: "I don't know if I ought to tell this. But Mr. Scranton said if I confessed he'd see that I got an easier sentence."

Allhoff achieved something between a sneer and a grunt. He made a note with a fresh pencil.

SCRANTON PICKED up the conversation. "When Searle discovered that there was something between his wife and Richardson, he faced him with it. They quarreled. Searle threatened to kill him. Eventually he did so."

"Sure," said Allhoff. "He went up to Manning, borrowed his gun, shot Richardson in the head and tossed the gun down a sewer. Manning, also, possessing a great golden heart, took the rap rather than blow the whistle on a pal."

"Damn it!" yelled Scranton. "Will you let me finish?"

"You can finish in the death house," said Allhoff, "watching your client burn."

Scranton controlled his temper with an effort and continued. "Searle was night watchman at Manning's mill. He had access to Manning's office at night. He took the gun from a drawer of Manning's desk. Now, as the absolute clincher, the D.A. has permitted me to bring the social security tag and the photograph over to show you."

"I've already heard about them," said Allhoff. "But even if I see them I won't believe it."

Scranton took a wallet from his pocket. He withdrew an envelope from it and handed it to Allhoff. Allhoff extracted a torn photograph and a gilded metal tag. He put them on the desk before him. I craned over his shoulder for a better look.

The social security tag was an ordinary square piece of painted tin. It bore a six-figure number on it and a name. The name was that of Richardson. The snapshot which had been torn, then pasted together, was a young woman with a sullen face wearing one of those recently current ridiculous hats. There was an inscription on it which read—*To Richie with love, Janet.*

"All right," said Allhoff, as he replaced them in the envelope. "And what speech goes with these?"

Searle was drunk and wild with jealous

rage on the night he killed Richardson. He took his wallet. He spent what money there was in it for more whiskey. He took that photograph of his wife and the metal tag home with him. He tore up the snapshot in rage and threw them away."

"And I suppose you found them on the city dump," said Allhoff.

"No," said Scranton. "Searle wasn't making much money. He sold old paper to the junkman. He kept it in bags in his basement and delivered it every six months or so. It was in one of those bags that Battersly found those things."

Allhoff raised his eyebrows. "Battersly?" he said. "Battersly found them?"

"Yes," said Scranton, "Battersly. A man from your own office. It occurred to Miss Manning and myself that there might be some evidence in Searle's house. We told Battersly our idea. He agreed to search the bundles of old paper in the basement."

"Neat," said Allhoff. "Very, very neat. Battersly, a cop who assists the man who sends Manning to the chair, finds the evidence that absolves him. What did he do with this evidence when he found it?"

"Took it to the D.A., of course."

"Then what are you doing with it?"

"As a great favor the D.A. let me bring it over to you. He realized you'd want to see all the evidence. Of course, it's irregular, but he thought you'd want to understand the whole thing."

Allhoff nodded slowly. "I do," he said. "I'd give my right arm—ill as I can afford it—to understand."

"Anyway," said Scranton, "I can assure you from a legal angle we're O.K. We've got our evidence and besides that we've got a cast-iron confession. So, what do you think now, Inspector?"

Allhoff picked up the coffee pot again. "I think," he said deliberately, "that Manning killed Richardson. I think, further, that he'll burn for it."

I heard a little sibilant intake of breath as Ruth Manning moved away from Battersly and walked across the room. She stood before Allhoff's desk, stared, enraged into his mocking seamed face.

"You beast," she said and there was stinging fury in her voice. "You stubborn pig-headed beast. You're the murderer, not my father. You'd rather see an innocent man die than admit you're wrong. You—you—" She broke off, inarticulate with anger.

Allhoff regarded her with narrowed ugly eyes. Then he uttered two words. One was an ugly adjective. The other, an uglier noun.

The girl shrank back. She turned appealing eyes to Battersly.

"Paul," she cried. "Paul, don't let him say that to me. Paul, you can't stand there and let him talk to me like that?"

But that was precisely what Battersly was going to do and there was no help for it. He stood there miserably, his eyes on the floor. Allhoff watched him with amused diabolical eyes.

I SAT still, aware of the desperate futile rage beating within me. I knew Allhoff had insulted the girl, not because he had been angry, but to smash at Battersly through her. Now he was grinning from ear to ear, perfectly happy.

"Well," said Scranton, "I don't care how you figure it, Allhoff. Manning won't burn. The governor has already issued a reprieve. When the D.A. sends him the data on the case, he'll undoubtedly grant a pardon."

"If he'll hold it up for forty-eight hours," said Allhoff, "he won't have to bother."

"What do you mean by that?"

"I mean," said Allhoff, and his voice rose, "that I put Manning in the death house for keeps. Since little golden-heart over there has got him out, I'll have to put him back again." He stopped and looked over at Searle. Searle's grayish-yellow face resembled the immobile countenance of a mud mummy. "I'm afraid," went on Allhoff to Searle, "that I'll have to spring you to do it. But that can't be helped. Now if you'll all get to hell out of here, I'll do some thinking."

Scranton grinned. "Think your vindictive brains out," he said. "But Manning doesn't die tonight. Within two days he'll be a free man." His grin grew broader and he licked his lips. "Furthermore," he added, "there'll be a Roman holiday in the city-rooms when the papers get hold of this. INNOCENT MAN RAILROADED BY ALLHOFF. EX-OFFICIO MEMBER OF POLICE DEPARTMENT TRIES TO SEND BLAMELESS MAN TO DEATH. God, they'll love that!"

Allhoff bounced up in his chair. "Get out, shyster," he screamed. "Get out! Get out! Manning'll burn, I tell you! Burn! Burn! If I send him up he's guilty. He's got to be!"

Scranton stood in the doorway looking at him.

"Allhoff," he said, "you're a madman. A raving lunatic. I'm a fool to talk to you. I won't do it again. I'll never enter a this

filthy slum again as long as I live. I'll wait and visit you in the madhouse."

The door slammed behind him.

The plainclothesman with Searle stood up nervously. "If you're through with this guy, Inspector—" he said inquiringly.

"Take him back to the Tombs," snapped Allhoff. "Let him have a good time. He won't be there long."

He turned his head and glanced over at Battersly and Ruth Manning. Battersly's arm was thrown protectively about her shoulders. Her head rested against his uniform coat. She sipped water from a glass Battersly had handed her.

"Listen," said Allhoff acidly. "This is not a bus stop, Battersly. If uncontrollable passion persists in beating within your breast, take it to hell out of here."

Battersly did not answer. His face was pale and the old tortured shadow was in his eyes. Yet there was the ghost of a smile on his lips. No matter what Allhoff handed out this time, Battersly, for once, held the top cards. He had outwitted his persecutor. He had snatched Allhoff's prisoner from the chair. For the first time since the pair of them had clashed, young Battersly had actually won a round.

"Come on, Ruth," he said quietly. "Let's go downstairs."

Allhoff did not look up as they passed him, went on through the doorway.

He drank his viscous coffee and poured more. His back was hunched over his desk and he stared at the grimy panels of the door opposite with dark and brooding eyes. After a long while he struck the desk-top with his fist. He spoke to me without turning around.

"Symonds," he said, "Manning killed Richardson. I know it. That Searle confession is as phoncy as an Ethiopian bond. I put Manning in the death cell once. And by God, I'll put him there again."

I looked over at him and sighed. Allhoff's ego demanded that he be always right. That was as necessary to him as air to a normal man. The day that Allhoff admitted a mistake would be a week from the Tuesday after Hitler, Mussolini and God confessed that their handiwork was a complete and total error.

"Allhoff," I said, "look at the facts."

"I'm looking at them," said Allhoff. "In fact, I'm looking through them and beyond them. When I'm finished one single fact will remain visible to the naked eye. That is, that Manning is guilty."

He lapsed into silence again. From time to time I heard him mutter to himself. His pencil scratched industriously upon his pad. I interrupted him once.

"Allhoff," I said, "why must you be so damned opinionated? Can't you be wrong just once? Innocent men have been sent up before. So what? I don't blame you. Anyone can make a mistake. You're hopelessly wrong this time. It's obvious to a child that Manning's a victim of circumstantial evidence."

"Sure," said Allhoff. "So was Hauptmann. So was Judd Gray. My God, do you think killers send out complimentary tickets before they commit a crime?"

I gave up at that and turned back to my work.

ALLHOFF DID not speak for fully twenty minutes, then I heard the tiny squeak of his chair as he swiveled around.

"It could be," he muttered softly, more to himself than to me. "It's possible. The more I think of it, it's the only possible answer. The problem is to break it down, to make them crack wide open."

I put down my pen. "Look at the evidence, man," I said. "Look at the evidence."

Allhoff snorted. "Evidence!" he said with vast contempt. "That's all you routine flat-feet know. Evidence!"

"Well," I said, "what do you work with? Voodoo?"

"Logic," said Allhoff. "Though it may well be voodoo to you. Logic—thought in the abstract. I not only figure what, I figure why. And I've figured it here. I've got the only possible answer."

"That's great," I told him. "But grand juries still prefer evidence. You're going to need some of that along with your logic."

"That's what I'm working on now," he said. "I've got to manufacture some evidence for those dimwits. Get over to the Tombs. Ask Doc Randolph and the warden if they'll drop over here for a minute."

His arrogant confidence, his superb ego, thoroughly exasperated me but—

I went downstairs, delivered his messages at the Tombs, then repaired to Noonan's to drink steadily until it was time to go home.

3. Crazy Like a Fox

ALLHOFF SAT at his desk wearing the expression of a cat who has just dined on canaries and cream. Battersly stared gloomily into Centre Street while I turned the pages of the morning *Times*. Allhoff sipped coffee and chuckled between sips.

Curiosity got the better of me. "What are you beaming about?" I asked him.

"I'm waiting for a phone call," he said with astonishing geniality.

"Bearing what glad tidings?"

He swiveled around in his chair and though he spoke to me, he looked at Battersly.

"Tidings that Morris Manning is going to burn. Tidings that Searle has retracted his confession, that Scranton will face an indictment for conspiring to defeat the ends of justice."

Battersly jerked his head around. "That's impossible, Inspector," he said. "Why, it—"

"I don't believe it myself," I said. "Searle's guilty as hell. Anyway, why should he confess, then within twenty-four hours retract. It doesn't make sense."

"The hell it doesn't," said Allhoff. "If you've got enough brains to see it, it's the only development that does make sense."

"Now, Allhoff—" I began, when the telephone on my desk interrupted me.

"Pick it up," said Allhoff. "It's the end of the Searle confession."

I picked it up. A voice spoke rapidly at the other end of the wire. I listened dazedly for three minutes, then hung up. Battersly stared at me tensely. Allhoff retained his expansive grin.

"Well," he said, "was I right?"

"Partly," I said slowly. "It's not only the end of the Searle confession. It's the end of Searle."

Allhoff hunched forward in his chair. "What are you talking about?"

"Searle's dead," I told him. "Stabbed himself in his cell ten minutes ago."

Fury and amazement distorted Allhoff's features. "What?" he shrieked.

I told him again.

"No," he said. "No! It can't be." For a moment I remembered the ancient tale of Canute who ordered the waves to stand still. He leaned forward and banged his fists on his knees like a child in a tantrum. "It can't be! Not now. Not under the circumstances. No. No!"

I didn't know what it was all about, but I rubbed salt into his wound.

"Yes, Inspector," I said mockingly. : "Yes. And all the pure abstract logic in the world won't bring him back to life."

"It seems logical, Inspector," put in Battersly. "He knew he was headed for the chair. He just took the easiest way."

"Damn you!" roared Allhoff. "What the hell do you know about it? Nothing. You haven't the slightest idea what's been going on. You—" He broke off suddenly and shot a question at me. "What were the circumstances? Who found the body? Who saw him last?"

"A guard—and Scranton. Scranton was in the cell a half hour ago. He left to return to his office to get a paper he had forgotten—a paper he wanted Searle to sign. Searle was all right when he left the first time. The guard heard Searle talking to him on the way out. When Scranton came back, the guard unlocked the cell. The pair of them found Searle on his bunk—dead. A knife in his heart."

ALLHOFF FROWNED. His lips moved as he muttered to himself. His brow was corrugated and there was cold sweat upon it. He sat thus for fully three minutes. Then, finally, he threw back his head and uttered a Gargantuan roar.

"I've got it!" he screamed. "Into my hands. Delivered into my hands. The dirty little shyster. I'm not sure how he did it, but I know he did it. I start with one killer and I finish up with two!"

He stopped, out of breath. Battersly and I stared at him. For a moment I honestly believed that he had cracked completely, that his erratic mind had crashed through the borderline where it had hovered for so long.

"Battersly," he said more quietly, "go over to Scranton's office. Tell him to come over here. You might bring the Manning girl, too. And make it fast."

"Wait a minute, Allhoff," I said. "Scranton won't come over here. He's still sore at you."

"The hell he won't," said Allhoff. "Arrest him, Battersly."

"Arrest him? For what?"

Allhoff grinned from ear to ear. He rubbed his hands together like a pawnbroker gloating over the Kohinoor.

"Murder," he said. "The murder of Robert Searle."

"But, Inspector—"

"Get going," said Allhoff. "You have your orders."

Battersly got going and I continued to stare at Allhoff.

"Boy," I said, "when you go nuts, you go all the way. You—"

"Shut up," said Allhoff. "You get going, too. I've an assignment for you. Get Searle's wife. Bring her up here. We might want to hear from her."

"Hear what from her?" I said. "Listen

Allhoff. Listen to a sane man for a minute. Why the hell should Scranton kill a guy whose confession is springing a rich client? Why—"

"Why don't you get to hell out of here?" he screamed. "Bring me Searle's wife! It's an order, *Sergeant*."

He underlined the *Sergeant* to put me in my place. I sighed, picked up my cap and made for the door. As I gained the stairs, I heard him yelling into the phone asking for the warden at the Tombs.

BATTERSLY RETURNED before I did. When I came in he was sitting on my desk looking extremely uncomfortable. Scranton stood in front of him verging on apoplexy. His face was purple and the room echoed with dire threats of the things he was going to do to Allhoff, once out of here.

Ruth Manning sat perched on the edge of one of our uncomfortable straight-backed chairs. Her cheeks were paler than usual, her eyes more somber.

Allhoff was quietly drinking coffee, deaf to Scranton's vehemence. He again wore his purring feline expression. There was a large cardboard box on top of his desk that had not been there when I left. Seated near the desk was a florid-faced Irish cop, O'Malley, who had worked with us on occasion. I nodded to Allhoff and drew up a chair for Searle's wife.

She was blond and pretty in a moronic sort of way. She was scarcely half the age of her deceased husband. Though she had heard of his sudden death a scant half hour ago, she was entirely composed. On the way up in the taxicab I had come to the conclusion that she hadn't cared a hell of a lot about Searle.

Allhoff put down his cup. "Shut up, Scranton," he said evenly. "Everybody's here, and I'm taking over now."

"If everybody's not out of here damn quickly," snapped Scranton, "I'll have your job for this, Allhoff."

"Sit down," said Allhoff. "Get used to sitting down. You're going to die sitting down."

"My God!" said Scranton to me. "He's gone crazy, Sergeant. He's a madman. I demand the right to counsel. I demand the right to telephone."

Ruth Manning turned her face to Battersly. "Paul," she said, "get me out of here. I'm really afraid of him. I—"

"You ought to be," said Allhoff. Then he grinned up at us. "Sure," he said, "I'm

mad as hell. Just listen to me and I'll show you how completely crazy I am." They were all silent now, silent and looking at me inquiringly.

"All right," I said, "Listen to him. If he hasn't got anything, Scranton can make his squawk at City Hall. If he has—"

"He can make it in hell," said Allhoff gloatingly: "Scranton, you're a damn lousy purchasing agent. You had a million dollars with which to buy Manning's freedom. You've only succeeded in buying yourself a one-way ticket to hell."

"Listen, Allhoff," I said, "you've been talking in circles all day. If you have anything concrete to say, will you say it?"

"All right," said Allhoff. "Let's review the situation. I put a millionaire murderer in the death cell. Then in comes that millionaire's lawyer with a guy who confesses all. On the very face of it, it smelled of decaying halibut. So I put my brains to work."

"Those brains will be off the payroll when I get out of here," Scranton said.

"The hell they will," said Allhoff. He sipped his coffee. Then, "The first crack in Scranton's fairy tale. Searle had cachectic pallor."

"I don't know what that means, Allhoff," I said. "But how does it indicate that Scranton killed him?"

"It doesn't," said Allhoff. "It merely indicates that Manning killed Richardson and that Searle's confession was a complete phoney. I worked on the premise that Manning was guilty. Now, if that were so, I was confronted with the question as to why Searle would confess to a crime he did not commit. There was one obvious answer to that—money."

"Money?" I said. "But you don't need money in a grave."

"Right," said Allhoff. "So we arrive at the second conclusion. Why would a man sacrifice his life for money? Obviously, to pass that money on to someone whom he loved."

"He'd have to love her one hell of a lot," I remarked, looking at Janet Searle.

"He would," said Allhoff. "And I doubt that he would love her that much if he were convinced of her infidelity."

A dim light glowed in my brain. "You mean," I said, "that Searle did not believe Richardson and his wife were seeing each other? Even so, he'd have to care for his wife one hell of a lot to die for her."

"True," said Allhoff. "But you forget the cachectic pallor."

"Just what the hell does that erudite phrase mean?" Scranton asked.

"A cachectic pallor is a medical description of the condition of Searle's skin," Allhoff sneered. "Did you notice that grayish-yellow face of his? It indicated a morbid unhealthy condition."

"So," I said. "And that proves what?"

"It proves a number of things," said Allhoff. "Including the presence of cancer."

Scranton's face was white as bleached ermine. Ruth Manning's fingers beat staccato on the wooden part of her chair. Janet Searle regarded Allhoff with mild wonder. The ray of light in my brain grew stronger.

"You mean," I said, "that Searle had cancer? That he wouldn't have lived long, anyway?"

"He wouldn't have lived a year," said Allhoff. "He knew it. Scranton was looking for a man with only a few months to live. He found one with a young wife and a night watchman's job in Manning's own mill. Those last two items were velvet. They made it absolutely perfect, didn't they, Scranton?"

"It's a lie," snapped Scranton, and there was a tiny tremor in his tone. "He said so himself. Why, he told me—"

He bit off the last word and was silent. He stood, breathing hard, forcing himself to meet Allhoff's mocking eyes.

"Sure he told you," said Allhoff. "We're coming to that in a minute."

"Wait a minute," I said. "What about that inscribed photograph? What about that metal social security tag?"

Allhoff sneered like Claude Rains. "Those things were so damned obvious, even Battersly should have figured them, to say nothing of the D.A. Those social security plates sell for half a dollar. The stores don't give a damn who they sell 'em to. All Scranton had to do, was to find out Richardson's number and have the plate printed."

"And the photograph?" I asked. "How about that?"

"That's even easier," said Allhoff. "If you remember that snapshot, it shows Janet Searle wearing a soup plate on her head. Those damned silly hats haven't been on the market that long. That picture was taken at least three months after Richardson was killed."

4. Ruthless— But No Louse

IT WAS unmistakable fear I saw in Ruth Manning's eyes now. Scranton licked dry lips. He wore the expression of a man who is desperately lashing his brains. Janet Searle still regarded Allhoff as if he were an interesting oddity. Battersly turned his head and stared out the window, finding compelling interest in the Centre Street traffic.

"So," continued Allhoff, thoroughly enjoying himself, "I came to the conclusion that my theory of Searle's short life-expectancy was correct. By every rule of logic it had to be. I asked Doc Randolph over at the Tombs to examine Searle. He did. We also checked the cancer clinics. Both Randolph and the Cancer Institute, which had been treating Searle, agreed that he had malignant cancer."

"But—" said Scranton, puzzled, then stopped.

Allhoff grinned like a cannibal. He lifted his cup, sipped, replaced it on the saucer. It clattered like the roll of a tumbril's wheel.

"Do you want to finish that sentence?" he asked. "Or shall I finish it for you?"

Scranton didn't answer.

"All right," said Allhoff. *But*—Searle sent for you this morning. He told you he didn't have a bad case of cancer after all. He told you that a simple operation would enable him to live for years. He told you he wanted to repudiate his confession. So you killed him."

I sighed. The little light in my brain was growing fainter.

"Allhoff," I said, "you're going storybook detective again. If Randolph said he had malignant cancer, why should Searle think he would live for years."

"Ah," said Allhoff, "Randolph didn't confirm to *Searle* his knowledge that he was dying. He only told me. At my request, he told Searle that there was little wrong with him. That the Institute had made a mistaken diagnosis. As soon as Searle heard that, he wanted to live. He wanted to withdraw the elaborate confession Scranton had worked out for him."

An almost imperceptible expression had come over the face of Janet Searle. She transferred her gaze from Allhoff to Scranton. There was an unspoken query in her glance. The lawyer stood meeting Allhoff's eye. It seemed to me that he had regained some of his self-possession.

"Then," he said with heavy irony, "I killed him, eh?"

"Right," said Allhoff. "That's the first time you've said a true word since you started this damned thing."

"Oh sure," said Scranton. "I killed him. Listen, I went to his cell this morning. I talked to him. I had forgotten a legal paper I wanted him to sign. I called the guard.

Searle was lying on the bed. As I left I spoke with him. The guard heard me. Ten minutes later, I returned. Naturally the guard was with me, unlocking the cell door. We entered together and found Searle dead. Personally, Allhoff, I don't think your false confession theory will hold up. I'm damn certain the murder rap against me, won't."

Allhoff shook his head in mock commiseration.

"Desperate men take long chances," he observed. "When Searle squawked, you saw a cool million-dollar fee slipping out of your dirty hands. You had only a minute to save it. Searle would have summoned the warden and the D.A. in another half hour. So you stabbed him. You put the body on the cot and called the guard. You told your tale about the forgotten document. With magnificent histrionics, you kept up a one-sided conversation with the corpse to fool the guard. Then you went away."

"Yes?" said Scranton evenly. "And will the guard testify that Searle did not answer me?"

"No," said Allhoff. "In all honesty, he doesn't remember. You handled that part well. The guard really thought you were talking to Searle. But there was one other thing."

"What?" said Scranton. He was cocky again now. "I suppose you've got moving picture of me killing Searle."

Allhoff's eyes snapped. "Not quite," he said slowly. "Not quite, Scranton. But I have this. A red thread was found under one of the dead man's fingernails. Apparently, he clawed out at his killer as he died and his finger caught in the fabric of a necktie."

"Marvelous," said Scranton. "So what?"

"Guards don't wear red neckties—any neckties at all," said Allhoff. "But you do. And there was no one else in the cell but you."

Janet Searle inhaled deeply. She opened her mouth as if to speak. Allhoff saw her.

"Never mind," he said. "You can talk later if you want to. What have you got to say, Scranton?"

Scranton bit off the end of a cigar. He was far more assured than he had been before.

"Say?" he repeated. "I'll say what I've always said. That you're mad, Allhoff. You should be in a psychopathic ward. After all, what have you got? That necktie business doesn't sound very convincing even here in your own slum. They'll laugh it in your face in the Grand Jury Room."

I nodded my head at that. The trouble with Allhoff's theory was that it had not provided the tangible stuff that a jury can understand. As things stood now, it was

fifty-fifty that he would be unable to break the Searle confession. It was a hundred to one he couldn't make the murder rap stand up against Scranton.

THEN I looked over at Janet Searle. She was still staring at Scranton. There was a puzzled, hesitant expression on her face. Then my mental light flared brilliantly. There was the witness who could doom Scranton. If Janet Searle talked, if she corroborated Allhoff's theory, it was all over.

I stood up excitedly. "Allhoff," I said, "let Searle's wife talk. If you're right she can prove it. She's your key witness. Go to work on her. Without her we're licked."

Allhoff turned to me and his little eyes were blazing.

"We?" he said with heavy sarcasm. *"We,* Sergeant?" Then his voice took on biting contempt. "You fool," he went on. "Do you think I'd stake my case on the testimony of a neurotic woman? Damn it, I prove my own cases. When I send anybody to the death house, he burns. If Searle's wife wants to talk, she can talk afterwards."

Now we all watched him. Battersly turned from the window, and even O'Malley pricked up his large red ears. How the hell he could clinch his case against Scranton without the aid of Janet Searle was beyond me. But it was Allhoff's moment and he played it to the hilt.

"I'm crazy," he said bitterly. "Old screwball Allhoff, that's me." His fist pounded on the desk and his voice rose to a shout. "But, by God, I'm the only man in the whole damned department who could think this thing through! The only guy with brains enough to make Searle tell the truth! The only guy with brains enough to put a dictaphone in his cell while he did it!"

I expelled breath slowly from my lungs and cursed myself for a fool. Invariably, when Allhoff explained something, it was so obvious I could never understand why I hadn't thought of it myself.

He tapped the cardboard box on the desk.

"Here it is," he said. "Every word of it. I had it planted in Searle's cell while he was being examined in Doc Randolph's office. It's all here, Scranton. Every word that you spoke to him. Every word that he spoke to you. Even the last sentence he ever uttered, when he said, 'God, Scranton, you've stabbed me!' Would you like to hear it, Scranton? No? Well, of course, it would be dull. You've heard it all before."

Now for the first time, Janet Searle's face

showed a spark of animation. She half rose in her seat and glared at Scranton.

"So," she said in a thick strangled voice, "you did do, it. Inspector, I want to talk."

She talked—in a low dead voice sultry with anger. Searle had loved her, had always regretted that he earned too little to lavish luxury upon her. He had to do anyway. Cancer had doomed him. When this chance came, she might as well gain by it. He had insisted upon it. Perhaps she had been wrong, but she would not sit by, for any amount of money, and tacitly approve the murder of her husband.

SCRANTON'S ARMS were on his knees. His head was in his arms. Ruth Manning's lips trembled and Battersly stared at her, while his brain propounded a question which his lips dared not ask.

Allhoff looked at him for a long moment, then said: "Battersly, why don't you ask me?"

"Ask you what?" said Battersly in a high thin voice. "How do you know what I'm thinking?"

"You're a crystal ball to me," said Allhoff. "You want to know if Ruth Manning took you for a ride. You want to know if she knew everything all the time or if she went along, an innocent sucker like yourself."

"Well," said Battersly huskily, "which was it?"

Allhoff grinned diabolically. "She knew," he said. "She knew. She played you for a beautiful sucker."

Battersly swallowed something in his throat. "You can't prove it. You can't—"

"Listen," said Allhoff. "That photograph— you said that you found it. That it went to the D.A.'s office. According to your story, Ruth Manning never handled it. So how does it happen that her fingerprints are all over it. They check with those she left on that glass she used for water yesterday. She handled that snapshot before it was planted. That's why? What about it, Miss Manning?"

Ruth Manning stood up. Her eyes flamed and there was a magnificent defiance about her.

"Why not?" she said. "My father's life means more to me than anything else. Why shouldn't I play him for a sucker if it would help save Dad?"

Battersly's face reflected the despairing misery in his heart. Allhoff watched the dead expression come into his eyes. He smiled sadistically.

"O'Malley," he said, "take Scranton across the street and book him. You, Battersly take the two women over to the D.A. He'll want to hold them as material witnesses, if for nothing else. Come on, get going."

O'Malley escorted Scranton through the door. Battersly stood up. He took Ruth Manning by the arm without meeting her eyes.

"Come along, Mrs. Searle," he said as he walked across the room. He strode through the door like an automaton, like a man who is so numbed with pain that he is beyond all feeling. The door slammed. I heard disappearing footfalls on the stairs and Allhoff and I were alone.

I was aware of that old sickish sensation at the pit of my stomach. This time he had hit Battersly squarely in the heart. I thought, for a moment, of a fiendish child who enjoys sticking pins into butterflies.

"Allhoff," I said, "did you have to do that?"

He looked at me over the rim of the coffee cup. "Do what?" he asked.

"Crucify the kid? You didn't have to tie a rap on the girl. You had Scranton. You didn't need her."

He shrugged his thin shoulders. "She confessed, didn't she?" he said. "I had nothing to do with it."

"You didn't have to check those damned fingerprints," I said. "You went to all the trouble to have that glass sent over to the Fingerprint Bureau. You didn't have to do that."

Allhoff put down the coffee cup. "My God," he said, "you're dumb. That photograph had been handled by about eighteen guys in the D.A.'s office. It had been handled by Scranton, Battersly, and myself. If Ruth Manning's prints were on it, how the hell do you think they could ever dig them out? What the hell sort of a copper are you?"

I stood up and walked across the room. This was the last brutal straw. I faced him across his desk and looked him in the eyes.

"Allhoff," I said, "you're a ruthless, bitter, little louse."

He put his cup down on the saucer.

"Ruthless?" he said thoughtfully. "Well, yes. Bitter? I concede it. Little? Without argument. But I'm no louse, Symonds. I'm no louse."

I walked to the door and gained the stair-head.

"I'm no louse!" he shouted after me, and his voice held an odd quiver I had never heard before. "Remember, Symonds, a louse has legs!" ◐

SLIPPERY FINGERS

by Dashiell Hammett

YOU'LL HAVE the time of your life trying to solve this crime before you get to the end of the story. You'll think some of the characters don't act logically, but when you figure it out afterward you'll decide they were all pretty wise.

"You are already familiar, of course, with the particulars of my father's—ah—death?"

"The papers are full of it, and have been for three days," I said, "and I've read them; but I'll have to have the whole story first-hand."

"There isn't very much to tell."

This Frederick Grover was a short, slender man of something under thirty years, and dressed like a picture out of Vanity Fair. His almost girlish features and voice did nothing to make him more impressive, but I began to forget these things after a few minutes. He wasn't a sap. I knew that downtown, where he was rapidly building up a large and lively business in stocks and bonds without calling for too much help from his father's millions, he was considered a shrewd article; and I wasn't surprised later when Benny Forman, who ought to know, told me that Frederick Grover was the best poker player west of Chicago. He was a cool, well-balanced, quick-thinking little man.

"Father has lived here alone with the servants since mother's death, two years ago," he went on. "I am married, you know, and live in town. Last Saturday evening he dismissed Barton—Barton was his butler-valet, and had been with father for quite a few years—at a little after nine, saying that he did not want to be disturbed during the evening.

"Father was here in the library at the time, looking through some papers. The servants' rooms are in the rear, and none of the servants seem to have heard anything during the night.

"At seven-thirty the following morning—Sunday—Barton found father lying on the floor, just to the right of where you are sitting, dead, stabbed in the throat with the brass paper-knife that was always kept on the table here. The front door was ajar.

"The police found bloody finger-prints on the knife, the table, and the front door; but so far they have not found the man who left the prints, which is why I am employing your agency. The physician who came with the police placed the time of father's death at between eleven o'clock and midnight.

"Later, on Monday, we learned that father had drawn $10,000 in hundred-dollar bills from the bank Saturday morning. No trace of the money has been found. My finger-prints, as well as the servants', were compared with the ones found by the police, but there was no similarity. I think that is all."

"Do you know of any enemies your father had?"

He shook his head.

"I know of none, though he may have had them. You see, I really didn't know my father very well. He was a very reticent man and, until his retirement, about five years ago, he spent most of his time in South America, where most of his mining interests were. He may have had dozens of enemies, though Barton—who probably knew more about him than anyone—seems to know of no one who hated father enough to kill him."

"How about relatives?"

"I was his heir and only child, if that is what you are getting at. So far as I know he had no other living relatives."

"I'll talk to the servants," I said.

The maid and the cook could tell me nothing, and I learned very little more from Barton. He had been with Henry Grover since 1912, had been with him in Yunnan, Peru, Mexico, and Central America, but apparently he knew little or nothing of his master's business or acquaintances.

He said that Grover had not seemed excited or worried on the night of the murder, and that nearly every night Grover dismissed him at about the same time, with orders that he be not disturbed; so no importance was to be attached to that part of it. He knew of no one with whom Grover had communicated during the day, and he had not seen the money Grover had drawn from the bank.

I made a quick inspection of the house and grounds, not expecting to find anything; and I didn't. Half the jobs that come to a private detective are like this one: three or four days—and often as many weeks—have passed since the crime was committed. The police work on the job until they are stumped; then the injured party calls in a private sleuth, dumps him down on a trail that is old and cold and badly trampled, and expects—Oh, well! I picked out this way of making a living, so….

I looked through Grover's papers—he had a safe and a desk full of them—but didn't find anything to get excited about. They were mostly columns of figures.

"I'm going to send an accountant out here to go over your father's books," I told Frederick Grover. "Give him everything he asks for, and fix it up with the bank so they'll help him."

I caught a street-car and went back to town, called at Ned Root's office, and headed him out toward Grover's. Ned is a human adding machine with educated eyes, ears, and nose. He can spot a kink in a set of books farther than I can see the covers.

"Keep digging until you find something, Ned, and you can charge Grover whatever you like. Give me something to work on—quick!"

The murder had all the earmarks of one that had grown out of blackmail, though there was—there always is—a chance that it might have been something else. But it didn't look like the work of an enemy or a burglar: either of them would have packed his weapon with him, would not have trusted to finding it on the grounds. Of course, if Frederick Grover, or one of the servants, had killed Henry Grover… but the finger-prints said "No."

Just to play safe, I put in a few hours getting a line on Frederick. He had been at a ball on the night of the murder; he had never, so far as I could learn, quarreled with his father; his father was liberal with him, giving him everything he wanted; and Frederick was taking in more money in his brokerage office than he was spending. No motive for a murder appeared on the surface there.

At the city detective bureau I hunted up the police sleuths who had been assigned to the murder; Marty O'Hara and George Dean. It didn't take them long to tell me what they knew about it. Whoever had made the bloody finger-prints was not known to the police here: they had not found the prints in their files. The classifications had been broadcast to every large city in the country, but with no results so far.

A house four blocks from Grover's had been robbed on the night of the murder, and there was a slim chance that the same man might have been responsible for both jobs. But the burglary had occurred after one o'clock in the morning, which made the connection look not so good. A burglar who had killed a man, and perhaps picked up $10,000 in the bargain, wouldn't be likely to turn his hand to another job right away.

I looked at the paper-knife with which Grover had been killed, and at the photographs of the bloody prints, but they couldn't help me much just now. There seemed to be nothing to do but get out and dig around until I turned up something somewhere.

Then the door opened, and Joseph Clane was ushered into the room where O'Hara, Dean and I were talking.

Clane was a hard-bitten citizen, for all his prosperous look; fifty or fifty-five, I'd say, with eyes, mouth and jaw that held plenty of humor but none of what is sometimes called the milk of human kindness.

He was a big man, beefy, and all dressed up in a tight-fitting checkered suit, fawn-colored hat, patent-leather shoes with buff uppers, and the rest of the things that go with that sort of combination. He had a harsh voice that was as empty of expression as his hard red face, and he held his body stiffly, as if he was afraid the buttons on his too-tight clothes were about to pop off. Even his arms hung woodenly at his sides, with thick fingers that were lifelessly motionless.

He came right to the point. He had been a friend of the murdered man's, and thought that perhaps what he could tell us would be of value.

He had met Henry Grover—he called him "Henny"—in 1894, in Ontario, where Grover was working a claim: the gold mine that had started the murdered man along the road to wealth. Clane had been employed by Grover as foreman, and the two men had become close friends. A man named Denis Waldeman had a claim adjoining Grover's and a dispute had arisen over their boundaries. The dispute ran on for some time—the men coming to blows once or twice—but finally Grover seems to have triumphed, for Waldeman suddenly left the country.

Clane's idea was that if we could find Waldeman we might find Grover's murderer, for considerable money had been involved in the dispute, and Waldeman was "a mean cuss, for a fact," and not likely to have forgotten his defeat.

Clane and Grover had kept in touch with each other, corresponding or meeting at irregular intervals, but the murdered man had never said or written anything that would throw a light on his death. Clane, too, had given up mining, and now had a small string of race-horses which occupied all his time.

He was in the city for a rest between racing-meets, had arrived two days before the murder, but had been too busy with his own affairs—he had discharged his trainer and was trying to find another—to call upon his friend. Clane was staying at the Marquis hotel, and would be in the city for a week or ten days longer.

"How come you've waited three days before coming to tell us all this?" Dean asked him.

"I wasn't noways sure I had ought to do it. I wasn't never sure in my mind but what maybe Henny done for that fellow Waldeman—he disappeared sudden-like. And I didn't want to do nothing to dirty Henny's name. But finally I decided to do the right thing. And then there's another thing: you found some finger-prints in Henny's house, didn't you? The newspapers said so."

"We did."

"Well, I want you to take mine and match them up. I was out with a girl the night of the murder"—he leered suddenly, boastingly—"all night! And she's a good girl, got a husband and a lot of folks; and it wouldn't be right to drag her into this to prove that I wasn't in Henny's house when he was killed, in case you'd maybe think I killed him. So I thought I better come down here, tell you all about it, and get you to take my finger-prints, and have it all over with."

We went up to the identification bureau and had Clane's prints taken. They were not at all like the murderer's.

After we pumped Clane dry I went out and sent a telegram to our Toronto office, asking them to get a line on the Waldeman angle. Then I hunted up a couple of boys who eat, sleep, and breathe horse racing. They told me that Clane was well known in racing circles as the owner of a small string of near-horses that ran as irregularly as the stewards would permit.

At the Marquis hotel I got hold of the house detective, who is a helpful chap so long as his hand is kept greased. He verified my information about Clane's status in the sporting world, and told me that Clane had stayed at the hotel for several days at a time, off and on, within the past couple years.

He tried to trace Clane's telephone calls for me but—as usual when you want them—the records were jumbled. I arranged to have the girls on the switchboard listen in on any talking he did during the next few days.

Ned Root was waiting for me when I got down to the office the next morning. He had worked on Grover's accounts all night, and had found enough to give me a start. Within the past year—that was as far back as Ned had gone—Grover had drawn out of his bank-accounts nearly fifty thousand dollars that couldn't be accounted for; nearly fifty thousand exclusive of the ten thousand he had drawn the day of the murder. Ned gave me the amounts and the dates:

May 6, 1922,	$15,000
June 10,	5,000
August 1,	5,000
October 10,	10,000
January 3, 1923,	12,500

Forty-seven thousand, five hundred dollars! Somebody was getting fat off him!

The local managers of the telegraph companies raised the usual howl about respecting their patrons' privacy, but I got an order from the Prosecuting Attorney and put a clerk at work on the files of each office.

Then I went back to the Marquis hotel and looked at the old registers. Clane had been there from May 4th to 7th, and from October 8th to 15th last year. That checked off two of the dates upon which Grover had made his withdrawals.

I had to wait until nearly six o'clock for my information from the telegraph companies, but it was worth waiting for. On the third of last January Henry Grover had telegraphed $12,500 to Joseph Clane in San Diego. The clerks hadn't found anything on the other dates I had given them, but I wasn't at all dissatisfied. I had Joseph Clane fixed as the man who had been getting fat off Grover.

I sent Dick Foley—he is the Agency's shadow-ace—and Bob Teal—a youngster who will be a world-beater some day—over to Clane's hotel.

"Plant yourselves in the lobby," I told them. "I'll be over in a few minutes to talk to Clane, and I'll try to bring him down in the lobby where you can get a good look at him. Then I want him shadowed until he shows up at police headquarters tomorrow. I want to know where he goes and who he talks to. And if he spends much time talking to any one person, or their conversation seems very important, I want one of you boys to trail the other man, to see who he is and what he does. If Clane tries to blow town, grab him and have him thrown in the can, but I don't think he will."

I gave Dick and Bob time enough to get themselves placed, and then went to the hotel. Clane was out, so I waited. He came in a little after eleven and I went up to his room with him. I didn't hem-and-haw, but came out cold-turkey:

"All the signs point to Grover's having been blackmailed. Do you know anything about it?"

"No," he said.

"Grover drew a lot of money out of his banks at different times. You got some of it, I know, and I suppose you got most of it. What about it?"

He didn't pretend to be insulted, or even surprised by my talk. He smiled a little grimly, maybe, but as if he thought it the most natural thing in the world—and it was, at that—for me to suspect him.

"I told you that me and Henny were pretty chummy, didn't I? Well, you ought to know that all us fellows that fool with the bang-tails have our streaks of bad luck. Whenever I'd get up against it I'd hit Henny up for a stake; like at Tiajuana last winter where I got into a flock of bad breaks. Henny lent me twelve or fifteen thousand and I got back on my feet again. I've done that often. He ought to have some of my letters and wires in his stuff. If you look through his things you'll find them."

I didn't pretend that I believed him.

"Suppose you drop into police headquarters at nine in the morning and we'll go over everything with the city dicks," I told him.

And then, to make my play stronger:

"I wouldn't make it much later than nine—they might be out looking for you."

"Uh-huh," was all the answer I got.

I went back to the Agency and planted myself within reach of a telephone, waiting for word from Dick and Bob. I thought I was sitting pretty. Clane had been blackmailing Grover—I didn't have a single doubt of that—and I didn't think he had been very far away when Grover was killed. That woman alibi of his sounded all wrong!

But the bloody finger-prints were not Clane's—unless the police identification bureau had pulled an awful boner—and the man who had left the prints was the bird I was setting my cap for. Clane had let three days pass between the murder and his appearance at headquarters. The natural explanation for that would be that his partner, the actual murderer, had needed nearly that much time to put himself in the clear.

My present game was simple: I had stirred Clane up with the knowledge that he was still suspected, hoping that he would have to repeat whatever precautions were necessary to protect his accomplice in the first place.

He had taken three days then. I was giving him about nine hours now: time enough to do something, but not too much time, hoping that he would have to hurry things along and that in his haste he would give Dick and Bob a chance to turn up his partner: the owner of the fingers that had smeared blood on the knife, the table, and the door.

At a quarter to one in the morning Dick telephoned that Clane had left the hotel a few minutes behind me, had gone to an apartment house on Polk Street, and was still there.

I went up to Polk Street and joined Dick and Bob. They told me that Clane had gone in apartment number 27, and that the directory in the vestibule showed this apartment was occupied by George Farr. I stuck around with the boys until about two o'clock, when I went home for some sleep.

At seven I was with them again, and was told that our man had not appeared yet. It was a little after eight when he came out and turned down Geary Street, with the boys trailing him, while I went into the apartment house for a talk with the manager. She told me that Farr had been living there for four or five months, lived alone, and was a photographer by trade, with a studio on Market Street.

I went up and rang his bell. He was a husky of thirty or thirty-two with bleary eyes that looked as if they hadn't had much sleep that night. I didn't waste any time with him.

"I'm from the Continental Detective Agency and I am interested in Joseph Clane. What do you know about him?"

He was wide awake now.

"Nothing."

"Nothing at all?"

"No," sullenly.

"Do you know him?"

"No."

What can you do with a bird like that?

"Farr," I said, "I want you to go down to headquarters with me."

He moved like a streak and his sullen manner had me a little off my guard; but I turned my head in time to take the punch above my ear instead of on the chin. At that, it carried me off my feet and I wouldn't have bet a nickel that my skull wasn't dented; but luck was with me and I fell across the doorway, holding the door open, and managed to scramble up, stumble through some rooms, and catch one of his feet as it was going through the bathroom window to join its mate on the fire-escape. I got a split lip and a kicked shoulder in the scuffle, but he behaved after a while.

I didn't stop to look at his stuff—that could be done more regularly later—but put him in a taxicab and took him to the Hall of Justice. I was afraid that if I waited too long Clane would take a run-out on me.

Clane's mouth fell open when he saw Farr, but neither of them said anything.

I was feeling pretty chirp in spite of my bruises.

"Let's get this bird's finger-prints and get it over with," I said to O'Hara.

Dean was not in.

"And keep an eye on Clane. I think maybe he'll have another story to tell us in a few minutes."

We got in the elevator and took our men up to the identification bureau, where we put Farr's fingers on the pad. Phels—he is the department's expert—took one look at the results and turned to me.

"Well, what of it?"

"What of what?" I asked.

"This isn't the man who killed Henry Grover!"

Clane laughed, Farr laughed, O'Hara laughed, and Phels laughed. I didn't! I stood there and pretended to be thinking, trying to get myself in hand.

"Are you sure you haven't made a mistake?" I blurted, my face a nice, rosy red.

You can tell how badly upset I was by that: it's plain suicide to say a thing like that to a finger-print expert!

Phels didn't answer; just looked me up and down.

Clane laughed again, like a crow cawing, and turned his ugly face to me.

"Do you want to take my prints again, Mr. Slick Private Detective?"

"Yeah," I said, "just that!"

I had to say something.

Clane held his hands out to Phels, who ignored them, speaking to me with heavy sarcasm.

"Better take them yourself this time, so you'll be sure it's been done right."

I was mad clean through—of course it was my own fault—but I was pig-headed enough to go through with anything, particularly anything that would hurt somebody's feelings; so I said:

"That's not a bad idea!"

I walked over and took hold of one of Clane's hands. I'd never taken a finger-print before, but I had seen it done often enough to throw a bluff. I started to ink Clane's fingers and found that I was holding them wrong—my own fingers were in the way.

Then I came back to earth. The balls of Clane's fingers were too smooth—or rather, too slick—without the slight clinging feeling that belongs to flesh. I turned his hand over so fast that I nearly upset him and looked at the fingers. I don't know what I had expected to find but I didn't find anything—not anything that I could name.

"Phels," I called, "look here!"

He forgot his injured feelings and bent to look at Clane's hand.

"I'll be—" he began, and then the two of us were busy for a few minutes taking Clane down and sitting on him, while O'Hara quieted Farr, who had also gone suddenly into action.

When things were peaceful again Phels examined Clane's hands carefully, scratching the fingers with a finger-nail.

He jumped up, leaving me to hold Clane, and paying no attention to my, "What is it?" got a cloth and some liquid, and washed the fingers thoroughly. We took his prints again. They matched the bloody ones taken from Grover's house!

Then we all sat down and had a nice talk.

"I told you about the trouble Henny had with that fellow Waldeman," Clane began, after he and Farr had decided to come clean: there was nothing else they could do. "And how he won out in the argument because Waldeman disappeared. Well, Henny done for him—shot him one night and buried him—and I saw it. Grover was one bad actor in them days, a tough hombre to tangle with, so I didn't try to make nothing out of what I knew.

"But after he got older and richer he got soft—a lot of men go like that—and must have begun worrying over it; because when I ran into him in New York accidentally about four years ago it didn't take me long to learn that he was pretty well tamed, and he told me that he hadn't been able to forget the look on Waldeman's face when he drilled him.

"So I took a chance and braced Henny for a couple thousand. I got them easy, and after that, whenever I was flat I either went to him or sent him word, and he always came across. But I was careful not to crowd him too far. I knew what a terror he was in the old days, and I didn't want to push him into busting loose again.

"But that's what I did in the end. I 'phoned him Friday that I needed money and he said he'd call me up and let me know where to meet him the next night. He called up around half past nine Saturday night and told me to come out to the house. So I went out there and he was waiting for me on the porch and took me upstairs and gave me the ten thousand. I told him this was the last time I'd ever bother him—I always told him that—it had a good effect on him.

"Naturally I wanted to get away as soon as I had the money but he must have felt sort of talkative for a change, because he kept me there for half an hour or so, gassing about men we used to know up in the province.

"After awhile I began to get nervous. He was getting a look in his eyes like he used to have when he was young. And then all of a sudden he flared up and tied into me. He had me by the throat and was bending me back across the table when my hand touched that brass knife. It was either me or him—so I let him have it where it would do the most good.

"I beat it then and went back to the hotel. The newspapers were full of it next day, and had a whole lot of stuff about bloody finger-prints. That gave me a jolt! I didn't know nothing about finger-prints, and here I'd left them all over the dump.

"And then I got to worrying over the whole thing, and it seemed like Henny must have my name written down somewheres among his papers, and maybe had saved some of my letters or telegrams—though they were wrote in careful enough language. Anyway I figured the police would want to be asking me some questions sooner or later; and there I'd be with fingers that fit the bloody prints, and nothing for what Farr calls a alibi.

"That's when I thought of Farr. I had his address and I knew he had been a finger-print sharp in the East, so I decided to take a chance on him. I went to him and told him the whole story and between us we figured out what to do.

"He said he'd dope my fingers, and I was to come here and tell the story we'd fixed up, and have my finger-prints taken, and then I'd be safe no matter what leaked out about me and Henny. So he smeared up the fingers and told me to be careful not to shake hands with anybody or touch anything, and I came down here and everything went like three of a kind.

"Then that little fat guy"—meaning me—"came around to the hotel last night and as good as told me that he thought I had done for Henny and that I better come down here this morning. I beat it for Farr's right away to see whether I ought to run for it or sit tight, and Farr said, 'Sit tight!' So I stayed there all night and he fixed up my hands this morning. That's my yarn!"

Phels turned to Farr.

"I've seen faked prints before, but never any this good. How'd you do it?"

These scientific birds are funny. Here was Farr looking a nice, long stretch in the face as "accessory after the fact," and yet he brightened up under the admiration in Phel's tone and answered with a voice that was chock-full of pride.

"It's simple! I got hold of a man whose prints I knew weren't in any police gallery—I didn't want any slip up there—and took his prints and put them on a copper plate, using the ordinary photo-engraving process, but etching it pretty deep. Then I coated Clane's fingers with gelatin—just enough to cover all his markings—and pressed them against the plates. That way I got everything, even to the pores, and...."

When I left the bureau ten minutes later Farr and Phels were still sitting knee to knee, jabbering away at each other as only a couple of birds who are cuckoo on the same subject can.

THREE GUN TERRY

by Carroll John Daly

MY LIFE is my own, and the opinions of others don't interest me; so don't form any, or if you do, keep them to yourself. If you want to sneer at my tactics, why go ahead; but do it behind the pages—you'll find that healthier.

So for my line. I have a little office which says "Terry Mack, Private Investigator," on the door; which means whatever you wish to think it. I ain't a crook, and I ain't a dick; I play the game on the level, in my own way. I'm in the center of a triangle; between the crook and the police and the victim. The police have had an eye on me for some time, but only an eye, never a hand; they don't get my lay at all. The crooks; well, some is on, and some ain't; most of them don't know what to think, until I've put the hooks in them. Sometimes they gun for me, but that ain't a one-sided affair. When it comes to shooting, I don't have to waste time cleaning my gun. A little windy that; but you get my game.

Now, the city's big, and that ain't meant for no outburst of personal wisdom. It's fact. Sometimes things is slow and I go out looking for business. About the cabarets; in the big hotels and even along the streets I find it. It's always there. I just spot some well-known faces playing their suckers, and that's my chance. A bit of trailing; I corral the bird, offer my help, and then things get lively. Blackmail it is mostly, but it doesn't matter to me. And then the fee; a hard-earned but gladly paid fee—that's me! I'm there forty ways from the ace.

So it comes that things is slow, and I'm anxious to chase down and corner a little of the ready. I guess I blow in nearly twenty bucks, jumping from joint to joint; but it's expense money, so I just shrug my shoulders when nothing turns up. Oh, I see crooks galore, but they ain't having no more luck than I am; which ain't the usual run of things.

Along about one-thirty I start for home—I got a car, but I ain't using it—the subway is my ticket that night. I just come out of a high-class robbers' den over on Sixth Avenue, and start toward Broadway; it's Fifty-sixth Street that I trot down, and it strikes me a wonderful place to pull off a murder—dark and quiet.

Then, when I'm halfway down the block, a woman shoots out of a brownstone front and skips down the steps toward a waiting taxi. She's just about to pull open the door and jump in when I see her draw back suddenly, stand undecidedlike a second, and then, turning, make a sudden dash for the steps. But she's too late. Two chaps hop out of that taxi and go after her. Now, I don't say that

she mightn't 'a made it, for she had a start on them, but another lad steps out of the basement way and heads her off.

And let me give those boys credit for working fast; they sure turned the trick like professionals; there ain't no more than a scream and a couple of kicks when them birds have whisked her up and run her into the taxi. A crank of the motor, and the car is speeding

away. Is that young lady lost forever? Not so you could notice it, she ain't! If they worked fast, so did I. I couldn't stop them—not me—but I had run across the street and as the car shot past me, I made a grab and swung up on the spare tire.

As we turn into Sixth Avenue, I see a window go up in the brownstone house, and I think I catch a shout. Then we ride. Things weren't so dead after all, and it looked as if I might get some return on that twenty.

There's three men and a driver, and you think the best thing I can do is to holler at the first cop we pass. But not me! He might stop us, and then again he might not. Also, I might get shot off the back of that speeding car, which was not exactly my most cherished thought. Besides, at the best, the police could only make a capture and give me a vote of thanks, with a misspelling of my name at the bottom of the page of the evening papers. No, I'm not looking for honor—there would probably be jack in this for yours truly.

It ain't cold, and the ride ain't so bad; not so good either, but then I couldn't be particular. As far as being worried about the end of the trip—not much! There were four of them—all armed I guess—but then I had a couple of guns of my own, and I'd be the one with the drop.

At last the ride was over, and we pulled up on a lonely street in the Bronx. It was an empty street, but on the next block was a row of two-story frame houses. I guess they didn't want to attract attention by arriving in style and would hoof it the rest of the way. There is some delay about them getting out of the cab, and I drop off the tire, and stretch my legs, and shake out enough kinks to account for a fifty-mile trip in a lizzy; also I might make mention of the fact that I played with my automatics—being overfond of such toys on certain occasions—and this was one of them. Of course, those birds couldn't know I had come along with them; they was too busy with the struggling girl when I swung aboard. So everything was rosy.

At length, they opened the door, and after stalling around a bit, one of them got out and leaving the door open beat it up the street. I guess he was going to get things set before he took the girl in. Well, I give him a chance. I like to do things right, and I waited to see which house he went into. Then I stepped around from the back of that car and slipped in. Yep, just slid right in and took the empty portable seat which he had left.

I get a laugh yet when I think of the expression on them lads' faces—the two of them, with the girl bound and gagged between them. There in the pale light of a dull moon, she sat, every muscle tense—her eyes wide and frightened.

But the two lads—regular tough birds they were too—no, their muscles weren't tense, they just sat there loose and staring, their eyes near popping out of their heads. Prepared! Why one of them held a gat right on his knees, but he never made no move to use it. Not that he got the chance, for I had rapped his knuckles with the barrel of my gun—not the butt but the barrel—and his gun just slid down his feet, to the floor. Of course, it's a bit risky using the barrel for such things; once in every so often the gun goes off, 'specially a light shooter like mine; but then you can't really bother about such little accidents; you can see where it would be his hard luck, not mine.

Say, there wasn't a yip out of either of them—their hands went up with such a goodwill that I thought they'd stick them through the top of the car. Very obliging they were, and I hadn't said a word yet. I just grinned. As for the lad in the front—well—I had the other cannon poked so hard into his spine that he was sitting straighter than he ever sat before in his life.

"Young lady," I says to the girl. "You got to help, as I can't keep more than half an eye on the driver—so just please close your left eye if he don't keep his hands well up and empty. That's the girl," I added as she nodded. "If you wink the left, I'll plug him. And don't be overparticular—I'm not of a sentimental nature."

Now most of this was only for effect. I didn't really think that the girl was able to help much, but it would give the chap in the front something to think about and make him behave. I didn't

need much time because I work fast. Even this kind of a situation wasn't new to me.

In thirty seconds, I had them gunmen standing on the sidewalk, their backs to the car and their hands stretched toward the heavens, like they were listening to Walter Camp.

"Now," I says to the driver. "Let the hands drop and we'll go back to where you came from. And pray that nothing happens to your car. For the first time that she slows down, I'll drill a hole in the back of your neck and do a little driving myself."

I didn't have to shout at him—you see, the window was down, and his attention was perfect.

And now for the first time, one of the lads on the pavement got his wind back and opened up.

"Better stay out of this," he warned me. "It will mean death for you—sure."

He spoke in broken English and his voice trembled with rage.

"All right Mr. Wolf," I chirped cheerfullike. "But Little Red Riding Hood and me will trot along. If she wants to come back to you later—why, well and good." Then turning to the driver I said sharp, "Let her go!"

And the driver being a man of sound judgment, we went.

I let him drive along for about a mile, and then I stop him and frisk him for a gun; he only has one, which shows a poor eye to the necessity of his profession. After that, we shoot along real merrily, and I give my attention to the girl. I guess it took about ten minutes to get her all straightened out, for I had to keep an eye on the driver, and take a look behind every once in a while. By the time I was finished, we were well down in Harlem.

Say, but that girl was scared; why, she didn't do nothing but hang close to me and keep her head up against my chest as she clung to my coat. And she was mighty little and mighty young too, I think, though I couldn't tell much about her, there in the dark of the cab. Somehow I felt almost like a father as I patted her little dark head and ran my fingers through her soft black locks. I could 'a laughed, but somehow I didn't. It certainly did seem strange to find myself putting my arm about a kid again. I don't know when I did it last—if I ever did it. And there I was, telling her that she was all right, and that I'd take care of her and—and— oh—just acting like a regular nut. What I should 'a been doing was questioning her and finding out just what her old man was worth and how much there would be in it for me. But somehow I didn't do anything but just try to comfort her like she was a baby.

After a bit, she calms down and gets out her handkerchief and snuffles a bit, but she never says a word, just clings to me like some frightened animal.

And then, when I'm about to ask her a few questions, the car suddenly comes to stop and I see that we have turned into Fifty-seventh Street and have stopped around the corner from Sixth Avenue.

"What's this, my lad?" I hail the driver. "Your memory is sorta weak, but mine ain't—come shake a leg and drive us around the block."

"This is as far as I go," he says sulkylike.

But at the same time there seems to be a note of determination in his voice.

"Oh, is it?" And I lean over and tickle him with the gat. "Come, I'll count just ten, and if we ain't off, then I'll give you the surprise of your life—and your death too." And I ain't bluffing either. I never bluff. And not being a chap what wastes time I start in counting:

"One, two, three, four, five." I run them up fast. I ain't no moving-picture director looking for suspense.

Would I have plugged him—well, he didn't wait to find out; he wasn't curious.

"Wait a minute, boss," he says. "I want to say something."

"Make it snappy—and if you ain't inclined to do what you're told, make it prayers."

"There's a cop down the street," he chirps. "If you don't get out here I'll holler to him."

It sounded like he meant business, too, though I couldn't get his game. Also, his English is pretty good.

"Call a cop! You!" I laugh. "Ten to twenty years for kidnapping—that's what you'll get."

Then he turns around sudden and looks at me.

"You ain't no Italian," he says, after a long look.

I only laugh. I'm too old in the game to take offense at such slander. Besides, there is something deadly earnest in the way he speaks.

"I guess you ain't in on the game. If you was, you wouldn't ask me to drive to that house, and you wouldn't go within miles of it yourself," he says half aloud.

"I wanta go home—I wanta go home!" The girl suddenly flings both arms about my neck. "Just around the corner!" She points down the street. Her voice is low—hysterical—foreign.

I shake the girl off and give him the once-over, and then I poke him with the gun.

"Now drive," I says. "Or I'll find a way to make you and the car move so fast that it will surprise both of you. Six, seven, eight—" I start in where I left off. I'm mighty sore and mean business—besides, I can see the cop coming down the street.

And then the girl suddenly takes things out of my hands. She opens the door and slips out, and is around on Sixth Avenue before I know she's gone. That settles the argument with the driver—I'm out and after her. One last look at the car, and the number is firmly in my mind as it goes rapidly down the street.

I'm only about ten seconds behind as she turns into Sixth Avenue, and then I swing around the corner myself and stop dead. There ain't a person in sight; the street is quiet and deserted.

It didn't seem possible that she could have made the length of that block in that short time, but I took a run down to the corner of Fifty-sixth Street to make sure. I could see well down the street—clean to Seventh Avenue—and there wasn't a soul in sight. I sure was stumped. She must be hiding in one of the hallways along the avenue. But why? Anyway, I'd take a look. And just then along came a cop. Now I ain't afraid of any cop—not me. But they sure ask embarrassing questions, and I don't stand in good with most of the dicks. I've made good when they have failed so many times. So I just loitered around and played safe. And this bull is a good-natured fellow, who smiles at me and says, it's a fine night, as he goes by. He's trying all the doors and is mightily slow about it, and all the time I'm expecting him to come across the girl. But I just stand there and stretch and look around; then I light a butt and walk slowly about.

But that cop was a gentle trusting soul, and pretty soon he shoots across the street and passes down the next block; and he's faster there because there ain't no one to see if he tries all the store doors. Things look good, and I decide to have a peek.

There were several dark entrances to the flats above the stores—dirty, ill-smelling hallways that I'd have to look into. I just come

out of one of them when I hear a voice, and there she was, popping up from behind a newsstand that had been pushed flat up against the building for the night.

"What are you doing there?" I says, some relieved and some mad.

"Oh—has he gone? I was frightened," she whispered as she come timidly out and clutched me by the arm. My, but she was a slim, delicate little thing.

"Who went?" I asked. "The lad with the car—yes, he went, all right." I still felt a bit sore about that.

"Oh no—not him—the policeman."

"The policeman," I exclaimed. "Why, what would you be afraid of him for? He'd be a good friend of yours—anyway."

"Oh—no, no. Uncle says no. I have had a lot of trouble since I have been in America. At the convent, things were so different, and I was so happy."

"How long have you been over?" I asked, to try and get her mind working easy; she was beginning to tremble again.

"Over?"

"Yes—in America?"

"Oh!" she said. "Three weeks—nearly."

"Is that all? You speak mighty fine English—almost as good as mine."

Why, there wasn't hardly any accent at all, just enough to make it sound attractive.

"I always knew the English, I think—my mother was an American—she died when I was a little girl."

She kind of sniffled a little.

"Never mind," I said. "You'll be with your father in another few minutes. It's your father that lives here?"

I paused; we were in front of that same brownstone front again—the one she had run out of earlier in the evening.

"I have no father—he died—a little while ago—and I came here—to my uncle."

I looked down at her again as we mounted the steps; she seemed so young.

"How old are you?" I asked. Fourteen, I guessed.

"Nineteen—almost twenty," she told me.

I whistled softly. Well, we never can tell, and the next minute I was ringing the doorbell. A moment later, an electric light flashed on above us. I felt that someone was observing us from within, and then the door was flung open.

Two men, fully dressed, whom I took for servants, stood one on either side of the door, and a tough-looking pair of citizens they were. They looked like they'd cut your throat in a minute. But that didn't bother me; a minute would have been too long—I'd 'a got them both—besides, just at present it seemed to me that these birds would be on my side of the fence.

And then, as we stepped inside and the door closed behind us, a stout man of about fifty, all dolled up in a trick bathrobe that would knock your eye out for color display, came down the stairs.

"Nita!" he yells. Then both clinch, and everything is jake.

After that I'm forgotten, except for those two rough-looking lads who watch me mighty careful—and what's more, I'm watching them too. There's a lot of Italian flung back between uncle and niece, and then I guess he starts in to question her; then they clinch again, and she beats it up the stairs.

Then the fat lad takes a tumble to himself and comes across the hall and takes me by the hand.

"The señorita calls you friend—she has told me of your chivalry, and I cannot thank you enough."

With that, he drags me by his cold, clammy hand into his library, and we both sit.

For a couple of minutes he just sits and looks at me and his smile grows bigger and bigger, and then fades and comes again. But he ain't fooling me none. Of course, I'm the light-haired boy with him now. I can see that, but behind that smile I can also see that he's a tough egg. His smile is broad enough, but then, I've seen too much of life. This bird I spot for a bad actor. And he's a buck with uncertain age, one of them half-bald fronts; he might be ten years older than what I think him, and then again he might be ten years younger.

So he has me tell him the whole story of the night's events, and he smiles some more, and I gather that he's thinking up an explanation of some kind. Then I pull a wisecrack, and I see that he's puzzled.

"You don't have to explain to me," I tell him. "I ain't interested unless—unless I got to be."

Well, that took the smile clean off his slate, for I suppose he was hatching up a barrel of lies. Then he starts to walk up and down the room. After a bit, he stops and looks down at me.

"You don't want to know about this—why—and why?" was the best he could get out.

"Not a word. It came out all right and I'm satisfied, if you are."

That fetches him up fine, and the smile comes back, and I see that he's getting ready to dismiss me without a yip. But he don't yet; he rings a bell and orders some refreshments—which is some pretty fair wine and a half-dozen slim sandwiches.

"You are a remarkable man—a real gentleman," he starts in to make a speech. "It is not often today that we find young men, who for the love of adventure and for their pride in the strong for the weak, succor women in distress. I wish I could reward you, but a gentleman cannot—"

And that's where I bust in on him. I don't want him to commit himself, and I see no reason why he should waste all them flowery thoughts. So I up and give him another shock.

"My reward for tonight's services—now that you suggest it—is exactly two hundred and fifty dollars. Fifty for the night's work and two hundred for the successful finish. I generally charge a little more at the end, but seeing how I came in uninvited—"

But I didn't get any further,

"Am I to understand that you wish money—money for what you did?" And his eyes grew big, and his wine slopped over his glass a little. I had touched him this time, for the foreign accent crept into his voice for the first time, and I knew that he was the brother of Nita's father. Before that, I wasn't sure which side of the fence he was on.

"Sure," I said. "You don't take me for no Sir Lunchlot, do you? This is business with me." And to keep him from having a stroke of apoplexy, I tell him my trade.

At first, I think that he's trying to hold out on me, but then I see that he's just thinking. His eyes go up and down, and his mouth too, for that matter; then his eyes get small, and he looks closely at me. Whatever he sees don't start a row, for he turns and, ringing a bell, tells the chap that comes to the door to send the señorita down. I get that much even if it is Italian.

And in about five minutes she comes in, and she's a wow. I didn't get a good look at her before, and I tell you it's a lucky thing that I ain't romantic. She sure was one swell-looking dame. Even me, a hardened citizen like me—yep, I was nearly ready to take ten

dollars off the bill if the fat lad had suggested it. She sure looked grand, all fixed up.

But he didn't make a crack about money; he just talked to her for a bit and they seemed to be having a bit of a row about me. At length he gives a wave of his hand that she shall go, but she don't—she just stays there. He says something, and she stamps her foot, so I see that she ain't so timid when she's in her own house. For a minute, I get the idea that they are arguing about the price, and she don't look so beautiful, for I can't tell which side she's taking.

At length the old bird gives in on some point and turns to me.

"We'll pay you what you ask and—perhaps much more."

Things are looking up. I just nod.

"Yes," he goes on. "There will be money for you if you are as brave as the señorita says you are—but you must be very brave."

Now he's hitting my gait and talking turkey. So I just smile and tell him:

"Show me the coin, and I'll make the boys at Valley Forge look like pikers."

Then his shrewd eyes went over me again, and his lips opened wide and his teeth showed, but no smile came this time—just a bit of a dental display—he couldn't make a go of the smile because he had forgotten to open his eyes wide enough. Then he took another drink and without further preliminaries opened up; yep, opened up considerable. But he talked so fast that I couldn't get for sure which was the bull and which was the real thing.

"It is this way," he makes a break. "The señorita, Nita Gretna, is my niece. She is my brother's child; Michel Gretna who, if he had lived, would have been recognized as the world's greatest scientist. Well, he made a formula—a formula of great value. The result of it will someday—I hope—startle the world. It is for his daughter—the glory, the honor and the money. To a friend who was his assistant, he entrusted this sheet of paper; this young man, Manual Sparo, brought it here to America. Certain things about it were not quite clear; Manual would work on it—perfect it before he married the señorita and turned it over to us. And when all was ready and the great moment at hand, enemies who desire this paper more than life—great powerful enemies—fell upon him and bore him away."

"Then they got the formula?" I said. Of course, I felt that they didn't, but he paused so long that it seemed up to me to show a little interest. And this talk of marriage was sudden.

"No—they got it not," he said backward. "Wild horses would not tear the secret from him, and the formula was hidden away. Tonight, the señorita went out in answer to a message which she thought came from him. She was indiscreet and should have consulted me, though she says she could not find me. What they would have done with her, I do not know; frighten her, perhaps."

"But they talked of torturing me to make him tell—" the girl started, but the uncle stopped her.

"Tut—tut," he said. "You were frightened and nervous." He turned to me again. "We will pay you much for that formula."

"Do you want me to know what the formula is about?" I got to admit I was curious; it's as well to know how valuable your services are. Besides, I didn't quite like the whole story—it sounded fishy, at least parts of it.

"I do not think that that is necessary. For the paper we will pay much money," he repeated.

"How much is that?"

I don't take much stock in promises.

He thinks a while.

"A thousand dollars," he says at length.

Well, he might have said ten thousand; it wouldn't 'a made no difference to me. I don't work on that kind of speck.' I draw a regular salary. So I up and give him an earful:

"That may be all right," I say, "but I have a regular charge. Fifty dollars a day, and five hundred bonus when I deliver the goods; also, I am willing to take all sorts of chances, but if I get pinched, it's up to you to hire the best lawyer that money can buy—also, I get thirty bucks a day for every day I spend in jail. And for every man I croak—mind you, I ain't a killer, but sometimes a chap's got to turn a gun—I get two hundred dollars flat. It ain't that I don't count this as part of my services, but there's a certain nervous shock to it—and besides, they're your enemies and should be cheap at that price. Also, your game must be strictly honest—I ain't no crook."

I tell you his eyes sure did open wide enough now—wide enough to pop out of his head, almost. He sure was hearing a trunkful, and I could tell that I wasn't falling none in his estimation. I generally let the killing business go by the boards until the time comes, but this time I didn't. You see, if I had to hunt around Italian joints, there was almost sure to be some gunplay and—and I got to protect my interests.

After a bit he says:

"You make this quite a business, but a man would be a fool to sign up to any such agreement."

"Oh, you don't have to sign nothing," I tell him. "When you agree, we just shake hands like a couple of gentlemen. And that's that."

His smile this time was a real one.

"But that protects you not at all," he twists up his English again.

"It gives me all the protection I want. It makes me feel that I've done the right thing."

"But if one don't play fair, what then?"

"Then…" I rubbed my chin. "That's the only point I forgot to tell you. You see, that only happened once and—but why go into unpleasant details; let's just say that they buried him anyway."

This time he actually rubbed his hands together, and chuckled. These foreign gents sure do have a real appreciation of art.

And then, when he's all set to agree to everything, the girl suddenly breaks in with an Italian marathon. I don't think he agrees with what she says, but she turns to me anyway and says:

"Uncle is doing all in his power to recover that paper of my father's, and now it is my turn. I will shake you by the hand, and I will pay you for this service; it is my turn to do something, Señor—" She pauses, and knowing the proper thing to do I get up and bow.

"Mack," I says. "Terry Mack."

And with that she puts out her little hand and mitts me.

It was near four when I got home, and nearer five before I got to bed. Yep, I sat up there in my big easy chair and killed nearly a double deck of butts; I had something to think about, you'll admit.

In the first place, even with the long talk I later had with the fat bird, whose whole moniker was Gustave Gretna, I didn't get any information worth a hill of beans. He made it clear enough that he didn't want the police to know anything about the game. He said if they did, why, the Italian government would mix up in it and make him turn over the formula for about one-tenth of what it was really worth, and he didn't want his niece to lose all that money. I also gathered that she was worth considerable change in her own name. But with real dope, that lad wasn't there at all. Oh, he talked a lot, but he didn't say anything, and of course it was my game to look wise and act like I could settle everything in no time, which was probably what I would do once I got started.

As for the girl, well, she puzzled me; yes, and bothered me some too. When the uncle went upstairs to get the two hundred and fifty bucks for me, which he kept in the house, she spilled out some conversation that even rattled me.

"I am not going to marry this Manual Sparo," she tells me lowlike. "I think I am going to marry someone else—oh—I hope I am. He is an American and—and I love him." With that, she kind of ducks her head and turns red.

"Good for you," was the best that I could pull off—I didn't quite like the way she looked up at me through them thick lashes of hers.

"Yes," she goes on. "But I don't know if he loves me—what do you think?" And she turns them big, black glims of hers full on me. "He's so brave and so handsome and—but I have known him such a short time." Then she breaks off sudden, for her uncle is coming down the stairs.

"Terry," she whispers, leaning over and laying a little hand upon my arm. "You are hired by me, you know, and I want you to promise that you'll see me once every day—without fail."

With that, her uncle trots into the room, and I must say he was a welcome sight.

Now, that's part of what I was thinking over, alone in my room along about four-thirty in the morning. She loved someone else—and that someone was an American—and was brave—and she lived in a convent all her life and had never been out of the house alone since she came to this country—and—and she had called me Terry. Well, I didn't need no more than three guesses. That dame had fallen for me, and fallen hard.

Of course, there wasn't nothing so terrible strange about that, except that I'm off dames—they don't go well with my business—good or bad—women don't have no place in my life. And yet as I stretched myself and looked my reflection over in the glass, something seemed to say: "Why not?" A home in sunny Italy, an open garden beneath—but rats—I snuffed out my last butt and climbed into bed. No more thinking then. I don't do nothing but sleep once I hit the covers; I used to plan then, but queer ideas come to you in bed—great and glorious ideas—but when you turn them over in the morning they ain't worth a thing—you just find them a waste of time.

But the next morning, when I have breakfast, I do a bit of real brain work. You see, Bud brings me my coffee and chops—Bud is my man, my valet, my chauffeur, my assistant—in fact, Bud is the whole works; not much of a thinker, but he can carry out instructions to the big T.

The first thing I figure on doing is having a talk with that taxi lad who drove me and the girl the night before; he was a real funny citizen, and the way he had acted bothered me some. Of course, you might think that would be a tough job, but not for me; it would be easy. I know the ropes in the underworld and the way to get my hooks on these lads. You see, I had the number of the car, a fake number to be sure, but then me and the bird what drove it would know and that was enough.

Along about two o'clock, which is about an hour after I finish breakfast, I trot down to Larkin's Saloon in the Thirties. Now, this Larkin sells booze, but he's also a dope peddler. I've done him more than one good turn because I can use him a lot, and he's always ready to turn a trick for me, if none of the boys—his boys, that's what he calls the crooks—suffer by it. Larkin has a suspicion that I'm a big gun in the dope traffic, and since it leaves a good impression on him, I let him have his think—yes, and help it along. And this same Larkin has got a system of communication that ain't been beat from here to Frisco. So I brace Larkin.

"Larkin," I says, leaning over the little desk in that tiny private room of his, just off the corner of the old bar, "Larkin, I'm looking for a gink what drove a car last night—number 19964—fake, I guess."

Larkin don't say nothing, but just screws up his face and wiggles his fingers, which I know is the sign to slip over the regular fee, so I dig and produce the ready.

"I can only do my part, Mr. Smith." Larkin makes it a point of calling everybody Smith—it don't make no difference how well he knows you. "The word will go about, and of course I can guarantee that no hurt will come to the—the boy?"

"Absolutely. I'm looking for information with money, not force—at least when I use your system, Larkin. I always play fair with you."

He just nods.

"You may expect him at eleven, if he's alive. In my little room, eh—that'll be ten dollars more." His palm is itchy, and though he keeps his hand by his side, his fingers go nervously back and forth.

"I'll pay now," I tell him. "You can give it back to me if he don't show up." I knew that old boy's weakness.

"Good," said he, and taking the money, we both walked out of the little room. He ain't much of a talker, is Larkin, but he's clever, or maybe just shrewd in his own way.

When I leave that joint about ten minutes later, I see the number 19964 in small figures over his cash register. But it was big enough to read, and I knew that that same number would be in more than a hundred places within the next two or three hours. It was so that Larkin worked his system; the chap what drove the car would see it and know what it meant. Larkin had called, and he would answer. Yes, there had been something in that chauffeur's eyes which told me he would come—I couldn't be mistaken about them same eyes.

After that, I take a bit of a walk, and then I beat it up to the brownstone house on Fifty-sixth, partly to keep my promise to the girl, and partly to see if I couldn't unbutton something of real value out of her Uncle Gus. And that bimbo meets me with a sure-enough startler. Señorita Nita had gone away!

Suspicious! I should say I was; if my face ever betrayed anything, it betrayed it then. But I like to think it didn't; I have a regular poker face and am mighty proud of it.

"Where has she gone?"

This seemed a natural enough question, and I put it to him suddenlike.

But he didn't show any more expression than an oyster.

"Off to Lake—but there, she's away for a rest—Manual and she are to be married soon. I might as well tell you that the gang of cutthroats who were after that formula took fright last night and Michel has returned. You believe me, of course."

And he pulled that last sentence louder than any of the rest; and to me it sounded like he was giving it as a signal or warning to someone listening. But he smiled all over as he watched me closely. I could see that he didn't expect me to believe him, and wouldn't believe me if I said I did.

"No—I don't get you," I says. "What's the lay?"

"It is enough that you should know that everything is now all right. The formula is back—your appearance of last night was of great value. Nita is pleased and has left this for you."

He brought forth a wad and counted a number of bills out on the table.

But I wasn't watching him. I was looking over his shoulder, and I was sure that the curtains moved behind him and that someone peered in. There was something intensive and strained in the whole atmosphere of that room, and I knew, just as well as if I had seen it, that a gun was behind that curtain.

"Ah—you don't believe." He stretched out the money toward me. "Will this five hundred make you believe and—and forget? Nita and I will not need you now—you understand—we are paying you this for silence."

The constant use of that plural "we" grated on my nerves. I guess it was done to hand me the impression that his niece and he were acting in consort, and that she was all right, but it hit me exactly opposite. But then the waving curtain with death probably lurking behind it! It was best to play the game into his hands.

"For five hundred dollars I'll believe anything," I chirped with a grin. "Trot over

the coin. When I wish to be, I am as silent as the grave."

He fell for it, and why wouldn't he, after the way I had represented myself last night. I was nothing more than a gunman in his estimation. It was quite evident that he didn't see the ethics of my profession and the good that I did—but I made up my mind that he'd see it later. You see, he had forgotten one thing: I had been hired by the girl—not him. He'd change that grin of his when he seen how a real gentleman played the game.

Then he up and patted me on the back.

"I knew you for a sensible rascal," he said. "Someday we may use you again—Nita and I."

So he bid me good night, and it was all I could do to keep from backing out of the room. I tell you it took real nerve to turn and walk to the front door and then go carelessly down the steps. I sure had a longing to put a bullet through that curtain. But I had five hundred dollars, and a mighty mean suspicion—also, I knew for a certainty that I was going to do that girl some good yet. As for her Uncle Gus—well, of course I didn't believe a word that hummingbird told me.

There was plenty to think about as I went down the street; there were the girl's last words to me, of the previous night, about seeing her every day. Did that just mean that she had fallen for me, or did it mean more? Did it mean that she was growing suspicious about her uncle? Well, I like to think that it meant both.

And there was more than just a feeling of money, and a feeling of pride to make good to the girl who had hired me. For one thing, I never fail—for another thing—well, somehow I just seemed to want to know that that little girl was all right. If I had 'a been sure of my ground and really thought it would 'a done her any good, I'd 'a thought nothing of forcing the truth out of her uncle or—yes—of bumping him over the hurdles. And the gun behind the curtain wouldn't 'a made no difference neither. I knew the gun was there, just as well as I knew that that fat crooked Italian had lied to me.

For the first time in my life I'm worried, and what's more I'm followed. I look at my watch; it ain't but five o'clock and there won't be nothing doing until eleven. Of course, I could shake off the lad what's following me—there ain't nothing to that—but I think it will leave things clearer for me if I can send him back to Uncle Gus with a good report. There ain't really nothing for me to do. I could go and search the house in the Bronx, of course, but if I had thought there would be any chance in that direction, I'd 'a been up there before I went home in the morning. I know that's useless; that gang was out of the dump twenty minutes after I lit out in the taxi—any cluck would know that.

So I play a high-class joint for a feed and spot a dapper little foreigner, sitting over in one corner, as my meat. But I don't give him a tumble; just act like a lad who was out for a good time—blowing in Uncle Gus's jack. I gotta laugh when I think how snug they're feeling and I figure along about midnight I'll have my fingers in their pie up to my wrists. Yes—all I want is plenty of leeway, and then, when I get my earful, there sure is going to be some fireworks.

And I'm right; that lad ain't got the sticking power. He follows me home, and twenty minutes later, when I look out the window, that street is as deserted as a poetry graveyard.

It's near eleven when I slip out of my apartment window—which is on the ground floor for just such occasions—and Bud meets me with the car around the corner. Away we go to Larkin's, and pulling up about a block away, I hop out and beat it for the saloon.

My bird's there; Larkin gives me the high sign as soon as I bust in the door. Into his little private room I slide and shut the door. My man looks up—a little frightened, but smiling just the same.

"Good!" I says. "The system worked."

"Larkin wanted me to see you and—and here I am." I could see he wasn't going to be none too cordial.

"Know me?" I sit down.

He just shows his teeth and nods his head.

"How deep were you in last night?" I ask.

"Deep enough," he answers.

"Want to double-cross?" I ain't going to waste time if he seems agreeable.

"Not me," he grins.

Then I look at him close.

"Snowbird, ain't you?" I shoot at him sudden. Those eyes couldn't fool me. It was those same eyes which had told me he would answer Larkin's call—Larkin was pretty well looked up to by the hopheads.

"What's that to you?" His eyes blaze a bit and the smile does a fadeout.

"Hard guy, eh?"

"Dick, eh?" he retorts.

"Ask Larkin—you know better."

"Did!"

I see he's a man of few words and we ain't getting no place, so I open up on him, tell him what's under my hat; that if he don't give me the information I want, I'll see that Larkin cuts off his supply. The thing registers a bit, and I see him get white under the gills, so I guess Larkin has tipped him off that I'm a big gun in the traffic. But I don't get much out of him; I see that he's in deadly fear of this Uncle Gus.

"He'd kill me in a minute," he says, his eyes wide with terror. "All I'll say is that he used to run a fruit stand down in Mott Street—just before the girl come, he fixed up the house on Fifty-sixth Street and then—no! My God! No! He'd find out who told and—no—not another word."

He wasn't smiling no more now; his face had turned a chalky white, and his teeth were chattering. In another minute, he had gone all to pieces like his kind do—he was between the two fears: of Larkin cutting his supply and Uncle Gus cutting his throat. Changed? Why, you wouldn't know him for the same man—cringing and whining and kneeling at my feet. But nothing came out of him, and then he suddenly turns, and I see him roll up his sleeve and give his arm a long scratch with a safety pin; then into the blood went a few drops from a tiny bottle. Blooey! Just like that he was himself again—and any chance I had, which wasn't much, was gone. But I was working on another idea.

"A hundred dollars for the information—where is the girl?" I rip out quick.

"The girl—again—"

Then he stopped short, but he eyed the money which I held in my hand longingly. But he wouldn't open up, so I pulled my best and last card; time was passing and something was telling me that the girl needed me.

"I tell you how you can avoid all trouble—with the gang and with Larkin," I told him. "Give me the name of one of the gang. One that knows all, and one that I can reach tonight—now. I'll get the information out of him just the same as I would have gotten it out of you, if I hadn't passed my word to Larkin." Oh, I felt like shoving my gun down his throat and getting the truth out of him. But my word had gone to Larkin and—well—I couldn't break it. I know that don't sound like common sense, but we'll call it my weakness. Terry Mack's word is good, and weak or not, it always will be good.

I see I had him interested, and I took out three hundred and offered it to him. Then I told him if this Gustave was sure to find out everything, why, he'd find out that it wasn't him that told, but the other fellow.

"Ain't there some fellow—just give me his name and address—just one who knows what's going on tonight—perhaps you have an enemy—someone what done you dirt." And that caught him.

He grabs the bankroll and spills a mouthful.

"Daggo Joe," he says, and gives me an address which is less than five blocks away. "He's there now alone—and will be there until six-thirty, when he goes on duty."

"Good," I eye him, "and if you have lied to me, why I'll hunt you up and make you eat every one of them bills and then—then I'll cut them out of you again." Which may sound like a lot of wind, but it was the kind that he would understand best, and I don't know but what I meant it.

With that, I beat it over to the Thirties and step up and down in front of Daggo Joe's for a few minutes. You can't fool these birds and give them a surprise visit; they have a way of knowing you're coming. And this Daggo Joe knew, for I seen a figure at the window which I spotted for his, and then the light went out in that window. But I want him to know that I'm coming and coming alone—he won't beat it—not him; he'll stay and play it foxy on me—kind of get revenge for the previous night. So eleven-thirty finds me entering the dusty old building and climbing the stairs to the third floor, where this Daggo Joe parks his noble person.

Of course, my electric flash covers every jump of them hallways; there ain't a chance for a lad to jump me in the dark—also, my gun is mighty convenient. When I reach his door, I tap lightly, and there ain't no answer, but I know that he's listening in there, and I know that he takes me for a soft one announcing myself like that.

I don't waste much time, but try the door—just a turn of the knob, and it gives—the door ain't even locked. Do you get the game—well, I do. He wants me to walk right in so he can croak me off. It nearly makes me laugh—the simplicity of the whole thing; why he's almost like a kid.

And I know just where he's standing, as if he told me so himself; he's behind that door, and he's got a blackjack or a knife in his mitt. And then I start to do what any dick would do, and just what Daggo Joe figures I'll do—push the door open slowly.

That's what ninety-nine in a hundred would do—play the game very cautious.

So I push the door very softly, and this Joe waits behind it, all smiles, I guess. Then I suddenly up with my foot and give that door a kick—a real healthy kick. If I do say so myself, that's the only way to enter a room what you got your doubts on.

Bang! Crash! You could hear his head connect with that door in one heavy thud. After that, there was nothing to it. I had my flash out and my gun on him, and the door closed and locked before he knew what had happened. It was five minutes before he recovered enough to speak. He didn't fall to the floor—I guess his head was too thick for that—but he slumped up against the wall and stayed slumped while I lit the gas.

"Howdy, Joe," I says, as I took the blackjack from his useless fingers and chucked it under the bed. And then, while he was recovering his manners, I dumped some water from the pitcher over his head and watched him swim ashore.

"I kill you yet," he says in a feeble voice, as he clutched at his aching head.

I could have laughed, but I didn't; there wasn't time. I saw now that that duck was able to talk and understand me, which was more to the point. I wasn't there for any fooling—not me—he had information that I wanted, and I hadn't passed my word that there'd be no force used.

"Joe," I says, whipping my gun into his stomach. "I want you to blow the whole game—first, where's the girl—quick!"

There was nothing gentle about me then—I'm a different man when it comes to business—that's why I'm a success. I always play that the end justifies the means.

"I tell you nothing!" He pulls himself up straight and folds his arms across his chest. "Your girl, eh—pretty soon they be through with her—and she my girl—the—"

But he never finished that string of dirty epithets. I up with the butt of my gun and gave him a swipe across the face that made his lordly air look mighty cheap. And right here come the tactics that you may not agree with. You may question the ethics, but the results are good. Poor morals perhaps, but good, sound, common sense.

It ain't pretty to tell, so I'll skip over it. But I beat and choked the truth out of him, anyway.

His tongue was hanging out, and he was black in face and pretty near gone when he nodded he'd tell. And tell he did.

"You'd torture that girl," I said. "And I'll torture the whole truth out of you," and I thought of that poor little kid and meant what I said. I don't bluff, and that gink knew it when he opened up.

It was in spasmodic jerks, and between the real fear of me and the imaginary fear of Gustave, he give me the lay of the game. Here's what I get:

In the first place Gustave ain't her uncle at all—his real handle is Boro, and him and her uncle ran a fruit market together down on Mott Street. The uncle had already kicked off when the word came that Nita was coming to America. This Boro got hold of the letter, fixed up the house, and posed as the uncle, whom Nita had never seen. It wasn't hard; he used to write all the letters for her uncle—that bird couldn't read nor write, and didn't feel overproud about letting his family know that America hadn't done much for him.

Nita comes and falls heavy; then comes this Manual Sparo, and things ain't so good; he spots the game at once. But he's a bit of a crook himself and loves Nita, so he offers not to spill the beans if he can marry Nita and connect with half of the formula money with Boro, the fake uncle. The uncle agrees, but Nita ducks on the marriage, and Boro, getting frightened that Manual may cash in on the formula, kidnaps him and tortures him to tell where he's hidden the paper.

Enough of that—he won't tell, and Boro hits on the plan of torturing Nita—for deep down in his black heart, this Manual really loves the girl.

That would hold me for a while—Joe didn't know what the formula was about, but he knew there was much money in it. A final shake and he tells me where the girl is hid. And that stumped me—she was right in that house on Fifty-sixth Street, and they were dead set on getting the formula that night.

The dirty swine; I just looked down at him—if he'd 'a smiled then I'd—but I had seen to it that there wasn't enough left of his map to smile. So I just cracked him over the head once—one good one that would put him to sleep for the rest of the night. I didn't want him to come butting in on the grand finale. Leaving him lying on the floor, I beat it; locked the door on the outside and, slipping the key in my pocket, turned the corner and whistled for Bud.

We sure made time uptown. It would be too late to call for help, and besides, I didn't figure I'd want none. When I left the car on Sixth Avenue, about a block away, I said to Bud:

"Give me an hour, and then if you don't get word from me, why—send the police—tell them it's murder."

"Police! Police!" Bud's mouth opened wide.

"Yes—police," I says. "It's the first time you ever had that kind of an order, but obey it to the letter—let the police know and then beat it."

Not that I thought that there was a chance of failure—I never fail—but that girl was trusting me and I was— But I turned my back on Bud and beat it down Fifty-seventh Street. It was like I was a bit ashamed of showing weakness.

So I pick my distance and make my approach from the other street. I duck through an alleyway, hop a high fence and land in the backyard of the house next door to the gang's. I got to figure out the best way to make it. Oh, I'm going in all right if I have to bust straight through the big French windows in the front with a gun in either mitt. But that's my last stand. I ain't one that goes in for dramatics; not me. I got the two big guns and one little one—the little one I always have—it's a sleeve gun and is used in an emergency; also, I have my flash and am ready for business.

I guess I take about five minutes studying all of them rear windows: I want to make sure that there ain't anyone spying out the back; it don't seem likely, but then I don't take no chances. There are only two lights—one high up which you can hardly see—the other one comes from a window about seven foot from the ground. I think it's the kitchen. Now, there is a water pipe running up to the top light, but I ain't no acrobat. Another look around, and I jump the adjoining fence and land in the yard of the brownstone house.

Edging up close to the back of the house, where a lad at the upper windows couldn't see me without raising one and looking out, I try to peer in the kitchen window, and it's a success; the shade is up just enough to look in under. There's one man in there, a dirty-looking bird, and he's in his shirtsleeves and fiddling around the coal stove.

Now, there ain't no trick ways of entering houses without people knowing it when they are awake—least I don't know of none. Open windows are nice, but you don't find them in a joint like this one. I'm good with a gun, and in my line that's near enough, but I might say that I have brains too and know how crooks think. For another thing, I ain't a lad what waits around all night for what is called an opening. I don't spend the rest of the night planning when some client's life is at stake, not me; I earn my money and act.

So—I just up with my fist and knock lightly on that kitchen window. If that boy goes for help, I'll be in that window before he ever comes back, for there ain't no bars on it. But if he ain't scared and uses his think box, he'll get to figuring that only a friend would knock. And that's what he done—he comes to the window and looks out.

It's dark, and he can't see nothing but my outline, which I stand there and let him see. Then I lift my hand cautiously like and signal him to lift the window. He stands undecided a minute, and then plays into my hand—he opens the window, but I ain't altogether in luck, for he don't stick his head out. He whispers something in Italian. I don't get what it is, but I make a sucking noise which he can take to keep quiet, and I hand him up a slip of paper which I pull out of my pocket. Out comes his hand to grasp it, and then—with all my strength I take hold of his wrist and pull. Say, there ain't a shout out of him as he comes out that window. But there is one unfortunate circumstance which I had hoped to avoid. I don't figure enough on the play of his heels—they crack that windowsill some wallop, but no glass breaks. He don't holler none as he lands; guess he's too surprised, but he sure did kick up the woodwork. One belt on the head, and the cry dies on his lips, and I'm up and over that sill and into the kitchen. Down comes the shade again; from an upper window someone might see the light and the shadow of the limp body on the ground below.

Just a jump and a brace and a swing, and I'm standing in that kitchen; believe me, I didn't waste no time. I wasn't going to get caught half in and half out of that window. Now, if any of them lads wanted to take a potshot at me, well and good—I was ready. Let them come. I was now in a position to return the compliment; in fact, I was perfectly willing to start the show. A fellow don't have to take a shot at me to arouse my interest; you don't have to give me a good moral reason to shoot. Show me the man, and if he's drawing on me and is a man what really needs a good killing, why, I'm the boy to do it.

Well, luck is with me or with them; you can take your choice, for I ain't dodging no gunplay, but there ain't a sound in the house. I'm inside, without anyone being the wiser.

I stand around for several minutes, though, to make sure, and then I hear a tap tap of feet in the room above me—just pounding on the ceiling—slow, like slippered feet that were treading heavily up and down in the same place. It would stop and then go on again, but listen as I would by the kitchen door, there was no other sound of life in the whole house. Still, that didn't mean so much. It was an old house and the walls were thick, and sound don't carry much—but it sure was a deathly stillness and that tap, tap, tap just above me.

I took a look around the kitchen to see if I could find out why that lad was down there, and I did—my heart missed a beat, which is something for my heart to do, I can tell you. What had I seen—well, I had seen two pokers flaming red hot, there in the open stove. Now, if it had 'a been one, it might have been there by accident, just dropped in when I knocked on the window. But two, I knew they were being heated for some purpose, and it was the realization of that purpose which made my heart give a sudden beat and a quick jump. The pokers were to be used to torture the girl and… A sudden scream—a woman's scream of terrible agony or fear came sharply through that heavy silence. I was out in the hall in a moment—it was Nita who had given that piercing shriek.

But I didn't lose my head none. Like a cat I went sneaking up the heavy wooden stairs, my sneakered feet making no sound there in the darkness. Oh, I had my flash, but I didn't use it. I ain't much stuck on suicide.

But the cry don't come again, and I reach the second-floor landing. I grope about in the darkness, following the banister along the hall, for that cry had come from someplace near the top of the house. Then, when I'm about to start that second flight, the tap, tap, tap comes again, and I stop dead listening. The sound is right behind me— just about in the middle of that hallway. Then I turn and catch a tiny speck of light creeping under a doorway. I sneak toward it carefully and listen again—the tapping stopped, but I hear a moaning now, and then a feeble foreign voice.

I push my hand along, feeling for the knob, and my fingers strike a panel—a sliding panel—just a tiny one, like they have in the speakeasies. I work it slowly just a crack and peer in. The room is only lit by a candle, which stands on an old table right in the center of the room; the rest of the place is bare, and then—came the groan again, and I see a figure laying on the hard boards, in one corner of the room.

There ain't a spot in the room for a cat to hide in, so I turn the knob; the door opens and I walk in, shutting it gently behind me. One look and a flash of light tells me that there ain't no cause to fear that gent lying in the corner—his hours are on the run; just another groan, and I don't need to be a doctor to know that that guy is going out.

Right off the bat I spot him as Manual Sparo, and I'm right. He half turns his head, and his eyes are glassy and he don't seem to be sure if there is someone in the room with him or not; then he mutters something, but I don't get him.

"Speak English," I says. I'm none too gentle because it won't do him any good now, and if he has anything to say I want to get it before he slips over.

"I'll tell—I'll tell," he says, in good English. "The girl don't know—I wouldn't tell her. The formula's in one of Boro's books—downstairs—third shelf—Modern Italian Poets. I tell you the girl don't know—spare her."

And his voice is getting louder with the final effort. Partly because I'm afraid he'll spill my chances all over the house, and partly because I fell sorry for the poor cuss, I up and tell him that I'm the rescue party.

At first he don't understand, but then things kind of get into his head and he grabs me by the hand. He knows I'm friendly, and he takes me for his brother back in Naples. So half in English and half in Italian, he gives me a lot of chatter. But I gather enough to learn this: They had carted him down from the Bronx early that morning, and they told him that they would torture the girl if he didn't tell. He wouldn't tell, and they sent the girl in to him; and he started to tell her where the formula was, and then he changed his mind. Some of the birds were trying to listen outside and got enough to make them think that he had told her— that was about two hours ago. He guessed that they were torturing her, and he had been knocking on the floor with his bare feet—he was ready to blow the game and save the girl, which I don't think would have helped her none.

And you should 'a seen him; his whole body had been hacked at, and his feet and hands burnt to the bone; he had grit, that boy—they didn't get nothing out of him, with all their deviltry. Yep, he had grit and bullheaded stupidity.

Now, you see, I just about did the right thing when I choked the truth out of that murdering villain a short while before—this was no crowd to fool with.

"How many are there in the house?" I said, lifting up his head so that he could breathe better. "How many?" I repeated again a bit louder, and then I look down at him.

There I'd been, listening to his story and trying to ease him up a bit and—well—he had gone out on me—living through all that he did, and then kicking off sudden like that. But I just shrug my shoulders—I can't expect all the luck—the poor devil was better off; he'd never have walked again anyway; that was certain. I let him down easy; he was a bad egg, but way down in his black heart he had loved the girl, and even if it was a selfish love, why—oh, well, I let him slip down to the boards easy.

I straightened up for one last look around that room, and then that shriek—that terrible cry—came again, a bit longer, more penetrating and piercing. This time I didn't wait to take things easy; I just dashed out of that room and up the stairs, my flash going full blast. And it was a good thing I had it, too, for it shines right on a lad sitting on the top of the stairs. Oh, he fired—yes—and I don't know what kind of a shot he was under ordinary circumstances. My light, a mighty powerful one, too, had struck him right between the eyes, and he didn't see none too well, or he shot in a hurry. Anyway, he only shot once—none never do shoot more than once at me. I guess our guns spoke together. I felt nothing and I didn't need to give a second look to him. When I fire, there ain't no guessing contest as to where that bullet is going. Often I poke for the heart, 'specially if there is any distance to cover; its surer. But this was shooting uphill like, and the light was directly on his face, so I let him have it there—someplace about the center of that ugly map of his.

There ain't much to that sort of shooting; you just kind of see a hole for a second; a tiny speck of red, and then the face fades out of the picture. So I just step over him as he rolls down the stairs.

Of course the shot is heard, and another bimbo ducks out of a side room, just as I make the landing. He don't do no shooting—he don't even get a look—just a spurt of flame and I get him. He falls pretty, blocking the doorway which someone is trying to close, but having no luck. And then for the fireworks!

I got the jump on them now; I've made a mighty good impression, and it'll have a good moral effect; there is nothing like following it up. Two of them dead—oh, they're dead all right—none ever come back and

fire just one more shot after I plug them. Once I hit a lad, he stays put. So I jump to the door, kick it flying, and, dropping my flash, I stand there a gun in either fin.

And then things ain't so good; to this day I can't explain how they happened to be so well prepared. I just stand there like the avenging angel, with a smile of greeting, when something like a ton of brick comes down and cracks me on the head. I remember firing at a sneering brown face and muttering number three as the clouds come down—after that, curtains—everything goes black.

How long, I don't know, but I come to after a bit and sit up. I ain't tied or nothing—just dazed—I see near a million stars and then I see worse. Over in one corner of the room I see Nita, and she's bound hand and foot on a bare hard bed. There's Boro and another lad close beside him, and one stretched dead out in the center of the floor—so I figure that even with the weight on my head, my aim was good because he ain't dressed like the bird I copped in the doorway.

And Boro is playing the game hard now, and there ain't no smile on that mean, wicked kisser of his. He has a gat stuck close up against my chest, which don't give me much of a chance even if I did feel like pulling something—which I don't. It's a good thought, but my brains are dusty—hitting on one cylinder like. But there's one thing they overlooked, one thing what brings a gleam of hope. They got both my big guns, yes—but their search hadn't been a good one, or was it the way I was lying? Yep, tucked up my sleeve is still the little automatic twenty-five; it's little, yes, but as I get the feel of it there, it seems as big as a cannon. Just let me get my head clear and give me a chance to drop my hands, and those birds will receive a treat—a little treat what they won't enjoy long.

I can shoot in a split second on an open draw—none faster. I'll pull a gun with anyone, even if he comes from the cow country; and I'll beat him to the draw too—there ain't no two ways about that. But on the sleeve business—oh, I'm fast—like lightning—but it takes a second, a whole second, and that's some time in a matter of life and death. But to pull my arm down and shoot takes one full second; I know, I've timed it.

But Boro has that gun bored into my chest and my hands shoved up in the air; through instinct, I guess, for there ain't no will to hold them there, for I don't hardly know what I'm doing. But I was trying to

think—place exactly where I was—what was happening—and behind it all was the reassuring pressure of hard steel just below the elbow.

"Get up!" says Boro, and though his hand is steady, his voice trembles with rage.

And I get up. I can see he's mighty willing to shoot and wonder why he don't. Then he backs me up against the wall.

"You say everything is all clear downstairs, Pedro, and that no one heard the shots," he says to the only other lad left, but he keeps his gun and his eyes on me while he talks. I guess his English is for my benefit, though why he wants to shower me with happiness, I don't know.

"No one heard," Pedro answers, and his English is punk.

"Go fetch some rope," Boro chirps, "and we'll tie up this swine—but first—well, you shall see something amusing when you return, Pedro—and Pedro, another hot poker—very hot—it is for his eyes."

So Pedro beats it. Well, you don't need three guesses to tell you that I'm going to take chances at the first opportunity, or without any opportunity, for that matter.

Boro holds me, with his gun, against the wall a moment, and then he backs away about three paces.

"You are one who shoots well, but so do I," he sneers. "Watch—first I will cripple you. The arms and then the legs—a bullet for each; and then when Pedro returns, it will be the eyes, but that will not be so pleasant—you would play a game with Boro, eh?"

Get what he was up to; why, he'd just stand me against the wall and wing me, and then burn out my eyes. I tried to think. I said to myself, now or never, and did nothing. I was like a man in a dream, and a mighty bad dream—just acting mechanically.

Bang! He had fired. There was a sear of red hot flame just below the elbow, and my left arm dropped to my side. I heard Boro laugh and Nita give a little smothered cry—just the quick intake of breath.

As the blood streamed down onto my wrist, my head seemed to clear, and then my brain hit suddenly back to normal. I was Terry Mack again, and believe me that is something.

Bang! The report came again and I thought it was too late, but no—his bullet had jammed against the hard steel of my little twenty-five, without ever touching my arm.

I don't know if he saw me smile as my right hand started to slink to my side. I think he did, for he was suddenly raising his gun again when I fired. But he never used it; Boro had fired his last shot.

The tiny splash of red appeared for a moment between his eyes; he stood so, his great eyes bulging in surprise more than pain—the surprise of death—then without a groan or a cry he pitched his length upon the floor. He didn't roll over and give a last convulsive groan or a kick—some may do it—none that I ever hit at that range. Boro died standing; died before he fell, and when he fell, there was not so much as a wiggle of his fingers.

As he hit them boards, the door opened and Pedro appeared for a moment in the aperture—but only for a moment. Why I didn't wing him I don't know—but he was gone—whining like a dog as he ran down the stairs, and that was the last I ever heard of Pedro. Of course I bolted the door before I went over to the girl. And I spotted the weight, too, which had put me out of business—it was fixed so that the rope didn't loosen it from the ceiling until someone pressed a catch near the door. Oh, it was good stuff all right, and I admired the pretty way it was pulled off.

I guess I must have staggered across to the girl—my arm didn't bother me none, but my head had gotten about as big as a church again. But somehow I released her. It seemed like I was two persons, and I'd ask my other self what I'd do, and my other self would answer me. Like this it went:

"Any now, Terry, my boy, what's on the program—they've all gone, you know."

And then I'd answer:

"Get a knife, Mack—there's one in the corner there—and cut the rope."

And I did, and afterward Nita told me that I talked to myself like a man in a fever. It was then that I told her about Boro not being her uncle at all, and about Manual being dead, and all that I had learned from Daggo Joe. But I never mentioned the formula; somehow I kept that to myself. And she wasn't hurt at all. Her feet were all right, for they had only just started the torture and hardly touched her tender skin. She had cried out more in deadly fear than in pain—but her mental suffering must have been terrible just the same.

It was she who took the chances, while I just sat there on the floor and mumbled to myself; she went downstairs and got water and bathed my head and tied up my arm, which proved to be only a flesh wound, and not much to bother about at that.

And then, when I come about all right, she turned around and fainted on me. I tell you it was a tough proposition, there with her in that house of death. But I was as clear as a bell now; it's wonderful what water will do for a man, and I tell you it's been a good friend to me in many an emergency.

Water helped her, too, and just as I got her able to sit up and was thinking of helping her downstairs, there came a ringing at the doorbell, followed by a heavy pounding on the door. I left her a moment and, opening the door, listened. The rapping came again, louder than before; and then came the crash of an ax, and I remembered—the hour was more than up and Bud had sent for the police. Good old Bud—I felt like wringing his neck; I wanted to do some talking with a first-class lawyer before I paid my social obligations to the police.

I turned to the window and looked out—there was the lead pipe, the one I couldn't climb up, but I felt that even with my bad arm I could slide down it— especially now that I had the proper incentive behind me. You see, this was no kind of a situation for Terry Mack to be found in. The girl would be all right—they couldn't possibly suspect her of all that slaughter.

"It's the police," I told her in a hurry. "You'll be all right, but for me—a quick getaway. You can tell them about me, but I'll hang low till my lawyer has proven a case against this gang. If they got me, they'd frame me sure—they love me like poison—you'll be O.K. Nita—I'm going to duck."

And then she up and staggered across the room and threw her arms about my neck and hung there; in fact, I had to hold her—she was so weak that her hands couldn't even retain their grasp about my neck.

"Don't leave me, Terry—you're all I got—and the police—oh, Terry, I'll die if you leave me."

And that shows you what fear of the police the fake uncle had instilled in her.

And right there is another thing that I can't explain. Maybe it's weakness, but I like to think it ain't, though I can't account for it. You might think that I had done enough for this girl and earned my pay—well, perhaps I had. But there was soft little hands about my neck and silken hair against my cheek—great innocent, childish eyes looking through pools of water into mine—and—well, I stayed—yep, I just played the fool and stayed.

So it was I held her in my arms when half a dozen cops busted into the room.

My cap is still sticking on my head, and I retain sense enough to pull it down close to my eyes.

Then there is questions and warnings and one thing and another. But I don't need no warning—my trap is shut tight—I'll have my mouthpiece when I do any talking, and he's a good lawyer, too. As for the girl, well, she opens up a bit but don't say nothing about the formula, which I think is wise but don't get her real reason for it; though I put it down to the money what's behind it, and her distrust of the police. And I tell you another thing—they are some surprised cops after they look that house over. I hear some of them in the backyard, where they have found the first lad what I socked.

Then in walks Detective Sergeant Quinn, and I know that things are going to get lively. This same Quinn has been trying to hook something on me since George Washington was a boy.

"And the story goes that this one man killed these four—pretty thin," he says, and then he walks over to me. "We'll just have a look at that mug of yours, my man."

With that he jerks off my cap, and me and Quinn look straight at each other.

"Good evening, Sergeant." I can't help but grin. Quinn's fizz is a scream.

"Terry Mack! Terry Mack!" he says twice as he steps back, but he can't hide the feeling of joy that comes over him. "Well, after all it does look like it might be a one-man job—with Mack that man," he says to one of his men. "Hooked at last!" His ugly face screws up in satisfaction. "We'll trot this pair out—separate them—you can keep the girl here until after the coroner comes. But keep your eye on her, and trot this fellow along."

Just as the cop comes up to me with the cuffs in his mitts, I turn to the girl!

"If you have any friends, know of anyone in the city that can help us—now's the time—we're in bad."

And I meant every word of it. I knew the police system, and knew that they'd put me through the jumps before I ever got my lawyer.

Nita seemed to recover somewhat.

"I know one who would help me—who would do anything that I ask. Can—how can I get him?" She was looking at the ceiling while she talked.

That's what I wanted; I wanted her request registered while all them cops were in the room. One of them would be looking for Quinn's job, and if Quinn did anything to hamper the cause of justice, one of them might be glad to blow it—secretly.

"Quick," I says. "Who do you know—who that can help us on the outside?"

"I know Mr. James Roland Williams," she said quietly, though her voice shook a bit. "I think he would do anything for me."

Quinn drew back; I gasped! And why not? James Roland Williams was the commissioner of police.

"Well—well—we'll see about that in the morning." But I noticed that Quinn's voice lacked its usual air of authority.

"How about it now—Quinn?" I chimed in. "This young lady is not used to being treated like a common crook, and from what I know of her friendship with Mr. Williams, it might cost you your shield."

Of course, I didn't know nothing about it, but it didn't strike me as a good time to show my ignorance.

Quinn just scowled at me and told me to hold my tongue, then he turned to the girl. Her honest, quiet air of refinement evidently impressed him.

"Do you know him very well—Miss?" He added the "Miss" after a moment's hesitation.

"Oh yes—I should say—oh, very well indeed." She nodded her head.

"Well enough to disturb him at this hour of the morning?" Quinn bent those hard, stern eyes of his full upon her. "You know, he only got back from a trip south last night."

"No—I did not know that. But it does not matter. He would be glad to come to me at any hour—he has told me so—told me—oh, please call him." Her voice broke.

Another glance, and Quinn turned toward the door. He paused undecided a moment, and then:

"Who shall I say—what name?" he said, and his manner was almost courteous.

"Sen—Miss Nita Gretna—Nita will be enough—he will come at once." There was a certain calm dignity in her manner.

One more close scrutinizing look, and Quinn turned again and left the room.

"And make it snappy, Quinn, even if you are getting a bit on for so many stairs."

I could not resist the temptation to call after him as he descended the stairs. I could see now that pretty soon everything would be jake, and I'd be the light-haired boy; a commissioner has a way of hushing up unpleasant events. Of course, I never doubted the girl—just one look at those clear, honest glims of hers was enough to convince anyone.

It was five minutes later when Quinn returned, and although he had run up the stairs his face was white—white with anger.

"Take them away!" he roared. "Keep them apart—watch that girl." He pointed a finger which shook with rage at Nita. "What do you mean by lying to me—Mr. Williams never heard of you. And he had other things to say to me, things that you'll pay for, my fine girl. Take them away!" he spoke to his men. "And keep an eye on that gunman—Terry Mack." With that, he showed us the width of his shoulders as he stamped viciously from the room.

As for me, I didn't look at the girl—she must'a felt pretty cheap, I thought. But what a superb bluff she had made! That innocent-appearing kid had looked the tough Quinn straight between the eyes and handed him out that earful of bull—and me—oh, I fell for it too.

But I shrugged my shoulders as they slipped on the bracelets and led me away.

"Holler for the best lawyer you can get," I called back over my shoulder to Nita. "We'll see it through together if they don't railroad me. And if you need any money, why—why, I got a bit saved up."

And that last line will pretty near show you that my head wasn't altogether clear yet.

And there you are; I spent the night behind bars. I didn't like the ride they give me neither. I should have been taken to an uptown station, but they booked me further downtown, which sure did look bad. You see, I had a sneaking fear that they might jump me through the hoop; there were several little things that the bulls would have liked to have gotten out of me. I ain't afraid of nothing, mind you, but I was a bit worried; this third degree which you hear so much about ain't all wind—not by a jugful it ain't. I know them birds.

Of course, I was searched all right, but there wasn't a thing on me. I had dropped that sleeve gun when the cops broke in the door, and frisking me was about as exciting as searching a Sunday school superintendent. But this Quinn was a lad who would railroad a bishop, if he felt like it, and—and I ain't no bishop.

A cop what knows something about medicine looks over my arms and sniffs at the wound and says it ain't nothing—so I don't even see a doctor. But I guess he's right, and although it smarts a bit, there ain't much to it as for my head—well, it's a pretty tough head, and I ain't looking for any sympathy, and what's more I don't get any.

I slept pretty well, though, for I felt they'd be too busy to put over any rough stuff that morning; just like a baby I sleep until breakfast. The turnkey was agreeable, and I got a pretty good breakfast. But I didn't like the idea of eating there—I should 'a been brought before a magistrate—the whole thing didn't look good.

At eleven o'clock a dick comes to my door and has it opened and smiles in at me:

"Come on Terry," he says. He's grinning from ear to ear and looks real friendly, which, of course, makes me suspicious. But he walks me right out of the side door of the jail and lands me on the street. Then he hands me out my things that they took from me when I was booked.

"You're sure in luck this time, Terry," he says. "You fitted in right last night, and Quinn is having forty fits—that car there is waiting for you." And he indicates a big touring car with the jerk of his thumb. "Good luck, Terry, you're a game boy, if a tough citizen, and I don't hold anything against you."

I take his outstretched fist and turn toward the car like I had expected it to be there; they ain't going to faze me.

"Good-bye and thanks—" I wave to the dick from the backseat.

"Casey's my name," he says, "Richard Casey!"

"Casey it is."

I shake again as the car speeds away. Then I look around a bit to get my breath; it's an expensive car all right, and there ain't no one but me and the driver. But the chauffeur don't seem to need any instructions, so I don't say anything. Just sit tight; that's my game.

Right up to the restaurant entrance of the Bolton Hotel we pull, and I hop out as live as life. I even start to enter the front door when a great big strapping boy of about twenty-five comes running out and grabs me by the hand.

"Mr. Mack—Mr. Terry Mack!" He smiles all over as he pump-handles me. "I'm James Williams—James Roland Williams, Jr. How's the arm?" he asks suddenly.

I almost forget myself for the moment:

"You're the police commissioner's son!" I guess I kind of gasp.

"That's it," he laughed. "Nita has told me all about you. She forgot the Junior last night when she rang up. You see, father was south when I returned from Italy, and I didn't get a chance to tell him the good news. Besides, there really wasn't any until this morning. Nita slipped away from me on the dock; she was to let me hear from her when she would say yes. She said it this morning."

He laughed again.

But I was to lunch with him and Nita, and there she was, waiting for us in a little private dining room upstairs. She didn't seem much the worse for last night. Young Williams said he wouldn't let her remember; he'd keep her going under high pressure until she forgot. Of course, his old man would see that everything was fixed up properly, and not a reporter had found out who had done the bumping off, nor that Nita was mixed up in it. The papers had just set it down for a general feeling of discontent among the Black-Handers.

And then I learned that he had met Nita on the boat, and that a wedding was all cooked up for the next day.

"It'll just be a quiet affair." Williams smiles all over his good-natured map. "Nita don't know anyone but you, so you'll have to show up." Then he tells me the church, and both of them get my promise to be on deck at eleven the next morning.

"Yes," she looks up at me from across the table, and I notice that there are dark rings under her eyes and that her fingers are twitching nervously. "We must have you Terry—it could not be a wedding without you and—oh—that old formula." She half closes her eyes. "I guess that it is gone forever."

And that's where I shine once again:

"Oh, is it?" I said. "Not so you could notice it—it ain't. Miss Nita, I was hired by you to get that formula, and I most generally get what I go after."

Then I turn to young Williams. I don't give him no information, but just make him promise to go and bring that copy of poems about them Italians to me, without opening the book, and I give him full instruction as to the lay of the book.

It ain't nothing to him, being the commissioner's son, to step right in and turn the trick, and in a half-hour or less he's back with the book. I open it, and there's the envelope. I guess I play the actor a bit when I hand it over to Nita, unopened. There sure was a certain air of satisfaction in that delivery.

Do their eyes open? Well, I should smile; Nita breaks the seal and opens it. She reads it a minute and then chirps:

"That is it." And leaning over the table she takes a match and lights the thin tissuey paper that she holds in her hand. We just sit and stare as she drops it in the plate—a burnt, blackened, unrecognizable mass.

At first I just scratch my head; it's like seeing all your good work literally going up in smoke. Then curiosity gets the better of me for once, and I break my rule about not asking questions.

"Would you mind telling me what it was?" I can't help but ask; you must remember that at least five met their deaths on account of that same piece of paper.

She gives a wan little smile:

"All I know is that it is a formula—a chemical for making poison gas—a gas far stronger and more deadly than any used in the last war, or ever invented. I understand that a small quantity dropped in a container, from a plane, would be enough to wipe out hundreds upon hundreds of people. It may be worth much money, and I do not doubt that it is—but—but it is worth more to humanity there in that dish." And she stirs up the ashes with her spoon.

Personally, I don't take much stock in such sentiment, and I look at Williams to see how he's taking it. But he's only looking at her, cowlike and grinning. Well, he's either dough-heavy or he's in love—or I guess both, for he looks like money and I think the car is his.

And then when I'm leaving them, Nita up and throws her arms about me and kisses me—yes, kisses me full on the lips.

"Oh, Terry, Terry," she says and her voice breaks a little, "you've been more than a father to me—much more."

More than a father! Grandfather, she must mean. But I don't say that. I look at Williams to see how he's taking it, but it seems that his only aim in life is to carry a perpetual grin, which he does to the queen's taste.

"There—there! Be a good girl," is all I say as I pat her on the back. And wasn't that a fool remark for a full-grown man with all his senses!

So I left them.

I guess it's near three o'clock when I see Bud and wrap myself into my easy chair. You see, my arm's all right, but I feel like taking it easy. And then along about eight that night Bud brings me in a envelope.

It's a check, and a good big one; I can see at a glance that everything has been taken into account, and she ain't forgotten the little matter of the four lads what got bumped off. And then the bonus—guess the extra was for Boro. But the check was big—very big—yet I can't honestly say that it was more than I was worth.

So I smoke and think; after all, it was an American that she loved and she hadn't fooled me none. Well, that little garden and the sunny sky of Italy had all gone blooey. I stood up and looked at myself in the glass—not a gray hair appeared—so she might have spared me that father scene. Did I feel bad—not me. I was mighty relieved; for a time, it looked like that dame was going to hook herself onto me for life. With a shrug of my shoulders, I picked up my hat and coat.

And how did I take it? Why, like the gentleman that I am. I just went out and bought her the very best wedding present that the swellest pawnshop in the city could produce. And believe me, that little gift, marked with the best wishes of Terry Mack, would hold its own alongside of anything that she got.

NOBODY'S FALL GUY

by Frederick Nebel

1. Something Special

MAYBE IT was her voice I fell for.

I hung up and said to Marge, "You sign those letters, kid, and lock up."

She looked up without stopping the typewriter and said, "I thought you didn't go out on jobs after five."

"This is something special," I told her.

"I could see that by the grin on your face."

"You're wise, you are."

"Any time there's a woman client it's something special."

I pulled a grin, said, "Sour grapes."

"Says you. Says I: A jane with you usually gets a hundred-dollar job done for half price—if she's pretty."

I crossed the room, picked up the Homburg and put it on. I passed back of her on the way out, poked her between the shoulders. "Toodle-oo, kid."

"I'm still waiting for that raise," she said.

Going down the corridor toward the elevator, I could hear her typewriter rattling on.

It was half past five. Forty-Second Street was crowded, and there was a nice smell after the rain. I ducked beneath the Sixth Avenue Elevated, fought the crowd to Times Square and jammed into a West Side subway express. I got off at Seventy-Second Street, walked over to West End Avenue and turned north.

The Hudson Arms had its name raised in bronze on either side of glass swing doors three marble steps from the sidewalk. I pushed one of the doors in and walked through the lobby on black and white tiles. An elevator full of mirrors took me to the fourth floor, and I walked down a quiet corridor on a carpet that was soft and resilient. No. 440 was at the end, and I raised a knocker shaped like a harp.

She fitted her voice. She was tall and lean-hipped and looked pliant in a pale blue peignoir. Her hair was blue-black and clung to her head like a silk helmet, tight over the ears, revealing just the lobes. Her face was shell-pink, angular but pretty, and her eyes were dark and luminous.

"You hurried," she said.

"It wasn't far."

Little oval-shaped sidelights glowed in pairs on the walls, though it was still light out. She closed the door and asked for my hat and I gave it to her. She put it on a console and I sat down at one side of a maroon divan. She joined me there.

"I'm so glad you came," she said.

We lit cigarettes from the same match.

"You'll be honest with me," she said after a slow puff.

"Of course."

She regarded me with wide open eyes that looked troubled and at the same time candid.

"It's about my husband."

"Before you begin, Mrs. Cassilly, I don't take cases that have to do with getting evidence to be used in a divorce action—"

She raised a hand. "Oh, it's not that—not that at all."

"Then be frank with me."

She kept staring at me—candidly. "Then I'll tell you. It's about my husband, as I said—Rupert Cassilly. Maybe you can help me, maybe you can't. I've thought it all out, however, and I think perhaps you can. I hope you can.

"You see, we're from Indianapolis. We've been in New York several weeks, though the Lord knows we should have been on our way long ago. That's the trouble. Rupert came into quite a bit of money and it's gone to his head. He's been gambling and drinking and then—three days ago—we had an argument. He packed a bag and went off to another hotel. You understand?"

"I think I do. You want to get your husband back."

She brightened, but a tremor still touched her voice when she went on: "Yes—yes, that's it. But not quite all. I not only want to get him back; I want to get him out of New York—to-night. Every night since we've been here he's come home terribly drunk. So drunk that he would fall in the door and go to sleep right on the carpet. Until, of course, he got angry and moved.

"Please believe me—I want to save him. I want to get him out of this city. We were on our way to Maine, to spend a couple of months there. We're driving, you see. Do you think you can help me?"

"I don't know yet. Where does he go?"

"That's what I must tell you. It's a gambling place on Lexington Avenue, just south of Grand Central Station. He goes there every night. He told me about it. They have roulette and other games and they have a bar, too. He's been losing frightfully. And he'll make an acquaintance on the slightest provocation.

"Now this is what I'd like to have you do. I'd like to have you get him out of there—to-night. It will be easy for you to strike up an acquaintance. He'll be drunk. In fact, to-night he must be drunk. You must get him out of there, get him in a taxicab, and meet me at a rendezvous. I'll have our car, and all the baggage. We'll put him in the car and then I'll start for the Boston Road. I

can be in Boston by morning, and if I get him that far I'm sure I can get him on to Maine. Do you think it's foolish of me?"

Emotion pulsed in her voice. She was massaging her palms together nervously. Marge was right. I fall for a pretty face. And this girl was not only pretty; she was trying to keep her marriage out of shoal water.

"Have you got the address of this joint?" I asked.

"Yes. And I have one of the cards. Rupert left it lying around. I guess you have to have a card to get in."

She got up and went to a secretary and came back holding a small white card. It had *Albert* engraved on it, and down in the right-hand corner was the address. On the back was scrawled a combination of initials I could not make out. But I knew the place. I knew Albert, who was not Albert but Nick Apostos, a fancy Greek. But I took the card anyhow.

She was regarding me with an expectant look. "Will—will you?"

I fingered the card, thinking. I'd been in Nick's place before. I knew his reputation. To fool around with Nick usually meant trouble, though ordinarily he wasn't a bad guy.

The woman was saying, "I so want to save Rupert from himself. He's really just a boy—just a boy."

"Where would you meet me?"

"Well, I thought somewhere on Riverside Drive—say at Ninetieth Street. I'll park a block down and when I see you get out with him I'll drive up to meet you. I'm all packed. You can ring me when to start."

"Have you a picture of him?"

She went into the bedroom and returned with a picture of a good-looking blond-haired man of about twenty-five. I studied it and then handed it back, stood up and crossed to the console to get my hat. I turned and looked at her and she seemed to be half smiling with a kind of subdued ecstasy.

"You think you can do it?"

"Maybe," I said. "Anyhow, I'll call you."

"Oh, thank you—thank you! And—and how much will—"

I thought of Marge and compromised. "It may be dangerous, Mrs. Cassilly, I think it's worth seventy-five—if I get him out. You can give me twenty on account."

She gave me two tens. "Oh, I hope it will work! If I stay here much longer I'll go crazy! I've got to do something. And I'll give you the rest at the rendezvous."

"Swell," I said.

2. The Bird with the Mustache

I BACHED in an old brownstone in Sixty-Fifth Street, between Ninth Avenue and Central Park. One big living room that at night became a bedroom.

Knowing Nick's, I put on a tux. There was no hurry. I went down to Forty-Eighth Street, just east of Sixth, and put on the feed bag at Mme. Paul's. Paul died a couple of years ago, but his wife still carries on. The Martini was good, the antipasto better, the Sauterne doubtful. I killed an hour over two tots of Martel and a cigar and told Mme. Paul she was looking great. She gave me a drink on the house and I breezed.

I walked across town and reached the address at ten thirty. It was a gray-faced house of four stories with a vestibule. The vestibule door was open. The inner door was locked. I pressed a button and after half a minute the door opened and I saw a white shirt-front and a Jap face above it. I handed the Jap the card and he let me in.

He took my hat and gave me a check. I climbed a staircase that had a broad, shiny balustrade, and began to hear voices. Double doors were open on the second floor, and I saw one end of a bar with high stools in front of it. Five men were at the bar; none interested me. There was a room beyond, heavily draped, where a few men and women were drinking at tables.

I looked in casually and then came back to the bar. The barman mixed me a brandy-and-soda and I took my time with it. I was lighting a cigarette, looking in the mirror behind the bar, when Nick Apostos came in. He touched my elbow.

"Hello, Nick," I said.

"Hello. You working for the Watch and Ward Society?"

"In these pants?"

He didn't look pleased. He was a chunky little Greek, big-nosed, and used oil on his thinning black hair. He had sagging, dull eyes and dead-white skin and wore black pearl studs in his front.

"I don't like having you here, Gallagher," he said.

I took it as a joke. "You'll get to like me, Nick. I really have personality once you get to know me."

"I don't care for personality. A guy needs more than case-dough to hang around here."

"I had some luck bulling the market."

Two guys at the end of the bar were watching us. They looked like a couple of torpedoes to me. Well, that was all right by me. If trouble broke, I knew where to expect it from.

"Have a drink, Nick."

"I don't drink." He put a white index finger against my lower stud. "Remember, I got no use for a private shamus. All you guys are rotten. And none of you guys make enough dough to play in my scatter."

"Be reasonable, Nick."

"Just blow wise," he said, and went into the room off the bar.

The two torpedoes at the end of the bar looked after him. One went into the room, came back to the bar, muttered something to his partner. They gave me a sliding look and then started rolling poker dice.

I finished the brandy-and-soda and figured that things weren't going to be la-de-da. The gambling rooms were upstairs. The first room I drifted into was large and hung with purple drapes. There were two roulette wheels and the upper East Side was well represented. There were as many women as there were men grouped around the whirring wheels.

Cassilly was there—a tall guy in evening clothes, good-looking in a lean, greyhound way, even if he bagged a bit under the eyes. A slab of blond hair lay down over one temple. He wasn't strictly sober. He was kidding a fat woman beside him. He didn't look like a bad guy. I drifted through the chemin de fer room, through another room where they were shooting craps; came back to the roulette tables.

With fifty bucks in my pocket I felt like a piker. But I bought ten dollars worth of chips and played the corners conservatively.

I lost the ten and bought more and then won thirty dollars with a load on number twenty-five. Cassilly lost like nobody's business, good-naturedly. I was at his elbow.

I put five chips on twenty-five and said offhand, "This for the wife in Indianapolis."

"Say, you come from Indianapolis?' "

"Just outside of it."

"Say, that's great!"

Five minutes later we went down to the bar. A lean, hard-faced guy with a thin, black mustache crossed eyes with me as I guided Cassilly to the stairs. But he looked away quickly. I didn't figure him in Nick's spread.

Cassilly ordered a Bacardi cocktail. It can put a man under quicker than any drink I know of. His wife was right; he was a kid, a big, overgrown kid whooping it up in the big town. I couldn't help liking him. Even when he started to bawl.

It was about his wife. He wasn't doing right by his wife. He was gambling and drinking and he'd had a fight with his wife, and he was playing around with other women. He was a cur. He was sorry he had ever left Indianapolis. He worshiped the ground his wife walked on. He rambled on, maudlin. I kept ordering Bacardi cocktails for him.

"Call me Rupe—just poor old Rupe."

He was calling me Jake.

Nick butted in. "Mr. Cassilly—"

"Lemme alone. Lemme alone with my old pal Jake."

I grinned at Nick. "You see, I have friends."

Nick looked surprised. But he seemed to feel better when he walked away.

The guy with the black mustache came into the bar and stood at the other end, near the two torpedoes. He took whisky straight. We crossed eyes in the mirror sometimes. I was trying to figure him out. I couldn't.

At a quarter past twelve Cassilly was wabbling. He was perspiring and he kept dragging his hand across his face.

"How about some fresh air?"

He blinked, nodded. I told him to hang onto the bar a minute and then went into a telephone booth. The nice voice answered, and I told her to be at the rendezvous in fifteen minutes. She said she would.

I got Cassilly off the stool and steered him toward the corridor. Nick ran into us.

"He needs air, Nick," I said. "I'll walk him around the block or take him home."

Nick shrugged, scowled, and went past.

We got our hats in the hall downstairs and the Jap let us out. I had to grip Cassilly's arm firmly. His legs buckling and he was no half-pint to begin with. But I walked him half a dozen blocks across town to kill time. He was practically asleep on his feet. He fell into a cab and I had to heave him up to the seat. We headed up the West Side.

I lit a cigarette and felt better.

We struck the Drive at Seventy-Second Street and hummed north. There were lights on the river, and lights kept blinking high up on the Jersey shore. The boy friend was sound asleep, snoring.

The cab drew up at the southeast corner of Ninetieth Street and I paid the fare. Then I had a time lugging Cassilly out. He was a dead weight on me. The cab driver grinned, got into gear and went off.

Cassilly wanted to sit down on the curb. I held him up, looking south, waiting for the car. Then I saw one pulling in. It was a Packard sedan. I was holding Cassilly with both arms. His legs had given way.

The car stopped. The front door swung open and a man jumped out, tugging at his pocket.

I dropped Cassilly and went for my gun. I wasn't quick enough. The guy's automatic jabbed me in the stomach.

"Easy, you!" he muttered.

Two other guys jumped out and grabbed hold of Cassilly, swung him into the car. They came back toward me.

"Get in, you!" the guy with the gun said.

"Look here, you punks," I began.

A blackjack put my lights out. But not before I recognized the man at the wheel.

He was the bird with the black mustache I'd been wondering about down in Nick Apostos's.

3. Escape

I BEGAN to hear wind rushing by, and the sound of tires on a cement road. I was on the floor of the car, gagged, blindfolded, my hands manacled behind my back. That made it uncomfortable. I was lying on my side, knees up against my chest, unable to move because of other legs and another body. When. I tried to move somebody put a foot on my neck and forced me down roughly.

It was no bed of roses. Cassilly and I must have been tailed from Nick's, But what, about Cassilly's wife? Perhaps she hadn't told me everything. Maybe she knew Cassilly was in danger, danger other than a constitutional one caused by dissipation. Maybe Nick was in on it. Maybe my phone call to Mrs. Cassilly had been tapped by some one in Nick's scatter. One thing was certain; they had had designs on Cassilly before to-night.

But why was I dragged along?

The road became less smooth. No cement beneath the wheels now. Old macadam, full of patches and inequalities. A woods road, because I could hear the echoes of the engine thrown back in a way peculiar to a narrow woods road. Twenty minutes or so of this. Then the car slowed down, made a sharp turn, and the tires turned muffled in soft dirt, the car lurched slowly. Then it stopped.

The men moved, spoke in low-clipped voices. A hand shoved me, a voice said, "Come on, you, get out."

I fumbled my way out of the car. A hand gripped my arm and I stood motionless in low grass, and I could smell the lush dampness of earth.

"You'll have to carry that souse."

"Okay. We'll carry him… You got that guy?"

The hand tightened on me. "Yeah. Go ahead, you guys."

"Dead drunk… He's pie-eyed, this guy."

The hand jerked my arm. "Walk, you."

We walked on a dirt road or path and then across cinders. The man who guided me began to jangle keys.. We entered a door and there was an old smell—old wood, old dust. Boards creaked under our feet. We climbed a staircase; another. My guide unlocked a door, gave me a shove. I staggered, struck something, slammed to the floor and thought it just as well to stay there.

I heard shades being pulled down. Heard the snap of a match. Footsteps came toward me. The gag and blindfold were removed. I was in a small dusty room and there was a candle burning,

"Goin' to lay there all night?"

I turned my head and saw a big, leather-faced man looking down at me. I got up and flexed my muscles and looked around. The candle was on an old-fashioned washstand. There was an old four-poster against the wall with nothing but a battered mattress on it. I could hear wind in trees; it sounded lonely. Frogs were croaking somewhere.

The big man had cold, steady eyes that looked white and were probably light blue.

"How about a butt?" I said.

He had a mirthless grin, cold as his pale, hard eyes. He stuck a cigarette between my lips, struck a match. I puffed up. The cold grin faded, but a look of indecent humor lingered. He turned and went to the door, stepped out, closed the door, locked it.

After a minute I moved to one of the two windows and edged the shade aside with my shoulder. It was moonlight. There were dark woods beyond a field where tall grass and weeds grew. There was a big barn. The croaking of the frogs made it all desolate and for a moment I had slow chills moving up and down my spine and the hair stood up on the back of my neck.

I smoked the cigarette down, spat it to the floor, stepped on it. I went over and crawled on the four-poster, wriggled to the side against the wall and sat propped against the wall. I had no idea where the house was; no idea how far we had come; no idea what it was all about. The manacles made me mad. I hadn't a ghost of a show.

The sound of voices startled me. They were in the room below. I couldn't make out any words, but there was no mistaking Cassilly's voice. It was strident now, angry, aggressive. He was probably indignant. He looked like a guy who would be indignant. There was a crash, like a piece of furniture going over. Then complete silence. Then a low muttering voice—not Cassilly's.

I fell asleep later and sunlight woke me up in the morning. Through the window I could see the yard and the ramshackle barn and the fields that once must have been farmland. But I saw no road, no other house. My walking up and down must have attracted some attention. The pale-eyed man came in with a mug of black coffee and a couple of hunks of bread. He drew a gun, unlocked the manacles.

"This is sure a horse on me," I said.

"Eat that."

He leaned against the door holding the gun. I ate the bread and drank the coffee.

"What have you heels done to the boy friend downstairs?" I asked.

"He's funny, he is."

"What am I in this for?"

He grinned. "I wouldn't know."

"You don't know a hell of a lot, do you?"

"Are you goin' to be funny, too?"

He came toward me jangling the manacles. I didn't get up.

"Get up," he said.

I said, "How's to leave my hands in front so I can smoke?"

"Get up, then," he said.

I stood up and held my hands out. We watched each other's eyes. Suddenly I jammed my right foot down on his left and crowded him. He tried to heave back. My foot held him rooted. It was an old trick. He swung his gun close. Its barrel slapped into my left hand, and I gripped it and shoved it away, then upward. My right fist sank into his ribs, drove his breath bursting between his lips.

He tried again to yank his left foot free. I must have been crushing his toes. But I kept close to him. His left fist came swishing around and banged against my ear. It hurt. It made my head ring. He used his left knee, missed, and then I used mine—missed—and for a moment we stood toiling, twisting slowly, but strenuously, grunting behind clenched teeth. We made no noise. Our eyes were locked. I had his gun arm up in the air. He had my right hand in an iron grip. I had his left foot under mine, and I was grinding it. It hurt him. His lips were flattening tighter against his teeth, a blue vein was standing out on his forehead, sweat began to make his face shiny.

"I'll blow your heart out for this!" he groaned.

"You'll blow hell out," I told him.

I kept screwing my heel on his toes. I was flat against him, straining to keep his gun clear. He let go my right hand and clouted me on the cheek. A ring he wore gashed me. I grabbed that hand and forced it outward and upward. He swore. He began kicking my shins with his right foot. He tried to get his teeth on my ear. I had to wheel my head. He kept at it. I slammed my head into his face, and he cursed and wrenched with both arms and I saw I had opened his lips. Blood trickled down his chin.

His face lost color. I ground down on his toes. His body was starting to sag, his breath puffed from his cheeks. He groaned loudly and shut his eyes tightly and muscles bulged alongside his mouth.

I took a chance. I stepped back, still held his gun-hand, drove my right fist to his jaw. His head snapped back and he reeled. I hit him in the mouth and as he was sagging I twisted his right arm backward, wrenched it until his fingers opened. I had his gun. His teeth sank into my left wrist and his left fist walloped my stomach, low. I coughed and felt sick, but I brought the gun barrel down on his head, stumbled over him as he fell, and sprawled beyond him, crashing into the door.

He was out. He was flat on his back—spread-eagled—out. We'd made a lot of noise toward the end. On my feet again, I squared off in the middle of the room, hefting the gun, watching the door. They would come, two or more. I couldn't drop to the yard; it was too far below. There was only one way out—the way I must have come in.

I waited to hear footsteps. I wondered if I'd cracked the guy's skull. I wondered how many would come. I was in a hot sweat and far from cocky. And impatient—waiting for them to come. How many bullets could I stand? I hadn't been shot in a long while, in three years. Two bullets that time. A month in the hospital. I'd have to take more than two to get out of this scatter.

But nobody came. I waited five minutes, and there was not a sound in the house. Then I opened the door and listened again. I looked back at the man on the floor. His eyes were open. I stared at him for a minute. Then I went over, closed his eyes, stood up and walked into the hall. I locked the door and went downstairs.

Cassilly's room, of course, was directly beneath. I had the ring of keys in my hand. I tried three keys before the door swung open. The hinges creaked. The room was dim, the shades down. As I stepped across the threshold a figure loomed. A chair crashed into me, the main force striking my shoulder. But it was enough to floor me, to choke any words in my throat. I lay half stunned and heard doors banging and feet running.

It must have been five minutes before the fog cleared. I rose by fits and starts and felt my way out of the room. I had to keep shaking my head to clear it, and the fresh air smelled good when

I stumbled into the yard. I found a well and drew up a bucket of water, ducked my face and head in it. Then I found a narrow dirt road and followed it. It seemed like a mile before I reached a macadam road. I remembered that last night the car had turned right into the dirt road, so now I turned left.

Picture me tramping along that road in a soiled tux, with cuts on my face.

4. Fifty Thousand

IT WAS two that afternoon when I let myself in the brownstone. I stripped, took a hot shower, shaved, and thought I looked pale. Dressed again, I walked over to Ninth Avenue, took a Sixth Avenue El and got off at Forty-Second Street.

Marge stared at me as if I were a ghost.

"Hello, kid," I said. "How is every little thing?"

The shock was over; she relaxed. "What kind of a date did you say you had?"

I glanced down at my mail, said, "Any important calls?"

"No. Business is rotten."

"Don't you believe it."

"Why," she said, "you're cut!"

I planted myself in the swivel chair, grabbed the phone and called the Hudson Arms. Mrs. Cassilly had checked out last night around twelve. I hung up.'

"Now I wonder what happened to her?" I said out loud.

"How should I know?" Marge said.

"Listen, Marge."

I told her about it, getting around finally to: "The place is up back of Yonkers, way back. An old farmhouse. I walked for almost two hours and then I came to Yonkers, where I could get a cab. It was a long ride in."

"And you didn't see Cassilly?"

"No. He socked me with the chair and beat it. At least it must have been Cassilly who socked me."

"That puts you in a nice jam, doesn't it?"

"What do you mean?"

"What do I mean!" she echoed. "I mean that you're going to have a hard time explaining that your motives were innocent when you walked Cassilly out of that gambling joint."

I shrugged. "Don't be an idiot. Cassilly's back in town by this time. He will have communicated with his wife after a time like this, and she'll straighten things out."

"Where's his wife?" Marge challenged. "How do you know that these birds haven't swooped her up too? Can you locate her? No. Where is she? Besides, even if she is here, even if she hasn't been touched, what makes you think she won't think that you decided to kidnap her husband?"

"You're becoming involved now, Marge."

"Not half as involved as you are."

I thought for a moment, then said, "It was a kidnap all right. Cassilly has money. A lot of it. They must have got his wife too, but I don't think they held her prisoner. Not for long, anyhow. They probably released her and told her that her husband would be killed if she didn't turn over a certain amount of money."

"And why were you included?"

"I've been thinking. They took me for one reason. Nick saw me take Cassilly out. The barman saw me. The Jap saw me. That would have thrown the guilt in my direction. They probably intended to keep me out there a long while—then probably bump me off. It was neat, Marge. I would have been the fall guy."

"Boy," she said, "you're still the fall guy. Cassilly will put up a yell. Shall I tell the police you're in when they come?"

"Don't be a wet blanket."

I got up, troubled, and went to the window, looked over at the public library. Marge had a lot of sense. I couldn't kid myself. I could explain that Mrs. Cassilly had hired me, but beyond that I couldn't explain how these other guys had muscled in on my case and turned it into abduction. It's never been a policy of mine to crack wise with the police; a private dick can't afford to.

I turned, saying, "Well, there's one thing I can do: I can go to Nick's tonight and try to find out things."

At five I left the office and went uptown on the EL I wasn't going to dress, but I wanted a gun. They'd taken mine when they hustled me off last night, but I had another home, where it wouldn't do any good if I had to get nasty at Nick's.

Walking east on Sixty-Fifth Street, I was about to walk up the steps to the brownstone when two men stepped out of a car and came toward me. I'd never seen them before.

"We'll go in with you," one said.

They looked like rats from the word go, even though they wore expensive clothes. They came up on either side of me and each one had a hand in his pocket and the pockets bulged. They were pale-faced guys, with sideburns and tight soft collars, loud ties.

I tried to laugh it off. "Where did you get that idea?"

"Come on—get going," the little bird said.

I walked up the steps and we went down the hall, into my one big room. The little guy locked the door and his pal, a narrow-faced guy with thick lips, kept a gun on me.

The little one was sure of himself in a snarly voice. "You think you're pretty damn good, don't you?" he said. He frisked me while his pal held a gun against the small of my back, and slapped my face. "Well, you ain't. How d' you like that?"

I couldn't help it—" Cut that out, you greaseball!"

He started handling a gun negligently. His lips were thin like two strips of red silk.

"Well, where's the jack?" he said.

"What jack?"

"You know what jack."

"The hell I do."

He was high-tension guy. He snarled and jabbed his gun hard against my stomach. "You're gonna come across, wisenheimer— you're gonna come across or you're gonna be cold meat."

"Easy on that roscoe, you dumb hood. It might go off."

"It sure might."

"I don't know what you're talking about," I said. "I haven't got any jack. There's forty bucks in my pocket and three thousand in the bank. Take the forty if you want it, and bust the bank if you want the rest."

"I ain' talkin' about small change, buddy. You know what I'm talkin' about. You were in big on the fifty-thousand, and we're get tin' back the whole dough or you and some other guys are goin' to get the heat."

"Not this guy," I said. "You're up a wrong tree. You sure are. I work for my money. You and your lock-jawed boy friend get to hell out of here."

The little one said, "Frank, frisk this joint."

The narrow-faced guy started turning my place inside out. He emptied the old highboy, ransacked my grips, my clothes, the closet. He hauled the mattress off the bed, cleaned out the bathroom, turned up the rugs, took the cushions out of two easy chairs and turned all my shoes upside down. The place was a shambles when he gave up.

"There ain't nothin', Tony," he said.

The little one looked exasperated. He kept moving his rod up and down before me, and his lips twisted tightly against his teeth.

"Listen," I said, "I'm strictly on the up and up. I was damned near killed this morning. I was taken for a ride last night along with a man named Cassilly. It looked liked a kidnap to me. But Cassilly got away this morning. So did I. I've been trying to locate Cassilly ever since I got back in town—"

"Says you!" Tony snarled.

"What I'd like to know is where you birds figure in this?"

"Never mind that, bozo. You can't song and dance yourself out of this."

"Do you know where Cassilly is?"

"What's it to you?"

"Well," I said, "I want to see him."

The little one looked suspicious. His eyelids thinned way down, his thin lips worked. Then his eyes sprang open.

"Oh, you do! You do, eh?"

"Honest."

"Okay. Come on."

5. The Fall Guy

THERE WAS a guy sitting at the wheel of the car outside. I got in and Frank and Tony sat down on either side of me. I couldn't figure them out, couldn't figure Cassilly and these birds in the same breath. We went a block north to Sixty-Sixth Street, took the transverse through Central Park and hit Fifth Avenue at Sixty-Fifth. We went over to Park Avenue and turned south.

The car pulled up in front of a gray-stone house in East Thirty-Seventh Street. The driver stayed at the wheel. Tony got out. Frank got out behind me and they flanked me on the way up the steps. Tony rang a bell and the hall door opened. We went in. I heard voices, and then I was being shoved down the corridor. Frank opened a door and I saw Nick Apostos standing in front of a mantel smoking a cigarette.

I went in saying, "Hello, Nick."

Then I saw Cassilly getting up from a divan, looking pale and bitter, his fists clenched.

"So you're from Indianapolis!" he said.

He wasn't drunk now. He looked very righteous and very neat in a tweed lounge suit.

"I hear," Nick said acidly, "you're from Indianapolis."

"That was just an idea I had," I said.

Nick said, "Mr. Cassilly has been a very good patron at my place. I run an honest place. No man comes to harm in my place. If he does, I know what to do about it. I always said you private dicks were the bunk. Where'd you get him boys?"

Tony said, "In his flat. We waited outside. Frank and me went in with him, but we couldn't find anything. He handed us a line about wanting to see Mr. Cassilly. It was just a bluff, if you ask me. The heel's a red-hot."

Cassilly laughed nervously, "So you wanted to see me! Well, by God, I want to see you!"

"Not half as much," I said, "as I want to see you."

"Remember," Nick put in, "I run a good place. I was glad Mr. Cassilly looked me up. If the police gets wind of this, my place might be closed down. I get the money, see, or you get finished—and nobody'll know about it."

I was becoming acclimated. "You men are under the impression, I suppose, that I helped kidnap Mr. Cassilly."

"Impression!" mocked Cassilly. "It's just an impression, is it? When you win my confidence, while I'm drunk, by telling me you're from Indianapolis! Don't be ridiculous!"

"I can explain everything. Have you seen your wife since you came home?"

"I should say I have. She was at my hotel, waiting. She paid out fifty thousand, the little fool—to save me. But you know that. You probably made the phone call to her demanding it by noon to-day."

"Not me. I was a prisoner in that house the same as you. I opened your door to get you out when you whaled me with a chair."

"That wasn't you. It was another man—another man."

I sat down and lit a cigarette. Nick hadn't moved from the mantel. Frank and Tony were standing silently behind me, holding their guns. This was Nick's residence.

"Mr. Cassilly," I said, "I can prove that my intentions were honorable. Just telephone your wife and ask her if she didn't engage me to get you out of Nick's so that she could get you away to Maine before you sobered up."

"What nonsense!" Cassilly scoffed.

"Call her," I said. "Tell her my life's in danger and that it's necessary she tell the truth."

Still dubious, Cassilly went to the telephone. He called a big mid-town hotel.

"Joyce," he said. "Listen, Joyce. Did you hire a private detective to follow me to that gambling place… Listen, Joyce, this is important. His life's in danger if you don't admit it… You're sure, honey…. All right."

I jumped up and tried to grab the phone. He stepped back and hung up, eying me coldly.

"Call her again," I said. "Let me talk to her."

"Get back," Nick said.

Frank and Tony moved across the room and I was surrounded by four men, all quiet, all deadly.

Then Nick began to shake his head, said, "It's no good. You're in the hot grease, shamus. You tried to step into big time and stubbed your toe."

I said. "She's a liar. She hired—"

Cassilly took a swing at me. I fell backward over a chair and landed on my back. Tony kicked me in the ribs, and after that stopped hurting I rested on both elbows and looked up at them.

"You did a dumb thing, Cassilly," I said, "to come around whining to Nick. He's not doing this for your sake. He's afraid the cops'll put the clamps on his joint if the news gets out. You should have gone to the police. The police would have given me an even break. I won't get it here."

"You get just what the hell you deserve," Nick said.

"That's all in the point of view. I know what I deserve. I'm on the level. I deserve a break."

"I just want that money back," Cassilly said.

"Well, you're not going to get it by dressing me down, because I'm as much in the dark as you are. And I tell you your wife hired me. I'm made the goat, the fall guy. I'm taken for a ride. Then I come home and these two guys turn my place upside down and then you go and take a crack at me. And now I'm on the spot, with these guys here itching to give me the works."

"You just come clean," Nick said.

I stood up, continued to work on Cassilly. "I want to make it clear, Cassilly, that you're putting yourself in a dangerous predicament. These men don't want the law in on it. They want you to get the money back, but merely because it 'll quiet you. If they don't get it they'll kill me. You look like a decent enough guy. I don't think you want to be an accessory in a little private killing. And that's what you'll be. Because I don't know where your money is. These guys don't believe that. They'll give me the works."

Nick was looking sinister. He didn't like my line. Cassilly began to look thoughtful, so I went on.

"You've got to believe me. I'm a business man. I have an office and a secretary and a pretty good reputation. Circumstances are against me. But you've got to think that circumstances don't mean anything. You've got to realize, Cassilly, that I'm on the spot, and that if these guys bump me off you'll be just as guilty as they are. All I ask for is a break. I want to meet your wife. I want to talk with her."

Nick said, "Be careful, Mr. Cassilly. This guy is a slippery one with a line of gab.

Leave it in my hands. I promised to get your money back. I'll get it."

Cassilly looked worried.

I hammered on— "All right, Cassilly. Here's a promise to match Nick's. I'll get that money, or as much of it as I can. I'll get one or more of the guys responsible. It's in my line. If that doesn't suit you, call the police, turn me over and place a charge against me. But first let me speak to your wife."

"Be careful, Mr. Cassilly," Nick warned.

Cassilly was hesitant. "I don't want murder on my hands. I don't want that." He looked at me. "All right. I'll take you to meet my wife. Lend me a gun, Nick."

"This sure is rich!" Tony snarled.

"Mr. Cassilly, I warn you against him," Nick said. "I know him. You don't. I know he's a smooth guy, a fancy talker—"

Cassilly was grim now. "Lend me a gun, Nick. It's my money that's lost."

"But the police—"

"He won't get as far as the police," Cassilly said, "if he tries any tricks."

Going out, I said, "Toodle-oo, Nick."

Don't think I felt nonchalant. My palms were sweating.

6. A Twisting Trail

CASSILLY WALKED me to Third Avenue and steered me into a taxi he hailed.

"It's not far," he said. "And mind you, no tricks."

"Ah, don't be like that, Cassilly. For crying out loud, do I look like a gunman? Anyhow, I want to thank you for getting me out of Nick's."

He was still grim. "You're not out of trouble yet. I still think you're lying."

I tapped his knee. "You've got a lot to learn, son."

He blushed a bit. I was really a bit sorry to see a kid like him mixed up in a scatter like Nick's.

The hotel was on Park Avenue, north of the ramp. We walked through a swell lobby and went up in a silent elevator. Even the air I breathed smelled expensive. Cassilly knocked on a door, then opened it and stood aside for me to go in. I entered with a slight grudge against Mrs. Cassilly.

"Joyce," he called.

"Coming."

She came in hurriedly from an adjoining room, stopped short, stared blankly at me.

Cassilly was saying to her, "This man swears you—"

"Wait a minute," I cut in; "Mrs. Cassilly, I'd like to have a few words alone with your husband."

She looked puzzled. And I guess she was frightened too, because now Cassilly was holding the gun in his hand.

"Leave us alone, Joyce," he said.

She retreated into the other room, closed the door.

Cassilly was staring grimly at me, his face white and set, his lips tight.

I held up my hand. "Please, Cassilly, turn that gun the other way. It's shaking like hell. You're nervous, my boy."

"You've got to explain," he muttered, trying to be impressive, and failing. "I'll not stand any nonsense."

"Cassilly," I said, "your wife appears to be a very charming little woman. She might, however, be irreconcilable if she found out that a picture of you was in the boudoir of another woman."

"What do you mean?"

"Put down that gun, Cassilly. I begin to see light. I've been a gopher—a dupe."

"By God, don't fool with me!"

"I'm not fooling. I'm deadly serious."

"Blackmail on top of—"

"Blackmail," I said, "if you don't give me a chance to clear myself. You can help me, Cassilly. You can help me get back a lot of that fifty thousand. Believe me, I'm on the square. I was hired by a woman who posed as your wife and who had a cabinet photo of you."

He looked shocked. I took advantage of it and gave him the details from the moment I'd walked into the apartment in the Hudson Arms. It bit into him. His shoulders drooped. He put the gun away in his pocket. He sat down. I sat down. His eyes began to stare transfixed at the carpet and I talked quickly, keeping my voice low, making it earnest.

He had heard the sounds of a fight in the room above his at the farmhouse. He had not known I was there. He'd thought it was just a scuffle among the gangsters. He had not recognized me when he heaved the chair. He'd gone right to Nick, first charging Nick with planning the job. Nick had convinced him of his innocence, had promised to get me.

"How deep were you with this woman?"

"Just a friendship," he said. "I thought she was pretty wonderful. I never even kissed her. She wanted the picture to remember me by, as a good friend. She was compassionate. I guess I got tight and told her about my leaving Joyce. I guess—she was playing me all the time."

"Where did you meet her?"

"One night at Nick's."

"What name did she give?"

"Rhea Palms."

I put a hand on his knee. "You just leave it to young Gallagher. You have been duped. I've been duped. You're sure there was nothing serious between you two? You never wrote her any letters? You didn't inscribe the photo?"

"No."

"Was she with a man when you met her?"

"I don't know. Apparently not."

"Where was she living then?"

"Hotel Lausanne."

"Well," I said, "I met her at the Hudson Arms, where she was on the books as Mrs. Cassilly."

He stood up, looked at the closed door. "Joyce wouldn't understand. I've been a fool—"

"You got into a bad jam," I told him, rising. "The woman's a crook. Clever. Well, she fooled me. I would have fallen for her myself. All right, Cassilly, make believe nothing happened. Leave this to me. And stay away from Nick's. Say nothing to anybody."

I gave him the office telephone and the one at home.

He was bewildered. "What are you going to do now?"

"One thing will lead to another," I said, and borrowed his gun.

I walked over to Lexington Avenue, entered a telephone booth, and called the Hudson Arms. I found that "Mrs. Cassilly" had taken a suite there two days before I met her. She had paid for a week in advance. I telephoned the Hotel Lausanne and found that Rhea Palms had lived there for a month; had checked out an hour before taking up residence at the Hudson Arms. She had not come back to the Lausanne.

Then I took a cab to the Hudson Arms, arrived there at half-past nine. I asked for the manager, showed credentials, mentioned a few minor points in the case and asked for cooperation. He called in the house officer and I was given free rein upon a promise of no publicity.

My client had checked out at midnight, or a little past. This much I got from the clerk at the desk who had been on duty at the time. Her checking out at that hour had caused a little attention. She had had two bags. I found that out from the bellhop who had carried them down.

No car had called for her. The bellhop had carried her bags out to the street and had called a taxi parked at the corner. He knew the driver, because the driver parked there every night to pick up calls from the five hotels in the block. Up until 10 p.m. there were four cabs at the stand; after ten, two; after twelve, one.

McHugh was the driver's name. He wouldn't be at his post until twelve. The boy didn't know where he lived, but he knew the name of the taxi company he worked for. I went over to Eleventh Avenue and entered the office of the company. McHugh was out, cruising the theatrical district. When the after-theater rush was over he would go up and take his post near the Hudson Arms, at midnight.

Well, I wasn't going to run all around Times Square looking for McHugh, so I killed some time in a speak in Fortieth Street, just east of Eighth Avenue. I ate there, too. At a quarter to twelve I went uptown and waited for McHugh.

When he pulled up I approached him and told him who I was. He lit a butt and looked unimpressed.

"You picked up a fare last night at little past twelve. A girl. She had two bags. Out of the Hudson Arms. Do you remember that?"

"Sure."

"Do you remember where you took her?"

"I think so."

"Well-?"

He looked at me bluntly. "How the hell do I know who you are?"

I showed him papers. "This girl is crooked," I told him. "She's a mob's front. She got a good guy in Dutch and she damned near had the cross put on me."

"Ah, them janes—them janes… Get in."

"Where is it?"

"The Wellington."

I climbed in. We went down the West Side to Forty-Second Street, shot east to Seventh Avenue, then south. The Wellington was hear the Penn Station.

"Should I wait?" the driver asked.

"No," I said, and tipped him for the ride and the information.

It took me ten minutes to work myself into the good graces of the clerk and a five dollar bill. He showed me the register. At twenty minutes to one, while I was being taken for a ride out of New York, a woman registered at the Wellington. She was the only one who registered between midnight and eight that morning. Claire Drexel, of New Haven; room 1005. I went into a booth and rang 1005. A woman's voice answered. I said, "One, oh, oh, nine?" She said, "No." I hung up.

I didn't want to start a row in the hotel if I could help it. I went over and explained that to the clerk. I asked him if any telegrams had arrived for Miss Drexel. He called over the bell-captain. There had been one at 9 p.m. I asked the clerk where the station was that usually sent the telegrams over.

My next move was a long chance, a little irregular. I made a flying trip home, got a fake badge of the New York Detective Bureau. I went down to Penn Station and in to the telegraph office. I showed the girl the badge and she was impressed.

I asked, "Have you got a copy of a telegram you forwarded to Claire Drexel, at the Wellington, between 8 and 9 p.m.?"

She looked through the file. She had a copy. It said:

TAKE AN EARLY MORNING TRAIN AND JOIN US AT THE BRADDOCK NEW LONDON.
ED.

I thanked her, went down to the subway and caught a northbound local. I got off at Sixty-Sixth Street, walked over to the brownstone and packed my Gladstone. I added my spare thirty-eight to the one Cassilly had given me, went out, carried the bag around to a garage, and climbed into my old roadster.

I drove north on the East Side and crossed the Willis Avenue Bridge. At three in the morning I was burning the wind on the Boston Post Road.

7. The Pay-Off

IT WAS drizzling when I rolled into New London at eight in the morning. The Braddock was on the main drag. I didn't stop. I drove past, made a right turn and found a garage a block away. I put in the car, grabbed my bag and walked back to the hotel. I entered the lobby, but did not register. I went to a large leather divan, put my bag down, went over to the cigar counter, bought some papers and then sat down by the bag.

At a little before noon my ex-client came in, followed by a black boy carrying her two bags. She registered. She looked swell. When she had gone up I walked over to the desk, picked up a pen and looked at the register. She was still Claire Drexel, in room 603.

"I'd like a room on the fifth or sixth floor," I said.

"We have one for two-fifty on the fifth floor, and one for three on the sixth floor."

"Is the three dollar room in front?"

"Yes."

I took it—607. It was two doors from 603. The even numbers were on the opposite side of the corridor. When the black boy went out I left the door on a crack, pulled a chair near it, sat down, smoked and listened.

Half an hour passed before I heard a door open, close. A key-tag jangled. I peered out. Claire Drexel was walking toward the elevators. I drew back, waited till I heard the elevator doors open and close. Then I stepped out, and walked rapidly, stopped, looked, up at the indicator that moved around like a hand on a clock. The indicator stopped at the eighth floor. Then it moved; went all the way around to the ground floor.

That was that; they were on the eighth floor. It was the pay-off. The men had probably come by car; the woman had come by train to get her end. Somewhere on the eighth floor was Cassilly's fifty thousand.

There was no use going to the house officer. If I explained the case to him he would see only one way out—the police—and that naturally enough. I didn't want the police in on it if I could help it. It would mean headlines. It would drag in Cassilly, the woman; and that might send his wife home to her mother, if she had a mother, and likely to the divorce court by way of a climax.

I had a master key along. It would be possible to get into the woman's room, but I didn't think I would find anything of importance there. The men had the money. I wanted the money, had no intention of making a pinch, only as a last resort. If it came to a matter of saving my skin or Cassilly's reputation, I was certainly going to save my skin. But I was at least trying to give the guy a break.

I went downstairs and sent a wire to Marge to put her at ease.

As I reasoned it, there were three men and the woman. There had been four, but I'd finished one in the farmhouse. I went back to my room, took the extra gun out of the Gladstone and shoved it in my pocket. The woman's room would be the best bet after all.

The master key worked almost immediately. I entered the room, locked the door, went over and drew the shades down most of the

way. I had not come into the room to find anything. I didn't even bother opening the woman's bags. I took a seat facing the door and waited, after I'd cut the telephone wire.

I waited twenty minutes. Then a key grated in the lock. I stood up, drawing one of the guns, and moved a hit to face the door more squarely. I respect most women. When I don't respect one, it's usually just too bad for her.

She came in quickly, bending over to remove the key from the outside and put it in the inside. She caught sight of me and gave a startled little cry.

"Lock it," I said.

"What do you mean being In my—"

"Lock it and shut up."

She locked it and then flattened back against the door, pretty as ever. She arched her neck. In one hand she carried a large pocketbook. I stepped close to her and ripped it from her hand; snapped it open with one hand, saw layers of bills, a small pistol. She remained motionless, white-faced, tight-lipped, her dark, luminous eyes steady on me.

"I'll keep this," I said.

"No doubt," she said. "But you won't keep it for long."

"I'll keep this, sister, and I'll get the rest of it. You're pretty clever, but not quite clever enough. You're in one bad spot, little girl, and I'm going to turn you over to the cops if you don't play ball. One peep out of your rosebud mouth and you'll get landed on like a ton of brick."

"You're pretty good, Gallagher," she said mockingly. "You're certainly pretty good. And pretty tough."

"Get away from that door. Get over and sit down."

She sauntered and sat down slowly, pulling a droll half-smile. I sat on the edge of the bed and eyed her intently.

"What room are your boy friends in?"

"Don't be a fool," she said. "You'd be going into bad company and you'd surely get hurt."

"That's my lookout, not yours. You've got a chance of sliding out of this. If you don't come across, so help me you'll spend the best part of your life behind bars. I'm not kidding, sister. I'm a tough baby, and I'm aching to get even with you for the dirty trick you pulled on me. So talk. Where's the room?"

A sly look came into her eyes. "What kind of a break do I get?"

"A clean one. You walk out of this hotel

and go where you please. Otherwise, I grab that phone, call the police, and use every bit of power I have to get you a long stretch."

She got up and walked around thoughtfully, biting her lip. Then she stopped, turned and looked at me blankly.

"They're in 810."

I went to the door, unlocked it, took out the key, held it up. "I'll lock you in—just to keep you honest."

Her expression didn't change. I knew that as soon as I got out she would try to telephone 810. Since the telephone wouldn't work, that was all right by me. I backed out, locked the door, ran to my room and left the bulging pocketbook in my Gladstone. I took the stairway to the eighth floor and walked down the corridor. Number 810 was near the end.

I knocked on the door, then lifted a leg and braced my foot against the door.

A voice called, "Who is it?"

"Telegram," I said.

"Slide it under the door."

"I'm sorry, sir. It has to be signed for."

Somebody growled. The key turned. I watched the knob turn. Then I drove my foot against the door and sent a man reeling to the floor. I heaved in, hefting the two guns.

One man was lying on the bed. The third was sitting on the edge. There were stacks of bills on the bed and a lot of sheets of paper.

"Not a move out of you guys," I said.

The guy who had fallen still lay there. I told him to get up. The guy on the bed had started toward his gun; so had the guy sitting on the edge. He was the dark bird with the black mustache. I kicked the door shut.

"All of you, get your hands up. You on the floor, I told you to get up. Come now, all you heels—hands high. Get over in front of the bed. Snappy."

"The jane two-timed on us!" the man getting up said.

The man with the mustache glared at him.

The other snarled, "Sure she did! She got her end and then two-timed!"

"She did not," I said. "I've been tailing you birds ever since you left New York. Shut up and crawl under the bed, all of you. Head-first, your heels toward the door."

"Listen," said the man who had accused the girl, "I ain't gonna crawl under no bed."

I took a step and cracked him with the barrel of a gun. The other two started. But I had them covered. The man I'd hit got to his knees and began crawling under. The others followed. When they were all under, with only their heels showing, I put one of the guns away. Then I doubled up four corners of the counterpane. All the bills on the bed were in it. I carried it like a sack and backed to the door.

One of them was saying, "It was the jane. I'm gonna get that jane."

"You're dumb," I said. "I got the jane's money, too, and I locked her in her room. I cut her telephone wire so she couldn't call you. You guys have been on the spot since you came here, I was just waiting for the pay-off. Here's her key." I threw it on the floor.

I backed out, closed the door and ran down the stairway, into my room. I opened the counterpane. It was a load of money, in hundreds and fifties. I counted forty-nine thousand and then stowed it in the Gladstone, locking it. I rang for a porter. When he came in I told him to send the

bag by express to my office in Forty-Second Street. He went out.

Then I sat down at the desk and wrote a couple of telegrams. I called up the garage and told them to load my tank and look at the oil.

There was a knock on my door.

"Who's there?"

"Ice water, sir."

It was a boy's voice, but I said, "I didn't order ice water."

I could hear the ice tinkling. It was an old trick. One of the mob had sent in an order for ice water for me. That was to get the door open. Then they'd rush it.

"You're mistaken, son," I said, and he apologized and walked away.

I waited an hour and then decided to take a chance. I opened the door and ran smack into the guy with the black mustache, took a crack on the head, went for my gun. Another guy crowded me from behind, got my gun.

In less than a minute they had me back in my room, the three of them talking hard. One searched my room, found nothing.

"Where is it?"

"It's gone," I said.

They whaled me, knocked me to the floor, beat me until everything began to dance before my eyes.

"Where is it?" was the question.

"I sent it to New York by express."

They turned the room inside out. They came back to me and hammered me until I passed out.

When I came to I took a cold shower. I had a welt over the left eye, a split lip and a number of sore ribs. Outside of that I felt pretty swell.

KENTUCKY KICKBACK

by T.T. Flynn

1. Old-Man Money on a Saw-Down Horse

HE DAWN over Churchill Downs turned from gray to scarlet-and-gold as a voice at the grandstand rail spoke with unconscious excitement. "Danny Moore's taking the wraps off El Conde!"

A score of binoculars were trained on the same sight. Two score stop-watches clicked at the same instant. Silence fell over the top-coated and sweatered railbirds standing singly and in groups at the edge of the track. Glasses and keen eyes followed the black horse and rider sweeping along the backstretch.

And just then the rim of the golden sun burst up in the eastern sky. East of the bright gay flowers and deep green sward of the infield. East of the old green-and-white stables huddled in serried ranks beyond the backstretch where El Conde was making his run. Another spring morning at Churchill Downs. Another spring day of Derby Week.

The Kentucky Derby!

And on the stretch-turn El Conde streaked through a shaft of golden sunrise in an effortless rush that eased off abruptly.

A gaunt, hook-nosed little man excitedly shoved a weathered hat back on his head and caught the arm of the man beside him. Face working, long nose twitching, he thrust out an old stopwatch.

"Look, Maddox! One-twelve-three for six furlongs! And breezing! He coulda done two seconds better and still made the Derby route! Man O' War was only a plater! I seen it when the Conde was a yearling! 'Don't sell a Derby winner!' I begged Cap'n Jim's girl. An' wha'd she do? Wha'd she do?"

"What did she do, Sully?" Mr. Maddox repeated. "She sold to Gloria Gerryman. And Gloria Gerryman boasts that she's already bet eighty grand that she's got a Derby winner."

Mr. Maddox glanced down at the expensive stop-watch cupped in his own big hand.

"One-thirteen even, Sully. You're so hipped on that black nag you're edging on the time."

"I've clocked 'em since I was in short pants!" Sully retorted heatedly. "If somebody's two-fifths off, it's you, Maddox! Maybe you've got reasons! You bookies oughta be worried about the dough you musta laid against the Conde! Serve you right if he cleaned you!"

Men near enough to hear the exchange were smiling.

One called out: "You'll have long white whiskers, Sully, when you see Joe Maddox cleaned!"

"Yah?" Sully snorted. "I've seen him cleaned! In twenty-eight I seen him so busted at Belmont he couldn't cover a double-buck

You could be ready to join Mr. Maddox in a resentful sneer and a sharp retort to Sully's slander.

But a grin was on Mr. Maddox's broad bland face. A chuckle shook Mr. Maddox's vast girth as he instinctively touched the great gem on his finger and nodded.

"It was tough that year, Sully. I lost forty pounds from not eating and looked like I'd been tailored by a tent-maker. How much are you betting on El Conde, Sully?"

"Huh?"

"How much?"

Sully looked embarrassed. His long nose twitched. He spat, grunted, started to turn away. Mr. Maddox put a hand on his arm and chuckled again.

"How much on El Conde, Sully?"

Sully shook off the hand and managed to look irritated, defiant and sheepish at the same time. "I'll handle my dough an' you handle yours, Maddox!"

"Two to one you're talking El Conde and laying cash on Jeanne's Hope, that oat-bucket of Jeanne Cavanaugh's," Mr. Maddox offered.

"So what?" Sully snapped defiantly. "So what, Maddox? Is it my dough or ain't it? I got a right to back Jeanne's horse if I like him!"

"You've got a right to jump off the New Albany bridge if you like it," Mr. Maddox chuckled.

One of the listeners laughed. "Sully'll get his money back faster by jumping off the bridge. Jeanne's Hope hasn't got a chance."

"Yah?" said Sully. "Yah?" and stamped away muttering to himself.

Mr. Maddox pocketed the stop-watch and looked after the gaunt little figure with an understanding smile.

"Sully knows a horse," Mr. Maddox said. "He's tossing away his money just because Jeanne Cavanaugh has got a horse entered and he can't bear to bet against her."

"Damn fool!"

"Just Sully," said Mr. Maddox.

El Conde had drifted past the hawk-eyed railbirds before the grandstand. The big black horse was breathing easily and worrying the bit that held him back. A great horse. Chances were he'd take the Derby. And that would be another feather in Gloria Gerryman's fabulous cap. Another tribute to the Gerryman millions that seemed bent on buying in a few years what others had taken generations to acquire.

Oil money came fast, spent easy. The Gerryman stable of thoroughbreds and great breeding-farm in the Kentucky Bluegrass, the

from Avenue A. He'd lost that chunk of ice there on his finger an' peddled the hock-check on his benny. If they can take him once, they can take him again. An' maybe the Conde's the one that'll do it."

HEAD AND shoulders Mr. Maddox towered above the gaunt and shabby Sully, who'd been Tim Sullivan to his mother and plain Sully to a host of turf followers from Bay Meadows to Saratoga and points between.

And when you looked at the vast and prosperous bulk of Mr. Maddox, and gauged the great white diamond on his left hand, you could doubt that so much assurance and prosperity had ever hocked an overcoat, been without an expensive diamond or a fat bankroll.

Gerryman yacht, the Gerryman villa at Palm Beach, the Gerryman Long Island estate, the Gerryman private plane, the Gerryman oil interests, had all been a matter of money.

And like a jewel topping a fabulously constructed crown was Gloria Gerryman herself. The rotogravure, gossip and society columns filled in the picture….

Breathing deeply of the cool crisp dawn, Mr. Maddox walked back under the grandstand to the clubhouse entrance. This was the best part of the day, these early mornings when only the rail-birds and stable hands were out to watch the morning workouts. In these early hours the turf belonged to those who loved it.

A SCATTERING of automobiles were on the parking-space before the clubhouse entrance. More were arriving. By breakfast time there'd be still more. The eyes of the world were on Louis-ville, here by the broad Ohio. Visitors already were swarming over the town. Uncounted thousands more were starting the annual trek toward the Bluegrass classic of the turf. By tomorrow night, just before the Derby, they'd be sleeping in shifts, and overflow-ing into the parks.

"Mist' Joe!"

Mr. Maddox paused at the door of his big blue sedan, stared inquiringly, and then nodded recognition of the monkey-like little Negro who had slipped furtively around the back of the car and jerked off his cap in a bobbing, grinning greeting.

"Hello, Chimp. So you made another Derby? What's on your mind?"

"Chimp" was short for chimpanzee—and there was a resem-blance, even to the hunched way Chimp moved and the long arms and big hands that almost touched his knees. Chimp was so ugly you hardly noticed he had only one ear.

"Sho' made hit heah again, Mist' Joe," Chimp chortled, fum-bling inside his ragged greasy coat.

"Need a couple of dollars to eat on!" Mr. Maddox guessed, reaching for his billfold.

"Naw, suh, thankee, suh. I'se been workin' eround de stables. Plenty greens an' fat meat for ol' Chimp dis spring. I'se got feen-ancial trouble, suh."

Chimp drew a clenched fist from under his coat and looked warily around. "You still makin' book on de Big Race, Mist' Joe?"

Mr. Maddox put back his billfold and chuckled. "As usual, Chimp. Want to make a bet?"

"I ain't got white man's money," Chimp mumbled, looking around again.

"Seeing as it's you," said Mr. Maddox solemnly, "I'll lay you from a quarter up. Track odds or how'll you have it?"

" White folks odds de folkses gitten eround de Brown Hotel corner," Chimp decided. "How dat pay me on dat saw-down lil Jeanne's Hope?"

"Jeanne's Hope?" said Mr. Maddox, lifting his eyebrows. "Have you been working for the Cavanaughs too, Chimp?"

"Naw, suh."

"Just got a soft spot for old Cap'n Jim and the horses Miss Jeanne and her brother own, I suppose?"

"Naw, suh," Chimp mumbled uneasily. "Never knowed de Cap'n, suh. Never done no work for dat family. Dat lil saw-down horse jus' my style, suh. An' does I win, I wants de winnin' money, suh. White folks style. You de payinest man I knews, Mist' Joe. You ain't hold out no winnin's on of Chimp."

"That's right, Chimp. You'll get your money if you win." Mr. Maddox frowned thoughtfully, cleared his throat, and decided: "I'll lay you twenty to one."

"Thankee, suh. An' please, suh, you won't say nothin' 'bout of Chimp bettin' he own money on dat Jeanne's hope? Jus' don't say nothin' is you asked?"

"Not a word," agreed Mr. Maddox solemnly.

Chimp looked furtively around again, then opened his sooty fist and disclosed a wad of grimy, much-folded bills. Twenty-dollar bills.

"Hit's two hunr'd an' fawty dollars, Mist' Joe. I bets de whole on de nose. Jeanne's Hope—an' I gits twenty to one."

"Wait a minute," said Mr. Maddox sternly as he leafed through the money. "Where'd you get all this, Chimp? Does it belong to you?"

"Yes, suh. I knowed you believe me, Mist' Joe. Hit's de dice some. But mostly hit's jes' ole Chimp savin' back er doller now an' then. Takes me long time to hold back so much, Mist' Joe. I been waitin' fer de jack-pot time to git me old-man money for when I gits old. Dis de time an' dat's de jack-pot money."

Mr. Maddox eyed the ugly little black man sharply, and then nodded. "All right, Chimp, I believe you. You're on Jeanne's Hope to win, two hundred and forty at twenty to one. And if it's your old-man money, I hope you make it. Forty-eight hundred and your money back if you win. That'll keep you in hog jowls and turnip greens for a long time if you stay out of crap games."

" 'Deed hit will, suh," Chimp cackled—and broke off suddenly with a contortion of his money-like face that might have meant anything. "Lawdy God, I done talk too long! I knowed hit!"

Mr. Maddox stared in amazement as Chimp vanished around the back of the automobile.

MR. MADDOX was putting the money in his billfold when an automobile horn blared peremptorily. Mr. Maddox looked, recognized the big cream-colored sedan rolling into the parking space. He'd seen the car back at the stables two days before, seen it disgorge its owner the evening before at the Hollister House on Broadway, where Mr. Maddox was staying.

O'Toole owned the car. Honest John O'Toole, the well known betting commissioner, race-horse owner and big-time gambler. Slim Pasternik was driving the O'Toole car as usual and was alone.

Behind the wheel of his car Mr. Maddox lighted a cigarette and dallied a moment before leaving, watching the big sedan.

And a thoughtful frown came on Mr. Maddox's forehead as Chimp shambled to the side of O'Toole's car.

"Now what," Mr. Maddox muttered as he drove off, "do you make of that? Is O'Toole or Pasternik trying a fast one with that nigger? Trying, maybe, to put me behind the eight-ball?"

A small two-hundred-and-forty-dollar bet seemed to refute the suspicion. And Chimp had always been an honest colored man. His story had sounded straight. His grimy much-handled money backed up the story.

But Honest John O'Toole being what he was, Mr. Maddox carried a lingering suspicion over to Third Street, and downtown to the hotel and breakfast.

THESE DAYS before Derby Day were busy. Churchill Downs was a mutuel track and bookies were not wanted in the city. Hourly now, horse money was flooding in on trains, automo-biles and airplanes.

Men and women were arriving who knew Joe Maddox of

old, at other tracks, in other cities about the country. And it was good business to be seen where the race fans were gathering. At the better hotels and restaurants, along Broadway, out at the track and stables.

And while Mr. Maddox moved in the public eye, his man Oscar stayed in the hotel suite taking bets and quoting odds over the telephone—on the Derby. This one week of each year, Mr. Maddox laid only against Derby money.

At lunch they met in the hotel suite over sandwiches while Oscar brought the betting-sheets up to date.

"Got to cut the odds again on El Conde," Oscar warned. "He's getting a play. If it keeps coming in and he takes the Derby, we'll be out on a limb."

"My guess is he'll take it," said Mr. Maddox. "He worked like a black ghost this morning."

"Yeah," said Oscar. "It's all over town. What's the matter with the dope who's training the Gerryman Stable? Why don't he cover up a little if he's got a good thing? Why let every tout on the rail know all about it?"

"The Gerryman girl should worry about the odds," guessed Mr. Maddox. "She's got her money bet, I hear. She's out to win a Derby—and if half what I've read and heard is right, the more publicity the better. She's a headline hog. A horse that wins that race is as good as a murder in the family when it comes to publicity."

Oscar's thin shrewd face puckered in distaste.

"A lot of crummy people are cluttering up the tracks these days. You could peel 'em down to their last bank account and wouldn't find anything a horse would go for."

Mr. Maddox laughed. "Styles change, Oscar. When I was a yearling, the Gerryman type bought diamonds and pearls for the yokels to read about. Now horses rate bigger headlines and show up better in the roto and society sections."

"And sometimes you can't tell which is the horse," Oscar groused. "There's a few regular folks left anyway. We got a grand and another five hundred on Jeanne's Hope this morning. That Cavanaugh horse. Old Cap'n Jim Cavanaugh's Stable. I heard his daughter and son took over after he died."

Mr. Maddox's bland, Buddha-like face grew thoughtful as he nodded.

"Jeanne and Jerry Cavanaugh. They were youngsters the last time I saw them." Mr. Maddox suddenly chuckled. "Cap'n Jim had Jerry over a knee in front of the tackroom door, whaling the dust out of his pants and cussing him. And Jeanne was standing by wringing her hands." Thoughtful again, Mr. Maddox asked: "Who's betting on Jeanne's Hope?"

"Harley Smith bet the grand. Girl called Norlene Bell telephoned and then brought the five hundred up. Said she'd bet with you in New York, and when she heard you were in town she looked you up. Said when her boy friend got in, she'd have some more to be covered."

"I don't remember her," Mr. Maddox said. "Don't give her any credit. Smith's good for a grand—even if he is as crooked a louse as ever cluttered up Chicago. Here's two hundred and forty more on Jeanne's Hope. The name is Chimp."

"Initials?" said Oscar, writing on his sheets.

"Just Chimp," said Mr. Maddox, smiling as he stood up. "Watch the Jeanne's Hope money. I'm interested in who likes that horse."

"Something doing?" Oscar asked alertly.

"I don't know," said Mr. Maddox. "But just in case there is, I

want to know. I'll call you from the track. Kopper King might cop that third race and we'll make some easy money."

Oscar grunted disgustedly. "Those four horses you ship around the country wouldn't win a race if they were running together in a four-horse maiden race. Why you waste dough on four cheap platers and get the ha-ha for running them now and then is too much for me, Joe. They ain't race horses. They're walking glue pots stuffed with oats an' too lazy to waddle."

"I've got Gerryman blood," Mr. Maddox chuckled. "If Kopper King wins the third, I'll get a headline."

The door closed on Oscar's derisive: "If Kopper King *finishes* you'll deserve a headline."

2. Little Miss Millions

THE THIRD race that afternoon was a ten-horse race. Kopper King dashed under the wire ninth by a nose. Mr. Maddox was not too cast down as he went to a telephone booth to call Oscar. Kopper King had beaten one horse at least.

"Another grand on Jeanne's Hope," Oscar reported. "Fellow named Starky."

"Don't know him."

"He brought cash up, so it's all right, Joe. Says he knows friends of yours. And here's a hot one. That punk, Stiffy, telephoned and said a dame named Cavanaugh wanted to see you."

"Jeanne Cavanaugh?"

"I should know," said Oscar. "Stiffy said she'd been crying. Said he told her you'd probably be around the barn some time this afternoon."

"I'm on my way over there now," Mr. Maddox decided.

Stiffy was the seventeen-year-old exercise boy for the Maddox Stable. He'd come in on a horse van and stayed on the payroll because all the gossip of the stables rolled out in Stiffy's endless stream of talk—and because Joe Maddox was soft-hearted.

Now, talking to his employer, Stiffy's big Adam's apple jumped in his thin neck and his pale-blue eyes blinked rapidly as he nodded jerkily.

"That's her all right. I knowed her before she tol' me her name. Got that runty little Jeanne's Hope that's entered in the Derby an' a couple platers that nobody'll ever claim offen her. Kinda pretty too. I hear that wise-crackin' guy on the other sida Stable Five made a pass at her an' got his face slapped. She shore looked like hell too when she come askin' where you was. Kinda sniffin' back up in her nose like a stable bitch that's lost a pup. I ast her what was—"

"Stiffy!" said Mr. Maddox sternly. "My lady friends don't sound like dogs, don't look like hell, and it's none of your blasted business what they want. I told you what'd happen next time you started swearing near me!"

"My God, I forgot!" Stiffy gulped, and ducked as an open-hand clout knocked him rolling.

Choking, Stiffy scrambled up. His raw-boned young face was agonized. Tears filled his eyes.

"Too bad, but I'll learn you," said Mr. Maddox gruffly. "Here's a dollar. Cut out that crying."

Stiffy grabbed the dollar and dived toward the nearest stall, gasping: "Ain't cryin'! S-swallered my chawin'!"

Mr. Maddox was smiling as he headed toward the barn which held Jeanne Cavanaugh's horses. The hard-boiled little Stiffys of today would make the veteran haltermen of tomorrow—because they loved horses and horse racing. Because their life was the long pungent stable lines, picturesque stable hands, wise little jockeys and handlers, and the hard gamble of breeding, buying, training, racing sleek thoroughbreds.

There was plenty of activity at the Cavanaugh barn. Horses that had raced were being walked out and cooled off under blankets. Last touches of expert attention were being given to horses that would race later in the afternoon. Owners, friends, visitors, jockey agents, track officials were moving about. The drumming rush of horses in the fourth race pounded past on the nearby track.

Mr. Maddox saw Jeanne Cavanaugh before she saw him. She was walking nervously back and forth before the stalls.

Baled hay was piled there, clean straw scattered underfoot, leather tack and a metal feed basket hung on pegs. Jeanne wore slacks, a light jacket sweater. A gay silk handkerchief was tied around her forehead and blonde hair. She seemed oblivious of her surroundings, and probably was unaware that the square set of her shoulders was very like the wiry carriage of old Cap'n Jim Cavanaugh.

"Hello, Jeanny," Mr. Maddox said.

She gave him a blank look and then a forced smile. "It's Mr. Maddox, isn't it?"

"I hear you were asking for me."

"Was I?" she said vaguely. "It—it was nothing. I didn't mean to bring you clear over here."

HER EYES were red, although she'd effectively used a mirror and vanity. Her forced smile was almost good enough to seem natural. If Mr. Maddox had been in a hurry, if the memory of Honest John O'Toole and black Chimp hadn't lingered in the back of his mind, he might have smiled it off with a few bantering words and gone away. Instead Mr. Maddox walked over and sat down on a bale of hay.

"Some little girls do get mighty pretty when they grow up," he observed. "Where's Jerry?"

The simple question took the forced smile off Jeanne's face. If her look wasn't frightened, questioning, Joe Maddox had lost his astute perception.

"Jerry? Did—did you want to see Jerry for any particular reason?"

Mr. Maddox chuckled as he reached for cigarettes and matches. "I wonder how much Jerry's changed, too. Bet you can't guess how I remember him."

"No," said Jeanne, standing there with her hands in the sweater pockets and the fixed welcoming smile more frozen every moment.

"The Cap'n was whaling him over a knee and you were taking it harder than Jerry was."

"I—I think I remember," Jeanne said. "Wasn't it at Latonia?"

Mr. Maddox nodded. "Is Jerry as good with horses as his father was?"

"Jerry," said Jeanne in a stifled voice, "doesn't like horses very well. He—he's been working at a bank here in Louisville. I've managed the farm and stable for both of us."

"Sit down, Jeanny," said Mr. Maddox, moving over on the hay bale. "You must have the Cap'n's eye for a horse. Got a Derby entry, I hear. I want to look him over while I'm here."

Jeanne sat down and stared at her toes. "Would you like to buy Jeanne's Hope, Mr. Maddox?"

"Before or after the Derby?"

"Now."

"It'd have to be now if he stands any chance of winning," Mr. Maddox said genially. "Derby winners come high. Too high for old Joe Maddox."

"I mean *now,*" said Jeanne in a flat dull voice. She was still staring at her toes. "Twenty thousand cash—and I'll tell you what we've kept hidden. Jeanne's Hope is faster than anyone thinks. He stands a good chance of winning."

"Then twenty grand is robbing you," said Mr. Maddox. "Look at the Derby purse. Seventy-five thousand this year."

"You mean you don't believe me. You don't want to buy him."

"I can't," said Mr. Maddox regretfully. "I'm using all my money making a book. Anyway, I can't use a twenty-grand horse or a Derby winner. I'm a bookie and never have tried to be much of anything else."

"I thought so," said Jeanne in the same stony voice. "I've tried to sell him to everyone who might have the money. I've offered to run him against a stop-watch to prove how fast he is. Everyone thinks there's something wrong because I'm offering him just before the Derby."

"*Mmmmm,* I suppose so. Can't blame them, Jeanny. He might break the track record and still be a dog who'd quit when the heat went on in the stretch."

"I don't blame anyone," said Jeanne without looking up. "If I can't get twenty thousand from you, I can't. I'm sorry you had the walk over here for nothing."

Mr. Maddox quietly asked: "What's the trouble, kid?"

Jeanne swallowed. Her small hands were clenched. She looked like she was fighting tears. Her voice had a dry huskiness as she shook her head.

"No trouble. Please forget it. And don't bet on Jeanne's Hope. He probably isn't as fast as I thought he was. I—I might change my mind and scratch him."

Mr. Maddox protested: "That'd be a crime if he's as good as you think he is."

"He is."

"Funny, Cap'n Jim's stable turning out two horses good enough to rate the Derby," Mr. Maddox mused, watching Jeanne's profile. "Kind of slipped up when you sold El Conde, didn't you?"

JEANNE'S CHEEK muscles bunched. "I knew how good he was. But I had to have money and Gloria Gerryman was willing to spend it. The Gerrymans bought Green Acres, the Harmsworth breeding-farm, near us, you know. Or don't you?"

"Everyone in the game knew when Sam Harmsworth got rid of his father's horses and breeding-farm. Too bad young Sam didn't have the liking for a thoroughbred his father had. He didn't need the Gerryman money."

"The papers said New York business was taking all his interest," Jeanne said dully. "Anyway, the Gerrymans bought the place. And bought El Conde. And according to the papers, she's after Sam himself now."

"So?" said Mr. Maddox. "Well, why not? Sam Harmsworth has family and social position. That's all the Gerryman sideshow needs now, isn't it?"

"I suppose so," Jeanne agreed. "If Sam's fool enough to fall for it."

"Maybe Gloria Gerryman would buy Jeanne's Hope," Mr. Maddox suggested thoughtfully. "Have you tried her?"

"Tried her?" said Jeanne—and suddenly her small fists were beating her knees. "That—that cat! *Oh—*"

Jeanne's voice broke. Snatching out a handkerchief she ran into the next stall, which was empty.

Mr. Maddox lumbered to his feet in astonishment, shook his head, scowled, and went to the stall door. Jeanne's shoulders shook as she stood with her back to the doorway.

"What is it, kid?" Mr. Maddox asked gruffly.

"Go away!" Jeanne all but wailed without looking around.

Mr. Maddox entered the stall and stood behind her. "Listen, Jeanny, I'm only old Joe Maddox, the bookie. Maybe there's nothing I can do. But I won't make it any worse and I might be able to help."

"Go away!"

Mr. Maddox shook his head helplessly, cleared his throat, swore inaudibly and stood his ground.

Cap'n Jim probably would have known what to do. Or her brother, Jerry. Or any man who had reared a daughter. But a hard-boiled old bachelor like Joe Maddox could only flounder helplessly.

"I'll stay here until I get some sense out of all this," Mr. Maddox decided grimly.

"Go away, please!"

Mr. Maddox retreated to the doorway and bulked there with a helplessness alien to his usual vast assurance.

Jeanne wiped her nose. Her slim straight shoulders still shook. But she made no sound. Mr. Maddox swore again to himself. Jeanne was crying all right. Deep down inside she was crying, and there didn't seem to be anything to do about it.

Mention of selling Jeanne's Hope to Gloria Gerryman had set this off. But why? Nothing wrong about the suggestion. Jeanne herself had sold El Conde to the Gerrymans.

Perhaps, Mr. Maddox decided, it was too much to have to sell a horse like El Conde and then sit by and see what a great horse he'd become.

Funny though about Jeanne and her brother having to sell El Conde. Cap'n Jim Cavanaugh had seemed well-fixed. Nice string of horses, nice Bluegrass farm for his mares and yearlings. But you couldn't tell. A stable could be on top one year in the racing game and scraping bottom the next.

And there still was this matter of selling Jeanne's Hope. Only something near to desperation would drive a girl like Jeanne Cavanaugh out peddling a Derby entry the second day before the big race.

"Why don't Jerry get out and do it?" Mr. Maddox asked himself. And then had to admit that maybe Jerry Cavanaugh had done it, was trying even now.

LAUGHTER, VOICES, sounded outside the barn, to the right of the doorway. A feminine voice said loudly: "So this is the horse Gloria might have bought instead of El Conde? Gloria darling, how *terrific* you were to pick El Conde!"

Jeanne stiffened.

Mr. Maddox looked out the doorway as a man commented: "He's too small. Not enough leg for the Derby. How about it, Sam?"

It was a gay group, seven or eight, in front of the second stall over. One of the young men was patting the brown muzzle of the horse inside.

Mr. Maddox whistled softly, and then the tall young man patting the horse looked around, saw him and called: "Is the owner around?"

"Just a moment," Mr. Maddox replied, and turned into the stall. "They're asking for you, kid—and if I didn't see it, I wouldn't believe it. Honest John O'Toole's out there with a Club House bunch. I think one is Sam Harmsworth. And even money says the brunette in the middle is Gloria Gerryman."

Jeanne was already opening a vanity and starting to dab at her eyes and cheeks. Her reply was bitter. "I could expect her to do this."

And then, astonishingly, Jeanne was smiling as she went out.

Mr. Maddox paused outside the doorway and watched the tall young man smile broadly as he stepped to meet her.

"Hello, Jeanne!"

"I'm afraid…."

He was disappointed. "I'm Sam Harmsworth."

"Oh! Of course! How are you, Sam?"

Mr. Maddox handicapped Sam Harmsworth with a look and found him passable. Tall, rangy, with clean lines, a likable smile. Nice voice, too, when he introduced the others.

"You know Gloria, don't you? And this is Miss Anderson, Mrs. Lloyd, and Tony Lloyd, Mr. Sanders, Mr. Conwell and—er—Mr. O'Toole."

Mr. Maddox was watching O'Toole—Honest John O'Toole—who looked like a bluff, hearty Irishman, immaculately dressed, including Homburg, gloves and cane.

And O'Toole was watching Mr. Maddox. In a moment O'Toole stepped around the others and came to the empty stall.

"Hello, Maddox. I didn't expect to meet you here. Friend of Miss Cavanaugh's?"

"Hello, shyster," Mr. Maddox said with scant ceremony. "How'd you deal yourself a spread of suckers like this?"

O'Toole reddened and his mouth shut with a snap. "Going to be nasty, are you, you slob!"

"Louses like you bring it out in me," said Mr. Maddox, enjoying himself. "Which pocket are you getting set to pick?"

"Some day," said O'Toole, keeping his temper with difficulty, "I'm going to take a crack at you. I don't like you, Maddox."

"Thanks for the compliment," accepted Mr. Maddox blandly. "I'll have to be asleep or looking the other way when you get nerve enough to take the crack, shyster. Tell Slim Pasternik that too. Tell him you both smell like skunk to me. All smell and nothing else."

That harmless remark produced an effect. Honest John O'Toole stood scowling, and then his forced smile was white-lipped with strain.

"I'll tell Slim," he said, and turned on his heel and rejoined the others.

The Anderson girl had a sharp, catty face and the high-pitched voice that Mr. Maddox had heard first. She was saying: "Miss Cavanaugh, do you *really* think your horse is as good as Gloria's El Conde?"

Jeanne laughed. "Does Miss Gerryman think so?"

"Heavens, *no!* But Gloria's betting-commissioner, Mr. O'Toole here, says he's worried about the chance your horse has to beat El Conde."

MR. MADDOX, still beside the stall door a few steps away, almost grunted aloud. So O'Toole had been handling the flood of Gerryman money on El Conde. And keeping it quiet, too. Not even Joe Maddox had suspected.

You might know O'Toole would finagle himself into such a spot. But O'Toole worrying about Gloria Gerryman's losing a race? Mr. Maddox smiled sardonically. You could bet that O'Toole had already made sure of his cut. And you could "if" the bet that O'Toole didn't give a sour mutuel ticket what happened otherwise.

O'Toole's deprecating smile and almost humble reply to the Anderson woman brought another sardonic quirk to Mr. Maddox's mouth.

"A good horse always has a chance, Miss Anderson. Naturally I try to overlook nothing that will help Miss Gerryman."

Mr. Maddox had been sizing up Gloria Gerryman. Even prejudice had to admit she was an eyeful. Dressed like a certified check. Dark hair and make-up as near perfection as care and money could attain. She hadn't been bad-looking at the start. Experts had gone on from there.

That was it, Mr. Maddox decided. She'd been modeled in smart beauty salons for the daily parade. And looked it. And the hard pouting line of her mouth hadn't been changed.

Take Jeanne Cavanaugh now, in her slacks, old sweater, silk handkerchief carelessly around her blonde hair. Jeanne was like someone's casual kid sister. You might admire the Gerryman. Jeanne caught at your liking.

And now Jeanne was smiling as she remarked: "We never know what a horse will do until he's finished the race."

"Jeanne had an eye like her father for a horse," Sam Harmsworth remembered genially. "Better look out, Gloria. O'Toole may know what he's talking about."

"O'Toole is an idiot," Gloria said sharply. "Now that he's bet my money—and enough of it, heaven knows—he pretends to be worried. I don't believe him. The only thing that will beat El Conde is a trick. There are so many dishonest people around race tracks. Isn't that so, Miss Cavanaugh? Thieves, swindlers, and such people."

From where he was standing, Mr. Maddox could catch the quick bunching of Jeanne's cheek muscles. Jeanne's left hand clenched tightly and then relaxed. But she was still smiling when she replied.

"Race tracks have cheats and frauds about as often as other places. Most of us don't admire them any more than—than Sam would."

Sam Harmsworth laughed. "Which isn't much, Jeanne. Let's look at your horse—and then I'll duck from these folks and we'll talk old times." He grinned broadly. "I didn't tell them, but the reason I suggested walking over here to see your horse was to see you. It's been a long time since we used to race bareback on the road back of your farm."

Gloria Gerryman spoke sharply. "Sam, you were going to watch my horse run in the sixth race!"

"So I was," Sam said carelessly. "I'll see him run some other race, darling. You always have a horse running somewhere. I can't always meet Jeanne and talk about old times on the farm."

"You can see your farm at the house party tonight. After all, *I* own it now."

"You don't own what Jeanne and I have to talk about," Sam chuckled. "Now let's see your horse, Jeanne. Tony, here, says he's small for the Derby."

Jeanne was pale, but still smiling as she turned back to Mr. Maddox. "Do you mind?"

"I'll see you later," Mr. Maddox said genially. "I just remembered an appointment myself."

Mr. Maddox had no appointment, but questions baited him as he walked back to the barn where his horses were stabled. "That Gerryman cat took a dirty dig at Jeanne with that crack about thieves or I'm a liar," he muttered. "And if Jeanne didn't get back at her, I'm another liar. Bad blood there! And Jeanne's in trouble and needs twenty grand fast! And where does O'Toole come in? He's slick and he's crooked. And if he ain't got an extra ace, I'm a liar three times."

Stiffy was leading the blanketed and placid Kopper King in circles before the barn.

"Know a one-eared nigger called Chimp?" Mr. Maddox asked.

"Nope," said Stiffy warily. "Uh—maybe I've seed him around. There's so da—so dern many of 'em around, a feller can't keep track."

"After you're through with Kopper King, look around for Chimp. He's getting along in years and looks like a monkey. Find out where he's working. And keep your mouth shut. Don't mention my name. I'll see you in the morning."

No need to worry about Stiffy's delivering. He'd find old Chimp if he had to go down all the rat holes.

Later at the clubhouse Mr. Maddox saw Gloria Gerryman and her friends. Sam Harmsworth wasn't there. Gloria looked sulky, angry.

Mr. Maddox was gratified. "Her boy friend stayed with Jeanne and it's burning her. Good for Jeanne."

Meanwhile Joe Maddox had his bookie business—and it was work. He was weary when he entered the hotel suite after nine that evening and found Oscar dialing the radio and enjoying a Scotch.

"Build me a double one," Mr. Maddox said, collapsing in the easiest chair and grunting as he unlaced his shoes.

"Lady friend of yours called three times," Oscar said as he went to the tray holding the mixings.

Mr. Maddox looked up alertly. "Jeanne Cavanaugh?"

"Nope. That Norlene Bell who put half a grand on Jeanne's Hope."

"I'm not in tonight," Mr. Maddox growled.

Oscar squirted bubbling soda into the glass. "She'll call again. Says her boy friend's in town and wants to talk some important Derby money."

"Not tonight," Mr. Maddox repeated. "Not if they've got gold sacked and waiting." Mr. Maddox grabbed the glass, sloshed the ice cubes, drank deeply, and relaxed with a sigh of relief. "I work harder than a ditch-digger, Oscar."

"Sure," said Oscar skeptically, sitting down with his drink.

"I wouldn't go out again tonight for ten grand!"

"I'd sprout wings and fly out for ten grand," said Oscar.

A news broadcast was on. European news, national news, then local items. About the Derby, track gossip, the incoming crowds….

"A record number of automobiles are arriving," the drawling voice stated. "The Chief of Police has requested motorists and pedestrians to be unusually careful. The first traffic death of Derby Week occurred this evening. The body of an unidentified Negro was found shortly after dark beside the Bardstown Road, killed by a hit-and-run driver. There were no witnesses. Police are holding the body and state that a missing left ear is the only clue they have…."

"Missing ear!" Mr. Maddox exploded, jumping up.

"Are you nuts?" Oscar asked in amazement as Mr. Maddox slapped the glass on the table and snatched for his shoes.

"I'm suspicious!" Mr. Maddox snapped as he yanked on the shoes and feverishly tied the laces.

"You going out?"

"Yes!"

"Since when did a one-eared corpse look better than a bag of gold?"

"Since it was a corpse!" Mr. Maddox snapped as he caught his hat and made for the door. "Stick around! I may need you tonight!"

3. The Corpse with the Missing Ear

THE MORGUE room smelled of formaldehyde. Shadows cast by the dim light had a cold bleak look. The morgue attendant was matter-of-fact as he pulled out the slab.

"Get it on the radio an' folks start coming in. Lots of them just for a look. Here he is. Know him?"

Mr. Maddox looked and nodded. "His name is Chimp. Works around the stables at the track. When the broadcast said he had one ear, I wondered if it weren't Chimp."

A patrolman who had come in with them whipped out a notebook and pencil. "What's the initials, mister?"

"Just Chimp."

"Funny name. How's it spelled?"

"It's just short for chimpanzee. But as far as I know, that's the only name he ever had."

"Hell of a name. He work for you?"

"No. But I've seen him around the tracks for years."

The patrolman noted the imposing, prosperous figure and a note of respect entered his voice. "Do you own a stable? I'll have to take your name as the identifying party."

Someone chuckled behind Mr. Maddox. "He owns a stable—and there's not another one like it in the country. Eh, Joe? I saw your Kopper King put on another comic this afternoon."

"Cassidy," Mr. Maddox guessed without looking around. He was sarcastic when he faced the grizzled, stocky man behind him. "Bad place for you, Cassidy. Someone might get your number and lay you on a slab. Were you following me?"

"I'll get around to it," Cassidy promised. "Since when did you get interested in morgue stiffs, Joe?"

"Since I knew you," said Mr. Maddox blandly.

"Do you know this nigger, too?" the patrolman demanded of Cassidy.

Cassidy flipped open a small leather pocket case. "Masterton Agency. Track detective."

"Oh, sure—glad you dropped in on this," the officer said readily. "This gentleman says the nigger worked at the track."

"That's right," Cassidy agreed.

"I got to find out who he worked for."

"Someone at the barns can tell you." Cassidy pursed his lips and looked down at the slab. "So somebody smacked old Chimp with a car and left him on the road?"

"Caved in the back of his head and scratched him a little," the morgue man said. "I've seen 'em come in here all busted up. When a train hits 'em—oh, my! This fellow was lucky."

"Every man to his own kind of luck," Mr. Maddox commented. "That's all I know about him. Cassidy here can give you my pedigree. We're old friends."

"Old acquaintances, anyway," said Cassidy. "His name is Maddox. Joe Maddox. Staying at the Hollister House. He'll be easy to get if you want him. Wait a minute, Joe. I'm going your way."

"I was afraid so," Mr. Maddox growled as Cassidy fell into step beside him. "So you've been watching me again?"

"How's the book doing?"

"Who said I was making a book?"

Cassidy smiled grimly. "There's plenty who'll say it."

"And prove it?"

"Maybe I'll have to do the proving."

THEY WERE on the sidewalk now and Mr. Maddox stopped, put a heavy blunt finger against Cassidy's chest. "Cassidy, I brought horses here to run. Like Vanderbilt. Like Whitney. Don't bother me by trying to make a pinch on any grounds!"

"Vanderbilt, Whitney—and Maddox," Cassidy said and chuckled. "Don't make me die laughing, Joe. If an owner's badge and privileges didn't go with those nags you ship around, you'd peddle them for lion steaks at the first zoo."

"Like hell!" Mr. Maddox denied with the first genuine irritation he had displayed.

"Maybe you wouldn't at that," Cassidy was graceful enough to admit. "Look, Joe—cut the stalling. Any particular reason for coming around to look at old Chimp?"

"The radio mentioned his missing ear. It reminded me of Chimp."

"That all?"

"Any reason why it shouldn't be all?"

"No-o-o," Cassidy admitted slowly. "I just wondered. Running into you at the morgue and all. Listen, Joe, I never thought you were a fool."

"Thanks for nothing."

"You're pretty smart, in fact."

"If it's a touch," said Mr. Maddox with resignation, "don't bother to lay it on so thick. I'm a sucker for a touch."

"You can keep your mouth shut," Cassidy finished. "Listen, Joe. Homicide knows who Chimp is. He smelled of horse liniment and had horse hairs on his clothes. With the track open now, they didn't have to guess. A few questions at the stable gate proved Chimp belonged there. They got in touch with our agency."

"Then why the phony broadcast—and a cop watching the body?"

"Murder," Cassidy said. "He was socked on the back of the head. He'd done his bleeding and was plenty dead when he was chucked from a car out there on the Bardstown Road."

Mr. Maddox swore softly. He and Cassidy had started walking.

Cassidy went on with a hard grim edge to his voice. "Who'n hell'd want to kill old Chimp? I've seen him around the bangtails since before I went with the Masterton Agency. He was so damned ugly, and having only one ear made him easy to remember."

"Maybe," said Mr. Maddox, "it was trouble over a crap game. Maybe he just got into an argument."

"Maybe," said Cassidy.

"Who was he working for? So far, all they've heard is that Chimp was doing odd jobs for anyone who needed a hand."

"Not much to go on."

"Not much," Cassidy agreed. "I was hoping you might know something about him, Joe."

Never had Mr. Maddox looked more like a bland, regretful Buddha. "Sorry, Cassidy. My horses are at the track—but I don't spend much time with them."

"You're telling me."

"I'll leave you here. It's been a hard day," said Mr. Maddox. "If I run across anything you can use, I'll let you know."

Cassidy was rubbing his chin, staring blankly as they parted on the corner.

MR. MADDOX was scowling, thinking, as he walked in the opposite direction and hailed a taxi. Chimp murdered! What could you think of it after Chimp's agitation early in the morning at the track? Slim Pasternik seemed to have been the cause. And Pasternik was man-of-all work for Honest John O'Toole. All dirty work. And O'Toole was handling money for Gloria Gerryman. And there had been some hidden meaning when Gloria Gerryman spoke to Jeanne Cavanaugh.

"The girls had been talking about O'Toole," Mr. Maddox muttered. "Gerryman cracked about thieves and swindlers and Jeanny cracked back. Did they really mean something—or was it only a couple of the girls sharpening their claws?"

Granted there was meaning in the smiling exchange of words between the two girls, would common sense suggest a connection between black Chimp's death and Gloria Gerryman?

Mr. Maddox entered the Hollister House and was crossing the lobby when a smiling young woman stopped him.

"You are Mr. Maddox, aren't you?"

"That's right, sister," Mr. Maddox admitted after a quick look. "I'm Norlene Bell."

She was young enough, dressed well enough—if extremely. But life hadn't been too easy with her. The marks were plain to see under the make-up.

Mr. Maddox couldn't recall her—which was unusual. She'd told Oscar that she'd bet with the Maddox book before. But then thousands could say the same thing. Mr. Maddox couldn't remember them all, he supposed, though he didn't miss on many.

She knew him by sight. She'd bet five hundred cash on Jeanne's Hope. Which might mean anything or nothing. She'd suggested to Oscar that there'd be more. Anything connected with Jeanne's Hope was of interest at the moment.

Mr. Maddox smiled warmly. "I hear you've been telephoning for me, Miss Bell. You placed a bet this afternoon, didn't you?"

"I certainly did. And the way somebody on your phone has been stalling me sounds like I'm poison, or trying to borrow my money back instead of betting more."

"Sorry," said Mr. Maddox regretfully. "Commissions are always welcome. I've been out. Now," he finished with a flourish of gallantry that might have thawed even Gloria Gerryman, "I'm entirely at your service."

"It's about time someone trotted out the old oil," Norlene Bell told him briskly. "My gentleman friend's in town with a couple of his friends and a pair of bank-rolls that need a soft spot in the Derby. They want to talk to you."

"We like that kind of business," said Mr. Maddox heartily. "Any time tomorrow that you suggest."

"Tonight," said Norlene Bell firmly. "And if you don't get it quickly, I'll find a bookie who will. There's a big crap game at the Broadway Hotel. My friends are having some drinks out on Third Street and talking about rolling dice before they go to bed. If they get in that game, they won't have horse money left."

"They'll get action, at least, if it's Duke Major's game," Mr. Maddox commented. "It's at the Broadway, I hear, and the word is out that only high-rollers are wanted."

"The boys are waiting for me," she said impatiently. "And I'm taking a bookie back to get their horse money tonight if I have to kidnap one!"

Mr. Maddox had already made his decision. "If you'll allow me a few moments upstairs, Miss Bell, I think we can settle this quickly."

"Now you're talking," she said, pleased and obviously relieved. "Make it snappy, before the boys run out on me. I'll be in that chair."

AS MR. MADDOX entered the room, Oscar turned off the radio. "That dame called again, says she's waiting downstairs, Joe.

She's getting hot. Did you collect the dead man?"

"Ixnay on the wisecracks!" Mr. Maddox snapped. "I'm in a hurry! This lady collared me in the lobby. I'm going with her and smoke out a couple of bankrolls. Listen to this.

"Get Stiffy, out at the barn. He may be asleep. You may have to take a hack out there and find him. Or wait for him."

"What's up?" Oscar asked alertly.

"How do I know? I'm trying to find out! Ask Stiffy what he discovered about the colored fellow. See if he found out who Chimp was working for, and any other dope he got about him."

"Chimp? You brought a bet in under that name!"

"He's dead. Stiffy'll probably know about it already."

"I knew it!" Oscar exclaimed. "It's that damn radio report! Listen, Joe, are we going to have more trouble? What business have we got with a one-eared black man who got clipped by a hit-and-run car?"

"It was murder!"

"My God! That makes it worse! Joe, we're here in Louisville! The Derby's day after tomorrow! There'll be enough dough around town to sink a river barge! Ain't that enough to worry about, Joe, without you up to your old tricks? And over a one-eared black corpse!"

"I know what I'm doing!" said Mr. Maddox, not quite accurately. "Here's something else for you. Find a fellow named Jerry Cavanaugh. He works in a local bank. Must be living in town. If he's not in the directory, you might find out though his sister, who owns Jeanne's Hope. Stiffy can find where she's staying. Or you can telephone the Cavanaugh Farm. It's out on the Bardstown Highway near Mt. Washington.

"Bardstown—Bardstown! The Cavanaugh Farm and the Gerryman Farm are both on that road! I wonder if that has anything to do with Chimp's being pitched out on the Bardstown Road?"

Oscar begged: "Does any of this make sense? I don't like it, Joe!"

"Get through to Jerry Cavanaugh some way, if you have to yank him out of bed," Mr. Maddox ordered energetically. "Tell him I want to see him tonight. If he won't come here, I'll go where he is. But I want to talk to him."

"O.K." Oscar nodded. "But I don't have to like it—and I don't! You going out with that Bell girl now?"

"On Third Street, she says. I won't be gone long. She's cornered a couple of fat bankrolls that are itching to buck the dice tonight."

"I hope you have luck there anyway," said Oscar. He shook his head sourly as Mr. Maddox headed out again. "Ten grand wouldn't have got you outa here a little while ago—and a dead nigger with one ear starts you charging around like a college cheer-leader! If I had my way, I'd get you outa town so fast—"

The closing door cut off Oscar's voice….

AS THE elevator let him out in the lobby, Mr. Maddox's frown changed to his usual broad, beaming good nature.

"We'd better hurry," Norlene Bell said as they left the hotel. "I called the apartment. The boys are sore because I'm not back. They've had a few drinks and want to get going." And as Mr. Maddox stepped to the curb for a taxi, she said: "My car's parked around the corner."

Mr. Maddox kept pace with her hurried steps. He had forgotten that he was tired. Part of his mind was on the dead Chimp, part on Jeanne Cavanaugh, Honest John O'Toole and the Cavanaugh horse.

"So you like Jeanne's Hope?" he remarked.

"*I* do. My friend doesn't."

That suggested her five hundred on Jeanne's Hope had little significance. She was only another customer. But if her friends had good money to cover tonight, this inconvenience would be justified.

She unlocked a sleek new sedan, drove expertly, hurried through traffic to Third Street, and turned south. "What do you think of Jeanne's Hope?" Norlene Bell questioned.

"Maybe a chance."

"Don't kid me. Is that all?"

"'No horse in the Derby has much more than a chance."

"That's baloney," she retorted scornfully. "You bookies have a good idea what's going to happen."

"But we don't all agree," Mr. Maddox chuckled. "If I could nail the winner, I'd retire after the race. The dope makes El Conde a stand-out."

She sounded the horn vigorously, shot past a car ahead. "That's what they think," she said flippantly.

"Why shouldn't they think so?" Mr. Maddox asked, on guard quickly from the tone of her voice.

She laughed. "Don't pump me, big boy. I don't know anything."

Mr. Maddox tried again to remember her, and couldn't. But she knew her way around. She was as hard-boiled as they come.

"What did you say your friend's name was?"

"I didn't say," she parried. "It'll surprise you. Here's the place just ahead."

Apartment houses, mostly brick, three and four stories high, set back from the sidewalk, were scattered along this tree-lined stretch of South Third. The building before which they parked was like many others along the street.

The Bell girl brushed the horn button as she took out a cigarette and turned. "Got a match?"

Mr. Maddox gave her a folder and reached for the door handle. The match flare lighted her face for an instant. Mr. Maddox paused, looking sharply at her.

The matchlight revealed her hard, knowing smile. Her look through the flame was triumphant. She blew the match out. Her voice had a faint mocking edge that might not otherwise have been noticeable.

"Thanks for the match. Thanks for coming," she said. "I didn't think you would."

She started to get out. She'd pulled the emergency brake and left the motor running. That brief sound of the horn might have been a signal.

Something was wrong. Mr. Maddox wasn't sure just what. But he was suddenly certain that he had made a fool move in leaving the hotel like this.

He shoved the door open to get out and the answer was there on the curb before him….

The man standing there must have come from a parked car behind them. He hadn't been there when they stopped, hadn't come out of the apartment house. "Stay in there, Maddox," he said. He was reaching under his coat.

It didn't need this much to recognize a heist. And by the time a man could lunge out of the car, the stranger could easily clip him. Mr. Maddox did the next best thing.

He obeyed, stayed in the car. Yanking hard on the door handle, he slammed the door shut, pushed the handle to lock position and threw himself across the seat behind the steering wheel to the other door through which the Bell girl had vanished.

Outside the automobile, in the street, he'd have a chance. The girl probably had a gun too. She might shoot. Mr. Maddox still carried the day's bankroll, and plenty of it.

Ordinarily he wouldn't have taken a long chance against stick-up guns. Too often bandits killed when the victim made a break. Joe Maddox knew he could always get a new bankroll. But Joe Maddox was finished, through, if a startled and angry gunman or gun-moll cut loose with a clip of metal-jacketed bullets.

But when you'd been taken for a sucker ride like this, you blew up….

The girl tried to shut the door. Mr. Maddox struck it with his hand and shoulder. The door flew out again, carrying her stumbling back.

That much Mr. Maddox saw as he started out to where he could straighten up and have room. Only then, from the corner of his eye, did he see the man turning from the handle of the rear door and bringing up an arm.

It couldn't be the man he'd just ducked back from. That one couldn't have gotten around the automobile so fast. Two men had come up beside the car, evidently.

Mr. Maddox ducked and tried to guard his head.

The blow glanced hard off his arm, crushed in his hat in a glancing swipe, knocked his head down.

Off-balance, dazed, Mr. Maddox still tried to fight out of the car. He was rolling forward when the man lunged into him and shoved him back. Mr. Maddox grabbed the coat, tried to drag himself out and up. The man swore at him.

The Bell girl wrenched out with a trace of hysteria: "You'll kill him, Dave! You'll kill him!"

"I'll cave his head in!" Dave said furiously. The second blow he struck clashed hollowly against the metal edge of the car roof, skidded down the side of Mr. Maddox's head, crushed his shoulder into numbness.

It felt like pipe and rang on the car-top like iron or steel instead of lead. In the quick, savage, almost silent melée, one white-hot thought raced through Maddox's mind.

Pipe like this must have caved in Chimp's head! Probably the same pipe, the same man! Joe Maddox was slated to be next!

The thought helped him hang onto consciousness and keep fighting to get out of the car.

Suddenly his neck was grabbed from behind. He was hauled back in against the seat. Strong fingers dug into his windpipe.

Mr. Maddox released the coat, tried to tear the hands away. He couldn't reach the man, who must have jumped into the back of the car from the curb.

The two of them pushed, wrestled him back to his side of the seat. He was gasping, fast weakening from lack of breath.

"Keep still, Maddox, or you'll get it sure as hell! Right here!"

Mr. Maddox stopped struggling. The hands cautiously loosened their grip.

"Someone's coming!" Dave panted. "Hold him! Shove him down in the seat!"

THE GIRL stayed behind. Maybe she had already left, walking to another car or hurrying across the street. Doors slammed. The motor was still idling. Then the car was away from the curb smoothly, swiftly, and if anyone was aware of the trouble, or suspicious, they made no sound that Mr. Maddox could hear—or that the two men noticed.

Gasping, gagging, Mr. Maddox tried to get his breath through a painfully congested throat. Head, arm and shoulder hurt from the dull, heavy blows. More alarming was the thought that these two men must already have murdered once tonight.

Another thought almost brought a grim smile. "Cassidy will have a fit if Joe Maddox is found out on the Bardstown Road and brought back to the morgue!"

The man in the back seat kept a hand on Mr. Maddox's shoulder, dug a gun muzzle into his back. "Going to take it easy, Maddox?"

"Write your own ticket," Mr. Maddox said thickly.

"Hold still! I'm going to frisk you."

The car turned left off Third Street, shortly made another turn as a hand from behind emptied Mr. Maddox's pockets, made sure he had no weapon.

The dashlight was off. Street lights at the corners showed the man called Dave lounging behind the wheel. The flurry of rage had passed, leaving a deceptive calm. His blunt weapon was not on the seat beside him. Mr. Maddox's exploring hand drew back.

"If it's money," said Mr. Maddox, "you've got it."

"And you," Dave retorted without turning his head.

Mr. Maddox spoke again in a monotone. "You've got my dough and you've got me. So what? Nobody would pay fifty dollars to see me again."

Dave turned another corner. They were, as near as Mr. Maddox could tell, driving toward the outskirts of town.

The man in the back laughed shortly. "You carried enough dough yourself. A slob as smooth as you should have better sense than to walk around heeled like that."

"Live and learn," Mr. Maddox muttered.

The man laughed again. "If you live." His gun muzzle slid over the seat top and prodded between Mr. Maddox's broad shoulders.

"Meaning?" Mr. Maddox said, not turning his head.

The gun jabbed for emphasis. "Meaning we don't like you, Maddox. We don't like that big face. We don't like that big belly. We don't like to see you around."

"I gather you don't like me," said Mr. Maddox dryly.

"That's smart. You're spoiling the Derby for us. We don't like it."

Dave spoke impatiently from the side of his mouth. "Give it to the big lug straight. He'll be kidding you next."

"He'll get it quick enough."

They were fast leaving Louisville, somewhere south and east of the Third Street spot where they'd started.

They passed bright gas-station lights. Beyond each oasis of light the road was a little darker. The outlying tentacles of the city dwindled. Fenced fields bordered the road. The cool night became black beyond the boring headlights.

Mr. Maddox considered jumping from the car. The thought might have been read for the gun touched his back again.

"I'd hate to shoot you, Maddox, if you tried to jump. It'd mess up the car."

"I've been trying to place you two," Mr. Maddox said slowly.

"Help yourself."

That might mean he'd never seen them before. Might mean that it didn't matter whether he did know them.

MR. MADDOX had recovered his hat. Perspiration was damp under the sweatband. His shoulder and head ached, but he ignored the feeling as nerves grew tighter and tighter.

Dave turned into a side road, graveled, narrow, without visible

life besides themselves. Fields and trees alternated on a rolling landscape. The car slowed sharply, swung into dirt ruts that led back into a patch of woodland.

Dave stopped, backed out on the road again, and headed the car back toward town before he stopped once more with the motor softly idling.

Dave turned behind the wheel, warily poised.

"You've had time to think it over, Maddox," the man in back said, sharper now and cold.

"I've thought."

Will-power kept Mr. Maddox quiet against the gun muzzle. Straining nerves cried to make a fight of it while there was a chance—if a gun in your back gave you any chance at all.

Dave said: "This is a lotta damn foolishness! Let me take him!"

"I'll handle it!" the cold voice said. "Maddox, you get one chance. No more. Beat it out of town!"

Mr. Maddox relaxed. "Any particular reason?"

"We don't like you!"

"Why bring me out here to say it?"

"We brought you out here for this!" A fist looped from behind, grazing Mr. Maddox's cheek and knocking him over against Dave.

Dave was waiting. Dave slugged the other cheek.

Mr. Maddox drove an elbow into Dave, knocking him back behind the wheel. A grab caught the door handle and the door was opening when the gun slugged Mr. Maddox out into the road.

He fell flat, lay dazed. As from far away he heard the cold voice close above him.

"Get smart, Maddox! If you're in town tomorrow, we'll take you! Lam out of the state while you've got a chance!"

Mr. Maddox was trying to get up. A kick knocked him sprawling again. The car started so fast the spinning wheels drove a stinging shower of gravel. When Mr. Maddox lurched groggily to his feet, the twin red tail-lights were dim through dust and vanishing over the first rise in the road.

His fingers found a cut, bleeding cheek. He was coated with dirt, sick and dizzy. The bright stars and clear sky, the peace and quiet of the lonesome night were a mockery to this hurt and helplessness.

Trembling, Mr. Maddox brushed at the dirt. He lurched when he stooped for his hat. Vague night sounds came out of the trees. Far off across the fields a dog barked. Mr. Maddox's feet crunched heavily on the gravel as he started back to the highway….

4. The Weepstakes

IT WAS close to midnight when Mr. Maddox returned to the hotel. Quiet had not yet fallen over the streets. There would be little quiet now, day or night, until after Derby Day.

People in the lobby stared. The elevator boy stared. Mr. Maddox had brushed himself as well as he could without a whisk, but his suit still looked as if he had rolled on the ground.

The cut cheek had stopped bleeding, but the elevator mirrors showed a dried smear of blood, the raw cut itself and bruises. The broad bland face of Joe Maddox, usually so smiling and confident, was sadly battered.

In the mirror Mr. Maddox sighted a quick glance of understanding between two men behind him. Their faint smiles said they considered him just another drunk.

In the suite Oscar was smoking, walking about. He stopped, staring at Mr. Maddox. "My God, Joe!"

"Fix me another drink," Mr. Maddox ordered huskily as he stripped off his coat.

"You look like you ran into a buzzsaw!"

"Who gives a damn how I look? Stop babbling like a nitwit and give me a double Scotch, straight. What luck did you have with those calls I told you to make?"

Oscar jerked a thumb at an easy chair drawn up facing the window, its back toward Mr. Maddox. "Get up, punk, and spiel it," Oscar said as he turned to the Scotch bottle.

Stiffy slid out of the chair and eyed Mr. Maddox with wary fascination. Stiffy had donned a wrinkled blue coat, slicked down his hair, but still looked like a stable punk cornered where he had no business to be.

Oscar added: "He said guys out at the track could hear him talking at the telephone, so I told him to grab a taxi and come here."

"I'm glad somebody's using a head around here tonight!" Mr. Maddox said sarcastically. "Let's have it Stiffy. What about that black Chimp? Never mind trying to hide the tobacco in your cheek!"

Stiffy's Adam's apple bobbed in his long thin neck as he swallowed and smiled wanly. "I ast that damned—" Stiffy went mute, backing to the shelter of his chair. "Hit ain't my fault, Mist' Joe!" Stiffy pleaded. "Comes when I ain't a-lookin'! I was tryin' to think fast—"

"Never mind this time. What about Chimp?"

"I snooped like you said. Plenty knowed that ole crop-ear dinge. Nigger gal with a razor sliced his ear off when he two-timed her. She yelled if them black cats liked him so well she'd cut him into cat meat for them. Hit scared the bob-tailed hell outen him an' he lit runnin' with his ear in his hand and kept going!"

Stiffy swallowed. "He'd bought her a marriage license, too. He never set eye on that damned ear again. Oncet when he was goin' through town on a freight he mighty near hopped off an'—"

"Never mind Chimp's past history," Mr. Maddox snapped. "What was he doing at the track?"

"Workin' around," said Stiffy. "Mostly around them Green Acres Farm horses."

"The Gerryman Stable?"

"Uh-huh."

"I'll be damned!" said Mr. Maddox. "Doubly and triply damned! Here's ten dollars!" Mr. Maddox scowled in remembrance as he failed to find the usual fat billfold inside his coat. "Oscar, give him a tenner. Give me that drink. Go on, Stiffy!"

"Gosh! Thanks!" Stiffy grabbed the money that Oscar handed him. "I reckon that's all. There's a nigger works for the Green Acre Stables 'at's some kin to this ole Chimp. He's the one told me how-come him to lose that there ear."

Mr. Maddox almost choked on the double whiskey. "Chimp's got a relative working for Gloria Gerryman?"

"Uh-huh. Name of Yaller Sam. He come with the Green Acre Farm when it was sold. Yaller Sam's a high-steppin' little nigger. Says he ain't claiming the dead 'un for kin so's they can't make him pay for the buryin'. Told me that hisself. I mighty near hung one on him for being so derned smart."

"Did you get Miss Cavanaugh's address?"

"I got it," Oscar said.

"That's all, Stiffy," Mr. Maddox decided. "Keep your mouth shut about this."

OSCAR WAITED until the door closed behind Stiffy. "I couldn't

find a Jerry Cavanaugh in the phone book, Joe. So I long-distanced the farm. A sleepy nigger woman answered. She was all tangled up about what I wanted, but she finally got the idea. She hunted around a little and came back with an address and telephone number. It's on that paper by the telephone. South Third Street."

Mr. Maddox winced almost visibly. "Did you call Jerry?"

"Yes. A man answered and said he wasn't Cavanaugh. Said he didn't know when Cavanaugh would be back. He asked me who I was and I stalled."

"Who was he?"

"How should I know? All he said was he wasn't Jerry Cavanaugh. Anyway a dame came to the phone a moment later and started trying to find out who wanted Cavanaugh."

"And you didn't find out who she was either?"

"You didn't say to get the dope on everybody who answered Cavanaugh's telephone," Oscar complained. "She sounded too anxious to get a line on me. I stalled her, too—and when she said she didn't know when Cavanaugh would be back I told her I'd call later."

"Did you mention my name?"

"I wouldn't until I got Cavanaugh. I was getting ready to call again when you came in."

"Which shows how smart it is to be too smart—and maybe you were right after all," Mr. Maddox growled, turning to the Scotch bottle again. "I've got to change clothes and get patched up. Call a doctor."

"Joe! Are you going out again?"

"I am!"

"Next time you'll come back on a shutter," Oscar warned sourly. "And by the looks of you, it almost happened this time! I knew that one-eared nigger in the morgue would get you into trouble!"

"Get my clothes!"

"You didn't have ten bucks to give that boy. Where's your bankroll, Joe?"

Mr. Maddox hurled the empty whiskey glass on the floor. "I wish I knew! I wish I knew a lot of things! I wish you'd cut that damned bleating! If it'll make you feel any better, I got snatched, beat up and robbed! And warned that if I'm in town tomorrow, I get knocked off! Does that make you feel any better?"

Oscar groaned. "I knew it was too good to last! Fine weather, plenty of dough for the book! Everything hotsy-totsy—and this has to happen!, Want me to start packing, Joe?"

"Get my brown suit!" Mr. Maddox snarled. "We came here for the Derby, didn't we?"

THE THIRD STREET address of Jerry Cavanaugh was another red brick apartment house, severe, dignified. When a taxi deposited Mr. Maddox on the curb, it was so late most windows were dark. There was not much traffic on the streets either.

Apartment 3, Oscar's information said. The foyer mail box for Apartment 3 bore a small card lettered: *D.H. Crowder—J. Cavanaugh.*

The telephone, Mr. Maddox guessed, was listed in Crowder's name. Crowder must have answered Oscar's call. The woman could be anyone, wife or friend of either man.

A bell button and speaking tube were above the mail box. Mr. Maddox ignored them and walked heavily up the stairs.

Apartment 3 was at the back.

Mr. Maddox lifted the small brass knocker, let it fall with a bang.

A thumb lock turning quickly inside suggested the person had been waiting for a caller. Then the opening door framed the anxious face of Jeanne Cavanaugh.

She gasped slightly at sight of Mr. Maddox. She was uncertain, astonished, quickly fearful.

"I—I didn't expect to see you!" she said.

"Ditto." Mr. Maddox smiled ruefully. "May I come in?"

"Why—yes. I'm waiting for Jerry. You—you wanted to see Jerry?"

A yellow dinner dress threw gold in Jeanne's hair, now caught most properly on her head. She was a little lady in her own right now, with a slim natural grace that Gloria Gerryman would never have. For it was an inner grace that money and beauty salons could never attain.

"Sam Harmsworth should see," Mr. Maddox thought as he lumbered into the small living-room. "The boy's a fool if he can't tell which is the thoroughbred filly." But aloud, he said: "Jerry? Yes, I hoped I'd find Jerry."

Jeanne was looking at Mr. Maddox's face. "You've been hurt?"

"Slightly." Mr. Maddox chuckled. "So we're both waiting for Jerry. When do you expect him?"

Jeanne sat down opposite him. Her small strong hands moved nervously in her lap. "I don't know," she confessed, watching him. "What—what do you want with Jerry?"

She was worried. Afraid too. And she had no cause to fear Joe Maddox. It had to be fear for her brother.

"Are we alone?"

Jeanne nodded. "Sam Harmsworth brought me here and left a little while ago."

"Fine young fellow."

"Yes," said Jeanne. Color rushed into her face.

"So it's that way," Mr. Maddox thought. But to Jeanne he said: "I wondered what Jerry was doing to help—and what I could do."

"I thought so," said Jeanne. "Please—I told you this afternoon—"

"None of my business, eh?"

Jeanne stood up, as if nerves cried against calm. "There's nothing you can do."

"Except buy your horse," Mr. Maddox supplied calmly.

"You won't—can't. Please forget everything."

"Jerry might have an idea," Mr. Maddox mused.

"I don't want you to say anything to Jerry!"

Mr. Maddox said casually: "Sam Harmsworth has plenty of money. Perhaps—"

"No!" said Jeanne passionately. "Not one word to Sam about this! I—I hardly know him! Today is the first time we've met for years!"

"He seemed to like it." Mr. Maddox smiled. "Didn't I hear something about an engagement he had tonight at Green Acres Farm?"

Jeanne's face was flaming. "Leave Sam out of this!"

Mr. Maddox chuckled again. "If that's the way you feel about him."

"I didn't say I felt any way about him! Please stop insinuating such nonsense!"

"I seem to be saying all the wrong things," Mr. Maddox said, with contriteness somewhat spoiled by the understanding amusement in his eyes. "But while I'm here, can I ask a few questions?"

"About what?"

"Do you know a black stable hand at the track called Chimp? Has one ear."

"No. Why do you ask?"

"It's sort of a game. D'you know a thin-faced fellow called Dave?"

Jeanne thought a moment and nodded. "I know the Reverend David Jones, in Mt. Washington. He's tall and thin."

"Not the man, I'm afraid." Mr. Maddox chuckled again. "How about a woman who calls herself Norlene Bell?"

"I don't know her. I don't see what all this is leading to."

"Neither do I," Mr. Maddox admitted. "Here's one more. Do you know Slim Pasternik?"

"Slim Pasternik?" Jeanne repeated sharply. The fear was dark in her eyes again. "Who is *he?*"

"Gunman and gambler."

JEANNE'S MOUTH opened. Then she turned to cigarettes lying on the wall table. The match flame trembled in her unsteady hand. She was looking down at the table, toying with the cigarettes, when her strained voice answered.

"I guess I've heard the name. That's all."

The easy chair creaked softly as Mr. Maddox got up and stepped to her. Jeanne looked up at him. She was pale.

"So Slim's got a hand in it?" Mr. Maddox said quietly. "Jeanny, don't lie to me now. I was a friend of your father's. I'm your friend. What about Slim Pasternik? There was a murder tonight."

"A murder? Ah—*who?* Jerry—"

"Not Jerry. A colored stable hand. But it was murder. Where is Jerry?"

Jeanne's laugh had a hysterical note. She was near to tears. "You startled me. Jerry wouldn't know anything about a murder. I—I don't know this man Pasternik. The worst that Jerry can be doing tonight is gambling. I'm not even sure of that. I—I'm only afraid he is."

"Gambling?" repeated Mr. Maddox. "And Jerry works in a bank?"

Jeanne's tears were unshed but glistening. Her chin trembled. "Jerry's not working at the bank just now. He—he—" Jeanne groped for a handkerchief.

Mr. Maddox, towering above her, looked concerned and thoughtful. "Jerry's out of the bank now," he mused. "And you need a lot of cash quick. And Jerry's been gambling? That makes a picture, Jeanny. How long has Jerry been gambling?"

"Several years," Jeanne admitted in a stifled voice. "At first he won a lot of money. Then he lost. He—he wins a little and loses a lot. And keeps thinking that he'll win a lot any time. Jerry's always been reckless. He'd never listen to others, not even his father. He doesn't drink—but this gambling is like a fever. And he loses and loses."

"You sold El Conde to Gloria Gerryman to get money for him?" Mr. Maddox guessed.

Wearily Jeanne said: "Jerry has a half-interest in the farm. El Conde was half his. And I'd do anything if it would help him. Most of our horses are gone. The farm is mortgaged. And—and Jerry keeps thinking he'll help with his gambling and only makes it worse. He's in trouble now."

"At the bank?" Mr. Maddox guessed again. "Jerry took some money?"

Jeanne wiped her eyes. "Just a little at first and then a lot more. They discovered it several days ago."

"And now Jerry pays it back quickly or gets a stretch in stir?"

Jeanne nodded. "Unless it's paid back or—or I give Gloria Gerryman a bill of sale by tomorrow for Jeanne's Hope."

"What the devil," Mr. Maddox exploded, "does Gloria Gerryman have to do with it?"

"Jerry took the money from the Gerryman account and thought he could cover it up for a time," Jeanne said wretchedly. "Gloria discovered the shortage and told the bank she didn't want Jerry arrested until she thought it over. The bank thinks she's doing it because our two farms are close together. Because we're neighbors. The bank thinks it's kind and generous of her. The Gerryman account is so large that the bank is glad to do almost anything Gloria demands."

Mr. Maddox growled under his breath. "If I'm any good as a guesser, that gold-plated little tart never did anything generous unless she got plenty out of it. So she wants your horse, kid?"

JOE MADDOX was a kindly man, and never was more so than at a time like this. A moment later Jeanne was crying softly against his coat.

"She m-means to win this Derby no matter what she has to do. She told me so. And she's heard that Jeanne's Hope has a good chance of winning. She says she'll pay Jerry's shortage at the bank and keep him out of prison if I give her a bill of sale for Jeanne's Hope and let Jeanne's Hope run under the Gerryman colors, too!"

"If I know the lady, your horse wouldn't stand much chance of winning under the Gerryman colors," Mr. Maddox growled. "There's too much Gerryman money bet on El Conde to win. That girl is sharp and hard. That means El Conde had better win."

"Jerry thinks so, too," Jeanne said wearily. "He doesn't think Gloria would let Jeanne's Hope win. And he says Jeanne's Hope has to run and win. He won't hear of anything else. He's sure our horse will win. He says we'll have plenty of money then—much more than the purse—enough to pay the bank back and take care of any trouble. He made me promise not to say anything until he saw me again. Oh, I don't know what to do! I tried to sell Jeanne's Hope for cash to pay the bank—and I couldn't!"

"How much did Jerry take?"

"About nineteen thousand—from the Valley Trust Company."

"And Jerry's out gambling tonight, letting you worry?"

"He told me not to worry when I talked to him on the telephone tonight. He said he'd be too busy to see me, but everything would be all right. He sounded excited and confident when he hung up."

Jeanne's gesture was helpless. "He wouldn't tell me anything. All I could do was come here, have the janitor let us in and wait."

"How about this Crowder, whose name is on the mail box?"

"That's Dick Crowder. They went to college together. Dick's out of town."

Mr. Maddox thought a moment, and then smiled and patted her shoulder. "You've done enough worrying. Turn in here and

get some sleep. Maybe Jerry's right. Maybe everything will be all right."

"How can it be?"

"Let Jerry and me worry about it," chuckled Mr. Maddox. "You get your beauty sleep—and tomorrow keep an eye on your horse and Sam Harmsworth."

"I won't be seeing Sam again. I told him so tonight."

"And what did Sam say?"

"He got mad when I wouldn't tell him why."

"Don't blame him," said Mr. Maddox. "If he's got any sense he won't even listen to you. But if he's fallen in love with you he probably is dizzy and not thinking straight."

"Sam's not in love with me! He's practically engaged to Gloria Gerryman!"

"So you're going to dog it in the stretch-run and let her have him," Mr. Maddox snorted. "What kind of racing is that? You're crazy about him!"

"I always have been. And I've cried all over you and I feel better. Sam won't want to see me again after Gloria tells him about Jerry. So let's all forget it."

"If Gerryman's as smart as I think she is, she won't blab to Sam until she gets him," Mr. Maddox said shrewdly. "Forget it and go to sleep. I'm going. Good-night."

MR. MADDOX was smiling as he left the apartment—and scowling as he hurried downstairs. He'd given Jeanne encouragement that even Joe Maddox could hardly justify. He didn't have twenty grand to help. Borrowing such a sum at this time was almost impossible. Word would flash over town that Joe Maddox was borrowing and must be broke. A bookie was only as good as his prosperity. And if the book was tampered with, if reserve cash was used and the book couldn't pay off after the Derby, there's be hell for Joe Maddox to face.

Jeanne had told him things he didn't know or suspect—and it only made more puzzling the things that already had happened.

Swearing softly under his breath Mr. Maddox hurried out of the apartment house to his waiting taxi. He had taken only half a dozen steps from the door when a familiar voice spoke behind him.

"In a hurry, Joe?"

"Where," said Mr. Maddox irritably as he swung around, "in the devil did you come from, Cassidy?"

Cassidy joined him, bulking in the shadows. "Out of the shrubbery, Joe."

"Following me, huh?"

"Just watching you, Joe," Cassidy said with a hint of grimness. "What was the idea of stalling me about going from the morgue to bed?"

"Any law against staying awake—or dropping around to see a friend?"

"When you came back from your first trip out, you looked like a little law might have helped you," Cassidy said sarcastically. "Who put the slug on you, Joe? And why?"

"So you were watching me then too, were you?" Mr. Maddox growled.

"Murder," said Cassidy, "always did make me curious. The way you're acting tonight makes it worse. Who was the girl you went out with after you shook me near the morgue? I got the license number, but you two ducked into the car so fast you got away before I could follow."

"What is that license number?" Mr. Maddox asked quickly.

"Who's the woman?" Cassidy countered. They eyed one another.

"Maybe we can help each other," Mr. Maddox reluctantly decided.

"Yeah?" said Cassidy suspiciously.

"She said a couple of her men friends wanted to talk horses. We came out here on South Third—and it was a stick-up. They drove me out in the country, warned me to get out of town in the morning, slugged me and left me to walk back."

"You looked like it," Cassidy grudgingly admitted. "Did you report it?"

"Not yet. Maybe that car license will give me a chance to find out who it was."

"Or me," said Cassidy. "Come clean, Joe. You got heisted and slugged. But you don't fall for a trick like that without a reason. What else?"

"Can I trust you, Cassidy?"

"Sure you can, Joe. Why ask?"

"It's a waste of breath," admitted Mr. Maddox. "I know the answer. But my nose is clean, Cassidy, and I need some help. Maybe I can help you, too. I'll deny this if some of your copper friends start asking. But that one-eared nigger laid a bet on a Derby horse with me this morning. Two hundred and forty dollars. Big money for him. And later in the day comes five hundred on the same horse from this dame who drives me to the stick-up. Cash money she laid down. It sounded like a straight story when she said her boy friend had a roll of cash he wanted to lay. So I went with her."

"How much did they get off you?"

"Somewhere between eight and nine grand. Everything but my diamond."

Cassidy laughed with grim amusement. "Not bad. Not bad at all, Joe. Five hundred to take nine grand. That's better odds than you like to pay off."

"They didn't know I'd be carrying a roll. They wanted to slug me and warn me out of town."

"Why?"

"You tell me," suggested Mr. Maddox. "The girl called herself Norlene Bell. One of the men is called Dave."

"Never heard of the woman. There's a million Daves. Know anything more?"

"If I knew, I'd tell you," said Mr. Maddox virtuously. "They half killed me."

"Tough, Joe. Tough. But thanks for coming clean, even if you did have to be slugged to make you talk. My taxi is back up the street. You turning in now?"

"Why not? Now that you're working on it, I'll sleep like a baby."

"I don't like the sound of that," said Cassidy suspiciously as they parted.

Mr. Maddox was smiling grimly as he reentered his taxi. "Broadway Hotel," he said to the driver.

5. Mr. Maddox Hocks His Luck

IT WAS two o'clock of the new day when Mr. Maddox entered the Broadway lobby. The desk clerk did not flick an eye at Mr. Maddox's question. He knew the answer automatically.

"Mr. Major's suite is Six-sixteen."

On the sixth floor people were still awake. A radio or two was audible and voices in some of the rooms. Six-sixteen was at the back.

Two men came out as Mr. Maddox approached. A third man looked out, closed the door quickly on a chain and looked through the narrow opening.

"Tell Duke it's Joe Maddox."

Several seconds later another man looked out, said, "Hello, Maddox," and unchained the door.

Duke Major looked like a well-bred Englishman, quiet, keen.

The first man and another, both posted inside the door, were harder looking. A practised eye could mark gun bulges under their arms.

In an adjoining room voices murmured. Duke Major opened the door and the voices were plainer, tobacco smoke thick. But there was not much noise.

Fifteen to eighteen men stood around a portable dice table, intent on the game.

Some were in shirt sleeves. Tables around the walls held liquor bottles, glasses, ice, plates of sandwiches, carafes of drinking water.

It was not very impressive until one looked over shoulders and saw thousand-dollar bills, five-hundreds, hundreds, fifties scattered on the table, and wads of the same kind of money held carelessly by the players.

Most of the year Duke Major held forth in New York. His game changed location every night or so. But the play was always high cash play, honest dice, and no trouble.

Mr. Maddox knew some of the faces. You'd meet them in New York, in Chicago, Miami, Frisco. Some gambled as a profession, some liked their excitement high and costly, and could afford it. Most of them were here in Louisville because the Derby would be run tomorrow.

MR. MADDOX grunted with satisfaction when he saw Honest John O'Toole, in shirt sleeves, cigar in mouth, rolling the dice.

Slim Pasternik was across the table, dapper, smiling as usual, missing nothing with shrewd cold eyes. Not betting himself, Slim was watching Jerry Cavanaugh toss a fifty on the table.

A look told Mr. Maddox it was the same Jerry Cavanaugh that Cap'n Jim had turned over a knee. A young man now, rather handsome, and reckless, headstrong.

The dice rolled and Slim Pasternik looked up. He saw the big bland impressive figure coming around the table. His eyes narrowed. He shot a look at O'Toole, who was rolling dice again and missed it.

"Hello, Jerry," Mr. Maddox said.

Jerry threw a quick look and blankly replied, "Hello," before he looked back at the table.

Jerry might have had a few drinks by the edge of excitement that gripped him, by the way his fingers nervously clutched a thin sheaf of twenties and fifties.

"Jeanny wants you," Mr. Maddox said.

O'Toole lost. Jerry snatched his money off the table before he looked around. "Anything wrong with Jeanne? Say, your name is Maddox, isn't it?"

"That's right. I want to see you for a few minutes."

"I'm busy now," Jerry said impatiently.

Mr. Maddox stopped smiling. "Son, your sister is worried. I want to talk to you."

Slim Pasternik thrust an elbow between them. "Scram, Maddox! You ain't wanted here!"

"You *will* be tough, Slim…" Mr. Maddox said almost regretfully.

His big fist traveled only a few inches to Slim's cheek, but Slim hit the floor well back from the table. He was up like a snarling cat, reaching under his coat.

Moving with astonishing speed for such a big man, Mr. Maddox caught the hand as it was coming out. A twist made Slim yell with pain. A small automatic clattered on the floor.

Mr. Maddox caught up the gun and stepped back, blandly chiding: "Some day your lousy tricks will get you into trouble."

The players had crowded back from the fracas. Jerry Cavanaugh was angry, bewildered.

"Are you crazy, Maddox? He's with me!"

"Never mind—we're leaving," Mr. Maddox said coldly.

The hard quiet voice of Duke Major demanded: "What's the trouble, gentlemen?"

Duke Major was flanked by the two door-guards holding automatics. They'd been in the room within seconds after trouble broke out.

O'Toole snapped: "That tin-horn bookie started all this! I saw him!"

Mr. Maddox said calmly: "This is Slim Pasternik's gun, Duke. I'll have a word with you."

Duke Major was brittle as they faced one another in the entrance hall. "You know my rules, Maddox. No trouble."

"Has young Cavanaugh been losing or winning?"

"I don't know. Losing a little, I think."

"A local bank where he worked caught him in a shortage the other day. He'd been gambling. Pasternik and O'Toole are playing him along for reasons of their own. His sister is badly worried."

Duke Major did not hesitate. "Pasternik brought him. I assumed he could afford this and knew what he was doing. Just a moment please."

Duke Major was suave as he stepped into the other room. "Gentlemen, I regret this slight misunderstanding. Mr. Cavanaugh, your friend is waiting outside."

Hotly Jerry said: "He's no friend of mine! I don't want—"

"I don't believe you understand me," Duke Major said easily. "Your friend is waiting for you."

"I'll go with him! Gimme that gun!" Slim Pasternik raged.

"In fifteen minutes, Pasternik. You know my rule. No weapons. You'll not be admitted again. Wait your fifteen minutes in the hall. Gentlemen, the game is open again."

The two armed men added the one grim touch. Grim enough for obedience. Jerry Cavanaugh was red with mortification as he left with Mr. Maddox. "Damn you, Maddox, I ought to—"

"You ought to have some sense by now," Mr. Maddox cut in coldly. "What's the idea of bucking dice on borrowed money?"

"I won't talk to you, Maddox!"

"You'll come with me or have more trouble."

"I think you're crazy!" Jerry said bitterly.

AS THEY walked away from the hotel, Mr. Maddox broke the silence. "I was a friend of your father's, Jerry. I'd like to help you. What kind of a proposition is Slim Pasternik offering?"

Jerry walked in tight-lipped silence.

"Son," said Mr. Maddox, "Slim's a crook. So is O'Toole. Why do you want Jeanne to run her horse in the Derby, even though Gloria Gerryman will have you pinched if Jeanne does?"

Jerry's silence continued.

"O'Toole's got a hand in it," Mr. Maddox mused. "And O'Toole has been placing the Gerryman money on El Conde. Is it reasonable that O'Toole wants Jeanne's Hope running against El Conde?"

"Who said he did?" Jerry burst out.

"If not, why are you so damn set on risking arrest just to see Jeanne's Hope run the Derby for your sister? Let Jeanne sign her horse over to Gerryman, settle your trouble, and then start over again right. It'll make Jeanne mighty happy."

"I know what I'm doing!" Jerry said angrily. "El Conde hasn't a— I mean, our horse will take the Derby. We'll win far more than the purse and have our horse too! There'll be money enough then to make the bank listen to reason! I can stand a day or so in jail to get that!"

"Mmmm," said Mr. Maddox. "So El Conde hasn't a chance to win the Derby? Maybe, son. Maybe. But a fist full of cash won't always quash an air-tight case of embezzlement. Sometimes the bank, and prosecuting attorney, have ideas of their own, even if the money is returned."

"I'll gamble on that!"

"You've had a hell of a lot of luck gambling so far, haven't you? Why don't you get wise and cut it out? Suppose your horse doesn't win? Where'll you be then?"

"He will! I've got a hunch! I know what I'm doing! I know what's best for myself and Jeanne! We hardly know you! We're not interested in you! Just keep your hands off our business!"

Mr. Maddox shrugged regretfully. "I know now why Cap'n Jim was whaling hell out of you the last time I saw you. I was going to take you to my hotel for the night. I guess I won't bother. Go on with your sucker gambling."

OSCAR WAS sitting up in pajamas and dressing-gown when Mr. Maddox returned. "I lose," said Oscar with relief. "You got in without a shutter under you. Cassidy, that Masterton cop, telephoned for you a few minutes ago. I said you weren't here, and Cassidy said that was all he wanted to know and hung up."

Mr. Maddox chuckled as he telephoned Jerry Cavanaugh's apartment, and waited. "I don't believe Cassidy trusts me."

Jeanne Cavanaugh's voice came on the wire.

"Mr. Maddox, Jeanny. I just left Jerry. He'll be all right, even if he doesn't call you or show up. He was gambling a little but it's over for tonight. Better get some sleep."

"Oh, thank you. I will now!" Jeanne said with relief.

"So it's a woman now," said Oscar accusingly as Mr. Maddox took off his coat. "You got to mix a woman in this and ask for more trouble when the Derby's almost on us!"

"Not much time left," Mr. Maddox agreed. "Why wouldn't El Conde have a chance to win?"

Oscar did not hesitate. "I'd give him plenty of chance. You win the Derby on form, not hunches or whispers. What's this Jeanne's Hope show as a two-year-old?"

"He seems to have rounded into form lately."

"So has Father Time," said Oscar. "My money goes on past performance."

"Then why shouldn't El Conde have a chance?"

"He *ought* to have a chance."

"That's what I'd like to make sure of," said Mr. Maddox enigmatically, as he started toward his bedroom.

MR. MADDOX slept late in the morning, and went down to the coffee shop for breakfast. He was not greatly surprised when Cassidy slid on the stool beside him, lifted one of the fat black cigars from Mr. Maddox's breast pocket and asked: "Sleep like a baby last night, Joe?"

"I didn't cry once," said Mr. Maddox modestly.

"After slugging Slim Pasternik!"

"Followed me again, did you?"

"A friend who was there told me. And so this Cavanaugh that Duke ran out with you has a piece of Jeanne's Hope?"

"Has he?"

Cassidy lighted the cigar. "I hear that Cavanaugh was with Pasternik and Honest John. The three of them wouldn't be greasing an ace for the Derby tomorrow, would they? Jeanne's Hope maybe not running like he ought to? With O'Toole placing the Gerryman money on El Conde, he wouldn't be trying to scuttle the next best horse, would he?"

"Ask him," Mr. Maddox grinned. "How about that car license?"

"I wired and just got an answer. Florida tag issued to a phony Miami address. The local police are watching for it. Where do you come in on this Cavanaugh-Pasternik-O'Toole play, Joe?"

"I'm trying to raise enough money to buy Jeanne's Hope," Mr. Maddox answered.

Cassidy got up disgustedly. "Don't hand me baloney, Joe! And if I catch you or these others monkeying with the Derby, God help all of you!"

That raised another angle to consider. At noon Mr. Maddox was no nearer a solution when he paid off a taxi at the track barn where Jeanne's Hope was stabled and turned to see Sam Harmsworth stalking around the end of the barn.

"This," said Mr. Maddox quickly, "is luck. I've been wanting to see you, Mr. Harmsworth."

"Don't talk to me about luck today!" Harmsworth snapped. "This cab vacant?"

The driver was already opening the door. Sam Harmsworth jumped in and left. Mr. Maddox was not surprised to find Jeanne sitting listlessly beside the tackroom door.

"Something wrong with Sam?" Mr. Maddox asked innocently.

"I made him go away."

"Love," decided Mr. Maddox, "would make a sucker out of any handicapper."

Jeanne said stonily: "Gloria Gerryman saw me this morning. She was furious because Sam spent the evening with me. If I see him again, or tell him she said anything, she'll have Jerry arrested. And she wants a bill of sale for Jeanne's Hope by six this evening."

"Going to give it to her?"

"I can't. Jerry is half-owner by law. This morning he refused to sign any bill of sale until after the Derby. I don't know what to do. Six o'clock isn't far away—and she'll have Jerry arrested!"

"Then you'll be free to spend the evening with Sam," Mr. Maddox pointed out. "Gerryman will do you every dirty trick she can. Claw her back. Take Sam away from her."

"I don't want Sam just to hurt her. After Jerry's arrested, Sam won't even want to see me."

"Let Sam say that. Jerry isn't arrested yet. And it's about time," said Mr. Maddox sternly, "that you shook Jerry off your apron strings. He knows what he wants to do. If he guesses wrong, it may teach him the lesson he needs. Wringing your hands and messing up your own life won't help him. What do you think Cap'n Jim would do if Jerry tried this hard-boiled damn foolishness on him?"

"He'd tell Jerry it was his own race and he'd have to run it," said Jeanne after a moment. "And—and he'd be right, I suppose." Jeanne drew a long breath and stood up. "All right. I wash my hands of Jerry in this. I'll run Jeanne's Hope to win no matter what happens."

"Good girl! Now get Sam!"

"Sam's out," Jeanne said firmly. "I'll not let Jerry's guilt smear Sam with disgraceful publicity as a—a friend of Jerry's sister. It would do just that. Sam is too prominent. The Cavanaughs will wash their dirty linen alone. I won't see Sam again—and that's that!"

"Gloria Gerryman will get him."

"I know," said Jeanne. "But maybe I'll win the Derby: That would be something, wouldn't it?"

Mr. Maddox glowered at Jeanne's unsteady smile—and suddenly exploded: "You're a fool, kid! Just the kind of a game little fool young Harmsworth needs! Stick around here this afternoon until you hear from me!"

THE GERRYMAN horses were several barns over. Maddox found the man he wanted currying a chestnut colt. Yellow Sam was a small mulatto, younger than Chimp, dressed like a dandy in striped silk shirt and high-waisted slacks.

"Boy," said Mr. Maddox, "I hear old Chimp was kin to you."

Yellow Sam broke off humming the *St. Louis Blues* and turned uneasy. "Naw, suh."

"Too bad. Chimp laid a bet with me on the Derby. I won't have to pay off then."

Yellow Sam blinked. "Is I kin, do you pay me do he win?"

"If you prove to the police you're kin to Chimp. And if the horse wins, which I doubt. Chimp bet two hundred and forty dollars on Jeanne's Hope to win. I gave him twenty to one."

"An' you pays on dat?"

"If Jeanne's Hope wins."

Yellow Sam threw down the currycomb and cut a buck and wing. "God'lmighty, I got rich! After tomorrow I never hit a lick no mo'!"

"You're damn sure Jeanne's Hope will win," said Mr. Maddox dryly.

Yellow Sam's face lost expression as he picked up the currycomb. "Naw, suh—I jus' hopin'. Where I get de winnin' money do I win?"

"I'll bring it around," Mr. Maddox said as he started on to the barn which housed his own modest racing-string. There he spoke briefly to Stiffy.

"Here's twenty for expenses. From now until the Derby starts, keep an eye on that Yellow Sam, over at the Gerryman Stable. Watch who he talks to, what he does every minute. But don't let him know."

The next thing was a telephone call to Oscar, asking: "How much cash is in the room and down in the hotel safe?"

"Twelve thousand in the safe," Oscar said. "Thirty-eight hundred and seventy up here."

"Put it with the twelve grand. I'll want it all shortly."

Oscar was instantly apprehensive. "You lost over eight grand last night, Joe! Are you going to lose this? It's the pay-off dough!"

"You'll get more in this evening and tomorrow morning."

"And we'll still have to pay off after the race!" Oscar said with growing anguish. "Joe, don't do anything foolish!"

"Only a fool can afford to be foolish," Mr. Maddox chuckled. "Maybe that makes me a fool." He hung up on Oscar, waited a moment and called Duke Major at the Broadway Hotel.

"Will you be there until I can taxi in from the track, Duke?"

"I'm having lunch in the Club House restaurant," Duke Major said. "Can I see you there?"

IT WAS almost an hour later when a waiter summoned Duke Major from a luncheon party at the Club House to the table where Mr. Maddox sat alone.

People were fast filling the seats, boxes and the big inner courts of the grandstand. Most of the Club House tables were already

filled or reserved. Tomorrow was Derby Day. By the hour, by thousands upon thousands, the mighty Derby crowd was pouring into Louisville.

Mr. Maddox was smiling faintly as he twisted the glinting diamond ring off his finger. "How big a loan on this, Duke?"

Duke Major whistled softly. "Broke, Maddox?"

"Business is too good," said Mr. Maddox calmly. "I need more cash."

Duke Major examined the diamond. "I've heard this ring is your luck. Taking a chance on letting it go at this time, aren't you?"

"I'm using it for luck this time."

Duke Major nodded understandingly. "Five thousand is the best I can do. I'll have to give you a check on the Valley Trust."

"Perfect."

IT WAS almost two o'clock when Mr. Maddox collected the bankroll from the hotel safe…. Almost two-thirty when the lean president of the Valley Trust Company shook hands, eyed the prosperous smiling visitor and warmly asked: "What can I do for you, Mr. Maddox?"

Smiling, Mr. Maddox laid a neat stack of thousand-dollar bills on the desk and tapped them with a big finger.

"You can accept this money for a release on young Cavanaugh."

Stafford, the president, was startled. "Cavanaugh gave me to understand he couldn't make good. We haven't quite decided what to do about him."

"Miss Gerryman might make good and she might not," Mr. Maddox suggested blandly. "This—er—regrettable affair will make bad publicity for the bank. Young Cavanaugh comes from a fine old Kentucky family. It seems a pity to proceed on the uncertain whims of a headstrong young Yankee girl who might change her mind at the last minute. Wouldn't your stockholders prefer to have the money back without question now…."

It was five minutes to three when Mr. Maddox emerged from the Valley Trust Company with a sealed envelope which he dispatched to Jeanne Cavanaugh at the track, by Postal messenger, together with a telegram.

NOW DO WHAT YOU WANT TO DO STOP NOT A WORD OF THIS TO JERRY STOP GOOD LUCK AND CLAW HARD AND FAST.

Oscar was sitting at the tables which held

telephones and betting-sheets when Mr. Maddox strolled in some time later. Oscar was just answering one of the telephones.

"Just a minute. Here he is," Oscar said, and put a hand over the mouthpiece. "This guy's called several times for you, Joe."

The gruff voice on the wire had a familiar ring.

"Never mind having this call traced, Maddox. So you got tough and stayed on in town? What's the idea?"

"No cheap gunmen can run me out of any town," Mr. Maddox said grimly. "I'm making my book and to hell with you! What happens now?"

"We're giving you two more days! See that you stick to your book and nothing else! We're watching you!"

The wire went dead. Mr. Maddox swore softly as he put the hand-set down. "Now what did he mean by that!"

"What did who mean by what?" Oscar demanded. Oscar was jumpy. He shoved over a stack of five-hundred-dollar bills.

"You'd better hear about this first. Young Cavanaugh bet this on his horse, Jeanne's Hope. Five grand. I took it because we figured El Conde's got the edge. But I've been sweating. Cavanaugh must know something. He seemed damn sure his horse would win and it'd do him plenty of good to win from you. I telephoned Jersey City and Chicago. The play there is on El Conde. Plenty of it. No big money on Jeanne's Hope yet. What do you make of it?"

"Jeanne's Hope will be in there to win. Maybe he'll take the Derby."

"And then what? Have we still got the bankroll?" Oscar stared, and with sudden uneasiness, demanded: "Joe, where's your ring?"

Mr. Maddox looked down at his bare hand. A smile started on his broad face, and turned into a rising chuckle that shook the vast expanse of his well-fleshed figure.

"I traded the bankroll and the ring to Cupid for a sharp set of kitty claws that I hope will scratch like hell."

"Kitty claws? Cupid?" Oscar gulped with growing horror. "My God, Joe, what have you done? We're sunk! I gotta feeling! We're sunk this time!"

Still chuckling, Mr. Maddox agreed. "If Jeanne's Hope wins, we're scuttled. And we might as well make a hell of a splash as we go down. From now until the Derby starts, cover every dollar of Jeanne's Hope money that you can find. And may the Lord have mercy on us!"

6. Honest John O'Toole

OUT AT Churchill Downs the afternoon races ended—the last races before Derby Day. And as twilight deepened into night, the track crowd joined the host of newcomers pouring in from all parts of the country.

Hotels had no rooms, no beds. Lines of people waited patiently for restaurant tables to be vacated. Traffic tangled and crept along on the downtown streets. All through the night more cars, more trains, more people would be coming. In the morning, highways leading to Louisville would be filled with speeding cars.

Joe Maddox had seen it all many times before. But always there was the same pulse-tingling excitement, even for a hardened old bookie.

And in thirty years there never had been a pre-Derby evening like this for Joe Maddox. On the streets and in the hotels were an ever-increasing number of familiar faces. An increasing tide of money to be bet. There were greetings and handshakes, talk of past races and the Derby on the morrow. There was everything that Joe Maddox lived for.

And there was hardly an eye keen enough to mark the undercurrent of grimness behind Joe Maddox's broad beaming smile. Grimness such as Joe Maddox had never known before.

For this was the first time—the first time in thirty years—that Joe Maddox had gone so far out on the surface of disaster. For the first time in thirty years Joe Maddox had deliberately put himself in a position where there was a good chance he couldn't pay off.

Old friends, old patrons who trusted Joe Maddox as they trusted their bankers, had cash money to bet, and did. They bet with Joe Maddox on the street, with Oscar at the hotel. They slapped Joe Maddox's back, shook his hand, and went their way certain that if their choices won, they'd get their winning money.

And Joe Maddox had to take that money. To refuse would make disaster certain. Too much money already had been bet with the book, and it was gone.

In the Brown Hotel lobby Mr. Maddox met Jerry Cavanaugh, sarcastically smiling. "Will you cover more money on my horse, Maddox?"

"Take it up to Oscar," Mr. Maddox directed. "Any amount."

"Since you know so much," said Jerry, "notice that I'm still at my affairs. Tomorrow I'll be in the clear."

"El Conde may settle you," Mr. Maddox said grimly.

"Not a chance!"

The jeering voice was Jerry Cavanaugh's. The words and money came from others. Doubt grew on Mr. Maddox like a mist of gloom. There were only a few hours left to discover why El Conde didn't have a chance.

An hour later Mr. Maddox looked in on Oscar and the betting-sheets.

"Cavanaugh brought fifteen grand more on Jeanne's Hope," Oscar said huskily. "And that Harley Smith repeated with four grand. He wanted to go on the cuff for three grand more and I said cash."

"Take all the cash he brings."

Direly Oscar muttered: "Somebody knows something. If we ain't being taken to the cleaners, I've never seen it done before."

"Any word from Stiffy yet?" Mr. Maddox asked.

"I called the barn. He ain't around. That Masterton cop said he'd be down in the lobby for a while and wanted to see you."

"I'll go down," Mr. Maddox decided. "Have me paged if Stiffy calls."

Cassidy was at the cigar counter in the lobby. "Every dip and con man on the circuit is in town," he growled. "I'm tired of collaring them. For two cents, Joe, I'd have you vagged."

Mr. Maddox produced two coppers. Cassidy irritably waved them away.

"I hear a nigger nephew has claimed old Chimp's body. Says Chimp didn't have any enemies. But that isn't why I wanted you. I hear that Cavanaugh and Slim Pasternik are laying heavy money around town on Cavanaugh's horse. What's your idea of that?"

Mr. Maddox chuckled. "How would I know? I only brought a racing-stable to town." And as Cassidy reddened, Mr. Maddox said abruptly: "That boy's paging me. I'll see you in a few minutes."

MR. MADDOX got out of the elevator and was jovially greeted by a plump, smirking man waiting to go down. "Hello, Joe. Glad to see you, Joe. I just came from your room. Business is fine, eh?"

"Rushing," said Mr. Maddox shortly. "Got a horse you like tomorrow?"

"You ask me that, Joe? After the money I've left with you on Jeanne's Hope? A fine horse, Joe. I've been watching him."

"So?" said Mr. Maddox. "Maybe I'd better watch him too."

And just then an elevator took Harley Smith away, and Mr. Maddox hurried to the suite, where Oscar had an open telephone waiting. "Stiffy," Oscar said.

Stiffy's voice over the wire was husky with earnestness. "I was a-watchin' that nigger, Boss, an' I lost him."

"What did he do before you lost him?"

"He worked around the barn all afternoon," said Stiffy. "And then he rode in a street car to town an' seen the police, an' then he come back an' et supper, an' it wasn't till he took him a walk after dark an' talked to a guy drivin' a big white car that I lost him."

Carefully Mr. Maddox asked: "Was it a big cream-colored sedan, Stiffy?"

"Uh-huh. Yaller Sam took him a walk over past Central Avenue, an' clumb in the auto an' talked with a feller inside. It was dark along there an' I snuck up behind to see what they was a-doin'. Before I got me a chance to duck, that damn nigger jumped out an' the car started off an' I lost him."

"I see. He saw you standing there?"

"Hell, no!" denied Stiffy. "I ain't that dumb. I clumb on the rear bumper an' rode that white car clean around the corner an' the nigger never even knowed I'd been there. But my dern foot got caught in the bumper," Stiffy said apologetically. "Wasn't nothin' to do but hang on till the damn thing stopped. Wasn't far or I'd fell off an' been drug along the street. The driver went in a house an' never seen me back there. So I figured I'd better tell you, Boss."

"Stiffy," said Mr. Maddox almost prayerfully, "could you find that house again?"

"I ain't only two blocks away now, at a drug store."

"Give me the address and wait on the corner!"

"More trouble, I suppose," Oscar commented sourly as Mr. Maddox put the telephone down. "And if it'll make you feel any better, Harley Smith bet another three grand on the Cavanaugh horse. Must of cleaned him, too, by the looks of those greasy twenties he had to dig up."

Mr. Maddox glanced carelessly at the dirty, worn, much-folded bills Oscar indicated. Suddenly he snatched them up and examined them. He jerked one out that had a slightly torn corner.

"I remember this one! I got these twenties from old Chimp! They're betting my own money back with me! Where do I find that dirty crook, Harley Smith?"

"He didn't give an address," Oscar said weakly. "Joe, is this dough part of that bankroll you lost last night?"

Mr. Maddox was already leaving, swearing as he went…. There was no sign of Harley Smith in the crowded lobby or outside where Cassidy followed Mr. Maddox.

"Why charge around here talking to yourself, Joe?"

Mr. Maddox snarled: "I just saw some of the money that was heisted off me last night! He left it upstairs!"

Cassidy stared—and then began to grin. "Joe, that sounds like somebody bet your own money back with you…. By God, *it's so!* What a story this'll make! And you can't prove it on him unless you admit running an illegal book here in Louisville!"

Red-faced, glaring, Mr. Maddox realized the trap he was in. A shout of laughter would roll across the American racing circuits when this story on Joe Maddox started circulating.

Cassidy was snorting, shaking as the full humor of it struck him.

Mr. Maddox eyed him wrathfully, and then speculatively. "Suppose, you laughing hyena, I could tip you off about a hocus that's being cooked up in the Derby tomorrow?"

Cassidy stopped laughing. "Don't kid me, Joe!"

"A little help about my bankroll, and a tight lip about it afterward might pay you odds."

Now Cassidy was alert in his role of a track detective. "If you know anything, Joe, write your own ticket. I'll keep my end of it. It's a promise."

"Let's find a taxi and I'll tell you about it while we ride," Mr. Maddox decided.

STIFFY SAID huskily: "There's the damn car still a-sittin' there." The cream-colored sedan was parked before a bungalow not far from Churchill Downs.

"Wait here," Mr. Maddox ordered.

"O'Toole's car all right," Cassidy muttered as they came abreast.

Cassidy was hard and serious now, after all he had heard in the taxicab. Crooked work in the Kentucky Derby, with the murder of old Chimp in the background, was big, important. A crooked coup in the Derby would deal a smashing blow to racing on all American tracks.

"Stiffy didn't see who was driving," Mr. Maddox husked. "Maybe we can see through a side window."

The bungalow porch was empty. Lights were on in the front of the house. A radio was playing inside. Cassidy cursed softly under his breath, and then jumped as Mr. Maddox's warning hand caught his arm.

Another automobile was driving up in front. They crouched at the side of the house as two people hurried to the front door and entered.

Mr. Maddox risked a look as the door opened. He swore softly as it closed again.

"That's Harley Smith and the girl who decoyed me to that heist last night! So they're close to O'Toole—and feeding my own money back to me! I'm going to try the back door!"

The radio was turned off as they went to the back of the house. There was a small screened back porch. The back rooms were dark.

The porch floor-boards creaked. Cassidy tried the back door and it opened. The dark room inside smelled of cooking. Voices carried in the small bungalow. Mr. Maddox recognized Harley Smith speaking.

"They took it all and no questions. I almost laughed in the big sap's face when I met him at the elevators. O'Toole was smart to let him stay over a day and make his book. I'm like O'Toole. If you have to take a guy or shut him up, get his dough first. Slim, are you sure everything's right now? We've all socked every dollar on that Cavanaugh horse."

Slim Pasternik's thin voice answered. "I gave the stuff to the nigger. He'll slip it in the morning feed. We've used it before. It's sure-fire and won't show in the saliva. El Conde will run, but he won't be a Derby horse."

"Are you sure about that nigger?"

"Sure. He's smart. And he won't get careless, since Dave and Harry here fixed the old nigger I caught listening to us that night at the track. Dave, it looks like that old Chimp told the truth, too, before you conked him. He only bet a few dollars with Maddox. Didn't talk. And after Maddox pays off, Maddox won't have a chance to think it all over and make a squawk. I'll get him myself."

Another voice, a cold familiar voice said: "O.K. about El Conde. But supposing this Cavanaugh horse doesn't win—with all our dough on him?"

"Stop crying about your dough, Harry!" Slim Pasternik snapped. "Look at O'Toole—over a hundred grand on the same horse! Every dime he can raise and borrow, and all the eighty grand he was supposed to have placed out for the Gerryman girl. He was sitting pretty—eighty grand to the good. All he had to do was keep the Gerryman horse from winning."

"Honest John O'Toole!" Mr. Maddox breathed.

Cassidy jabbed him with a warning elbow as Slim Pasternik talked on. "The Gerryman girl tipped O'Toole. Her trainer had been watching the training track on the Cavanaugh farm and putting a stop-watch on this Jeanne's Hope when he worked. He was a flash, and no one else knew it. The Gerryman girl began to worry and blabbed to O'Toole. To check it I came to town a month ago and made a pal out of Cavanaugh himself. It wasn't hard. He's a sap, too. And short of cash. So when I told him I had dough looking for a good Derby shot, and I'd split with anyone who could steer me right, he fell for it and told me about the hot shot they'd been nursing along. El Conde was the only one that figured to beat him."

Slim laughed scornfully. "When I told Cavanaugh I had inside dope from the Gerryman stable that El Conde wouldn't last the Derby distance, he swallowed it. He said it must be so because the Gerrymans wanted to run Jeanne's Hope in the Derby as a Gerryman horse. He decided it was proof they didn't have a Derby winner in El Conde. So he's been playing along with me. I've been handing him O'Toole's dough—and he's been placing it as his own for a cut. It's perfect. There won't even be questions about O'Toole's betting heavily against El Conde. And with El Conde muffing the race, we'll all clean up."

"And Cavanaugh gets a cut?" the Bell girl questioned.

"Are we dumb?" Slim countered. "Cavanaugh's screwy about gambling. We've already got a play ready to take his purse money from him. And maybe his horse too. It's perfect, I tell you. We'll take everything like Grant took Richmond. Let's have a drink on it."

"I need one," Harley Smith said.

WITH NO more warning than that, footsteps approached the kitchen door. Mr. Maddox moved hurriedly, but before he could leave the kitchen, the door opened. An overhead light flashed on—and suddenly the Bell girl was screaming.

"Dave! Harry! Men in the kitchen!"

Cassidy reached her, swung her stumbling, screaming across the kitchen to Mr. Maddox.

She kicked wildly. Her sharp fingernails clawed Mr. Maddox's broad face as he caught her. Cassidy had plunged toward the front of the house.

"Keep quiet, you hell-cat!" Mr. Maddox panted as he twisted her around and held her arms from behind.

A gunshot crashed in the front part of the house, then another. Swearing, Mr. Maddox pushed the girl away and charged toward the trouble.

A short hall opened into a front room that ran clear across the house. Two more shots followed—and Mr. Maddox met Cassidy stumbling back into the hall. Cassidy had dropped his gun. He'd been shot in the right arm.

Slim Pasternik's thin voice raged in shrill alarm: "Don't kill him, Dave! This'll wreck everything, you fool! He's a track cop!"

"No cop takes me and sends my prints to Washington! I'll fix him!"

Cassidy lurched down to catch his gun with his left hand.

"I got it!" Mr. Maddox snapped.

A crouching figure with a gun jumped opposite the hallway door as Mr. Maddox scooped Cassidy's gun off the floor. "Maddox!" the man yelled in recognition. It was the voice of Dave. And as his gun blasted, someone flipped a light-switch and plunged the front room into blackness.

Mr. Maddox flattened against the wall. He could see Dave's gun muzzle spurting fire in the dark. He fired once, twice, automatically counting Dave's shots. Dave was as blind as he was. And now Dave's gun went silent. A chair clattered over. Dave's gasping voice cursed.

Out front automobile engines were racing.

"They're lamming!" Cassidy blurted, and shouldered Mr. Maddox aside as he got into the front room first.

Another piece of furniture clattered over. Dave's oaths in the darkness sounded strangled, almost sobbing. And suddenly the lights were on again. Cassidy was wheeling from the switch.

Dave had just staggered away from an overturned floor-lamp and clutched a chair to keep from falling. His empty gun lay on the rug. A hand pressed his side and when he coughed, blood showed on his lips. He looked dazed.

"He'll keep! Gimme that gun! They're getting away!" Cassidy snapped.

House doors had opened all along the street. People had run out in alarm. The two automobiles had reached the next corner and were swinging clumsily around out of sight.

Stiffy's wildly excited voice yelled: "When I heard the shootin', Boss, I stuck my damn

pocketknife in their tires! They ain't goin' anywhere fast with flat tires!"

In the distance a siren wailed. Cassidy excitedly blurted: "Boy, you hung it on them! They won't get out of town now! Joe, watch out here while I telephone for a guard to be put on El Conde."

7. *Kentucky Kickback*

THE MORNING papers had it in black headlines. Only the girl and O'Toole were missing… and the rising, electric excitement of Derby Day pushed it all in the background. From mid-morning on the great crowd went surging toward Churchill Downs.

Mr. Maddox was rocky from answering police questions and lack of sleep, but he was there. Cassidy was there, too, arm bandaged and in a sling, a satisfied smile on his face as he edged into the box where Mr. Maddox was sitting.

"Well, Joe, I saved your skin on this. How does it feel to be a hero instead of being pinched for making a book?"

"I'll tell you when I see if the Cavanaugh horse wins or not," Mr. Maddox said grimly.

"Cavanaugh was lucky his contact with Pasternik was based on good faith instead of guilty knowledge," Cassidy observed. "If he and his sister win the Derby, he'll come out of it better than ever. I wouldn't worry about him."

"Who's worrying?" Mr. Maddox said shortly. "I'm thinking about the dough I'll have to pay out if his horse wins."

The first races on the card had been run. The clear notes of a bugle floated through the yellow sunshine. The murmuring movement of the vast crowd heightened.

"Here they come!" Cassidy exclaimed as the red-coated leader rode out of the paddock tunnel, followed by the long file of slowly pacing horses and diminutive jockies gay in bright racing-silks.

Flags were fluttering in the slight breeze. Bursts of handclapping spread as the post parade moved slowly along the track.

The band struck up *My Old Kentucky Home*. And a lump came into Mr. Maddox's throat and the sentiment of the moment wiped out all thought of profit or loss or disaster to Joe Maddox. This was the great moment before the Derby start.

Then, very quickly it seemed, the horses were at the starting-gate… backing, plunging, fighting the assistant starters… and suddenly the roar of the crowd marked the start of the race.

Eager eyes and then binoculars could follow the pack of horses fighting for position on the turn. The amplifiers were calling: "Mad Money is taking the lead… Cantwell second… Jeanne's Hope third… El Conde fourth…."

The lengthening field swept down the back stretch, carrying the hopes of owners and millions of listeners out over the airwaves of the world.

Tiny horses, now, seen across the green infield, carrying tinier jockies…. And it was hard to believe that the fate of Joe Maddox ran there with one horse and its crouched rider….

"Jeanne's Hope first… Mad Money second… El Conde third."

Now there was a madness in the roar of the great crowd. Mr. Maddox caught himself shouting too. *"Come on, Jeanne's Hope!"*

Then he realized what that tiny running horse leading on the stretch-turn meant. Wealth and fame to Jeanny Cavanaugh—money for Jerry Cavanaugh—and ruin for Joe Maddox.

The race swept into the stretch. Jockey whips began to rise and fall. And the inexorable loudspeakers called fate for Joe Maddox.

"It's Jeanne's Hope by half a length… El Conde second… Clydesdale third… Mad Money and Sir Sam…."

The crowd was on its feet, delirious and screaming. Mr. Maddox and Cassidy were up.

"El Conde closing… Jeanne's Hope by a head… Jeanne's Hope by a nose…."

Cassidy was beating Mr. Maddox's arm. "Look at that black horse run! Look at that El Conde! What a horse! *What a horse!*"

El Conde was running under the whip like a smooth black machine, like a great ghost flashing faster each length to the wire….

"El Conde!" Cassidy whooped. "Jeanne's Hope couldn't hold it long enough! What a finish, Joe! What d'you think of it?"

Mr. Maddox was standing quietly, like a man who had faced doom and watched it move away. Mr. Maddox shivered slightly, and then a growing smile spread across his broad bland face, and he was himself again. He stood for a few moments watching El Conde come back to the horse-shoe wreath of flowers for his victorious neck, to Gloria Gerryman and the waiting photographers. To enduring fame and world-wide publicity for horse and owner.

"I'm thinking," said Mr. Maddox almost dreamily, "of the lesson Jerry Cavanaugh has learned, and all the dough I've made today, and of what that eighty grand of Gerryman money would have won if O'Toole had bet it as he was ordered."

A MOMENT later Mr. Maddox jogged Cassidy's elbow. "Look this side of where Gloria Gerryman's getting her picture taken! There's Jeanny Cavanaugh and Sam Harmsworth holding hands!"

"I see them!" said Cassidy. "You know, I feel kind of sorry for her, with the Gerryman girl getting the Derby after all."

Mr. Maddox chuckled.

"Don't feel sorry for Jeanny. Gloria Gerryman won the race—but I'm thinking Jeanny Cavanaugh really won the Derby. Let's go down and congratulate her—and Sam."

THE GREEN GHOUL

by Frederick C. Davis

1. The Crimson Axe

 **LAY OAKLEY,** ace private investigator of Hollywoodian affairs, leaned with an air of finality across his desk in the inner sanctum of Secrets, Incorporated, and regarded his three callers skeptically.

"Gentlemen," he said, "I am a detective, but I am not a seer, nor a spiritualistic medium, nor a yogi, nor an exorciser of ghosts. The matter is outside my field. I must decline to handle the case."

His trio of visitors glanced bitter disappointment at one another. Mr. Henry Wethering's abundant avoirdupois quivered with anxiety. Mr. Wallace Quinn's small being shrank perceptibly with despair. Mr. Samuel Tompkins' lean frame tightened with determination. He removed a wallet from his pocket, a check from the wallet, and placed it on the blotter before Oakley. Oakley studied the alluring four-figure amount, looked very thoughtful, said: "Let's get this straight."

His three troubled callers took new hope.

"You gentlemen," Oakley observed in summation while he glanced at the notes he had made during the interview, "hold valuable real estate on Sutter Boulevard in Beverly Hills. You, Mr. Wethering, own a large villa which adjoins Number Thirteen Thirty on the west. You, Mr. Quinn, own a sumptuous *hacienda* on the east of Thirteen Thirty. You, Mr. Tompkins, likewise own a large house which flanks Thirteen Thirty on the rear."

"That's exactly right," Mr. Tompkins said and all three nodded.

OAKLEY CONTINUED: "These properties you do not occupy yourselves, but lease. You are accustomed to letting them, at high rentals, to prosperous celebrities of the movie colony. During the past year, your tenants have come and gone with distressing frequency. They move in and promptly move out again. The undesirability of occupying your properties is rumored about, and as a result the three villas have long stood deserted."

"Right," said Mr. Wethering.

"The reason for the pronounced unpopularity of your houses," Oakley resumed, "is the adjoining property, Number Thirteen Thirty. The house and grounds there, you have been told repeatedly and emphatically by your departing tenants, are haunted.

Your leases have been repeatedly broken because no one wants to live next door to a ghost."

"That's right," affirmed Mr. Quinn.

"This particular phantom," Oakley continued, "though it appears only at night in the manner common to spooks, otherwise conducts itself peculiarly. Its unspectral habit is to indulge in setting-up exercises, broad-jumps, pole-vaults, and hundred-yard dashes. After a period of strenuous, unghostly athletics, it takes a plunge in the swimming pool. Your neighbors have seen it leaping and dashing about. They have even witnessed its fancy dives into the water—because it glows like a fire-fly."

"That's exactly right," Mr. Tompkins stated.

"You have already carried your troubles to the occupants of Thirteen Thirty," Oakley went on. "In the haunted house live two brothers. The younger is Mr. Philip Gately, a lawyer. The elder is Lawrence Gately, a confined invalid. They do not rent these ghostly premises, but own the property. To them you have complained that their athletic ghost is costing you a great deal of money. The Gatelys have answered that all this is sheer nonsense, because no ghost exists."

The three callers stated in chorus that such was the case.

"Philip and Lawrence Gately say they have never seen any spirit bounding through a pole-vault, trying to set up a new supernatural sprinting record, or execut-

ing any swan dives. Though the splashing of the water has been plainly audible to their temporary neighbors during the ghost's plunges into the pool, they say they have never heard a single suspicious ripple.

"In short, a score of people, unacquainted with each other, and at different times, have looked from the windows of the surrounding villas in the dead of night and have seen the phantom cavorting about. Their stories corroborate one another, but nonetheless the two men who live on the property laugh at them and say it is tommy-rot."

Again the troubled trio confirmed Oakley's resumé.

"Now, because you are completely baffled, and because the glowing ghost is costing you considerable money, you have come to me. You want me to drive it away. You want me to shoo it out of there, so that you may again collect high rents from your properties, and toward that end you offer me a tempting retainer."

"For God's sake, Mr. Oakley, something's got to be done!" Wethering blurted. "If this goes on I'll be a ruined man. That ghost has got to be chased away from there!"

"It's certainly not nonsense and tommy-rot!" the diminutive Mr. Quinn protested. "I don't blame my tenants for getting out. There is a ghost. I've seen it myself!"

"So have I!" Tompkins declared.

"And I!" Wethering added.

OAKLEY'S HEAD wagged. "Gentlemen," he sighed, "if I ran your ghost into a corner, what would I do with it? One can't handcuff a phantom. One can't lodge charges against a spirit. If I tried to arrest your spook, and the papers learned of it, I should be made a laughing stock." He reluctantly slid the check back across the blotter. "I'm very sorry, but I must decline to handle your case."

Again the three men regarded one another hopelessly. They began a concerted plea, but Oakley's gesture silenced them. They rose, with their check, worried and baffled. As they went toward the entrance, Oakley's telephone rang. He reached for it, as a door opened and a head of brilliant red hair beamed through.

"It's important, Oke," he was informed by Miss Charmaine Morris, his capable and eye-brightening assistant. "A matter of life and death."

Oakley began, "This is Oak—" but a breathless voice, carrying over the wire, cut him short.

"Mr. Oakley, I must see you!" it blurted. "As soon as possible— at once! My—my life depends on it. If you don't—do something to protect me—I shall be killed!"

Oakley straightened. "Who's calling? Why are you afraid? Where are you?"

The frantic voice rushed sibilantly. "I'm being watched! Someone

is prowling around the grounds. I've seen a face peering at me through the window. He has some kind of a big weapon. It's Jerome. For God's sake, Mr. Oakley, I'm alone—I'm sick. If you don't come quickly, you'll find me dead!"

Oakley frowned. "I can't come to your place until I know where you are, you know. If you'll tell me—"

"My name is Gately—Lawrence Gately."

Oakley went tense and snapped: "What?"

"The address is Thirteen Thirty, Sutter Boulevard, Beverly Hills!"

Oakley exclaimed: "I'll be damned!" He thought fast. "Stay right where you are, Mr. Gately. Lock yourself in. I'm coming right now!"

He broke the connection and strode from his desk as a dapper, lean, young man scissored in. Mr. Archibald Brixey, Oakley's first assistant, looked like a fop but was far from being one. He wore faultless clothes and a monocle; but he possessed a penetrating mind and two well trained fists. Now, as Oakley leveled a commanding forefinger at him, the monocle flipped from his eye.

"Bring those three men back here, Archie! I've changed my mind!"

Brixey squinted the circular lens between eyebrow and cheek and incredulously inspected Oakley through it. "Oke, you've jolly well taken leave of your senses," he said, "if you've decided to turn spiritualistic medium and—"

"Bring them back, Archie!" Oakley repeated. "They're equipped with a very beautiful check, and I want it."

BRIXEY SWUNG long legs out the door. Oakley slipped into his topcoat as the alluring Cherry Morris fluffed her resplendent hair. Brixey's urgent voice sounded in the outer office, and footfalls returned to the entrance.

Cherry said: "Did you find out somehow that the ghost is a beautiful blonde? I can't imagine any other reason that would interest you in it so passionately."

"Cherry," Oakley pointed out to her, "the ghost's gender and complexion have nothing whatever to do with it. I can't ignore a man who is frantic with the fear that he will be murdered at any second. Since he lives in the very house that's haunted, the ghost immediately becomes suspected. Stand by, my dear."

Into the office filed Wethering and Quinn and Tompkins. The three property owners were now animated with a new hope. Oakley told them: "I've reconsidered, gentlemen. I'm on my way to Thirteen Thirty now. Please hand Miss Morris your check, and give her whatever further information you can. I must make a hasty departure or I may have to tackle two ghosts instead of one. Come, Archie!"

Oakley ran down the steps with the angular Brixey at his heels. He crossed Hollywood Boulevard to the parking lot beside the famed Grauman's Chinese Theater, where banners fluttered in the sea wind and bright incandescents gleamed. Brixey angled down beside him in his sleek roadster and they swung in the direction of Beverly Hills.

"Jerome," Oakley said in an ominous tone. "Remember that name, Archie—Jerome."

Oakley weaved his gleaming car up the winding road in Beverly Hills and swung to the curb at 1330 Sutter Boulevard. Making a quiet approach to the sprawling stucco villa that lay beyond the gates and across gardened grounds, he avoided the graveled driveway and walked with Brixey on velvet grass. He studied the house that lay shadowed under shaggy palms; and once near it, he paused to listen.

Vaguely he heard a pounding sound. *Thump, thump!* It came from somewhere within the walls of the villa. *Thump, thump, thump!* Irregular, sometimes muffled, again sharp and reverberating, it continued while Oakley moved cautiously to the entrance. Again he heard blows struck inside. Wondering, he clacked the brass knocker.

Immediately the chopping beats ceased and silence reigned within. The quiet of the house was undisturbed while Oakley waited for a response, and looked about.

Visible on three sides of the Gately estate were the *haciendas* owned by the troubled Messrs. Wethering and Quinn and Tompkins. The windows of all three were black with the emptiness of desertion. A high hedge bordered the grounds, though any neighbors who cared to do so might look from their second-floor windows upon anything happening within the bounds of 1330. Beyond and below the hills lay light-spotted boulevards and the white purlieus of Los Angeles.

Oakley knocked again. "For a man who pleads for help," he observed, "Mr. Lawrence Gately is singularly slow in letting it in when it comes."

Finding that his second tattoo on the knocker brought no response, he twisted the doorknob. It was locked. He stepped back, surveyed the entrance, saw no light in any window. Signaling Brixey, he followed a gravel walk to the rear of the rambling *hacienda*. Under a moonless sky, the grounds lay black and silent, but in the starlight Oakley glimpsed outlines that stopped him.

"Hello!" he said.

HE WAS looking upon an array of equipment which made up a small outdoor gymnasium. In the darkness dangled a pair of flying rings, a trapeze, the rack of a pole-vault, and a tanbark track stretching off to the rear. The layout had been constructed beside a huge swimming pool, the surface of which lay mirror-still. Oakley saw that this spot was also plainly visible from the upper windows of the three surrounding villas.

"Here," he observed, "is where the ghost indulged in athletics. Tonight he seems to be otherwise engaged."

"I say, Oke!" Brixey protested. "You don't believe that guff, do you?"

"Many different persons have reported the phenomenon independently," Oakley pointed out, "and so I'm inclined to believe it—yes."

He strode along the rear of the house. Brixey stopped beside him and they peered inward through open French windows. The room beyond was utterly dark and soundless. Oakley called, "Mr. Gately!" and the echo of his voice was the only answer.

Suddenly Brixey blurted: "My word! There it is!"

Oakley inquired, "There what is?" and peered at his companion as the latter affixed his monocle with awed deliberation.

"The ghost!"

Oakley's gaze paralleled Brixey's. He sensed a presence—something hovering in the gloom that blackened the rear of the villa—but for a moment he saw nothing. Then a faint, greenish shine came out of the blackness and brought a chill to Oakley's blood. It floated at the height of a man's head, an ovoid glow that became sharper in outline, that became—a man's face!

Suspended in black night, disembodied, motionless, it peered at Oakley and Brixey. Its widened eyes emitted a spectral shine. Its parted, luminous lips exposed glinting, snagged teeth and a curling tongue that glowed! The phosphorescent features worked into an expression of terror—and abruptly vanished.

Empty darkness lay where the ghostly face had hovered and peered.

Brixey blurted: "I say!"

Oakley snapped: "Listen!"

Quick, quiet footfalls sounded at the corner of the house, at the spot where the apparition had materialized. Someone—or something—was running through the grass. Oakley broke into a sprint. Brixey swung long legs at his side. Once beyond the corner, they stopped, listening intently. Now the furtive footfalls were gone. In the spread of unobstructed lawn that reached to the boulevard beyond, there was no sound and no movement.

Oakley and Brixey peered at each other in bewilderment. They turned back. Again they paused, near the corner of the house.

"It was here," Oakley said quietly, "that the phantom appeared."

"I say!" Brixey blurted again. "We did see that thing, didn't we? A face shining like an alarm clock—a face without a body! It can't be anything human, Oke! It couldn't have been a real man we heard running—there's no place out there to hide! That thing melted away into thin air!"

Oakley's eyes narrowed. "We," he said earnestly, "are going to look into this!"

He strode back to the open French windows. Again, with Brixey, he peered into utter darkness, listened—complete silence. He stepped in, slipped a paper packet from his vest, and struck a match. Flickering yellow light played feebly across a spacious room and upon something black, of indefinite outline, lying on the floor.

The flame puffed out as Oakley strode to a light switch. Through the blackness Brixey blurted: "My word! Did you see—"

"A body," Oakley affirmed, and snapped the switch.

Amber light revealed the horror. Oakley peered at it and went pale. Brixey adjusted his monocle, stood transfixed. Between them, on the Persian rug, the body lay in a welter of blood. The conservative black suit which clothed it was slashed in a score of places. The wrists and hands, the feet and ankles, were savagely gashed and glistening with red. Above the starched collar was a ghastly stump of a neck. The cadaver had no head!

On the stained carpet beside it lay the weapon which had hacked the body into an almost shapeless pulp, which had struck off its head—an ancient battle-axe.

"It seems, Archie," Oakley said grimly, "we're a bit too late."

2. *Voice from the Grave*

OAKLEY TOOK slow steps. His eyes squinted with revulsion as he inspected the mutilated corpse. Blood had flowed from scores of deep cuts opened by the driven edge of the axe. The carpet was sodden with it. Oakley saw a diamond stud in the dead man's spotted tie, a heavy golden chain trickling across the vest. Gingerly he slipped a gold watch from the pocket, to find it marred by blows of the weapon, its crystal shattered. He noted the time at which it had stopped and the light in his eyes grew sharper.

"My word, Oke!" Brixey exclaimed. "Where is his head? It's nowhere in sight!"

"The head," Oakley affirmed in a tight voice, "is missing, Archie—yes."

His gaze had shifted to the odd weapon of murder. It was heavy and formidable. At the end of its long, time-seasoned handle a chain was affixed, connected at the end with a metal wrist-cuff. The edge of the blade was a sharp, gleaming, curved line. Near the stump of the cadaver's neck, the rug was cut and the floor bitten, where powerful blows of the axe had cleaved through.

"We heard the murderer hacking that poor chap!" Brixey gasped. "He was in this room while we were at the door. We frightened him away. I've never beheld such a horrible sight!"

Oakley was peering around. "The battle-axe," he said, "didn't come from this room. It's a valuable piece—it would have been hanging up somewhere—but there's nothing gone from the walls."

Again Brixey gasped. "Oke! A head missing—and we saw a disembodied face shining in the dark! What does it mean? Was that actually a spirit, carrying this poor chap's head away? That thing we saw—was it the ghost of only a head? My word, Oke, I simply can't understand this!"

"What it means," Oakley declared grimly, "is something I intend to find out!" He turned to a telephone sitting on an antique Spanish table near the entrance. "This is a case for the police. In a few moments we'll have our friend, the elephantine McClane, tramping in on us." He began to spin the dial. "As far as I'm concerned, the most horrible thing about any murder we run into, Archie, is McClane."

A new voice spoke from the door. It startled Oakley, caused Brixey's monocle to pop from his eye. It said, with an ominous gruffness: "You don't need to make that call, Oakley."

THEY STARED at the hulking man who was standing in the French doors. His face was as threatening as an English bull's and his eyes, bright as his polished box-toed shoes, were glinting with suspicion. He had drifted out of the darkness with scarcely a sound and now he regarded Oakley with condemning intentness.

"McClane!" Brixey moaned.

Oakley put down the phone. "What the devil are you doing here?" he snapped. "How long have you been in this place, McClane? I can tell by the way you're looking at me that you already suspect I'm the murderer!"

McClane grunted. "Huh! It's queer as hell how you get mixed right into the middle of every important case I handle. You've got a nerve! I find you in the room with a murdered body and you begin asking *me* questions!"

"As usual, McClane," Oakley retorted, "you're ready to grill hell out of the first person within reach. I'm here because I was called by a man who was afraid he was about to be murdered. To judge from appearances, he didn't call me soon enough."

McClane blurted "What? He called you too? That's damn funny! I'm here because a Lawrence Gately phoned me and said he was afraid for his life. He said there was somebody prowling around the grounds and trying to get at him. Whoever that guy was that he saw," McClane opined, gazing at the decapitated corpse, "certainly did get at him!"

Oakley asked shrewdly: "Did Gately, when he phoned you, mention anyone's name?"

"No." McClane marched to the body and grimaced. "God, what a mess! I just got here. I saw the lights go on, and I heard you talking. I warn you, Oakley, I'm going to check up on your story. There'd better not be anything fishy about it. If there is, I'll throw you into the cooler so fast you'll—"

"You seem to have dedicated your life to the purpose of making San Quentin my permanent address, McClane," Oakley cut in sourly. "For God's sake, get busy! The man who committed this murder hasn't had time to go far. He'll get all the way out of California while you stand around and threaten me!"

"Huh!" McClane grunted again. He took a long look at the corpse, and marched to the telephone. Oakley glanced around while the big plainclothesman called headquarters. McClane obtained connection with his superior and began growling the details of the crime into the transmitter. He turned from the instrument to command Oakley and Brixey, "Stay here!" and marched into the adjoining rooms.

"Oke," Brixey suggested gravely, "you'd jolly well better retire from this case as fast as you can. McClane's going to collar you if possible. He's waiting for a chance to throw us all into the jug, and I damn well don't fancy going there."

OAKLEY HAD taken a new interest in the corpse. He bent to examine more closely a tuft of black cloth lying beneath the decapitated body. He tugged on it, and found that it was not the fabric of the dead man's clothing. He began slowly to pull it away; and the shrill ring of the telephone stopped him.

Oakley spun to answer it as McClane came tramping back. A voice asked: "May I speak with August, please?"

Quickly Oakley noted the number on the dial and asked if there wasn't a mistake.

"This is Mr. Gately's house, isn't it? I want to speak with August Gaspar, the gardener. This is Mrs. Hepplehaus calling."

"So far as I know, Mrs. Hepplehaus," Oakley answered, "August Gaspar isn't here. I suggest that you call again later."

McClane tramped in as he broke the connection and growled: "What the hell do you mean by answering the phone? I'm in charge here! Just how're you mixed up in this case, shamus? Whatever way it is, you'd better be damn careful!"

"My God, McClane, you positively reek with unfounded suspicions!" Oakley retorted. "It was apparently a perfectly innocent call for—"

A chorus of sound from the driveway surprised them. Gravel

gritted beneath the tires of an approaching car. It braked; footfalls approached the entrance. A key clicked in the lock; the door opened. In the glare of light a man stopped short, hand on the knob, staring.

McClane thrust at him: "Who're you?"

The newcomer's face flashed white as his gaze went to the horror on the floor. An inarticulate gasp broke from his lips. He jerked closer, then recoiled. Stunned, frozen, he peered up and blurted: "God! God, it's—Lawrence."

"That's Lawrence Gately?" McClane snapped at him.

"My brother—yes! What—what's happened? Who're you—what're you doing here?" Then again, in abject horror: "Oh—my—God!"

Oakley said quietly: "You're Philip Gately, then. Try to pull yourself together, man! Your brother's been murdered. Can't you understand that?"

Philip Gately turned haggard eyes from the headless body. He had been carrying a briefcase, and now he dropped it. His bleared eyes met McClane's gaze, then Oakley's and Brixey's; and the headquarters man grasped his arm.

"Look here, now, Gately!" McClane growled. "This is tough on you, but you've got to take it. The law's in charge here. I want information, and I'm going to get it. Sit down! Answer my questions!"

Gately blurted: "For God's sake—not here!"

McClane scowled, and thrust him to a connecting door. "In there, then!" Gately stumbled through, mopping at his white face with palsied hands. "First of all I want an alibi from you!" McClane glared back at Oakley. "You, shamus—you stay here! Understand that?"

OAKLEY DID not move until McClane and Gately were out of sight beyond the door. He listened a moment to the big detective's bulldozing questions, to Gately's quavering answers. With a gesture that cautioned Brixey to watch, he stooped again beside the corpse.

He took the black tuft of cloth into his fingers and pulled. It slipped from beneath the body, spotted wet with blood. Oakley lifted it, eyed it in amazement. He shaped it out into a black hood. Two eye-holes had been cut in it. It was a mask fashioned to envelop the entire head of the wearer.

Brixey stared as Oakley passed it to him. Oakley's interest returned to the corpse. Again he fingered something that

lay beneath the body; and this was white. He drew it away—a strip of folded paper, closely printed in varying colors, bearing geographic names.

"This," he said, rising, "is an airplane ticket from Glendale to New York. Keep it, Archie!"

Again he listened, tensely, to McClane's growls and Gately's tremulous answers in the adjoining room. The telephone clattered and he strode to it. The receiver brought a familiar voice to his ear as McClane tramped back. Brixey whisked the cowl-mask and the airplane ticket out of sight and Oakley stated wryly: "It's for me, my friend. It's Cherry Morris, to be exact."

McClane said "Huh!" and tramped back to Gately. Oakley bade: "Go ahead, Cherry!"

"Oke, it's gone out over the air—the murder at the Gately place. Not five minutes later, just a moment ago, I took a telephone call from a girl who was so frantic she could hardly speak. I warn you—she's a beautiful blonde in distress and—"

"How the devil can you know that if she only telephoned?"

"Because she's in pictures. We've seen her. She's got lots of what it takes. You stay away from her, Oke, or she'll get you into trouble. She's desperate for help of some sort—she pleaded to see you right away, but mark my words, if you go rushing off to rescue Rona Jerome from her diffi—"

"What!" Oakley snapped. "Jerome?" He whispered it. "You're sure of that name?"

"You'll fare much better," Cherry told him, "if you let that blonde alone and buy me a hamburger instead, because I'm hungry and—"

"Her address, Cherry!" Oakley mentally noted it. "Get yourself to that place right away! Meet Archie and me in front of it."

A snap of his fingers electrified Brixey as he strode past the headless body. "Archie, keep that mask and ticket out of sight! Come with me—quietly. Unless I'm mistaken, McClane is going to be hot on the trail after us, and we've got to move fast!"

Brixey stuffed the strange objects inside his coat and tugged at Oakley's arm as they hurried to the French door. "My word, Oke! McClane will jolly well clamp down on us if we leave like this! Where're we going and why?"

Oakley slipped into the darkness beyond the French doors without speaking. He ducked into his roadster and Brixey angled down beside him; he tramped on the starter.

A door flashed open and McClane bel-

lowed, "Hey! Come back here!" as Clay and Brixey whirled down the winding road toward Wilshire Boulevard. Grimly, while the wind whipped past, and Brixey eyed him aghast, Clay toed the accelerator. He was well on his way before he answered Brixey's question.

"We're going," he said, "to the home of the man whom Lawrence Gately named to me as his intended murderer. The reason? Gately telephoned me at just twenty minutes past ten. The axe that killed that man struck his gold watch and stopped it at ten minutes *before* ten. If that evidence can be believed, Archie, Lawrence Gately telephoned me just half an hour after he was murdered!"

3. A Living Corpse

OAKLEY LEFT the wheel at a modest home nestling at the foot of the Hollywood hills. Charmaine Morris was waiting near the gate; now turned shapely pumps toward him. With Brixey they went to the door and rang. Disdainfully, Cherry powdered her nose and hitched at her garters, exposing exquisite legs.

"I am trying," Oakley sighed, "to keep my mind on the problem. Stop that, Cherry! Suppose you tell me why a dead man should telephone me a plea to be saved from a murderer half an hour after his violent demise."

"Suppose you tell me," Cherry countered, "why you persist in a case which is sure to get you into trouble. Never mind—I already know the answer. It's a beautiful blonde, as usual. Damn her!"

Steps approached the door while Oakley protested. "The blonde," he said, "is incidental. Somebody tried to trick me tonight. I can't allow that. If it was not Lawrence Gately who phoned me, it was his murderer. If it was his murderer, why the devil should he phone me at all? Why should he stay there to hack that body so frightfully—stay there so long, in fact, that my coming, in response to his own call, frightened him off?"

Cherry sniffed. "I can't think on an empty stomach," she said. "I still would like a hamburger sandwich."

The door opened to reveal a young woman as beautiful as Cherry Morris' worst expectations. Because it was Oakley's business, as ace private investigator of the film capital, to know all its faces, comely and otherwise, he recognized her at once as Rona Jerome. Her star was in its ascendancy; she was destined for fame. Many times Oakley had admired her smoothly beautiful face on the screen; but now it was deathly pale. Miss Rona Jerome was visibly shaken.

"Please come in," she begged when Oakley identified himself and his assistants. She followed them into a music room, then entwined her slender fingers nervously, her eyes uncertain upon Oakley's, her lips trembling. He had admired her histrionic ability too; but she was not acting now.

"You may trust me completely," he said quietly. "If you need my help—"

"I do need your help—desperately!" she exclaimed. "I hardly know how to explain. I've turned to you because—there's no one else. It—it's the Gately murder and—" She broke off.

"You are afraid," Oakley asked her, "that you will be involved?"

Rona Jerome's blue eyes widened. "How did you know?" Without giving Oakley a chance to answer she rushed on. "I'm not afraid for—for myself. If I'm involved, it will mean the end of me in pictures—but that's not the real reason. It's—my father."

"Suppose," Oakley suggested quietly, "you begin at the beginning."

The girl struggled painfully with words. "Please—please come with me."

SHE QUICKLY crossed the hallway, into a library. It was sumptuously furnished, lighted in amber, walled on three sides with shelves loaded with books. Rona Jerome paused near a desk and made a frightened gesture. Oakley found it unnecessary to ask the reason for her anxiety. He saw it— hanging on the wall.

It was an ancient battle-axe resting on wrought-iron hooks. From the end of its seasoned handle, a chain dangled, to which a cuff was affixed. Its broad, curved blade was polished bright—a blade such as might horribly mutilate a human body and decapitate it.

Very gravely, Oakley declared: "An exact duplicate of that axe was used to kill Lawrence Gately."

"I know!" The girl said it in a horrified whisper. "That's why I've sent for you. Father—father owns a pair of them, but one is missing. Mr. Oakley, he had nothing whatever to do with killing Lawrence Gately. You've got to believe that! You've got to prove he didn't!"

Oakley peered at two other wrought-iron hooks embedded in the wall at the other side. They were empty; but bright paint, in contrast to the slightly faded color which covered the rest of the wall, outlined unmistakably the shape of a second battle-axe that had rested there. It was there no longer.

"I'm afraid," Oakley said gravely, "that what you ask is a very difficult task. Just what about the axe—the one that is missing?"

"I didn't know it was gone until after I heard the radio news bulletin of the murder," the girl declared wretchedly. "Hearing that an axe had been used to kill Mr. Gately— naturally, I was startled. I came in here and found one of the pair missing. I don't know—I can't explain how—"

"Those axes are your father's property?"

"Yes. They are very old. The pair were used by the Honorable Corps of Gentlemen-at-Arms, the oldest bodyguard of an English sovereign, in Fifteen Twenty-six. My father found them in an old shop in London—they're really museum pieces. There is only one explanation—if—" Again the girl sought words. "Someone must have stolen one of the axes from this house tonight—deliberately—trying to put my father under suspicion!"

"Where is your father now?" Oakley asked gently. "And where was he at ten tonight?"

"He's in his room waiting to see you," the girl answered. "I came home from the studio—I worked late—about a quarter after ten. He was there then. He told me he'd been there all evening, reading. I know—"

"Alone?" Oakley asked.

"Alone," the girl admitted in a whisper. "Mr. Oakley, will you please help us? Before the police find out—won't you please try to prove that my father had nothing whatever to do with killing Mr. Gately?"

Oakley sighed. "Miss Jerome," he answered gravely, "your father's situation is very precarious. I received a telephone call tonight from Lawrence Gately, and Gately told me then he was afraid of being killed. He declared someone was trying to get at him—and he mentioned the name Jerome."

"No!" the girl gasped in protest. "Oh, no!"

"He did," Oakley insisted. "I have seen the axe that was used to kill Gately. It is an exact duplicate of the one hanging now on your wall. It is, without any possible doubt, the axe that is missing from this room. As for an alibi, your father has none. His saying that he was alone here, reading, at the time of the murder, is scarcely—"

"But it's true!" the girl pled. "Father couldn't be capable of such an act! Won't you please—"

"You place me," Oakley interrupted quietly, "in a painful situation. I want very much to help you. I know that if you become embroiled in this murder case, your career will come to an abrupt end. I know that once a certain detective, named McClane, gets his big hands on your father, distressing consequences will follow. All the evidence points to your father's guilt. Frankly, trying to prove his innocence seems hopeless. Please forgive me, but I must refuse the case."

THE GIRL stood stricken. Oakley bowed regretful goodnight, and turned back to the entrance. Brixey observed the girl's pale beauty through his monocle, sighed reluctantly, and went with him. Cherry Morris led the way, said: "For once, Oke, you've resisted a blonde in distress. Accept my congratulations and a reminder that I'd still like a nice, juicy hamburger."

Oakley sighed, "What a witch you are!" and began to step out. A plaintive call stopped him. He turned to see Rona Jerome hurrying toward him. The girl's eyes were shining with a desperate plea. She caught Oakley's hand as though she meant never to let it go.

"I—I haven't told you everything!" she exclaimed. "Won't you at least listen? Won't you talk to my father and let him tell you—"

Oakley avoided Cherry's cool eyes. "I should be very heartless," he answered suavely, "if I refused you that. Please take me to your father. I will listen, but I can promise no more."

Cherry Morris murmured, "I will still believe in Santy Claus, will I?" as she followed Oakley down a hallway. Rona Jerome opened a door and Oakley stepped through first. Inside the room a floor-lamp was throwing a bright cone upon a wizened man slumped in a chair. Sight of him immediately filled Oakley with revulsion.

The skin of his gaunt face was splotched; his hands were thin and scaly; he was almost bald, and his sunken lips meant he was toothless. He rose quickly as Rona Jerome went to him, and his lean arm curled around her. Oakley stood fascinated by the contrast between this beautiful young girl and this horrible figure as the introductions were made.

Sanford Jerome declared earnestly: "Mr. Oakley, I swear to you I knew nothing of this until Rona heard it on the radio and told me! For God's sake, you've got to believe me! I don't care about myself—but it will ruin Rona's life. I'm asking your help for her sake!"

Oakley observed: "You are genuinely afraid, Mr. Jerome—afraid of the police."

"I know the circumstances are damning. I'm afraid of the police—yes—because they will consider I had a strong motive for killing Lawrence Gately."

"A motive?" Oakley murmured.

Jerome's eyes blazed. "Look at me! I saw you wince when you caught sight of me—but I don't blame you for that. I am a horrible sight. I am dying, Mr. Oakley—slowly dying a ghastly death—and Lawrence Gately is responsible."

A light came into Oakley's eyes. "I remember, now. All evening I have been trying to recall the connection I made between your name and Lawrence Gately's, Mr. Jerome. I think I have it now. A law suit, isn't it?"

JEROME'S HIDEOUS lips curved in a mirthless smile. "Lawrence Gately is—was—a defendant in a suit for heavy damages that I was pressing against him—yes. No judgment against him could ever repay me for my lost health, for the suffering he's cost me. I have gone after him with all the power of the law because he has ruined the lives of scores of innocent people—and he has fought me with every legal weapon possible. He deserved death! I've said it countless times—I say it again, now!"

Oakley looked grave. "See here," he said. "You're not convincing me that you're innocent of his murder. On the contrary."

Sanford Jerome seemed not to hear. "Do you know why I've been fighting that man in the courts, why I've dedicated what life I have left to forcing him to pay, in some small way, for the horrible damage he has done to scores of human lives? It's because he has made me a living corpse!"

Oakley blinked. Brixey, fascinated, adjusted his monocle. Even Cherry Morris forgot her disapproval of Rona Jerome's plea as she heard the pathetic earnestness of Sanford Jerome's voice. The actress's hand clung tightly, reassuringly, to her father's.

"Listen, Mr. Oakley!" Jerome exclaimed; and his story poured out.

Years previous, weakened by an anemic condition which persisted despite the routine treatments of physicians, Jerome had turned to a new and costly patented tonic called Radelix. It was, he explained, a medication for which revivifying powers were claimed, the basis being the radioactive substance contained in it. He had consumed bottle after bottle of it and at first had felt a marked improvement in his condition. His betterment had soon passed. He had found himself wasting, consumed by a strange malady that sapped his vitality. His physician had declared the tonic to be the sole reason, that his ailment was—

"Radium poisoning!" Jerome spat. "Incurable! The radium salts in that devilish concoction lodged in my system. They permeated every organ of my body. They started a condition which cannot be controlled. They caused sores like burns. They are bringing on atrophy and cancer—death! One of the most horrible deaths a human can face! I'm dying because of the devil's brew that came out of the quack laboratories of Lawrence Gately."

Jerome's haggard eyes burned fever-bright, his scaled hands worked into bony fists as he rushed on.

"Gately made fortunes from his patent nostrums before he put Radelix on the market. He made groundless, extravagant claims for it and charged exorbitant prices. I am only one of hundreds he victimized. The government forced him to take it off the market with a cease-and-desist order—but there it stopped. All that man's wealth can't repay the appalling suffering he has caused. Not even the loss of his life can repay it! I'm glad he's dead! I wish I *had* killed him!"

Rona Jerome reproved him with a frightened, "Father!" The unfortunate man's fevered eyes exerted a hypnotic effect on Oakley. He stood motionless, listening intently to every word, as Sanford Jerome rushed on.

"Look, Oakley! See what he has done to me! See the horrible thing he has made of me!"

Jerome's one scrawny hand shot to the switch of the standing lamp. He snapped it off, and darkness filled the room. The move was a surprise; no one stirred. Until his eyes became accustomed to the blackness, Oakley wondered. His puzzlement vanished and cold amazement came when he saw, at first faintly, but brightening with every second, a dull greenish glow in the dark!

In that lightless room the hideous face of Sanford Jerome shone with a gleam of its own! His skin radiated a poisonous glow. His eyes sparkled with a phosphorescent light. Every feature of his face—even the deep, shadowed wrinkles—exuded a ghostly green radiance. For a full moment, in stark silence, Oakley peered at it—a phantom face such as he had seen hovering in the night that shrouded the house in which lay the mutilated body of Lawrence Gately!

THE SWITCH clicked again, and light blinded Oakley. He saw Brixey peering, aghast, at Jerome; and now the unfortunate man was clinging to his daughter's hand with pathetic tenderness. The girl's head was on his shoulder; she was sobbing softly. She raised tear-brimmed eyes to Oakley.

"This—this is why we are so worried," she whispered. "Father's damage suit has been sidetracked again and again. It has become a bitter, almost hopeless fight. Don't you understand now why the police will persecute him? They'll think father—"

"Killed Lawrence Gately because the courts denied him legal recourse," Oakley added to the girl's unfinished sentence. "I see that clearly. Once McClane gets his hands on you, Mr. Jerome, you'll be hounded to the chair. There's no doubt of that!"

"And you won't help us?" Rona Jerome pled. "You won't?"

Oakley studied the girl's drawn face. He gazed into her father's gaunt eyes. He said, very quietly: "On the contrary, I will."

"Thank God!" Sanford Jerome breathed. "Thank God for that!"

Oakley ignored Brixey's moan of protest, paid no attention to Cherry Morris' stifled exclamation of anxiety, went on calmly.

"I'll help you because I believe you both. I think you're innocent, Mr. Jerome. It would be a frightful pity if your daughter's career ended abruptly—now that she has such a promising future. I'll take the case on condition you'll do exactly as I say."

"Yes!" the girl exclaimed. "Anything!"

"Then," Oakley directed, "come with me."

He strode to the vestibule, with the dismayed Brixey and the anxious Cherry Morris following. He drew Cherry aside near the door and spoke imperatively.

"Hop down to the office in a taxi, darling. Archie and I are going to need the car. Get all the dope you possibly can out of the files, on everybody concerned in this case. Camp there until I show up or call you."

Cherry's very red lips pursed indignantly. "Don't you realize what you're heading into?" she asked. "This blonde is going to be your finish. Oke, you're a perfect fool!"

"About you, my dear," Oakley assured her gravely. "On your way!"

He hastened Cherry out the entrance. He heard her high heels clicking away over the pavement as he strode into the library. Sanford Jerome and his daughter hurried to Oakley's side as he lifted down the old battle-axe. He peered at the wall, where the shadows of the two ancient weapons were clearly visible in the unfaded paint, and spoke crisply.

"This, first and foremost, must he gotten rid of. You've got to deny ever owning the pair of axes. You've got to paint that wall as soon as possible—tonight, if you can—in order to get rid of those marks. Somehow, Mr. Jerome, you've got to provide yourself with a strong alibi. Occupy yourself with that problem while I get this damned axe out of sight somehow. Paper—wrapping paper—quick!"

His glittering eyes emphasized his directions to Jerome as the girl hurried into the rear of the house. "Your legal connection with Gately is sure to lead Detective McClane straight to you. He'll grill hell out of you, but you've got to take it. Whatever your story is, stick to it!"

RONA JEROME returned with a folded sheet of heavy brown paper. Quickly Oakley wrapped the ponderous axe in it. He curled his arm around the bundle, strode to the door, stopped; again fixed Jerome and the girl with an uncompromising eye.

"If McClane breaks you, Mr. Jerome, if he learns the truth, you'll certainly get the chair. Your daughter's film career will be at an end. Also, it will be the finish of one hitherto fortunate private detective. Remember that!"

He paused, scanned the street, strode to his roadster. He slipped behind the wheel; Brixey angled down beside him. He fumbled with the brown package, muttering maledictions. "What a devil of a thing to try to get rid of!"

"You're doing an excellent job of getting rid of yourself, Oke," Brixey said, with a quaver. "If McClane ever grabs onto you now, you're sunk!"

Oakley declared, in exasperation: "I'm trying to get this damned thing out of sight! Lift your legs, Archie!"

Brixey folded. "But I say, Oke!" he protested. "You're mad! Have you forgotten the face we saw shining in the dark behind Gately's place? It was the face of the murderer—or a ghost! There's nothing else to think. And if it was the face of the murderer, it was Jerome!"

Oakley was sliding the long-handled axe beneath Brixey's thin knees. "Where the devil can we dispose of this?"

The answer came in a chesty voice that spoke from the darkness on Oakley's right. It said, laconically: "I'll take it!"

Brixey's monocle popped from his dismayed eye. Oakley peered coldly at the hulking figure that had come silently upon them, and permitted himself a moan of despair.

"McClane!"

"I'll take it!" McClane said again.

Oakley slumped despondently at the wheel as the big detective's hands seized the brown-wrapped package. McClane rattled the heavy paper off. He gripped the axe by the handle, appraised it with an eye which gleamed as brightly as the axe-edge, and turned a triumphant grin upon Oakley.

"Did I ever tell you that some day I was going to send you to San Quentin for a nice, long stretch?" he gloated. "It'll begin pretty soon now. Just long enough to get Jerome convicted of murder and you for attempting to conceal evidence."

"Don't be tiresome, McClane," Oakley answered without heart. "You'll have a tough time proving that charge, and when you've failed, I'll sue the pants off you for false arrest."

"This time you can't bluff me with that!" McClane snapped. "I've got you absolutely cold! I suppose you were taking this down to headquarters, were you? That's why you were wondering so hard where to dispose of it. Sure! Oakley, you're sunk!"

A chill pervaded Oakley.

"I got the dope on Jerome from Philip Gately," McClane growled. "I know all about the big law suit and the reason why Jerome killed him. I come beating it here on a hot lead and what do I find? You on the job again! Trying to cover the murderer! Obstructing justice! Concealing evidence! Just between you and me, Oakley, I think you're a damn fool."

"Just between you and me, McClane," Oakley sighed, "I agree with you."

"All right!" McClane called across the street. "Lawton!" Out of the shadows of the hedge on the opposite sidewalk a short, stocky man materialized. He paced to McClane's side—Detective-Sergeant Lawton. McClane passed the axe to him and directed sourly: "Hold onto that. Take charge of the prisoners. Drive 'em down to headquarters. I'll be coming right behind you with Jerome."

OAKLEY WATCHED McClane tramp to the entrance of the house. He saw the door open, saw McClane shoulder in. Lawton's gesture turned his eyes away.

"Move over," Lawton commanded. "I'm taking the wheel. It's a nice trip, down to headquarters. You'll enjoy it." Oakley's eyes

glinted with desperation. He did not move over; he got out. He faced Lawton squarely and his voice crackled. "Sergeant," he inquired, "have you ever been presented with a very black eye?"

Defiantly, Lawton retorted: "Never!"

"Then," Oakley finished, "accept one now—with my compliments!"

His fist became a black blur that exploded terrific power on the point of Lawton's chin. The headquarters man emitted a bellow, dropped the axe, staggered back with arms windmilling. Oakley snatched the axe and tossed it to Brixey's lap.

Brixey bleated his dismay. Again Lawton bellowed, weaving in, and at the same moment McClane burst out the door of the Jerome home. Oakley made the car, swung it from the curb on whining tires. A gun blasted behind him and a bullet whipped across the top of the roadster. Oakley zigzagged madly at the corner.

"McClane will have every prowl car in town hunting us—in two minutes! We've got to abandon the roadster!"

"We're jolly well abandoning life, liberty and the pursuit of happiness, if you ask me!" Brixey moaned.

Wilshire Boulevard was close ahead when Oakley swerved to the curb. He jumped out, gripping the handle of the battle-axe. He fingered into the grips of a manhole cover, clanked it aside, dropped the keen-bladed weapon into the black cavity, slid the iron cover back, signaled Brixey. They loped toward the lights.

Oakley's wave stopped a taxi. They ducked into it breathlessly and it eddied into the stream of traffic. The driver, looking back, inquired: "Where to?"

"Head in the general direction of Mexico," Oakley ordered him grimly, "and head fast!"

4. Ghost Glow

THE ETERNAL California sun beamed its morning radiance upon a taxi that drew to the front of a house which bore a placard reading—*Rooms and Board*. Oakley and Brixey emerged from the cab. They glanced furtively around, trod to the entrance, hurriedly knocked.

Beards blackened their faces and fatigue sagged their shoulders. The taxi, which whirred away, was the sixth in which they had sought escape from the police during a night of constant shuttling about the expansive precincts of Los Angeles. Hard by, in this section of Culver City, sat the studios of several major producing companies. Their cautious glances assured them now that no squad cars were on their trail.

Oakley bowed when the door opened. "Mrs. Hepplehaus?" he inquired. "My friend and I wish to engage a room. You were recommended by a friend of ours, Mr. August Gaspar."

Mrs. Hepplehaus's smile came and went. "August? Have you seen him lately?" Her inquiry plainly came from the heart.

"I regret that I haven't," Oakley told her, not adding that this was because Mr. August Gaspar was a total stranger to him. He did not, moreover, explain that he had been led to this address through Mrs. Hepplehaus's telephone call to the Gately home—with the aid of a directory which disclosed the fact that her name was unique in all Los Angeles. "May we see a nice, comfortable, sunny, double room?"

Mrs. Hepplehaus nervously bade them follow her. "August didn't come home for dinner last night," she related as they climbed steps, "and it's the first time he ever missed one of *my* dinners." She opened a door and added: "He hasn't come back yet. I'm worried. Is this all right?"

"It's splendid," Oakley assured her, gazing upon a horror of clashing greens and reds and pinks in the furnishings. "A week in advance—is that satisfactory? Is August's room near?"

"Right across the hall," Mrs. Hepplehaus informed him, taking the banknote Oakley offered. "Breakfast at eight, lunch at two thirty, dinner at seven. The food's very good."

Oakley murmured his conviction that it must be, and bowed her out. Brixey sank into a chair upholstered in seasick green with overshades of jaundice yellow, and moaned his despair.

"Why," he beseeched, "have we come to this offensive hole? Why do you possibly think we can continue to elude the police? Why did you let yourself get into this dashed case at all?"

"Archie," Oakley answered wearily, "we're in what is technically known as a spot. It behooves me greatly to do everything possible to prove one Sanford Jerome innocent of murder. Unless I can do that very promptly, you and I will shortly be setting up housekeeping in San Quentin."

"Much," moaned Brixey, "to McClane's devilish glee."

"There is something very strange behind all this," Oakley continued. "First, the telephone call from a man who was then already dead. Puzzling, isn't it? The weapon of murder—there's absolutely no doubt of it, Archie, we were caught red-handed doing away with important evidence. One of Jerome's axes was certainly used for the kill. But why? Why not a good, old-fashioned gun?"

Brixey did not know why.

"One other thing, Archie. When we looked into the room where that mutilated and headless corpse lay, it was absolutely dark, wasn't it? Absolutely dark?"

"Absolutely," Brixey affirmed morosely, "dark. If that means anything."

"I'm beginning to believe it means a great deal."

OAKLEY LOOKED out the door. He trod down the stairs and found a pay telephone in the lower hall. Ascertaining that no one was within listening distance, he slotted a coin and called the number of Secrets, Incorporated. The anxious voice of Charmaine Morris answered.

"The top of the morning to you, darling," he greeted her. "How did you sleep?"

"Oke! Oke, you fool! Don't you know the whole police force is looking for you? Since you ask, I didn't sleep a wink!"

"Nor I," Oakley sighed. "Very distressing. Cherry, I need information. If you have any reports, read 'em to me."

"I have several reports," Cherry returned icily. "A particularly interesting one is that Oke Oakley is going into the pokey as soon as McClane grabs him. Sanford Jerome is under arrest and in general there's hell to pay. You're putting circles under my eyes, damn you."

"Alas!" Oakley sighed. "The reports, Cherry!"

"I have," Cherry continued, "very little information that promises to save you from being convicted of complicity in a very bloody murder. What Jerome told us last night, about the big law suit, checks up. Additional information concerns Lawrence Gately."

"Go on!"

"Gately, soon after the filing of the damage action, made himself a recluse at Thirteen Thirty Sutter Boulevard. He has not been seen in public for months. His lawyer brother was defending the legal action taken against him. Fully twenty people have been waiting to file similar suits against Gately, if Jerome should be awarded a judgment. All that's blown up now, of course. It doesn't help much, does it?"

"Don't ask questions," Oakley said, "answer 'em! Have you any dope on Jerome's strange affliction?"

"Yes. Radium poisoning is incurable, just as he says. It may be caused by quack medications containing it. In fact, it is on record that men have died from drinking water that was too powerfully radioactive. Accredited physicians use radium very carefully and very sparingly in special treatments. It's dangerous stuff."

"Evidently!"

"Radium salts, taken into the body, accumulate in their effects. The body itself becomes radioactive and degenerates. The effect is similar to those awful x-ray burns that sometimes attack doctors. You remember the case of the eight women who contracted radium poisoning in East Orange, New Jersey, several years ago?"

"Faintly," Oakley told her.

"They worked in a watch factory. Their job was to cover the numerals of watches with luminous paint containing a small amount of radium. The work required very fine brushes, and they pointed the brushes on their lips. Result, radium in their systems. Result, damage suits against the company and judgments awarded in favor of the women. Result, slow and horrible death for them all. They've been dying off one by one. Each of them shone in the dark and their bodies continued to glow after death."

Oakley's eyes widened. "Keep right on!" he urged. "We're getting places!"

"San Quentin principally," Cherry retorted over the wire. "In case it means anything, the axe used to kill Gately is similar to one wielded by Robert the Bruce when he felled Henry de Bohun with a single blow the day before the battle of Bannockburn."

"That clears up everything!" Oke jeered.

"Oke, I think I'm being watched!" Cherry added.

"In any case," Oakley directed her, "stay right there. Don't go out. Have your hamburgers sent up. Hold down the fort at all costs, because I've got to rely on you for further information. Next, reach Philip Gately and get all the dope possible on Lawrence Gately—but get it by phone. I'll call you again. Farewell, my dear."

Oakley returned to the garish room where Brixey was dozing. Brixey opened an eye and put a monocle in it. Oakley sank to the bed with a sigh.

"Better enjoy this while you can, Archie," he whispered. "The bunks in San Quentin aren't so soft."

BACK AND forth across the rented room Oakley paced. Drawn blinds shut out the shine of the street lamps. Lunch and dinner had passed and Mrs. Hepplehaus had brought her excellent cookery up to them. With her cooperation, they had obtained a razor and shaved. Brixey had slept soundly while Oakley had listened for sounds in the hallway. Now, nervously, he kept marching on the hideous, figured carpet.

"I do believe," Brixey mourned, "San Quentin will be better than this."

Oakley snapped: "Archie, our friend August Gaspar has not yet returned. Mrs. Hepplehaus is in a dither. Does that mean anything to you?"

"Very little," Brixey admitted.

"Then," Oakley retorted, "come with me while we add burglary to our many crimes."

He listened with his ear to the hall door, stepped out. At the door opposite, which Mrs. Hepplehaus had indicated as being that of Gaspar's room, he drew from his pocket a packet of skeleton keys which he always carried with him. His third try drew the bolt. With Brixey, he stepped into a room no less striking than their own.

In the glow of a pink-and-green table lamp, Oakley made an inspection. From a drawer of the bureau he removed a folder of snapshots which revealed Mrs. Hepplehaus at the side of a man whose arm was around her ample waist. Oakley knew he was gazing upon the likeness of August Gaspar. In another drawer Oakley found a diary belonging to Gaspar. He read entries intently, skipped pages, read more.

"It seems," he informed the distressed Brixey, "our friend has led an adventurous life. He enlisted during the war, stayed in the navy for a stretch afterward, shipped on tramp steamers, worked in an orange grove, then went to work as gardener for the Gatelys on the haunted estate. He notes here that he was selected for the job with great care and is proud that he was picked over a score of other applicants. All in all, a blameless life."

"I profess no interest in the elusive Mr. Gaspar," Brixey stated impatiently. "I think we should jolly well get the hell out of here."

"I agree." Oakley returned the snapshots and the diary to their places. "We are getting further the hell out of here than you think." They stepped out the door and Oakley's skeleton key locked it. "Once more I will see what luck Cherry has had, if any."

He trod down to the telephone. Ten times during the day he had called Secrets, Incorporated, and now he called it again.

Cherry's voice came over the wire a bit garbled, and Oakley deduced that she was munching a hamburger.

"Still no luck, Oke," she whispered. "Philip Gately won't discuss the case. He has taken to refusing to answer his phone. I see by the papers that the remains of Lawrence Gately were solemnly interred beneath the sod this afternoon."

Oakley muttered blasphemy. "Stay right there," he directed, "but stop trying to get Gately on the wire. That's evidently hopeless. A more direct attack must be made, and I'll make it. Pray for me, Cherry."

"Oke!" the girl exclaimed anxiously. "What are you going to do now?"

"Stick my neck out," Oakley told her grimly, "with the expectation of having McClane apply a billy to it."

HE BROKE away and ran up the stairs. Brixey eyed him in amazement as he slipped into his topcoat. "Follow along, Archie," he directed as he started out. Brixey obeyed under voluble protest, but Oakley led him into the danger of the open street. They ventured to Washington Boulevard, flagged a taxi. Oakley, settling to the seat with a sigh, directed the driver: "Thirteen Thirty Sutter Boulevard, Beverly Hills."

Brixey moaned. "This is the end!"

"On the contrary," Oakley answered. "It's the beginning—the beginning of a desperate attempt to clear ourselves, Archie. If it fails, the confining effect upon us will be permanent."

The cab carried them along La Cienega Boulevard and turned left on Wilshire. When it was close to the Gately estate Oakley amended his orders and stopped it short. With Brixey at his side, he turned from 1330, walked fast, entered the grounds of the adjoining deserted house owned by one Wethering. They crossed to the bordering hedge and peered into the haunted gardens.

Heavy curtains obscured the light of two windows of the lower floor of the villa at 1330. It indicated that Philip Gately was at home. Oakley's eyes shone with satisfaction as he surveyed the gloom-shrouded lawn. He took particular notice of the outdoor gymnasium and observed: "Again the ghost is not in evidence. We're going over."

He went over at a bound. Brixey strode at his side as he turned to the rear of the house. Suspecting that McClane was having it watched, he kept to the shadows. At the French windows he knocked, and Oakley heard quick steps within. The latch clicked,

and the drawn face of Philip Gately looked out through the crack.

"A furtive but very necessary visit, Mr. Gately," Oakley informed the surprised man. "May we come in?"

Gately opened the way for them without speaking. They noted, as they entered, that the Persian rug, on which the decapitated cadaver had rested, was removed. Gately's color faded while he stared at them.

"What—what does this mean?" he demanded. "I understand from McClane that you are charged with—"

"Whatever you understand from McClane is an exaggeration, Mr. Gately," Oakley interrupted. "See here. I'm in a very tight place. I've come here for information because you refused to give it to my assistant, Miss Morris, on the phone."

"I have nothing to say!"

Oakley's eyes glittered. "I can't force you to talk," he admitted. "I'm asking for enlightenment for the sake of a man innocently accused of murder, for the sake of a girl whose life will be ruined by scandal; and, frankly, for my own sake because I wish very much to stay out of prison. Considering that, can you remain silent?"

"But Sanford Jerome is guilty of murdering my brother! I'm convinced of it!"

"I'm convinced he's not," Oakley countered. "I'm convinced that this case is far stranger than anyone else suspects. Talk, Mr. Gately! If you don't, you'll have an innocent man's blood on your hands."

Gately blinked. "What—what do you want to know?"

"I want to know, first of all, if your brother, Lawrence Gately, was afflicted with radium poisoning."

Gately blanched. "I can't—"

Was he?

Reluctantly Gately answered: "Yes."

"Ah!" Oakley exclaimed. "He was suffering from the same incurable ailment as Sanford Jerome. Why, Mr. Gately—why have you wanted to keep that fact a secret?"

THE ATTORNEY'S lips tightened. "That should be obvious. Lawrence was the defendant in a very heavy damage suit. Jerome's case was based on his having contracted radium poisoning through the use of Radelix, a preparation once manufactured by my brother. If it became known that Lawrence was suffering from exactly the same affliction, that he contracted it from exactly the same source, his case would inevitably have been lost."

Oakley's eyes were glittering. "Jerome contracted radium poisoning from taking Radelix and your brother contracted it from making it!"

"From experimenting with the formula during his researches," Philip Gately corrected. "That damnable stuff drove Lawrence out of the patent medicine business. Jerome's suit, if successful, would have been immediately followed by twenty others. All of them would certainly have been won by the plaintiffs. Naturally, we did everything possible to avoid that by keeping it a secret that Lawrence was similarly afflicted."

"Naturally," Oakley echoed, "you denied the existence of the so-called ghost in your garden because that ghost was in reality your brother!"

Gately gestured painfully. "Yes. The horrible effects of radium poisoning on his appearance forced Lawrence to become a recluse. He hoped that fresh air and vigorous exercise would help him rid his system of the poison. That's why he exercised in the open at night. But what—what bearing can this possibly have on—"

"A very direct one!" Oakley snapped. "Your brother was in a desperate plight. He faced the loss of his entire fortune. Once he was put on the witness stand, the truth would have been forced out of him. The result would have meant utter disaster for him. That's true, isn't it?"

"Yes—yes!"

"What will happen to his money now, Mr. Gately?"

The question collapsed Gately into a chair. "Oh, God!" he breathed, and cupped his hands over his face. "I'm completely at sea. Today—today I began a check on my brother's holdings. I discovered that all his securities had been liquidated without my knowledge. I found that he had withdrawn large amounts of cash over a period of months. What he did with the money, I don't know. But—there is scarcely any left!"

"Ah!" Oakley exclaimed again. "He was spiriting his money away so that he could plead poverty and avoid paying the damages, wasn't he?"

Gately jerked up. "Lawrence is dead," he said throatily. "All this means nothing now. Sanford Jerome killed him, in spite of what you believe!"

"I still doubt it." Oakley turned away. "Mr. Gately, I'm going after this case with all I've got. With your permission or without it, I'm going to take a look around these grounds. Goodnight."

He strode out, and Brixey swung long legs at his side. From the corner of the house he peered searchingly across the spread of lawn which reached to the boulevard beyond. It was here that the shining, ghostly face had appeared just previous to the discovery of the mutilated body. It was across that expanse of green that the furtive footfalls had apparently raced away. Oakley's hand sought his fountain-pen torch.

"Oke, where is all this getting us?" Brixey asked wretchedly. "I'm all in a muddle!"

OAKLEY TROD along the garden that flanked the side of the house. He swung the beam of his light over bushes and cacti, studying earth baked dry under the hot sun. He went on carefully until he reached a small oblong window set flush with the ground. He bent to examine it carefully and then said: "Ah!"

The catches which held the sash in the frame were loose. Oakley slid the sash out, pointed his light inward. Beyond the opening he saw the joists of the floor, raw earth hollowed away, the reaching tentacles of an automatic gas furnace operated electrically from buttons in the rooms upstairs—a commonplace equipment in California homes. Abruptly he dropped to his knees, thrust his head through the aperture, wriggled in.

"Follow along, Archie!" he directed.

The amazed Brixey crept after him as he crawled along an excavated passage which led to the gas furnace. It was shallow; they hunched. Oakley's light disclosed fresh disturbances in the dry dirt-scraped footprints. His beam cut a tangent past the drum of the furnace and again he drew a breath of triumph.

"Someone," he declared, "has been hiding here. This is the place our ghost disappeared into, Archie!"

"It only means," Brixey sighed, "that Jerome planned his bloody murder with fiendish care."

The shaft of Oakley's light played on small cartons and cans piled on the floor. The boxes contained crackers, the tins condensed milk and sardines. Several had been emptied and tossed aside. Crumbs sprinkled the dirt. Oakley's torch played over a supply sufficient to last several days, and swept on.

He tensed when a thud sounded overhead, and heavy footfalls tramped on the floor. Each step was a hollow reverberation in the excavation. Oakley groaned when he heard the heavy rumble of a familiar voice.

"McClane! Directly above us!"

"A perfectly splendid position to be caught in!" Brixey deplored. "Oke, you display an amazing talent for getting yourself into tight places."

Oakley gestured Brixey to be quiet.

Alertly he played his light across the dirt. The ray shadowed a small area the size of a platter, recently disturbed. He crawled to it, found a spot between small mounds which was softer than the surrounding earth. He fingered into it as McClane's footfalls again hammered overhead—hard and fast.

Oakley pawed at the dirt quickly. Brixey, peering at the window, saw shining bulldog shoes appear in a gleam of light. The beam of a hand-torch shot inward at them. It flashed blindingly into their eyes and the voice of McClane bellowed.

"Come out of there, Oakley! I've got you! You're not going to get away this time!"

Oakley abandoned his digging and sat. "Good evening, McClane," he greeted wryly. "You're too big to get in through that window, you know. What if Archie and I choose to remain here? How could you get at us?"

"I'll get you out of there if I have to tear down the house!" McClane snarled. "It's no use, Oakley! You're got!"

Oakley sighed at Brixey. "I'm afraid he's right again. There's nothing else to it, Archie. We've got to make an undignified exit into McClane's clutches."

"I hope," Brixey sighed, "they'll give us cells with a southern exposure."

OAKLEY LED the way on hands and knees. He wriggled out the window and McClane's big hand clamped his shoulder. He straightened as Brixey unfolded, noted a steely glitter of triumph in McClane's eyes, asked resignedly: "Are you absolutely set on jailing us, McClane? Tonight? Forthwith?"

"I can't get you into the cooler quick enough to suit me, shamus!"

"In that case," Oakley sighed despondently, "I'll make a clean breast of it. God help Jerome, but—come into the house with me, McClane."

He freed himself of McClane's grip and, with the mournful Brixey at his side, strode through the French windows into the room where murder had occurred. Philip Gately faced them coldly. McClane straddled, blocking the way out, fondling an ugly-looking .45.

"All right!" he snapped. "Come across!"

Oakley extended a soiled hand to Brixey. "Give me," he said, "the mask and the ticket, Archie."

Brixey paled. He brought from his inner pocket, into which he had rolled it, the cowl of black cloth which Oakley had found beneath the decapitated body. He followed it with the ticket which was good for one passage by air from Glendale Airport to New York City. Oakley tossed them to the table.

"You might have had those sooner," he said, "if the exigencies of the case hadn't obliged me to take to my heels before I could mention them."

"More concealed evidence!" McClane snarled. "By God, Oakley! That's three counts against you, not to mention assaulting an officer!" He snatched up the mask and studied it in a puzzled manner. When he scanned the ticket he snapped: "So you were planning to skip, were you?"

"No, no," Oakley moaned. "Not I. Perhaps Lawrence Gately was planning to make use of that ticket." As Philip Gately blurted a protest that this was not true, Oakley added: "The murderer, then. He lost it in the death struggle, McClane. It calls for checking up."

"You're telling me how to handle this case, are you?" McClane snarled.

"I'm entertaining a forlorn hope that you might try a bit of thinking," Oakley sighed. "For instance, who has been hiding under this house and why? What did he bury down there? If Jerome is innocent of the murder, what is the only other answer poss—"

Oakley broke off short. The room became silent—and black. Black because, suddenly and without warning, every light blinked out!

The surprise of the sudden darkness held Oakley motionless when a swift movement sounded near the French doors. He glimpsed a figure silhouetted against the faint gleam of the stars, a figure that had darted out of an adjoining room. It sped to McClane and heaved him aside. McClane vanished in blackness while uttering a howl of dismay.

Oakley sprang close to Brixey's side. "Now's our chance!" Against the wall, beside the French windows, a violent struggle was jarring the furniture. "Out, Archie!" A lamp toppled with a crash. "Quick!" A sharp click followed, as of hard objects meeting violently. A moan, a scuffle of feet, a flutter, then again the black figure shadowed against the starlight, running with frantic speed into the deep gloom outside.

Oakley's hand had found a knob. He whirled through, thrusting Brixey ahead. He paused, one long moment, hearing McClane's wheezy breathing, the scrape of heels on the floor as McClane strove to rise. Oakley tore away and sped. He groped to a rear entrance that Brixey had already opened. He sprinted, leaped, slashed through the hedge. Brixey dashed beside him to the street and they kept running.

Five minutes later they were sitting breathlessly in a taxi, exchanging stares of dismay.

"Somebody got hurt in that fight, Archie!" Oakley declared when his breath came back. "Blood was spilled. I saw it on the floor. Saw it in the dark—shining with that same ghostly glow!"

5. The Green Ghoul

OAKLEY SOUGHT a telephone in a drugstore far from any busy street. Again, in a desperate attempt to elude searching patrol cars, he and Brixey had transferred from cab to cab. Almost two hours had passed since their precipitous departure from the Gately villa, and the seventh of the series of taxis sat now panting at the curb; Brixey huddled within it, as Oakley called the number of Secrets, Incorporated.

"Darling," he told Cherry Morris, "Archie and I are fugitives from a herd of wild elephants. Thank God you're still among the free! I need your help!"

"Blondes get you into trouble," Cherry retorted distantly, "and a red-head gets you out."

"Too true," Oakley sighed. "Cherry, listen! How to get this piece of information is up to you, but you've got to get it. I want to know if Philip Gately happened to get hurt in the fight in his house tonight—hurt so that he bled. And I want to know right now, this minute, in what cemetery the late Lawrence Gately is resting in peace."

Cherry's sniff carried clearly over the line. "The Kindly Light Cemetery," she said, "and you'd better be picking out a nice plot, with good drainage, for yourself."

"Not yet! Listen! Get that dope about Gately, then meet me at the Kindly Light. At the gate, Cherry. As fast as you can make it. Bring two shovels with you. Get them somehow and—"

"Two what?"

"Shovels, my dear! Large, spoonlike implements for—"

"And meet you at a lonely cemetery at this time of night?" Cherry inquired timorously. "Have you gone mad?" Suddenly her coolness melted. "Oke, darling, whatever you're planning to do, don't do it! What'll become of me if they send you to jail? I should have married you long ago, I know I should!"

"You'll probably have to marry me in jail, if at all. Hurry it, my dear! To the Kindly Light and—"

"Oke—listen!" Cherry whispered. "I've had the queerest feeling that I'm being watched. I know somebody's watching me. Maybe it's McClane. Maybe it—"

"Shake him, whoever it is, and start those lovely feet of yours moving very rapidly!" Oakley urged. "Archie and I are on our way!"

Oakley returned to the taxi, ducked in beside the mournful Brixey, gave the driver orders that sent them along a through street. Now and again Oakley added directions which whirled them out into the open country. They passed outlying *haciendas*, turned off the main road, swung at last along a lonesome byway which led past a high stone wall. There Oakley's orders stopped the cab.

HE PASSED the driver his last banknote, and the taxi whizzed away with alacrity. The vanishing gleam of the headlamps left Oakley and Brixey surrounded by darkness relieved only by the faint glow of the stars. Brixey stared, through his monocle, at a golden sign affixed above a locked gate. *Kindly Light*, it read. Beyond, in the gloom, stood headstones, like silent ghosts.

"My word!" Brixey sighed. "What are we up to now?"

"We wait," Oakley answered impatiently, "until Cherry comes. I thought this would be a nice place for a picnic."

They walked back and forth along the stone wall. The ground rolled, and at a point where the wall was low, they gazed across the spectral gloom of the cemetery to see the windows of a caretaker's cottage glowing brightly. Oakley cautioned silence and they patrolled again. Presently a gleam far down the road sent them scurrying for shelter.

A taxi drew to a stop near the gate. From it Cherry Morris alighted, pulling two long-handled shovels after her. While the driver stared suspiciously, she paid him off and disdainfully ordered him back. Her manner made it plain that a lone young woman coming to an isolated graveyard at midnight, and carrying two shovels, was quite within her rights. Standing the shovels beside her, she waited in the darkness as the lights of the cab faded into the distance.

Oakley approached quietly. "Good evening, my dear," he said. "Be nice to me, Cherry. This may be the last time I'll ever see you without strong iron bars standing between us."

Cherry was too worried now for banter. "Oke, please!" she pled. "Somebody was watching the office. Somebody followed me. I tried to shake him off, but I was too anxious about you to do a good job of it. I don't think it's McClane. Oke, I'm scared!"

"Be brave, my dear," Oakley cheered her. "The worst is still ahead of us. Come with me."

He led Brixey and the girl along the wall to a point where the ground rose. He drew over, helping Cherry. When Brixey stood beside them, they listened intently, watching the lights of the caretaker's cottage. There was no sound save the whispering of the wind in the leaves.

"Did you learn," Oakley inquired softly, "whether or not Philip Gately suffered a wound tonight?"

"I did," Cherry breathed, "and he didn't. I got him on the phone and pled with him until he told me. McClane is at headquarters, wiring the governor to order the militia out after you."

"In that case," Oakley said, "we have work ahead of us."

Carrying the shovels, he trod along a walk. Quick glances sent him past graves that were plainly not freshly dug. When he paused, far at the side of the cemetery, it was on a plot spread with new earth, at a grave newly mounded. He leaned to read a plain headboard in the starlight and straightened to murmur: "Here it is."

Here, he meant, was the grave that bore the name of Lawrence Gately.

He tossed his hat aside, stripped off his coat, bade Brixey do likewise. Brixey complied with mumbled protests which Oakley ignored, took the shovel which Oakley thrust into his hands.

"Watch, Cherry," Oakley ordered. "Archie, dig!"

Brixey blurted: "Dig?"

"Dig," Oakley affirmed, "quickly and with as little noise as possible!"

GRIMLY HE drove the blade of his shovel into the soft earth of the fresh grave. Cherry shrank back in dismay as Brixey, with a resigned shrug, joined in the labor. Their shovels *chuffed,* swung, heaped earth aside. Bit by bit they cleared the outline of the grave and deepened it. In silent terror Cherry watched the lighted cottage while they dug themselves knee-deep.

"Grave robbing! One more crime," Brixey sighed, "added to our already long list."

"Oke," Cherry protested in a whisper, "you *are* mad!"

Oakley kept digging. Slowly the excavation deepened. Waists level with the ground, they swung their shovels building the heaps around them. Oakley glanced up as a whimper came from Cherry; then stopped, breathing hard. The girl was looking down at him, her face white in the faint light.

"I've got that queer feeling again, Oke! Somebody's watching us! There is! I know it!"

"Eyes sharp, Cherry!"

Oakley glanced around keenly, resumed his task. Brixey's monocle popped in and out of his eye as he labored. Their breath beat fast, their hands chafed against the shovel handles, their muscles throbbed with the exertion of swinging load after load upward. Now they were invisible to Cherry, in the hollow and behind the mounds, unless she leaned to peer at them.

A hollow thump sounded when Oakley's blade struck something solid beneath the soft ground. He said "Ah!" and began to scrape. The shovel cleaned loose earth from new boards—the top of a wooden box. When Oakley and Brixey paused, they were standing on the lid of a coffin container.

"At it, Archie!" Oakley commanded "Open it!"

Brixey was beyond protest now. At Oakley's side he pried at the lid. They struggled to thrust the shovel blade into a widening crack. They levered one side loose, then the other. Cherry Morris, holding her breath, saw the leaf of the box rise out of the darkness, saw it slide upon a black mound. She peered down, anxiously observed Oakley stooping at the head of a bronze casket.

"Help me loosen the clamps!" he whispered to Brixey.

Their fingers whitened with the pressure they applied to the wing nuts. They panted with the effort, loosening one fastening after another. When the last was free, Oakley stepped back and took a deep breath. He leaned again, gripped the edge of the head section, tensed for a pull.

"Now!"

Slowly, stickily, the metal leaf raised. Oakley lifted it high. He peered into the interior of the casket. Vaguely, in the dim shine, he saw the outlines of a body—a body without a head, the body he had discovered in the house of Lawrence Gately. For a long time he stood motionless, eyes upon the horror. He whispered at last: "No glow. No glow in the room when we found him. No glow here."

Suddenly he turned, toed up the earthen wall, heaved himself over the mounds of dirt.

Brixey clambered beside him as he pulled into his coat. His eyes were shining, his manner brisk, the curve of his lips triumphant.

"Stay here, Archie!" he ordered. "Watch that! It's important! Cherry, stick with Oke!"

He started away with the girl's hand curled snugly around his arm. Brixey, finding himself alone at the side of the open grave, blurted a dismayed, "I say!" but they went on. The concern in Cherry's eyes deepened when she realized Oakley was heading directly for the caretaker's cottage. Too bewildered to protest, she went with him straight to the door.

HE KNOCKED. The sound echoed emptily inside. Oakley twisted the knob, pushed, found the door locked. He stepped back, noted that a window was set in the wall near it, snugged the barrel of his automatic in his palm. One sharp swipe with it sent the fragments of a pane spattering inward. Oakley reached in, fumbled with the spring catch of the door, loosened it.

"What I want," he explained crisply to Cherry as he opened the way, "is a telephone!"

Cherry murmured, "I'll have some peace garnished with a little quiet for mine," as she followed him in.

Oakley charged at the instrument on the table, lifted it, listened for sounds. The dial clicked and spun beneath his flicking finger. The room was silent until Oakley asked: "Police headquarters? Give me McClane!" He waited while Cherry moved toward a closed connecting door, tightened, said. "Good evening, good evening, McClane, this is your old pal Oakley."

"What!" rasped in his ear.

Oakley hesitated. Something like a faint moan reached his ears from somewhere beyond. He saw Cherry open the connecting door quickly and step through. She passed from sight as an explosion in the receiver shocked Oakley.

"My God, Oakley! You've got a nerve, calling me! I'm looking for you, shamus! I'm—"

"Wait, McClane," Oakley cautioned briskly. "Keep your blood pressure down. I have important news. I'll tell you exactly where I am, but first—"

"I'll find you!" howled in the receiver. "You can't jump on me in the dark and beat me up and—"

"Listen!" Oakley interrupted. "I didn't do that. The man who attacked you was hiding inside the house. I saw him knock you down and beat it out and—"

"I know where you are!" McClane snapped in. "You're at Glendale Airport. You grabbed that airplane ticket in the fight, but you're not going to get a chance to use it, shamus! You—"

"The man who hit you wanted that airplane ticket, but it wasn't I," Oakley countered. "Listen, will you? He lost that ticket when he committed the murder. It was his prepared get-away and he found himself in a spot because he lost it. In a minute you'll understand why he didn't dare try to get another, why he had to get that one back. Have you dug into that place in the cellar of the Gately place, McClane? You'd better do it right away. You'll find something very interesting. A human head, I believe."

McClane roared: "What the hell are you talking about?"

"I'm explaining what happened!" Oakley told him impatiently. "Do I have to spell the words? Don't you know it was all planned out, and you and I were called there as part of the plan? Think, McClane!"

"I'm thinking you're crazy!"

Oakley moaned. "The murderer first stole an axe from the home of Jerome. The reason was to blame Jerome for the murder. The killing was done. The victim's head was amputated. The murderer buried it under the house. He returned to mutilate the body. My coming frightened him off. He hid under the house, he was there when we were looking for him."

"I'm having this call traced, Oakley, I warn you!"

"Go to it! And keep listening! The murderer didn't realize he'd lost his ticket and his mask until later. His means of escape was lost. He—"

OAKLEY'S WORDS stopped as a hoarse cry carried out of the gloom of the graveyard. It was Brixey's voice, choked, strangling. Oakley howled, "Archie!" but there was no answer. He started away, paused to hear serene silence, turned back.

"Listen fast, McClane! That mask was also necessary to the murderer in case he had to move about in the dark. He needed it because his face, his whole body, is phosphorescent. He couldn't keep out of sight unless—"

"Jerome, sure!"

"Not Jerome, McClane! Gately! Lawrence Gately!"

"Lawrence Gately's dead!"

"No! He's not the victim, he's the murderer! He and that slick lawyer brother of his planned this thing in order to escape heavy damage judgments against him. He'd been sneaking his money into hiding for months. They tried to make it appear he was dead so that he could slip away and keep his wealth. A desperate man, McClane—a desperate plan." Oakley peered at the door through which Cherry had gone.

"Cherry, what the devil are you doing in there?" he demanded. "Come on back!" His words rushed again into the transmitter. "He put his clothes on the man he killed. He beheaded his victim so that the dead man would be mistaken for him. He used the axe not only to incriminate Jerome but because it was capable of mutilating a body beyond—"

A stifled scream! It sounded strangled in the weird quiet of the cemetery and lodged Oakley's words in his throat. He stood motionless a second, and heard McClane's voice rasp in the receiver: "I've spotted you!. You're at the Kindly Light Cemetery! You're bagged!"

Oakley dropped the telephone, took a bounding stride toward the door. He moaned, "Oh, God!" and stopped beyond the sill. This room was a dirt-tracked cubicle in which shovels, headboards, rakes, tools were stored. Its rear door was standing open. In front of it a snake of rope lay on the floor, fallen from one of a row of nails on which other lengths hung. On the floor also lay a man in overalls, bound hand and foot, gagged, his head welted, staring in fear.

"Cherry!" Oakley shouted. He jumped to the door, peered out, whirled back. He snatched a pair of pruning shears from the bench, bit the blades upon the caretaker's bonds, tore the gag from the man's mouth. "Where is she? What happened to you? Where is she?" he asked.

The caretaker's free hand made a wild gesture toward the open door. "Somebody dragged her out!" he gulped as he struggled up, as Oakley turned again. "Same guy that sneaked in here and knocked me out!"

Oakley sprang across the sill. He raced into the spreading gloom, hearing the telephone inside the cottage clatter again with a shouted, "Police headquarters!" Oakley wound his way among tombstones toward the yawning grave.

He stopped short near it, coldly amazed, the snout of his little automatic twinkling in the moonlight. The shining eyes of Cherry Morris were upon him. She was writhing in the tightly drawn strands of rope that bound her to a monument at the foot of the opened grave! Terror whitened her face; and sight of it sent a chill through Oakley. Motionless, nerves snapping with alertness, he peered through the surrounding gloom and saw only the ghostly white of grave markers. "Steady, Cherry!" he whispered.

A MOAN floated to his ears from nearby, turned him quickly toward the black hollow. Peering over heaped earth, he saw Brixey folded on the exposed casket. "Archie!" Oakley called sharply; and Brixey's eyelids fluttered. Automatically he groped for his monocle as he dragged up. He swayed dizzily as Oakley reached and commanded: "Grab on!"

A warning sense of furtive movement flashed a chill into him as a cry of fright broke from the lips of Cherry Morris.

Oakley twisted to see a shadow figure stepping close behind him. A slashing sound cut the air as the darkly outlined man swung back with one of the shovels. The sharp edge whizzed and Oakley squirmed frantically to free his hand of Brixey's gripping fingers. Swiftly he ducked and the murderous blow fanned cold air on his face. He jerked back as the black figure began a second murderous sweep of the shovel.

Oakley sprang and his fist drove out to unnaturally soft flesh. The shovel clattered down and grappling arms clasped him. In the grave Brixey moaned as Oakley wrenched loose. His knuckles clicked between a pair of gleaming eyes; and the shadowy figure melted before him. He straddled a man who lay still at the edge of one black heap of earth.

From the grave came a mournful, "I say!"

"Steady, Archie!" Oakley reassured him. "That is not to be your last resting place!"

He hurried to Cherry Morris; he fought the knots and loosened them. The girl sagged away from the monument and into Oakley's arms. She clung close, quivering with suppressed sobs.

"You're all right!" Oakley told her. "What the devil happened?"

"I caught him sneaking out the door of that room, Oke—that man with the horrible face! He grabbed me before I could even scream! He carried me here, and saw Archie, and let me go, and hit Archie an awful sock. Then he had to grab me again—and Archie began coming to—and he had to tie me up to handle Archie again and—oh, he's horrible!" Cherry's arms tightened. "He threw Archie in the grave!"

"And Archie," Oakley said grimly, "is still in!"

He turned, again extended his hand. Brixey gripped it and Oakley heaved back. Out of the gloom of the open grave Brixey mounted. He stood fumbling for his monocle, gingerly feeling a welt on his head.

"I say!" Brixey shook loose earth from his clothing. "He was trying to bury me alive!"

"Undoubtedly," Oakley agreed as he stooped over the prone figure, "he was desperate to get rid of us all because we threatened the success of his plan. He was desperate enough to try to put us all permanently in what is supposed to be Lawrence Gately's grave."

"Supposed?" Brixey gulped. "It's jolly well somebody's grave, Oke! It is Gately's, isn't it?"

"Not Gately's," Oakley said. "The body in the casket is that of poor Mrs. Hepplehaus's lost love, August Gaspar. This—"

Oakley grasped the unconscious man's shoulder, turned him on his back. They stood silent, peering at the green radiance shining against the ground. The hands and the face of the fallen man were radiating a ghastly shine. Lax, horrible, phosphorescent, it was a poisonous, glowing thing before them.

"This," Oakley finished, "is Lawrence Gately."

When, twenty minutes later, Detective-Lieutenant McClane charged into the Kindly Light Cemetery, he found Oakley and Brixey and Cherry Morris surrounding an open grave in which their murderous prisoner crouched—a living thing shining in the dark!

CLAY OAKLEY leaned across his desk in the inner sanctum of Secrets, Incorporated, and smiled upon his three callers.

"Gentlemen," he said, "what I have just told you should assure you that no ghost will appear again on the grounds of Thirteen Thirty. Mr. Lawrence Gately is going the way of a convicted murderer. Your tenants will again be happy. I think that is all."

Mr. Henry Wethering rose, smiled and said: "Thanks!" Mr. Wallace Quinn beamed and echoed: "Many thanks!" Mr. Samuel Tompkins grinned broadly and emphatically, added: "Many, many thanks!" Oakley shook their hands; they paraded delightedly from his office; and he reached for the ringing telephone.

"McClane calling, Oakley," said a remarkably subdued voice. "Say, listen. The inspector's asking me some questions I can't answer. You've got to help me out. If I haven't got all the dope, how the hell can I make him believe I cracked this case?"

"Of course, McClane," Oakley smiled, "if you're quite sure I'm not to be pilloried for destroying evidence—"

"Aw, forget it!" McClane drawled. "I talk rough, but I mean well. You're a good guy, Oakley, and I like you. Listen. I'm coming over and—"

"Come right along," Oakley bade, "and we'll all have a spot of tea together."

He smiled upon the vastly relieved Brixey and the still doubtful Cherry Morris. From the blotter he lifted four varicolored oblongs of paper.

"A few additions to the exchequer, my dear. Here is a check from Mr. Wethering. Another from Mr. Quinn. Still another from Mr. Tompkins. A fourth from the grateful Rona Jerome. All exceedingly handsome, but hers," Oakley, sighed, "is the most beautiful of all!"

Printed in Great Britain
by Amazon